Praise for *The Phoenix Crown*

"An irresistible proposition for a gifted operatic soprano. The double lives of a talented young Chinese woman and her artist lover. A tenacious, globe-trotting female botanist. The legendary crown of an empress. The devastating San Francisco earthquake of 1906 and the ensuing rampant, deadly fire. Brilliant authors Kate Quinn and Janie Chang weave these threads together into a seamless, page-turning masterpiece of history and suspense—shot through with women rising up from the margins of society to claim their own singular futures. I could not put this triumphant novel down."

—Marie Benedict, *New York Times* bestselling author of *The First Ladies* and *The Mitford Affair*

"Oh my goodness, I couldn't put this book down! Heart-pounding, gasp-out-loud storytelling—*The Phoenix Crown* is the best book I've read all year."

—Victoria Christopher Murray, *New York Times* bestselling author of *The First Ladies* and *The Mitford Affair*

"When two masters of historical fiction team up, it's like 1+1=1000. I'm in awe of this impeccably researched, magnificently rendered, and breathlessly paced tale that kept me up late into the night reading, reflecting, and delving into the haunting true stories that inspired this novel. I cannot wait to recommend *The Phoenix Crown* to my own book club."

—Jamie Ford, *New York Times* bestselling author of *The Many Daughters of Afong Moy*

The
PHOENIX
CROWN

The
PHOENIX CROWN

A Novel

KATE QUINN
and
JANIE CHANG

wm
WILLIAM MORROW
An Imprint of HarperCollinsPublishers

THE PHOENIX CROWN. Copyright © 2024 by Paul Wehmeyer Productions LLC and Janie Chang. Excerpt from THE BRIAR CLUB © 2024 by Paul Wehmeyer Productions LLC. Excerpt from THE PORCELAIN MOON © 2023 by Janie Chang. All rights reserved. Printed in the United States of America. No part of this book may be used or reproduced in any manner whatsoever without written permission except in the case of brief quotations embodied in critical articles and reviews. For information, address HarperCollins Publishers, 195 Broadway, New York, NY 10007.

HarperCollins books may be purchased for educational, business, or sales promotional use. For information, please email the Special Markets Department at SPsales@harpercollins.com.

FIRST EDITION

Designed by Diahann Sturge

Library of Congress Cataloging-in-Publication Data has been applied for.

ISBN 978-0-06-330473-4
ISBN 978-0-06-333997-2 (international edition)

24 25 26 27 28 LBC 6 5 4 3 2

To Stephen and Geoffrey

Prologue

A rose by any other name," someone quoted, and Alice Eastwood was hard-pressed not to roll her eyes. When it came to Shakespearean quotes about flowers, hang *Romeo and Juliet*. She preferred *Julius Caesar*: "Nature must obey necessity."

Because Mother Nature was a carnivore: she ate what she wanted when hunger made it necessary. Alice had known that in her bones since that day five years ago, when the earth shrugged its shoulders and a city cracked in half.

"You've been on quite a pilgrimage of Europe's gardens and conservatories, Miss Eastwood! Will you return to San Francisco soon?" The question came from the director of the Royal Botanic Gardens in Kew as he trailed Alice toward the Palm House with its great glassed layers like a crystal wedding cake. "I understand you've been invited to resume your old position at the California Academy of Sciences—curator of botany?"

"Not yet." But she knew it was coming, the invitation to help rebuild the lost herbarium. Whether she could bear to accept or not, she hadn't yet decided, so Alice sped her footsteps to outpace both the question and her companion. She still had the vigor for the work, no question—perhaps she was fifty-two, but she certainly hadn't calcified with her advancing years: whether heading up a California mountain to investigate a poppy field, hauling herself into a pack mule's saddle for an expedition in the Rockies, or striding along raked gravel paths of formal gardens, Alice Eastwood was always first on the scene.

No, it wasn't the vigor she lacked—it was the heart. Set foot on that treacherous San Francisco earth again, after what had happened there?

The director hurried after her, a little out of breath. "The Academy's herbarium was destroyed during the '06 earthquake, I believe? Such a loss to science."

"Yes," Alice said briefly, eyeing the Palm House as though it were a thorny sample she had to yank out of the ground without her field gloves. She had a little bit of a Thing about conservatories (she wasn't going to call it a fear) ever since that particular day in '06, but you couldn't be a botanist and have a Thing about conservatories, so she squashed it down firmly and strode inside. Ah—the smell of vegetation, warm air, fern fronds. Life. The sun twinkled through the glass panes overhead, paths wound under shading palms, and she thought she could smell the elusive scent of orchids. "You have a sample of *Encephalartos altensteinii* I was interested in seeing . . ."

"Yes, this way. Someday I'm hoping to lay hands on an *Epiphyllum oxypetalum*, but—"

"A Queen of the Night?" Alice didn't often veer away from proper scientific names—it felt mildly rude, like addressing a woman by her nickname when you hadn't yet been formally introduced—but *Epiphyllum oxypetalum* was special.

"Yes!" The director of the Royal Botanic Gardens brightened, tugging on his whiskers. "I've never been lucky enough to lay eyes on one, much less in bloom. Difficult when it only flowers for one night, eh?"

"I've seen one bloom." Alice could see it now: a white, exotic blossom opening slowly in a dark room, almost seeming to cast its own light, emitting a heady and indescribable fragrance. She remembered her fingers trembling as she touched one exquisite petal, remembered the look on the faces of the women

around her. Four women who could not have been more different, united in vast, wondrous awe around the miracle of that
flower. *Miracle* had not seemed too momentous a word, after
what they had endured.

"Where did you see . . ."

"Oh, a long time ago." Alice fiddled with the Zeiss lens hanging around her neck on the same chain as her spectacles, bringing it up to her eye to examine a spot on a palm leaf. "Let's see
that *Encephalartos altensteinii.*"

Later, having said her goodbyes, after being introduced to a
dozen botanists and trading addresses for correspondence ("I
know of your interest in the *Genista* genus, Miss Eastwood,
and would be happy to send you some samples!"), Alice wandered the lawns outside the Palm House, clapping a hand to her
flower-laden hat to keep it from blowing away in the summer
breeze. The hat had come from Paris, made by a master embroideress at the Callot Soeurs atelier: the only remotely fashionable
touch on a woman who would always rather carry a plant press
than a velvet handbag. Her stride along the path was still brisk,
but she hadn't outpaced the question after all: *Will you go back
to San Francisco?*

Alice found a bench nearby and sat, picking up a discarded
newspaper and fanning herself. Later she thought how *random*
that was: she never read the society pages; and she shouldn't have
seen that article at all. But the abandoned paper had been folded
back on one of those gushy social columns, the sort that breathlessly reported which ball Lady So-and-So had attended in a
gown of pale green liberty satin and an eight-strand pearl collar,
or which earl's daughter had married in a cloud of mousseline
and Valenciennes lace . . . Only it wasn't a description of a gown
or a ball that caught Alice's eye on this bright summer morning.

—phoenixes carved in rare blue-and-white jade—
—fifty-seven sapphires and four thousand pearls—
—butterflies fashioned out of kingfisher feathers—
—carved ivory Queen of the Night flowers—

And she found herself reading, fingers clenched so tight the newsprint crumpled in her grip. Reading it once, twice, her hands shaking. Putting it down at last, staring blindly over the children bowling their hoops and the strolling women in their white summer muslins. Instead of banks of blowsy roses she saw a wall of flame, and instead of twittering birds she heard the crystalline shatter of glass.

She rose, not bothering to formulate a polite apology as she approached the first top-hatted gentleman hurrying past her bench. "Excuse me, sir, I don't know London at all well. Where would I go to send a telegram overseas?" The man stared at her uneasily before rattling off some directions, and Alice didn't blame him. She was drenched in icy sweat, white-faced and trembling—Alice Eastwood, who had not trembled as she climbed a railing six stories high over a shattered atrium in the old California Academy, who had laughed when she was nearly swept over a waterfall to her death at Cataract Gulch but struggled out of the river with a handful of wet plant samples instead.

Alice Eastwood, afraid?

Very, she thought as she hurried out of Kew Gardens, already parsing her words for that telegram. Three telegrams, actually. One to New York, one to Buenos Aires, one to Paris . . . but all beginning with the same four words.

The Phoenix Crown
Found

Act I

Chapter 1

April 4, 1906
Thirteen days, fourteen hours, fifty-two minutes
before the San Francisco earthquake

The birdcage was starting to squawk and vibrate indignantly on the seat, so Gemma Garland lifted the cover a crack and spoke down into it. "Almost there, I promise." The woman who had just settled into the seat opposite shot her a *look*, but Gemma had been traveling all the way from New York in a third-class compartment—she was travel-stained, weary, feeling every one of her thirty-two years, and certainly well beyond caring about censorious looks. Especially *looks* from hatchet-faced schoolmarms in navy bombazine and mouse-colored toques. Women like that had been giving Gemma *looks* since she was twelve years old.

"Chilly day," the woman finally said. She'd been moving from compartment to compartment with a stack of pamphlets, and Gemma already had a wary feeling about where this conversation was headed. "Stopping in San Francisco, are you?"

Why, no, Gemma considered replying. *I'm just going to keep riding the train straight into the bay.* There wasn't any farther west to go than San Francisco, was there? "Yes," she answered, lacking the energy to be acerbic. The train was already racketing through the city outskirts; she wouldn't have to endure this stuffy cigar-stinking compartment or its nosy occupant much longer. "Yes, San Francisco," she murmured.

"It's a godless place," the woman tutted. "Rotten with sin and depravity. Full of painted harlots, heathen Chinee, and wicked millionaires."

Just the town for us! Gemma imagined her oldest friend,

Nellie, laughing. Nell's first letter from San Francisco, in fact, had said much the same thing: *It's a rollicking sort of place— San Francisco's made its fortune, so now it's mad to improve itself. Galleries, theaters, mansions . . . not to mention rich men lying around everywhere like lumps of gold, just waiting to be picked up!*

"I hope you won't be staying long, dear," the woman opposite continued. "The Cesspit of the West is doomed, you know. Prince Benjamin has foreseen it."

"Mmm," said Gemma, not asking who Prince Benjamin was, but that wasn't going to save her, she could just tell.

"Patriarch of the Flying Rollers of the House of David," the woman said. "In Benton Harbor, Michigan."

"Benton Harbor, Michigan, is that so." *Explains the mouse-colored toque*, Gemma thought.

"The patriarch himself sent me here. I am to warn the people of San Francisco to give up their ways of vice—" Clearly nothing was going to shut the woman up, so Gemma fell back on stage-craft: chin on hand as if fascinated, widening her big blue eyes until they nearly clicked in doll-like innocence. The same expression she always donned when singing Olympia in *The Tales of Hoffmann*, right before she launched into "The Doll Song," and it always brought down the house. "—if they don't renounce their vile sinning, God will bring fire and earthquakes down upon them," the woman opposite finally finished up her rant. "Within the month."

"Goodness, fire *and* earthquakes." Still wide-eyed. "Wouldn't one or the other be enough?"

"The ground shall break apart beneath their hell-bound feet by May, if they do not repent!"

"How lucky I'm only staying through the end of April," Gemma murmured.

The Flying Roller looked her over, clearly approving of Gemma's plain traveling suit in London smoke cloth and ebony braid. "Visiting family, dear? I do hope it's not misfortune that brings you so far."

"On the contrary, I'm making my debut."

"Debut?" The Flying Roller blinked. "Into society?"

"Oh, no." Gemma knew her peach-fair skin was still good, and her Nebraska-corn-blond hair didn't need any tinting yet, but no one was ever going to mistake her for eighteen. "On the stage! I'm an opera singer." The woman recoiled as if she'd been confronted with a viper, and Gemma threw out her biggest, most glittering smile. "I'm making my debut with the Metropolitan Opera traveling company in two weeks, on the boards of the Grand Opera House—in Bizet's *Carmen*, in fact, opposite the great Caruso."

Praise be, that finished off the Flying Roller, who slapped a tract down on the seat and moved on to the next compartment with a great deal of muttering.

Not quite true, though, is it? Gemma's thoughts whispered, once she had the compartment to herself. *You aren't exactly making your debut opposite Caruso.*

"Close enough," Gemma said aloud, picking up the tract. She *was* making her debut; it *was* with the Metropolitan Opera traveling company; it *would* be in *Carmen*; and Caruso *would* be throwing that glorious golden tenor across the footlights at her . . . along with the rest of the chorus, because that's where Gemma was making this great debut: in the chorus. Laced into some cigarette-factory-girl bodice, swishing some Spanish petticoats. Maybe she'd get a bit of stage business in the tavern scene, get to flutter a fan at the bullfighter.

It's still the Met, Gemma thought. *It's still Caruso.* But the chorus, oh dear. Not exactly where a girl wanted to be at thirty-two, when she wasn't really a girl any longer. When she was headed into the absolute prime of her voice, her best singing years . . . By then you hoped you'd have made it out of the ranks of cigarette factory girls.

"By this time next year, you will be." She said it aloud to the empty compartment, adopting the steely tone of the matron in Red Hook, Nebraska's only orphanage. Gemma knew very well that *steeliness* did not come naturally to her—that was the trouble with having the sort of farm-raised childhood that involved cows and plains and white-steepled churches, not to mention parents who raised you with the belief that being kind and generous to everyone you met would ensure a good life. It wasn't until age fourteen that the farm, the cows, and the parents had all gone, and Gemma landed at the orphanage and realized just how wrong those early lessons were. The plain fact was, the only person a woman could rely on was herself, and she'd better be hard-nosed about it because otherwise she'd end up alone, humiliated, and stony broke.

Gemma shut her eyes hard against that particular train of memory before it could progress too far down the last few horrible weeks in New York, and skimmed the Flying Roller's tract with its lurid illustrations. (Thunderstorms, billows of hellfire; cracks in the earth opening up to swallow a crowd of shrieking San Franciscan sinners.) A new beginning, that was all she needed.

And a little bit of a holiday, too. Caruso and the rest of the company were on the road and wouldn't be arriving in San Francisco for another fortnight. *I'm being sent to replace a chorus soprano who's quitting after the Kansas City run to marry her beau,* Gemma had written Nellie several weeks ago. *I'll join the company when they arrive in San Francisco, and start in* Carmen. *I hear we're opening for the cream of San Francisco soci-*

ety (does San Francisco society have a cream, *exactly? Surely they do, if they can afford Caruso's fees!). Anyway, why don't I come out early? I haven't seen you in nearly a year, and to be quite honest, I need a good dose of your unshakable optimism. I've had such a horrible time lately, Nell, you can't imagine. I don't just need your optimism, I really need you.*

Darling Nellie was a patchy correspondent—her letters sometimes stopped coming for weeks or months, whenever she disappeared into some new passion or project—but she'd answered *that* letter at once. Of course she had, because Gemma's oldest friend might be scatterbrained and disorganized but she knew desperation when she heard it. *Hop the next train to San Francisco and come stay with me while you wait on Caruso, farm girl,* she'd written in her backhand scrawl. *I don't know what's gone wrong for you lately, but I promise we will fix everything. I've got a room on Taylor Street on Nob Hill; it'll be just like bunking together in the Bronx when we were wide-eyed greenhorns. Only with fewer roaches!*

Gemma smiled, thinking of that squalid cold-water apartment where they'd first met. Nellie had been a tall bony brunette of sixteen, brandishing an artist's sketchbook and a roll of brushes, throwing words like *cubism* and *perspective* around like jabs from her sharp elbows. Gemma had been plain Sally Gunderson, nineteen and a year out of the orphanage and terrified that the set of pipes in her throat wouldn't be good enough to make a splash in New York, even if they could nearly lift the steeple off the church in Red Hook—but even more terrified of being a hired girl with milkmaid calluses for the rest of her life, sleeping on a pallet in the cellar and getting the belt when she didn't work fast enough. She and Nellie had sized each other up as they stood in that roach-skittering Bronx apartment, both of them trying so hard to look like jaded professionals and not scared girls, and Nellie had been the one to burst out laughing.

"I don't have a *clue* what I'm doing," she confessed with one of her big infectious grins. "And I don't think you do, either, farm girl. Except that we both need new names, because who's going to take us seriously in this city with handles like *Nellie Doyle* and *Sally Gunderson*?" And they'd picked out new names on the spot—though to each other, even now so many years later, it was still *Sally* and *Nell*.

Oh, Nell, Gemma thought. *What would I do without you?* She hadn't been able to write about all the unpleasantness that sent her fleeing from New York (the shouting and the contemptuous gazes and the shame, no, don't think about that, not right now), but she could *tell* Nellie about it once they were face-to-face. Nellie would understand. She was the one person in the world who could be exempted from the general rule that everyone in the end would just let you down.

The train began slowing with a great screech of wheels. Gemma hastily folded up the Flying Roller's tract, cramming it through the bars of the birdcage. "Enjoy," she told Toscanini, lowering the cover again and reaching for her handbag. She had arrived.

EVERY CITY HAD a mood. As much as Gemma had traveled with one opera company and another over the years, she knew that for certain. New York was cynical, Chicago was energetic, Red Hook was sleepy . . . The mood she got from the great golden city of the West, as she stood on the railway platform flicking cigar butts off her skirt hem and inhaling San Francisco's smells of salt water, horse manure, and smoke, was *cheer*. Everyone in the crowd below seemed to be rushing somewhere, their voices noisy and exuberant. The clothes were a bright jumble: knot-buttoned tunics on the Chinese, loudly patterned kerchiefs around the necks of the sailors, tasseled shawls swirling around the shoulders of the prostitutes elbowing their way toward the docks. And music—Gemma's trained ear immediately found music. A sea shanty being bawled from a bar a few doors down . . . A lullaby in a minor key, hummed by a woman hurrying by with a baby carriage . . . "Kathleen Mavourneen" sung in surprisingly sweet harmony by a pair of laundrywomen sauntering by with their baskets.

"You looking for a drink and a meal, miss?" a hansom driver called, seeing Gemma crane her neck at the line of cabs. "I'll drive you to Sully's, best steam beer south of the slot."

"South of the slot?" Gemma echoed, puzzled.

"That means south of Market Street, ma'am, because it's got slots between the cable car rails. You hop in and I'll show you—"

"Never mind that. I'm going to Taylor Street." Gemma rattled off the address Nellie had written her and gasped at the price the driver promptly quoted. "I'm looking for Taylor Street by way of Nob Hill, not the North Pole!"

"Good luck hauling that trunk all the way up Nob Hill by yourself," he smirked, and Gemma took great pleasure in seeing his expression sour as she took her birdcage in one hand and the strap of her trunk in the other and began hauling everything down the street.

She made it almost as far as Third and Mission, gritting her teeth as her trunk's end bounced on the cobbles behind her. In an opera, a gallant young tenor would have offered to carry it for her and they'd be singing a passionate duet by the top of Nob Hill, but life wasn't as accommodating as an opera. "Shut up," Gemma told Toscanini, protesting inside his birdcage. "I'm not asking *you* to hoist an end." The opera house must be nearby;

she saw a brand-new poster tacked to the side of a saloon, with the name *CARUSO* in elaborately scrolled letters, and stopped to look at it with a flutter of cautious hope. There were billboards and ads everywhere, pasted on the sides of buildings, raised above scaffolded half-built constructions—everyone in San Francisco, it seemed, was selling something or building something. You could make your fortune in a town like this.

An elderly Chinese man trotted past with a two-wheeled pushcart, stumbling against Gemma as he tripped on an uneven paving stone. Gemma felt her trunk's strap slip from her hand and barely stopped everything from overturning. The slim Chinese boy running alongside the older man quickly stopped to right her trunk, tipping the unlikely-looking fedora on his head and bowing. "I'm sorry, madam," the boy said in surprisingly unaccented English. "Old Kow did not mean to get in your way. He begs forgiveness." A stream of Chinese from the older man, who had snatched the cap off his head and stood giving a tentative gap-toothed smile, as if hoping not to be shouted at.

"Oh, not at all. These streets—" Gemma broke off, looking at the pushcart. "I don't suppose I could hire you to take my trunk up to Taylor Street?"

Soon a price had been agreed upon (much more reasonable than the hansom cab driver's), the trunk and birdcage were perched on the cart, and the old man took up the handles and set off at a surprisingly nimble pace. Gemma fell in gratefully beside the boy, who had pushed his fedora back over a long shiny black plait. "You speak excellent English," Gemma couldn't help saying.

"I was born here, ma'am." The boy looked seventeen or eighteen, with a smooth delicate-featured face, a mouth in a firm line, dark eyes like wary twin shields.

"Perhaps you can tell me more about San Francisco, then."

Gemma smiled. "That great marble dome showing over there, what is that?"

"City Hall, ma'am." The old man laughed something in Chinese behind the pushcart; the boy seemed disinclined to translate until Gemma made an inquiring noise. "Old Kow says City Hall is worth more than the men in it, ma'am. He says they're such a greedy lot, they would eat the paint off a house."

Gemma laughed, stopping short as an automobile came barreling around a corner like a rattletrap nursery toy. "And *Nob Hill*, what exactly is that?"

"It's where the finer people live, ma'am. In the big houses." The boy didn't exactly unbend as the blocks rolled past and the cobbled street began to rise and climb under their feet, but he readily identified everything Gemma pointed out. "That's the entrance to Chinatown, ma'am . . . That's the flag over the Palace Hotel . . ."

"I've heard it's the biggest hotel in the West." Caruso and the Met company would be staying at the Palace when they arrived, Gemma knew, but she wouldn't have checked in there even if she *could* afford it. She'd seen far too many sopranos end up in debt and disgrace because they got a taste for the champagne life when all they had to work with was a steam-beer salary. No, she'd happily bunk down with Nellie, even if it meant a makeshift pallet on her friend's sofa. "How far are we from Taylor Street?" The wooden houses of the poorer districts, leaning against each other like tipsy friends, were slowly giving way to stone-faced mansions crowned with gilded cupolas and fenced around in spiked brass. Less raucous cheer, more keep-off-the-grass.

"Not far, ma'am." Soon the pushcart pulled up outside a tidy wooden four-story half sunk into the nearest rocky hillside— Nob Hill, but not the most luxurious side of it, Gemma surmised. She opened her handbag, trying not to pant at the steepness of the slope she'd just climbed, counting out coins to the Chinese boy. *Hard-nosed*, she reminded herself, looking at the thinness of her wallet, but found herself handing over a generous tip anyway. To be frugal was one thing, to be a cheap tipper was another entirely.

"Thank you, ma'am." The Chinese boy bowed, giving a quick curved smile that turned that solemn face into something completely different. Gemma found herself wondering if what she'd assumed was a boy was in fact a girl . . . All those operatic stories where girls dressed up as boys had to come from *somewhere* after all. But her guide, whether boy or girl, was already turning with a soft ripple of Chinese for the old man, both of them disappearing down the hill with the pushcart, and Gemma supposed it wasn't any of her business.

Besides, she was here at last: the house on Taylor Street where Nellie had invited her to stay, had told her they would *fix everything*. Through the open window with its crisp fluttering curtain, Gemma could hear the sound of a gramophone: the "Flower Duet" from *Lakmé*, and a strong contralto voice singing along. No one answered Gemma's first knock, but when she knocked again, both the singing and the gramophone stopped, and there was a rustle of footsteps.

"*Paeonia officinalis anemoniflora*," said the woman who answered the door.

Gemma blinked, still holding her handbag and birdcage. "I beg your pardon?"

"On your hat." The woman pointed at Gemma's narrow-brimmed gray crin with its black silk flowers. "Peonies. The only genus in the *Paeoniaceae* family. Though more normally pink, purple, white, yellow, or red, at least when found in nature and not on a hat. Though who knows? Who's to say there isn't a black peony blooming somewhere? Science is all about the un-discovered, and we never know as much as we think we do."

"I thought they were camellias," Gemma heard herself say. "I always try to have camellias on my hats—for *La Traviata*, you know, since it comes from *La Dame aux Camélias*."

"Oh dear, no, you could never mistake a *Paeonia officinalis anemoniflora* for a *Camellia japonica*." The other woman looked perhaps forty-five, face smile-creased and sun-browned as if she usually forgot to clap her hat over that sensible knot of gray-streaked hair before venturing outside. Her skirt was short, not even brushing her shoe tops, and a sprig of fresh violets was pinned to her crisply ironed shirtwaist. "Alice Eastwood," she said, offering her hand as forthrightly as a man. No wedding ring.

"Gemma Garland," Gemma responded in kind. "Was that you singing along with the gramophone, Miss Eastwood?"

"Yes, it was. I'm no singer, but I do like belting out a chorus or two when I'm puzzling a conundrum."

"What conundrum?" Gemma followed Miss Eastwood inside, rather enjoying this odd conversation.

"I found a new flower, and I'm not sure what it is." Miss Eastwood led the way into a parlor crammed with china bric-a-brac, crocheted antimacassars, and an upright piano draped with a fringed Chinese shawl. "Found some of these straggling at the edge of a vacant lot on my way to work."

Gemma examined the little purple blooms, pressed and glued against a stiff sheet of paper on the nearest overcrowded occasional table. "Prairie phlox. I have no idea what the Latin name is, but it grew in sheets near my family's farm in Nebraska."

"Did it?" Miss Eastwood beamed down at the flower, bending to write the words *Prairie phlox* in a careful pencil script beneath the sprig. "I wonder if this came all the way from Nebraska. It's amazing how far seeds can waft on the wind; they lodge in the most curious places. I wrote an article about the flora of Nob Hill, just on the plants I saw every day forcing themselves up between cobblestones. Sixty-four species, fifty-five of them not native to this state, all determined to thrive among the stones! Life is astounding."

"Yes, it is," Gemma agreed, looking around the parlor for some sign of Nellie. "Do you run this establishment, Miss Eastwood?"

"Gracious, no. I rent the garret on the top floor, since '92. Our landlady's longest-running boarder." Pushing back a graying strand of hair, Miss Eastwood smiled. "I'm a botanist, Miss Garland. Curator of botany at the California Academy of Sciences."

Gemma wasn't sure she'd ever met a woman who was a botanist. On the other hand, most people hadn't met a woman who was an opera singer, either—met one up close, rather than seeing one across the footlights like a creature in a zoo. "If you've been here so long, Miss Eastwood, I'm hoping you might know another local transplant who wafted here on the wind. Miss Nellie Doyle, though you may know her by another name." Nellie changed her artistic handle nearly as often as she changed clothes, unlike Gemma, who had stuck with *Gemma Garland* since age nineteen. "She might be going by Donatella Disogno"—that had come after Nellie's flirtation with Italian portraiture—"or by Thomasina Cray"—that had been her Hudson River landscape years—"or by Danielle LeMarq." Her French impressionist phase.

"Miss LeMarq, yes. The one who looked like a California poppy? Fragile on the outside, tough little weed on the inside."

Miss Eastwood smiled, and for a moment Gemma thought Nellie was about to come sauntering into the room in those outrageous trousers she'd started wearing as soon as she read George Sand. But then the botanist shook her head. "Your friend left, oh, six weeks ago? Had the room below mine, but she cleared out for new pastures."

Gemma felt the smile sliding off her face. "Did she leave an address?"

"No . . . She'd been spending less and less time here, the last six months or so. Working on a showing, hinting about big things to come. I think," Miss Eastwood added delicately, "there may also have been a man involved."

That sounded like Nellie. Maybe she'd moved, and her forwarding letter had gone astray? Gemma bit her lip, wondering what to do. Her trunk was still sitting on the front step, and she was starting to see the faint pulse around the room's lamps and windows that meant a migraine might be coming—oh God, not *now*. She massaged her temples discreetly, but Miss Eastwood had been distracted by the birdcage, which was rattling again. "Is that a bird in there, or a small earthquake?"

Gemma lifted the cover off the cage. "That's Toscanini."

"You have a famous Italian conductor in your luggage?"

If I did, I wouldn't still be in the chorus at thirty-two, Gemma thought. "No, just a budgie."

Toscanini greeted the daylight with a screech, ruffling his green feathers, looking decidedly cross. He'd made mincemeat of the Flying Roller's tract—shredded it to absolute ribbons under his perch. "Good boy," Gemma approved, wedging a finger through the wire bars and inviting him to cuddle along her knuckle, but Toscanini only glared. "Oh dear, he doesn't appreciate train travel. All those spittoons."

"What *is* it about spittoons?" Miss Eastwood wondered. "And why can't men seem to aim properly at them?" The two women watched Toscanini flutter around the cage, cracking a few seeds from his dish. "*Psittacidae* family? Fauna isn't my specialty, but isn't that the same as parrots? Does he talk?"

"No, but he imitates my vocal exercises. Annoyingly, he has an even better range than I do. I know an opera singer is supposed to travel with a yappy little dog, but . . ."

"An *opera* singer, Miss Garland?"

Gemma waited for the Look, like the one the Flying Roller had given her. The look that said *Harlot*. But the botanist's gaze was admiring, and Gemma felt her bruised, New York–battered soul start to preen just a little bit. "Soprano," she murmured, and couldn't resist singing just a line or two from the "Flower Duet" Miss Eastwood had been singing along with on the gramophone. "*Sous le dôme épais, où le blanc jasmin . . .*" Her voice fell into the room like sunshine, warm and full—Gemma could *feel* it, and a lump rose in her throat. She hadn't been able to sing in days, with the train journey and all the preparations beforehand. Go more than a day or two without practicing, and she always had the superstitious suspicion the voice would be gone the next time she tried to use it. Not the voice she spoke with, but the delicate contraption of skin and cords that gave her the ability to pour sunshine into a room when she sang.

Well, she still had it. Even after all the terrible things that had happened in New York, she still had it. And she was here, in a brand-new city, primed for a brand-new start.

(So where was Nellie, who had said she'd be here with open arms?)

"You sing beautifully," Alice Eastwood said, oblivious to

the roiling going on inside Gemma. But Toscanini sidled along his perch and consented to rub his head along her finger, and Gemma swallowed that lump in her throat. She scratched her budgie's throat gently.

"I don't suppose my friend's old room is available for rent?"

Chapter 2

April 5, 1906
Twelve days, twenty-three hours, thirty-
six minutes before the earthquake

Suling couldn't be seen entering the Palace of Endless Joy. If anyone told her uncle she'd been anywhere near the brothel, he'd lock her up until the day he married her off. It was a good thing she had ways of thwarting Third Uncle's wishes. She pulled on a plain unobtrusive tunic, dark green without a trace of embroidery, then loose-fitting black trousers. Pausing at the mirror on her bedroom door, she twisted her plaits into a loop at the nape of her neck. Just an ordinary Chinese girl, going out on errands. She wondered if the blond woman from yesterday would've recognized her as the laundryboy who had agreed to tote her luggage up the hill. Suling gave the woman a second thought only because she had been friendlier than most and the tip had been so generous. And because the Taylor Street address was familiar to her, a boardinghouse that used her family's laundry services.

Taking a deep breath, Suling opened the door and moved quietly across the floorboards toward the stairwell. The sickly sweet odor drifting out from Third Uncle's half-open door told her she needn't have bothered with discretion. Sunk in an opium-laced sleep, he was resting on the rattan daybed and wouldn't notice. He noticed very little these days, and the laundry business her parents had worked so hard to establish in San Francisco's Chinatown was slipping through his heedless hands. But she no longer cared. Now his lack of attention was to her advantage. When she was absent from the laundry, he assumed she was at one of her part-time sewing jobs. Like every other able-bodied adult in Chinatown, Suling worked an erratic hodgepodge of jobs to earn extra money. She did piecework above the Fung Tai Dry Goods store or sewed for Hing Chong Tailors; sometimes she taught embroidery at the Mission Home. It was all respectable work for a young woman, all close to home and inside Chinatown, which allowed her to come and go without arousing Third Uncle's curiosity.

It was still early as she set off along Washington Street to Hing Chong Tailors. At this hour shopkeepers were still busy setting up for the day. Produce vendors were arranging vegetables harvested from market gardens outside the city, and their sidewalk displays showed off boxes of spring vegetables: bright green bunches of scallions and asparagus, onions and peas, spinach and red radishes. At the butcher's, racks of pork ribs hung from hooks, along with whole chickens and ducks, freshly killed and plucked. Even before she neared the dry goods store, Suling could smell the pungent ingredients inside, familiar odors of dried shrimp and preserved turnips, fermented black beans and hard sausages.

Men jostled and joked with one another as they went to their jobs, some heading out of Chinatown to work at hotels and restaurants, others to the wharves for a day on the shrimp boats. They crowded in factories to roll cigars, sew garments, or stitch shoes and boots. The buildings where they worked might've been graced with grand names such as Everlasting Quality Broom Factory, but Chinatown's factories were not large businesses by any stretch of the imagination. They were no more than small sweatshops.

Gambling parlors on upper floors had flung open their windows to let in the cool April air, tempting passersby with the beguiling sounds of clacking mah-jongg tiles and shouts of triumph from customers who had been playing all night.

The only businesses still tightly shut at this time of day were the brothels. There were dozens in Chinatown—more white brothels than Chinese ones, but when newspapers went on a rampage against sin and corruption, they only denounced the Chinese whorehouses. Suling glanced up at the shuttered windows above a glossy sign, PALACE OF ENDLESS JOY. It was the most expensive Chinese brothel in San Francisco and a woman owned it.

Suling rounded the corner to Hing Chong Tailors, where the owner was busy draping fabric over a dressmaker's form. She tilted her head questioningly toward the door at the back of the shop and he nodded imperceptibly.

The door opened to a narrow stairwell that accessed the upper floors of the building behind the tailor's shop. It was a discreet entrance to the Palace of Endless Joy, known only to a few of Madam Ning's most valued customers—and to her friends. Suling sewed for Hing Chong Tailors so she'd have a way to enter the brothel without raising any eyebrows. When Suling's mother was still alive, there had been no need for deception; her father didn't mind his beloved wife visiting a dear friend. But Third Uncle was not so understanding.

The stairwell was dim, sunshine fighting its way through a dirty skylight. She climbed past the second-floor landing and its shiny red-painted door. The beautifully furnished rooms on this floor were for entertaining clients. The next floor up was where the women lived, rested, and ate their meals. The third floor was strictly forbidden to customers. Suling pulled the chain on the plain brown door and heard a bell inside tinkle. Then heavy footfalls shook the floorboards, and the door opened. A corpulent female shape, a pudgy face, mouth still yawning.

"So early in the day, Young Miss," said Amah Chung. "The mistress only just woke up. Well, you know where to find her.

I should get her breakfast ready." She padded down the hall on cloth-soled shoes and Suling heard another loud yawn.

The hallway was quiet and smelled of sandalwood and roses from the special incense Madam Ning used, the only kind she bought. Nothing but the best for Bai Meishen, the patron deity of prostitutes. The god's altar stood at the end of the hall. Offerings of coins and small pieces of jewelry littered the yellow silk brocade in front of the porcelain statue. Only eight women worked at the Palace of Endless Joy but they commanded high prices.

Suling knocked on the door across from the stairwell. "Auntie? It's me."

A husky voice bid her enter. The walls were austere, painted a soft sage green, with only a few watercolors decorating the room, all landscapes. A large rosewood pigeonhole desk dominated the space, a tall floor lamp beside it. The desk's drawers, Suling knew, were always locked, the key always on Madam Ning's person. Madam Ning was at her dressing table, wiping a thick layer of white cream from her face. "You're here rather early," she said, without turning around.

"I couldn't sleep," Suling said, sitting on the floor beside the woman she called Auntie, even though they were not related by blood. She put her head on the woman's lap.

"Those bad dreams again?" Madam Ning said.

Suling nodded. She didn't have to say more. Her auntie knew about the dreams, the ones where Suling stood at the edge of a cliff high above the beach over Mile Rocks, mute and unable to run or shout for help. An endless repetition of an awful moment of that awful day when she had been paralyzed by the steep path down the cliff, the long drop to rocks and beach if she should slip. Unable to run, powerless to do anything but watch as the current swept her parents out into the Pacific. It had been eight months since her mother fell off the rocks while foraging for seaweed and her father waded out to rescue her. Caught by the riptide, both were pulled out to the open sea. Madam Ning had been her mother's closest friend and since then always made time for Suling—outside of business hours.

Suling looked up at the older woman's reflection in the dressing table mirror. The brothel owner was a woman of around forty with beautifully arched eyebrows and flawless skin. Her full lips gave her oval face a perpetual pout that was girlishly charming, but only the most unobservant would think her easy to deceive. The formidable ambition that had taken her from prostitute to owner of the most exclusive brothel in Chinatown was there to see in the intelligent gleam of her dark eyes and the determined set of her chin.

"Do you want to take some of this face cream home with you, Suling?" the older woman said. "It's something new I'm trying out. Powdered pearls mixed with ginseng and camellia seed oil. You're still young, but it's a good thing to take steps before it's necessary." Madam Ning liked to chat about inconsequential things before discussing serious matters. Her voice, lilting and hypnotic, told Suling bits of news and gossip, worries about "her girls," none of which were serious because there had never been a problem in her establishment the shrewd woman couldn't resolve quickly and discreetly.

The door opened and Amah Chung shouldered her way in, carrying a large tray.

"Two bowls of hot soybean milk," she announced, "one sweetened with sugar for you, Young Miss, and the other salted for Madam. One steamed bun filled with sweet red bean paste, the other with salted duck egg yolk. You can argue over who gets which bun. I've got work in the kitchen." Amah Chung shuffled out and shut the bedroom door.

"She's my most valuable employee," Madam Ning remarked. "Whores come and go, but Amah Chung's cooking is always reliably excellent." She picked up the salted duck egg bun and bit into it with relish. "Drink your soy milk, my darling. Amah Chung pretends not to care but she will be very hurt if you don't eat something. Now, what is it that brings you here so early in the day?"

Her affectionate smile warmed Suling more than the sweet soy milk. She felt the tightness around her chest ease slightly. At least she could tell Auntie everything. Well, almost everything.

"My cousins have arrived," Suling said, ignoring the breakfast tray. "Their ship docked yesterday and now they're just waiting to get through Immigration. And when they do, I'll have to marry Dr. Ouyang." She sat on the bed and flopped backward with a groan.

American customs officials didn't make it easy for Chinese. They had been known to detain immigrants at the Pacific Mail Steamship terminals for several weeks, sometimes months. But the point was, her cousins would replace her at the laundry. And when that happened, Third Uncle wouldn't need her anymore, and he would marry her off to Dr. Ouyang. Who already had two wives.

"You're nineteen, it's time you married." Madam Ning lifted the bowl of soy milk to her lips and drank deeply. "Dr. Ouyang is one of the most respected men in Chinatown. He's a good man, a kind man. And it's not as though he's old and feeble. His hair is only just turning gray and for fifty, he's as trim and fit as a man of thirty."

Suling rolled her eyes. "But his wives! They were so rude to my mother. What will it be like living with them as his third wife, lowest in the hierarchy?"

"You'll be his favorite," Madam Ning asserted. "I know it.

When we were all much younger, Ouyang Lin was infatuated with your mother. He wasn't rich back then, but whenever he came to the brothel, it was always 'Is Ming Lee available?' even though your mother was one of the most expensive women there."

There were no secrets in Chinatown. Ming Lee and Madam Ning had been sold off by their families to men who shipped them to San Francisco, then resold them to brothels. In an industry where most girls died from abuse, illness, or suicide, the two became best friends and survived, Ming Lee by running away and Madam Ning by working her way up and taking over a brothel.

"Then why didn't Dr. Ouyang buy my mother from the brothel?" Suling said. "Or marry her after she escaped to the Mission Home, like my father did?"

"He would've bought out her contract if he'd had enough money," her aunt said, "but sometimes in life, timing is what matters."

Dr. Ouyang returned to China to raise money for an herbalist store of his own just as the US government passed the Chinese Exclusion Act, making it nearly impossible to immigrate. Ouyang endured months of questions and obstacles to prove he was a merchant—one of the few professions allowed to enter the country.

"And you know the rest," Madam Ning said. "During this time, your mother ran away to the Mission Home, your father, Feng, saw her there while delivering laundry, and after a few weeks, offered to marry her."

Feng didn't mind that Ming Lee had been a prostitute. There were so few Chinese women available that men were willing to buy out a prostitute or bond servant's contract and no one thought the less of them. If a man wanted a wife and family, Chinatown offered few other options.

"So you believe Dr. Ouyang will be kind to me for my mother's sake?" Suling said.

Her aunt shook her head. "No, my precious. Because you resemble your lovely mother."

"That's rather unnerving," Suling said with a shudder.

"Ouyang's wives know he was in love with your mother. That's why they were rude to her," Madam Ning said, "but you don't love Ouyang so your mind will be clear. With patience and cleverness, you'll find ways to carve out your own domain within Ouyang's household. Romance encumbers thought."

Suling straightened up. "I could be a terrible wife. I could be rude and uncooperative to the other wives, ignore his children, resist him in bed. Then he might divorce me."

"Or he might sell you to a brothel. Or to someone who supplies brothels." The words came out like a whip. "It wouldn't be the first time a husband got rid of a difficult wife by selling her."

"I'm an American citizen, born and raised here. I could run away, go to the Mission Home. Report my situation to the authorities."

"You wouldn't get the chance to run," Madam Ning snorted. "You'd be locked up until money exchanged hands, and afterward, too. It's what I would do."

"I could run away before the wedding," she said. "Miss Cameron would take me in, like she did Tye Leung. And now Tye helps Miss Cameron rescue girls from brothels and cruel employers."

"And Tye must live in the Mission Home," Madam Ning said, "where a policeman stands guard outside because they receive death threats from people for stealing their property."

Prostitutes and bond servants. Property. But still, wasn't Tye proof that a Chinese woman could earn her way? That times

were changing, especially for Chinese born in America, educated and fluent in English?

"You can't hide inside the Mission Home for the rest of your
life, Suling," Madam Ning continued. "Tye's parents eventually
agreed not to force her into an arranged marriage, and that's
why she's free to come and go."

Suling knew this. Just as she knew that most young women
who left the Mission Home did so after Miss Cameron arranged
marriages for them with Chinese Christian men. These men
traveled to San Francisco from other states to meet prospective
brides at the Mission Home. The legal protection of marriage
was one of the surest ways to deter former employers and owners from chasing after the rescued women.

But marriage to a stranger wasn't what Suling wanted, any
more than marriage to Dr. Ouyang.

"Your chin is jutting out, Suling, you have your stubborn
look." Madam Ning sighed. "It's that Reggie person, isn't it?
You haven't seen your Reggie in weeks. How often have I told
you those white devils just think of Chinese girls as novelties,
something exotic to try out?"

Just as Reggie had been an exotic novelty to her. Short black
curls, emerald-green eyes, and a generous mouth that smiled so
lazily, so invitingly. Suling pushed away the memory.

"What about you and Clarkson? You've been lovers for ten
years now," Suling said. "Is he a white devil?"

"He is a business arrangement, and fortunately he's grown
fond of me," Madam Ning said, rather primly.

Fortunate also that Sergeant Michael Clarkson happened to
lead the police unit tasked with investigating vice in Chinatown.
The Palace of Endless Joy was seldom raided, and if it was, nothing much ever came of it.

"Listen, my dearest," Madam Ning said, "the world doesn't

give women many paths to choose from. Worse yet, we are Chinese women in a country that hates Chinese." She turned to face Suling. "Whatever you do, keep in mind that you can't depend on others. Only yourself."

"I understand," Suling said, thinking of Reggie. Whose disappearance confirmed what Madam Ning often said, what her own mother believed: that the ones you love are the ones with the power to hurt you. Their own parents had sold them into prostitution. While Feng had been besotted with Ming Lee, Ming Lee had treated him with fondness and courtesy rather than love.

And she had not given in totally to Reggie, Suling reminded herself. And she'd been right not to give in totally to Reggie and romantic love.

It was just that Reggie was proving rather hard to forget.

IT WAS HALF past noon by the time Suling finished her class at the Mission Home. The girls were a pleasure to teach, motivated by her promise that if their embroidery work improved, she would try and sell their pieces. For the first time in their lives, they would keep the money they earned. Unfortunately for the girls, Suling reflected as she walked home, such meager earnings weren't enough if they hoped to support themselves. She knew this all too well from selling embroidered collars and cuffs to housewives along her laundry route.

She climbed up the stairs from the laundry to the living quarters above. The door to her uncle's room was wide open now and at the first squeak of floorboards he called her to enter.

"Niece, there's good news," he said, his thin, pockmarked face almost glowing with pleasure. "Dr. Ouyang has done us a tremendous favor. You just missed him."

"What kind of favor?" she said, not at all unhappy to have avoided the herbalist.

"He went down to Immigration at the Pacific Mail Steamship terminals," her uncle said. "He vouched for your cousins and made a few . . . ah, gifts of money here and there. They'll be processed quickly, out in two weeks. Guaranteed."

"Two weeks?" She bit her lip. So soon. Too soon.

"Ah, one more thing," her uncle said. "Dr. Ouyang tells me the fortune teller has picked the most favorable date for your wedding—April the nineteenth. So now you must work quickly on your wedding garments."

Suling shut the door to her room. She moved the wooden chair from her bedside to the wardrobe, felt for the small cloth bag hidden on top. It contained money she'd been putting aside, something she'd been doing even before meeting Reggie. She shook her head, pushing aside memories of Reggie, eyes shining as they pored over railway timetables.

But in the short time left before her supposed wedding day, she needed to earn as much money as she could. Because she was going to follow through with those plans to leave San Francisco.

With or without Reggie, she was going to escape from her marriage, from Chinatown. From this life.

Chapter 3

Gemma spotted Nellie's work the moment she made her way into the Grand Opera House. She didn't know a smidge about art, and even rooming with Nellie in the Bronx for five years hadn't taught her the difference between impressionism and art nouveau, or why oil paint was different from watercolor (except that it made their petticoats smell), but she knew *Nellie's* art. *I've been hired to touch up the frescoes in the Grand Opera House,* Nellie had written perhaps eight months ago in her careless scrawl. *I doubt they'd have hired a woman, but their usual artist hared off to San Diego without finishing the job, so here I am. Just the usual trompe l'oeil rubbish, cupids on clouds in nausea-inducing pastels!*

But Nellie could never resist putting her own irreverent touches into her work, even routine work. The cupids on the Grand Opera House's entry fresco had all been given droll expressions: this one smirking, that one batting his eyelashes, the pop-eyed one with a cloud added behind his bottom, so it looked like he'd just released some noxious smell. And the various Muses in Greek draperies on the ceiling, Gemma thought as she tilted her head back—the prim one with the lyre looked like the Taylor Street landlady, and was the one with the flower wreath Alice Eastwood? Yes, it was, right down to the friendly beam and the sprig of violets. Portraits had always been Nellie's specialty.

Gemma wandered farther into the building, not taking the double doors into the terraced tiers of seats, but the side doors that led backstage. All it took was a word with the dozing doorman, and a flash of her card as the Metropolitan Opera traveling company's newest member, and she was in. How many opera houses and theaters had she explored by now? The usual warren of dingy back passages, curling posters of old productions flapping on corridor walls, buckets parked out to catch the occasional leak . . . Gemma looped up her fringed hem as she wandered down toward the backstage area, inhaling the smells of violin resin, dusty velvet, and old scores, not seeing a soul. Opera houses were always quiet as crypts in the morning. Was there a musician alive who ever got up before nine? Noon if they could help it?

Normally she counted herself in that category, but she'd hardly slept a wink in her new Taylor Street lodgings. The migraine hadn't been so bad—only half a night of huddling in her darkened room with a cold-pack on her forehead, wishing she could scoop her eyes out with a spoon—but by the time she'd been able to sleep, wrung out and numb, her whole head still feeling fragile as glass, she'd slipped right into a nightmare about that horrible day in New York last month, scrabbling on her hands and knees and cringing as people laughed—so at dawn she rose, fed Toscanini a handful of seeds and a few chunks of apple, and headed out bleary-eyed into the already-bustling city.

But now she heard the distant sound of a piano and felt the night fog clearing away. It was the "Habanera" from *Carmen*, in fact, being played with considerable panache. Humming along, Gemma followed the sound to a practice room and poked her head around the door left ajar.

The man at the piano stool turned to look over one shoulder, broad hands finishing up the complicated final flourish of the "Habanera." "Looking for someone?"

"Looks like I've found someone." He was olive-skinned, burly, black hair mussed and sleeves rolled up. "I'm the newest member of the traveling Metropolitan Opera company," she said, giving him the day version of her stage curtsy—a flick of the train, a graceful sinking of the knees, a sparkling smile. Her armor, arriving at a new opera house. No one in San Francisco, after all, had any idea what had happened to her in New York. "Gemma Garland."

"You're a couple weeks ahead of Signor Caruso and the rest of the company," the burly man observed, swinging around on the piano bench.

"I'm to take the place of a soprano departing in Kansas City and thought I'd come early to see the sights. This morning I've already walked down a hill so steep it could have doubled as an Alp, seen a Chinese woman with the tiniest bound feet imaginable as I was passing Chinatown, and heard the latest city gossip about a local Pinkerton detective who has gone missing. Foul play is suspected, according to the trolley car driver who let me off past Market Street. That is, south of the slot," Gemma corrected. "Is that how a San Franciscan says it?"

"It is." The pianist lifted a hand to his head as if only belatedly realizing he didn't have a hat to doff. "George Serrano—" He pronounced it with a Latin roll, Spanish or maybe Brazilian, though his English was unaccented. "I'm one of the repetiteurs here. I imagine I'll be rehearsing you in the practice rooms once the company arrives."

Gemma was glad she'd turned on the charm. Repetiteurs, those invaluable rehearsal pianists and accompanists, were very good allies to have in an opera house. Win them over, and they'd rehearse you an extra half hour if you were feeling insecure in your Act III recitative. Alienate them, and they'd start your aria in the wrong key just to see you squirm. "I don't suppose—" she began, tilting her head under her narrow-brimmed straw laden with blush-pink roses, but he cut her off with a grin.

"You want to try the stage? Sopranos always do."

"Mezzos, too," Gemma protested, but smiled back. "Would anyone mind if I . . ."

"Help yourself. Straight back and up the stairs."

He gave a friendly wave, about to turn back to the piano, but Gemma stopped him on impulse. "I don't suppose you remember a woman artist working here, Mr. Serrano? She was hired to touch up the frescoes in the entryway—dark hair, often wore trousers?"

"I remember her. She quit last summer. Left the work half done, which had the management in a froth."

Gemma would like to say that didn't sound like Nellie, but it did. *They're only paying me half what they'd pay a man, Sal,* she'd say as she lit out for a better opportunity, *so they shouldn't be astounded if I only do half the work.* And of course, the opera house wouldn't have Nell's new address, wherever she was. After Gemma left their shared Bronx apartment flat for a traveling opera company in Boston and Nellie departed for the Hudson River Valley to paint landscapes for a summer, the two of them had conducted much of their friendship through letters—they'd fall back into room-sharing whenever they were both passing through New York, which was relatively often, and then Gemma would tease Nellie all over again about her mugs of brush water lying everywhere, and Nellie would tease Gemma about her ever-present throat lozenges, but letters had become their lifeline: a conversation carried on for nearly eight years. And in eight years, how often did scatterbrained Nell *ever* remember to leave a forwarding address?

She should have left one this time, Gemma couldn't help but think. *She knew I was coming to San Francisco, and she knew I was in a bad way.* But Gemma pushed that persistent, piercing little hurt aside for now, saying, "Thank you, Mr. Serrano."

"George," he said with a cheerful salute, going back to the piano. "Come back anytime you want to run some arias—" And she wandered back the way he'd pointed, ascending stairs and ducking through stage doors, until she found herself in the wings, looking at it.

The stage.

It's a splendid space, Sal, Nellie had written. *I can just see you up there draped in diamonds, slingshotting your big high C's over the footlights!* Gemma found herself holding her breath, as she did the first time she came onto any new stage. Just a raked expanse of boards, dusty in the harsh overhead lights, showing every scuff mark. None of the sets, the costumes, the music that turned it into an enchanted space; just a bare stage. The thing that lived on the back of Gemma's eyelids, had lived there ever since seven-year-old Sally Gunderson opened her mouth in church and poured out "Abide with Me" in such a pure, ringing flood of sound that nearly the entire congregation fell silent. Opening her eyes and realizing people were looking at her, and thinking *yes*.

Yes.

This is what I want.

Standing there in that Nebraska church in her achingly white spats under her frilly Sunday frock . . . that hard-backed pew had been her first stage, and it hadn't needed a spotlight for her to know it was where she wanted to be. "Little girls should be seen but not heard," her mother had told her, growing up, but Gemma had known from age seven that she wanted to be seen *and* heard. Her mother's gentle chiding hadn't nudged that desire out of her, and neither had the orphanage matron's birch switch, later.

Gemma looked out over the shadowed tiers of empty seats (twenty-five hundred of them, her new landlady had told her in that odd accent between Boston and Brooklyn that seemed to be the local San Francisco twang) and imagined this place two weeks from now: packed to the rafters, flashing with diamonds, the scent of expensive tobacco and even more expensive perfume wafting up, the drone of a hundred different conversations that stopped only when the conductor lifted his baton . . . everyone who was anyone in this brash, bustling city, come to hear the great Caruso. Maybe they wouldn't notice Gemma in the ranks of the chorus. But Caruso might. He was said to be a man who appreciated a pretty soprano, after all.

She walked center stage, hummed a little to wake the voice up, ran through some scales and vocalises. She didn't need a piano; she had perfect pitch—she'd warmed up before auditions in tiled washrooms, in crowded corridors, even once in a broom cupboard. Her vocal cords now thrumming, she started with some Mozart, Cherubino's aria from *The Marriage of Figaro*, simple and familiar, then on to the Countess from the same opera. One of Gemma's favorites, the Act III aria, sorrow giving way to hope, and that thrilling fall from the high A . . . She could hear her voice resonate, rising through these empty tiers, filling the nooks and crannies, and started on some Handel, feeling out her higher register despite the postmigraine tenderness of her head. What she'd give to sing the Queen of the Night here, hurl her high F's into the void like crystal bullets . . .

The sound of slow clapping followed her final tripping run. Gemma peered down into the house. "Hello?" she called.

He came toward the stage from the back of the opera house, still clapping. A man in a dark suit—she couldn't see more from this distance. "Zerlina," he said.

Gemma blinked. "I beg your pardon?"

"New York, '98 or '99. *Don Giovanni*." He nodded, as if flipping to the end of some mental index. "You sang Zerlina."

"That was '98. I only sang the role for one night—I was the understudy." Twenty-four years old, her first contract with a small opera company, steadily making her way out of the chorus into modest roles. That one night of Zerlina had been Gemma's first chance at a larger part; she'd been borderline delirious at her good luck. "How on earth do you remember me? I was just a last-minute replacement for—"

"I never forget a voice, and yours is unusual." The man came out into the light by the orchestra pit, doffing his hat, and she could finally take the measure of him. A lean, rather homely face; dark hair in need of a trim; a long jaw in need of a shave. His suit was expensive but he wore it carelessly, collar open to show a tanned throat, fine gloves half stuffed into his pocket. He stood with head tilted back, hat in one hand, the other jangling a charm on his watch chain, and he had yet to take his eyes off her. "Your singing has a silvery quality, but most voices like that sound silvery and cold. Yours has a warmth, like silver and Christmas incense."

"You flatter me, sir. I have to tell you, I'm not at all averse to being flattered." There hadn't been much of it lately.

"Oh, I'm not flattering you at all." He sounded businesslike, as though he were stating figures for a board meeting. "I don't really bother with people I need to flatter. I look for the best, the ones who don't need it. What you have in that throat of yours is something special. Better than it was eight years ago; it's put weight on. Gravitas. You should be singing Donna Anna now, not Zerlina. The leads, not the ingenues."

"Gracious," Gemma said, trying to catch hold of this odd conversation. "I didn't think a man could tell a woman she'd put weight on without sounding like a cad, but I was wrong."

"Pardon me, I have no manners at all. A complaint I hear frequently." He smiled, eyes still not moving away from her.

Gemma was suddenly glad she'd put on her best walking suit this morning, the blush-pink faille with blond satin collar and cuffs exactly the same shade as her hair. "Might I inquire after your name, Zerlina? The program from eight years ago didn't list the understudies."

She introduced herself, gave him her story—the Metropolitan Opera Chorus, her early arrival in San Francisco, coming to the opera house to look for a friend—but she gave it with a bit more verve and sparkle than she'd given to Alice Eastwood or George Serrano the repetiteur. *Silver and Christmas incense . . .*

"Chorus work?" The man in the rumpled suit tilted his head. "Why?"

Gemma evaded. "I don't believe I know *your* name, sir."

"Henry Thornton, of Thornton Ltd. Also Thornton Railways and Thornton Ironworks."

A man of means, then. Perhaps. Gentlemen did like to inflate their standing when looking to impress a woman. "A man of business, who knows something about music. How very rare."

"Business is boring. It exists to fund the things in life that matter."

"Such as?"

"I'm not certain how to answer that." He rubbed his jaw, reflective. "If I say *art*, then I sound like a pretentious boor. But it is what I believe. Business isn't worth much, in the grand scope of things. Art—beauty—music—those are the things that matter." A shrug. "So perhaps you'll think me a pretentious boor. I can't help that."

Gemma was inclined to warm to him, but reminded herself: *hard-nosed!* Pretty phrases did not make for sincerity. "Are you musical yourself?"

"Oh, no. Hopeless," he said promptly. "Can't sing, can't play, can't sketch or draw or dance. But I know great art when I see it." He bowed slightly. "And great artists."

"Favorite opera?" Gemma challenged.

"*Pelléas et Mélisande*. I saw it in Paris."

"How modern of you. I was sure you'd say something trite. *Barber of Seville*."

"Overdone."

"I admit it's never been my favorite."

"Because the starring role isn't a soprano."

Gemma burst out laughing.

"You laugh like a bell," he observed. "I'd give you a railroad to sing the 'Bell Song' for me."

"I sing the 'Bell Song' divinely, but what would I want with a railroad?"

"I would invite you to have dinner with me instead, but . . ."

"But?"

"You look like a nice girl, Miss Garland." He smiled again. "I'm not very nice. Better steer clear of me."

"I always steer clear of stage-door Johnnys," Gemma parried, even as she thought, *A nice girl?* Not exactly what a woman dreamed of being called when she was trying to reinvent into a tougher, steelier version of herself. Gemma busied herself with her handbag, crossing the stage with a rustle of taffeta petticoats. "If that's all, Mr. Thornton—"

"Dammit," he said. "I'm going to invite you to dinner anyway. Call it a business meeting."

"I should still say no. Since I've heard you aren't very nice."

"I'm not, but at least you're forewarned." He came to meet her, reaching up to assist her down the stairs. "Does tomorrow suit you?"

His hand was ungloved, and as her own alighted on it, she saw it had been badly burned at some point. Not a fresh injury:

his fingers curled inward slightly as if the skin had healed too tight to stretch; the last two fingers were missing their nails, and the scarred knuckles were as rough to the touch as a tree root. He could have easily hidden it with a glove, but he hadn't. Gemma didn't let so much as a flicker of reaction or curiosity show, and she thought she saw his eyes crinkle in response. He was clearly used to stares.

"The Palace Grill," he said. "Tomorrow?"

The best restaurant in San Francisco, Gemma already knew that much. *Take it*, she could practically hear Nellie crow. *Order the oysters* and *the champagne! Rich admirers should be soaked for everything you can get, Sal.* Nellie had always been better than Gemma at being hard-nosed.

Still . . .

"Perhaps I'll have dinner with you, Mr. Thornton." Gemma glided down the last step. "It really depends on what else you have."

"Shall I show you my stock certificates?"

"Your marriage certificate, if you have one. You see, I don't accept dinner engagements from gentlemen who are already engaged at home." She wasn't *quite* unscrupulous enough for that, and never had been. *Rich patrons pay the bills*, Nellie had said before, more than once, *and most of them are married. You think their wives don't know they keep dancers and singers and the odd painter like me on the side? With that voice and that bust, you could have your own suite at the Park Avenue Hotel and your own carriage driving you to rehearsal every day.*

I'm an artist, Gemma had protested, knowing she sounded like a prig. *Not a courtesan!* Nellie had looked a little wounded at that, clearly feeling her roommate was sitting in judgment, and maybe she was right—Gemma *did* judge. In most ways she'd left Red Hook, Nebraska, behind her, but not all. In her entire career, she'd never taken so much as a pair of gloves from a man with a wife at home.

And yet, where exactly had all her Nebraska morals and standards gotten her? In a very bad New York mess, that was where . . .

"No wife at home," Mr. Thornton said, breaking the scatter of her thoughts. He was nearly a head taller than she, looking down steadily. "Here, or in New York, or anywhere."

He might be fibbing, of course.

"You probably wonder if I'm lying." He read her mind easily, scarred fingers still holding hers. He made no effort to pull her closer. "I sometimes lie, but never in business. And it is a business proposition I wish to make to you, Miss Garland."

She raised her eyebrows. "Oh, really?"

"Not the kind you're thinking of. A true business proposition, from a hardheaded man to a clever woman."

"I'm clever now, am I?"

"Better than *nice.*"

He was still toying with the charm on his watch chain—a white jade disk with a hole in its center, polished smooth and shining. "Is there a story behind that?" she asked.

"I'll tell you tomorrow," he answered, releasing her hand. "At the Palace Grill. Eight?"

"Eight." Gemma nodded crisply, thinking of her lean wallet. In truth, she couldn't really afford to turn down a free dinner. She'd just keep the oyster fork at hand in case his proposition turned indecent (and didn't they usually? Sigh). She moved past him toward the opera house doors like a no-nonsense artist who knew her worth, a sensible woman who wasn't going to be bamboozled by pretty words, and he didn't try to crowd her or brush against her as gentlemen so often did. He just stood back, watching, and Gemma's hand tingled briefly inside her glove where he'd held it.

Don't look back at him, she thought. A no-nonsense woman wouldn't, so she didn't.

Besides, she didn't have to look back to know that he was still staring.

Chapter 4

April 6, 1906
Eleven days, seventeen hours,
twenty-nine minutes before the earthquake

Third Uncle was at his favorite mah-jongg parlor and Suling didn't expect him back until after midnight. She could get ready for the afternoon's deliveries without him discovering her ruse.

It was safer to leave the neighborhood dressed as a boy. Too many white men still assumed that a Chinese woman outside Chinatown was a prostitute. When she'd first put on boy's clothing, she had used strips of cotton sheeting to bind her breasts, which proved too time-consuming. Instead she'd sewn herself a sleeveless vest that buttoned up tightly to flatten her slim figure. Over this she now put on a boxy boy's jacket. Her hair was already plaited in a single neat pigtail so all she had to do was clap a fedora on her head. It had been her father's hat and was too large, the brim almost obscuring her eyes. But it hid the fact that the crown of her head wasn't shaved as it would've been if she were really a boy.

Her father would've been aghast to see her dressed like this, but Suling was no longer a sheltered daughter. It was even more imperative now that she go with Old Kow on his delivery rounds, opportunities to get out of Chinatown and sell her embroidery to earn a bit more money. Money for train tickets. For rooms and food. For bribes.

Suling touched the red silk cord around her neck out of habit, felt for the ring strung on it. A sharp lancet of pain in her heart made her wince and she considered throwing away the cord and the ring. But she decided to wear it until she didn't feel even a small twinge. It was a useful reminder of her folly in ever believing she had a future with Reggie.

Downstairs, the caustic smell of lye soap drifted up the stairwell. The workers' loud conversation and the metallic grinding of clothes wringers drowned out all other noises, including the squeak of the door as she slipped out to the street. Old Kow was waiting for her by the curb, standing beside the two-wheeled pushcart, which was stacked with packages of clean laundry. The elderly man greeted her with a gap-toothed grin. His dislike for Third Uncle made him a willing conspirator in this deception.

"Up the hill or toward the waterfront, Young Miss?" he said, calloused hands gripping the shafts of the cart. Eight months ago, before her parents died, she had been Kow's employer's daughter and he still treated her with deference even though Third Uncle now owned the business.

"The waterfront." She helped with the cart, guiding as he pushed it over the uneven paving stones of Washington Street. It was still early afternoon, not too warm yet, but enough that the stench of dried horse manure rose up from between the cobblestones.

"Miss Feng, you must be impatient for your cousins to get through Immigration," Old Kow said, as they turned south onto Stockton Street. "Then you can finally get married. Nineteen is rather old, if you don't mind my bluntness in saying so. By the time my wife was nineteen, we'd had three children."

He continued talking, more to himself than to her. Kow was one of the hundreds of aging men left without decent employment once the railways were built and the gold rush ended. Suling's mother had felt sorry for Old Kow and had given him a part-time job helping their delivery boy. Then, three months ago, the delivery boy quit and Old Kow had to make deliveries on his own. But Kow's English and memory proved so poor that he returned with incomprehensible messages, strange requests that caused confusion at the laundry and irritation to their customers.

"And what will I do when you're married and gone?" Kow continued. "Your cousins won't speak English yet; how can they help with deliveries to foreign customers?"

"I'm sure my uncle will think of something," Suling said, even though Third Uncle had yet to come up with a single useful idea, before or since her parents died.

For several weeks after her parents' death Suling spent her days almost doubled over with grief, battered by waves of intense and uncontrollable anguish. Third Uncle had made an effort to manage the laundry on his own. But all too soon, even in the depths of sorrow, Suling saw why her father had been so reluctant to turn over all but the simplest management tasks to his younger brother. Third Uncle's idea of running the laundry consisted of haranguing the workers even when all was well. The workers were longtime employees, diligent and well-trained. But one by one the men quit because Third Uncle insulted them unforgivably, then cut their wages as his gambling debts mounted. Now only the desperate and shiftless were willing to work at Fenghuang Laundry; opium addicts and gamblers who disappeared as soon as they had enough in their pockets for another pipe full of dreams or another game of mah-jongg.

Out of respect for what her parents had worked so hard to build, Suling forced herself to go down to the laundry each day and tried her best to keep everything running. She found that work helped keep grief at bay. She stared for hours at her father's ledgers until she understood how to keep the accounts, even though that was supposed to be Third Uncle's job. It was Suling who suggested sending for cousins from China to replace the succession of inept men who cycled through the laundry. Family did not quit a family business; they did what was required. Family did not ask for salaries; they lived together, ate together, and took a share of profits only if the business flourished.

Shortly after this, Third Uncle agreed to Dr. Ouyang's marriage offer—an offer that included a substantial payment. Couch it in whatever terms he chose, Third Uncle was selling her to the herbalist. Her parents, loving and indulgent, had never pressed her to marry, had always said the decision was hers even though there'd been many lucrative offers for her hand—in Chinatown, young women of childbearing age were rarer than white peacocks. Suling had been blessed to have such parents.

Now that Third Uncle was her oldest male relative, in the eyes of their community he was entitled to rule her life. Her tears and pleas meant nothing to him. The affable young uncle of her childhood who took her to watch Chinatown's festivities had never really cared about her. He only cared that she was the answer to his debts. He cleared out the cashbox every afternoon before going to a gambling parlor. At least he had enough sense not to demand more; he knew she held money back to pay wages and buy supplies.

What he didn't know was that she'd begun taking money from the cashbox for herself. She had no loyalty to Third Uncle anymore.

SULING AND OLD KOW began the afternoon's deliveries on Stockton Street at the edge of Chinatown, to some white shopkeepers. Their English-lettered signs stood out: a grocery store, a boardinghouse, a stable yard, and a carpenter's workshop. Chinese or white, families that lived above their own stores were squeezed into cramped rooms too small to hold the tubs and mangles needed to wash, let alone dry, their laundry. Thus all but the poorest households sent their washing to laundries.

When they crossed California Street and out of Chinatown, Kow's sauntering gait changed to one more purposeful, and at the same time, more inconspicuous and unassuming. "The trick," Kow said when Suling first began doing the rounds with him, "is to look busy, as if you're on an important errand for a customer. And you never stare or gawp. Look straight ahead, step out of the way if you must, but as though we inhabit different worlds."

Different worlds. She should've remembered this before getting involved with Reggie. Suling clenched a fist against her heart for a moment. She couldn't think about Reggie. Not now, not ever again. And certainly not while she was making deliveries.

Suling took an armload of string-tied packages to the servants' door at the side of the next house. When the door opened, she greeted the housekeeper politely.

"Wait a moment there," the lady said, looking at her more closely. "You're not the usual boy."

"No, madam," Suling replied. "He left. I'm the new boy." She had been accompanying Old Kow since the delivery boy quit. That was three months ago, and this woman hadn't noticed until now. Hadn't ever truly looked at her, or at her predecessor.

"Well, at least you speak English. Don't run away yet." She tore open one of the packages and shook her finger at Suling. "Now then, you tell your people to use more bluing on these sheets next time. I want a nice, bright white."

"I will tell them, madam."

"Your work's been shoddy for months," the woman said. "I've a good mind to go somewhere else. The only reason I haven't is because those other laundries don't know English and I can't abide that pidgin talk. Why can't you Chinamen talk proper if you want to live here? You and that other boy, you're the only ones I can understand."

"I was born here, madam," Suling said. "Good day to you." She gave a mental shrug as she walked down the wooden steps, remembering her father's advice. Once, after a white customer had loudly insulted them at the laundry, she'd asked her father why he wasn't angry. Feng shrugged. They lived among people who despised them. If they registered every offensive comment, expended emotion at every insult, they'd never manage to get on with their own lives.

She returned to the cart and grimaced in reply to Old Kow's inquiring look. "I think we might lose that one's business, too," she said. "Sheets not white enough."

He shook his head. "I tell those lazy beggars to soak the whites longer, but they want to hurry off and gamble. They take no pride at all in their work. Not like the old days, Young Miss. Not like when your parents ran a proper laundry."

But Suling wasn't paying attention to his words. A horse-drawn buggy had caught her attention, a glimpse of billowing white shirt and dark curls, the passenger's features shaded by the carriage awning. Then the buggy drove past and sunlight fell on a stranger's face. It wasn't Reggie. Suling exhaled, not even aware until that moment that she had stopped breathing.

She couldn't go on like this.

At the next house a petite woman in a gingham dress and matching sunbonnet was bent over a tiny strip of garden. When Suling approached she stood up and indicated that Suling could put the packages of laundry on the front stoop. Suling then gave the woman a small box.

"Oh good, you brought my collars." The woman lifted out twelve sets of white linen collars, each exquisitely embroidered.

"Daisies, roses, violets. Beautiful work as usual. Tell your mistress I'll need a dozen more again next week. Any kind of flower. Same price." She reached in her pocket. "Here you go. And here's a little extra for you, boy."

"Thank you, ma'am." Suling touched a finger to the brim of the fedora. The enterprising young housewife sold the collars to her friends for twice what she paid Suling. Since Suling could never get higher prices from a white customer, at least this meant the woman bought up most of Suling's work. Collars, cuffs, borders, these were all easy. She worked on them during her spare hours and late into the night, needle flashing through cloth, brain calculating how much more she had to save before feeling confident enough to buy a ticket out of San Francisco.

The last house on their route was on Nob Hill. It was an octagon house, an eight-sided structure on Hyde Street, four stories high, with an abundance of windows and topped with a cupola. A veranda decorated with intricate fretwork wrapped around the entire ground floor. A section of the veranda was glassed in, a solarium that served as a foyer connecting to a long conservatory filled with plants and flowers Suling had never seen anywhere else.

Suling took a deep breath as they crossed the street, willing herself not to think of how many times she had been here, not to deliver laundry but to steal some time with Reggie. She tamped down those minutes in her mind, memories now useless except as object lessons.

Kow, oblivious to the roil of emotions behind her smooth features, hurried to the gate. He enjoyed deliveries to this address because his friends worked here. The houseboy and cook's helper, known as Big Fong and Little Fong, had been hired only a few weeks ago, tipped off by Suling, who'd overheard the housekeeper voicing a need for more staff. In Chinatown, knowledge and connections created bonds, debts of honor and loyalty, transactions that did not involve money.

The tradesmen's entrance opened to a short flight of steps to the basement where the domestic servants worked. The hurried pace in the kitchen and short, barked orders from the cook made it clear preparations were underway for a large party. Meat roasted in the oven and a huge copper pot simmered on the stove. A scullery maid was shelling a mountain of peas, and across the kitchen table, Little Fong was bent over a cutting board.

When Suling called out a greeting to him, Little Fong merely waved and went back to deboning a duck. Suling pushed open the door to the laundry room across from the kitchen, and Old Kow stacked the packages of laundry at one end of a long table. At the other end, a maid toiled over a gray wool jacket, carefully sponging out a stain. The young woman glanced up, tiny auburn curls peeping out from her cap, perspiration beading on her freckled forehead.

"You takee this," she said, pointing at two canvas laundry bags in the corner. "You puttee more starchee on napkins. No good last time. Do like this again and we send linens to the Hospital."

Many Nob Hill homes sent their laundry to St. Christina's Convent and Hospital, which operated a laundry business. Their cost of labor was free, the work considered part of their mental patients' therapy. This competition bothered Suling more than the maid's pidgin English.

"I will let the laundrymen know, miss," she said. "Is Mrs. MacNeil in? I'd like to see her."

"What for?"

Suling stifled a sigh. "It's the first Friday of the month. This is when she pays the laundry bill."

"I'm busy," the maid retorted. "Wait until she comes down. Now get out of my laundry room."

"I'll see if Big Fong can spare a moment," Old Kow said when they left the laundry room. "He'll tell the housekeeper you're here."

He took the two bags from Suling and she followed him outside. After only a moment's hesitation, she turned and hurried along the brick path that circled the octagon house, berating herself for being so weak. The veranda contained the main door to the glass and iron confection that was the conservatory, but Suling ignored the steps to the veranda. She continued around the corner to the gardener's entrance, screened behind a pair of oleander shrubs. The door opened to a utility area in the conservatory hidden behind flowering trellises of scarlet bougainvillea. Reggie had shown her how to come in this way. Just across from the bougainvillea, beside a display of ginger lilies, they had kissed for the first time. Suling gazed at the spikes of white blossoms, breathed in the spicy scent that was now linked forever to Reggie.

But she had told herself not to give in completely to Reggie, either physically or emotionally. She had held back, paid attention to Auntie's advice. Because she never wanted to feel the pain of loss again. The overwhelming loss of her parents. The smaller loss, more of a disappointment, really, when she realized her uncle had never cared about her. The loss she would soon face upon leaving Chinatown, her community, and San Francisco, her city.

She touched the red silk cord around her neck, felt the cool metal of the ring between her breasts. If the ring lanced pain through her heart, the conservatory squeezed it through a mangle. Hot tears stung her eyes. She had not done very well at holding back her feelings. She had to accept that Reggie had left, abandoned her and San Francisco for some new interest. But remembering the feel of Reggie's lips on hers, Suling couldn't believe she had been just an exotic novelty. She wiped her eyes before returning to the house.

Old Kow was beside the tradesmen's entrance, sharing a cigarette with the two Fongs. The Fongs knew who Suling was, of course, and grateful for her role in their employment, they would never reveal her deception. She wished they'd been hired sooner, when Reggie still lived there. They might've known what happened.

". . . and the police barged into Ah Ling's home," Kow was saying, "as though a family of six living in one small room could hide a missing man. They're really worked up over this."

"The missing man is a Pinkerton detective," Big Fong said, "and there's a rumor going around that someone from Chinatown is to blame."

Kow snorted. "Someone from Chinatown is somehow always to blame. The police want to solve the case before the Pinkerton agency does. It's like a contest."

Big Fong waved at Suling. "The housekeeper wants to see you, Young Miss," he called. "She's in her office."

As BEFIT HER status, the housekeeper's room was large and served as both office and bedroom. A tall folding screen concealed the bed. The stout and stately woman sat behind a small desk, crossing items off a list.

"Mrs. MacNeil," Suling said. "You wished to see me about the monthly bill? I have it right here."

"We can deal with that later," the housekeeper said, standing up. "The master wants to see you. Let's go up."

Mrs. MacNeil patted down her hair at the mirror by the door and repinned the cameo brooch on her blouse. Suling followed her up the back staircase, used by servants to get to the service corridors on each floor. At the second floor, the housekeeper opened the service door and they entered the marble-tiled mezzanine. At its center, a circular staircase with gilded wrought-iron banisters spiraled up from the main floor to the top of the mansion. None of the servants, not even Mrs. MacNeil and the butler, ever used this staircase. Suling risked a quick look over the stairwell as they crossed the mezzanine and stumbled, a brief moment of vertigo, the corkscrew effect of the railings setting off her fear of heights. She much preferred the service stairs, enclosed by sturdy wood paneling.

The housekeeper stopped at a door flanked by two palm trees in large porcelain urns. The door was wide open and inside, Mr. Henry Thornton's office was as busy as the kitchen downstairs. A clerk sat at a table, fingers pecking away at a typewriter. Another clerk made marks on a large map that nearly covered one wall while a third stood behind him making notes on a pad.

"Get that paperwork to the land titles office at once," a commanding voice called. "I want that thousand-acre parcel tied up before Felix Brisac changes his mind."

A chorus of assurances that the matter would be dealt with immediately, and the office emptied with a shuffle of papers and a rush of young men in gray wool suits and stiff collars. Attaché cases gripped tightly in their hands, they hurried down the circular stairs. They lived in their employer's home as Reggie once did, available to Thornton any time of the day or night.

Suling knew about Thornton. He had business connections everywhere, even in Chinatown. But living at the octagon house, Reggie knew more. *He has an office in the Financial District*, Reggie had explained, *but when he's got a party, like he does tonight, he prefers his office at home because he can keep working until the last minute before guests arrive.*

They'd been snatching a few precious minutes in the conservatory before Reggie had to return upstairs. Suling twisted one of Reggie's curls around her finger. Coal black, darker than the deep brown-black of her own hair. *He makes me attend so many parties. He's relentless when he's after something*, Reggie had said, with reluctant admiration. Thornton applied the same intense persistence whether he was acquiring a tract of land, a railway, a silver mine, or a work of art. *And I'm part of how he'll succeed in what he wants.*

And yet, Thornton had let Reggie go. That was the most curious thing, the question that prickled at the back of Suling's mind. Had Thornton's plans changed so that he no longer needed Reggie? Or had Reggie disappointed Thornton and been fired?

Mrs. MacNeil now gave Suling's shoulder a tug and pulled her to the doorway. "The laundry delivery boy is here, Mr. Thornton."

"Send him in and you can go," the voice said. A confident, assured voice.

Suling stood on the Persian carpet in front of the large desk and looked around. The wall opposite the map was lined with bookcases that reached almost to the ceiling, their continuous ranks broken by a doorway that led to a smaller room, a private study.

"Take a message to Madam Ning," he said, coming out of the study. Without preamble, barely glancing at her. He set down a stack of documents on the desk.

Suling understood immediately. When their delivery boy quit, he'd given notice to her, not Third Uncle. Apologizing with every breath, the boy also explained to her the arrangement between Thornton and Madam Ning. Madam Ning spoke, but didn't read, English so the boy carried verbal messages between the octagon house and the brothel. This was the first time Suling had been called upstairs to take a message. Thornton hadn't given a party in a while, at least not one where he wanted Madam Ning's services.

"I'd like the usual, half a dozen girls; the party's on Monday," he said, shuffling through the paperwork on his desk. "It's an afternoon function. They should be here at one o'clock, they can leave at four. Same work and pay as always."

"Yes, Mr. Thornton."

Now he looked up. "You're not the usual laundryboy."

"He quit," she said, "but he told me what to do."

"Well then." A pause. "Be sure she sends Susie, or if Susie isn't available, some other girl who speaks English."

"Yes, Mr. Thornton."

THE FIRST TIME Thornton made his unusual request, he had sent a written note. Madam Ning had turned over the embossed letterhead, run her fingers across the thick creamy paper, then called Suling over to read it. The brothel owner had been suspicious at first, then bemused. Thornton wanted her girls to dress up in Chinese clothing, sumptuous gowns that he would provide, and serve drinks to his guests. "Living exotics" were his words.

There followed a discussion back and forth, conveyed every week through the delivery boy until Thornton, no doubt recognizing his equal in negotiations, agreed to all Madam Ning's conditions.

He would send a carriage to fetch the girls and take them back to the brothel, avoiding any possibility of their being harassed, kidnapped, or endangered in any way outside Chinatown.

He would pay Madam Ning the same hourly rate as what the girls could reasonably expect to earn at the brothel even though they would only be serving drinks.

He would pay double for one of the girls, who could speak English and who would translate his commands to the others. Madam Ning had put in this last condition for Suling's benefit. "It's a convenience for him and an assurance for me, since none of my girls speak English very well," she told Suling. "If you're there, everyone avoids misunderstandings. And for you, it's extra money. You need your own income now that your parents are gone, and your uncle is totally useless."

"But what about my uncle?" Suling said. "How can I explain why I'm going out at night?" Madam Ning pondered for a moment, then smiled. "Leave it with me. He won't ever know."

When the time came for the first engagement, Third Uncle suddenly hit a lucky streak at the gambling parlor. Flush with winnings and eager to try his luck again, he sent word to the laundry that he was busy and for Suling to do the closing up. Madam Ning assured Suling he would not return until the morning.

An hour later, her face powdered white, eyebrows penciled to the classic willow leaf shape, and lips stained a deep scarlet, Suling climbed into the carriage with five of Madam Ning's prettiest whores. At the octagon house, Thornton's housekeeper, features impassive, took them upstairs to the third floor via the back staircase. A sharp word from Mrs. MacNeil and they trooped into a room where gorgeously embroidered tunics and high-collared jackets hung on a rack. A second rack held an assortment of colorful trousers and paneled skirts. A selection of embroidered cloth shoes, some flat and some with tall wooden platform soles, were lined up against one wall.

Amid much laughter and raucous jokes, the women dressed,

elbowing one another away from the tall mirror by the window. The jackets were wide, the tunics flared out down to the knees, comfortable and easy to wear. They tried on the shoes, one pair after another to find the best-fitting ones. Suling wished she had time to study the intricate embroidery, some created using stitches she had never seen before.

"Do you really think we won't be required for sex?" Butterfly said. Her real name was far less dainty. "How can a man be willing to pay so much without wanting the game of clouds and rain?"

"Let's see what happens," Hyacinth said. "Perhaps he'll want to watch women having sex. Wouldn't that be nice?" She slipped her arm around Butterfly and pulled her into a passionate kiss.

"Not in front of the child," Butterfly giggled, but she returned Hyacinth's kiss.

"The child has seen worse," Suling said, "but the housekeeper will be shocked, so stop it. She's knocking on the door."

But it wasn't the housekeeper who entered, it was Thornton. "Which of you is the one who speaks English?" he asked.

"I am," Suling said. "My name is Suling."

"Sue Ling? All right, Susie," he said, "my guests arrive in fifteen minutes. Tell the girls they're going to be in the Chinese Room. The servants will make sure their trays are always filled with glasses of champagne. All they need to do is smile and offer champagne to any guests walking by."

The women couldn't help sighing with pleasure upon entering Thornton's Chinese Room. One wall was paneled in black lacquer painted in gold, scenes of arched bridges and pagodas. Red lacquer panels inlaid with orchids and butterflies in mother-of-pearl adorned the opposite wall. Against a third wall, cabinets with glass fronts held Thornton's collections: snuff bottles, jade figurines, enameled vases. But it was the glass case at the far end of the room that captured the women's interest: a blue-and-gold headdress mounted on a stand.

"Oh, a phoenix crown," Butterfly breathed, pressing her nose to the glass. "This must've belonged to an empress. Or a royal consort."

Only women from the royal family could've owned such a headdress. Sapphires, pearls, and rubies traced a pattern around the lower part of the headdress. Phoenixes carved from pale blue-and-white jade flew across the front and sides. Heavy white tassels, which on closer inspection were strings of tiny white pearls, dangled down the back, carved flower pendants at their ends. Strings of larger pearls looped down the sides. But the blue! The upper part of the headdress was covered in hundreds of blue flowers and blue butterflies trembling on gold wires. The petals and butterfly wings were inlaid with king-fisher feathers, a brilliant, intense color more enthralling to the eye than any gemstone or flower, so vivid Suling felt she had never truly seen the color blue before.

The evening had proceeded just as promised. Suling and the others only had to smile and hold out trays of champagne. Guests wandered about chatting to one another, peering with envy at the treasures in Thornton's collection. The male guests stared openly at the Chinese women.

"Your, ah, serving wenches are rather unique, Thornton," she heard one man say. "The men are titillated, and the women would be scandalized if they weren't so curious about the Chinese whores. Which brothel did you use and can I assume they're . . . ah, available later?"

This last sentence wasn't whispered, as though Suling couldn't hear. Or couldn't understand.

"The young ladies are here to add an exotic oriental atmosphere to the party and that is all they're here to do, Curran,"

Thornton said. "Touch them and you're off my guest list for life."

A roar of laughter from the cluster of men around Thornton. Suling bit her lip.

"He's an odious little toad, isn't he?" The voice was low and warm, slightly amused. "And I doubt he could afford Madam Ning's prices anyway. By the way, my name is Reggie."

SULING NOW WRENCHED herself away from the memory. The first time she'd heard that voice, the first time she'd seen that face. The first time she'd fallen into those emerald-dark eyes. Thornton was still talking.

"Speaking of Susie, one more thing." Thornton disappeared back into the study and returned with a bunch of pale pink camellias in his hand and a cardboard portfolio under his arm. He put the flowers on the table.

Except they weren't real camellias, they were silk. And Suling knew every cut and stitch of every leaf and petal because she had made them. Camellias were Reggie's favorite flower, so she'd made six. Flowers that would never wilt. Everlasting blooms, everlasting love. What she wanted from Reggie, but she never said those words out loud.

Thornton pulled a drawing from the portfolio, a botanical rendering of a pure white flower that at first glance resembled a camellia blossom. He took out a second drawing, one that showed the same flower from three different angles; now she saw the unusual outer ring of long, thin petals that could've belonged to a totally different plant.

"I understand that Susie makes silk flowers," he said, pointing at the artificial camellias. "Tell her if she can make twenty-five of the flowers in these drawings by April eighteenth, suitable for pinning on a dress, I will pay a dollar for each flower."

Suling almost gasped out loud. The most expensive hat she'd ever seen in a shop window cost five dollars. Twenty-five dollars for twenty-five silk flowers. It was an extravagant amount.

"I will tell her," she said. Then, hardly daring the words, "Please, sir, how did you know Susie made silk flowers?"

"A former employee told me," he said. He rolled up the drawings and slipped an elastic band around them. He handed the roll to Suling. "Tell Susie to be careful with the drawings. I want them back. And she doesn't need to wait until the eighteenth to deliver all the flowers. If she can get me a few in time for that party on Monday, I'll pay for those right away."

What more proof did she need that Reggie didn't care about her? Her labor of love was in Thornton's hands. Left behind, abandoned, like her.

Chapter 5

Miss Eastwood . . ." Gemma blinked, poking her head round her door into the hall. "What on earth are you *wearing*?"

"My hiking wear, since I'm just back from a botanical expedition up in the hills." The older woman paused on her way downstairs, looking down at her skirt: sun-faded blue denim with leggings underneath. "I designed it myself, after I was once nearly swept over a cliff in a waterfall in Denver—that corduroy skirt down to my boot tops would have dragged me down if I'd gone over. This may not be fashionable, but it's much more practical for striding up and down mountains, Miss Garland."

Do call me Gemma, Gemma nearly said. *Most theater people just swan about calling each other* darling, *with a terribly affected drawl.* It would be so easy to say that, to ask Alice to give her a hand with her corset strings, perhaps share a cup of tea . . . But that was how you became *friendly* with your boardinghouse mates, and that wasn't such a good idea. At her last boardinghouse in New York, Gemma had made friends with the entire building—how many hours had she spent making sympathetic noises about unreliable men or tightfisted employers, how many loans had she floated of two dollars here and five dollars there? And how many of those "friends" had come to her defense when she needed it so badly those last horrible weeks?

None. Not a single one. So it really was better to keep your neighbors at a distance. Alice Eastwood seemed perfectly pleasant, but so did almost everyone up until you had to rely on them. Then they let you down.

"Will you be joining the rest of the boarders for dinner

downstairs, Miss Garland?" Alice was asking, and Gemma cut her off.

"No, I have plans of my own."

"Then perhaps you'll join us in the parlor for a little music later. We like to sing a few songs round the piano in the evening—Mrs. Browning was so hoping you might lend your voice, but she's too shy to ask—"

"I'm a professional, Miss Eastwood, I don't have time for amateur musicales," Gemma made herself say firmly and shut the door to wrestle with her corset strings herself, looping them around her bedpost and leaning hard until her waist squeezed down. She wasn't ever going to make a fashionable seventeen inches, or even twenty-seven (a soprano needed to breathe) but dinner out with an interesting man, no singing required? "That's worth squeezing down to twenty-three," Gemma gasped out to Toscanini, who had been let out of his cage for the evening and was perched on top of her mirror.

Do-re-mi-fa-sol-la-ti, he sang with a flip of green wings, perfectly on pitch.

"Stop showing off," Gemma scolded, shrugging her bodice up over her corset cover and struggling to fasten the hooks. The room smelled faintly of linseed oil, as all Nellie's old rooms did, but Gemma had unpacked her mother's old patchwork throw, her stack of tattered scores, the pretty painted tins of lozenges and tea she kept on hand to soothe her throat. Performers learned to make a home wherever they went.

Of course, *a* home wasn't the same as *home*.

You're going to have a home, Gemma told herself grimly, looping jet beads around her wrists. A sunny city apartment with a screened terrace for Toscanini, and a concert grand in the salon for practicing. Pearls in the jewel box and money in the bank and no one, ever, to tell you *you're a stupid caterwauling bitch.*

"Heavens!" At the kitchen door downstairs Alice Eastwood paused with a plate of hasty pudding in hand, on the way to the dining room where the other boarders were clinking and chattering. "You look very smart, Miss Garland," she said, looking at Gemma's sheer black mousseline over electric blue silk, the band of blue silk sashing her waist, her pearl earbobs, and the black velvet ribbon around her neck. "On your way to a party?" she asked, not seemingly put off by Gemma's earlier terseness.

Gemma flipped her train over her arm—the best of her dinner dresses, two years old but every singer knew how to keep her wardrobe freshened up. A diva who didn't present herself like one was soon just an out-of-work singer. Someone who could be flicked into a gutter. "I am going to hear a business proposition, Miss Eastwood."

Or at least get some free oysters and try not to get her rump pinched.

"YOU'RE PROBABLY USED to being offered diamonds," said Henry Thornton, "but I'd offer you kingfisher feathers."

"I beg your pardon?" Gemma tilted her head, bemused.

"Kingfisher feathers are just the color of that gown, and Chinese royalty used them in jewelry for at least two thousand years. The feathers are cut and glued onto silver gilt, then set into haircombs, brooches, crowns . . . They're so delicate, only the best artisans can work with them. The electric blue in the feather will never fade because it's an optical illusion rather than a dye."

"Heavens, I had no idea. Your business is railroads and foundries; how did you come to know about kingfisher feather jewelry?"

"Chinese art fascinates me. I've been collecting pieces for years—jade, porcelain, screens." He showed her his white jade watch charm. "My very first piece. It brings me luck."

Gemma smiled. He wore dinner dress this time, but as casually as he'd worn his morning suit yesterday; his tie was carelessly knotted, his dark hair rumpled and still in need of a cut. Yet the staff of the Palace Grill turned nearly invertebrate in his presence; he had only to raise a finger of that burn-scarred right hand to send them leaping in all directions. They leaped now to freshen the champagne flutes with more Veuve Clicquot, and Gemma let her eyes drift over the marble columns lining the walls of the dining room, the coffered ceiling, the lights sparkling on a roomful of dazzling white-clothed tables and bejeweled diners. "What else has your lucky piece brought you, Mr. Thornton?"

"An octagon house on Hyde Street, up on Nob Hill."

A much more moneyed part of Nob Hill than Taylor Street, Gemma guessed. "Octagon—your house has eight sides?"

"Eight is a lucky number, in Chinese lore. Ever since I moved in, I've been filling it with beautiful things."

"Such as?"

"Paintings—I'm partial to art nouveau; I have a Toulouse-Lautrec and a Beardsley. Rare plants—I've put in a conservatory to house my botanicals. One is a Queen of the Night plant"—he raised his glass to her in toast—"which produces one of the rarest blooms in the world. It blossoms only for a single night, did you know?"

"No, I didn't." Though Alice Eastwood probably would have.

"You're an orphan," Thornton said suddenly. "Aren't you?"

Gemma blinked. "What?"

"An orphan. There's a certain look orphans have, weighing everything as it's set before you, because you've learned it might be snatched away."

The soup course arrived—gumbo for Thornton, cold creamy vichyssoise for Gemma, giving her time to parse a response. "On the contrary, I had a lovely childhood," she said in composed tones, very careful *not* to look at her bowl as if it might be snatched away. "The sort of rural Nebraska farm everyone thinks of when they say 'backbone of the nation.' Milkmaid calluses, ice cream socials, and singing in the church choir. So I'm afraid you're quite wrong, Mr. Thornton."

"Pardon me, then. I have a bad habit of reading people at a glance—useful in business, but I'm told it's very rude." He picked up his soup spoon, eating left-handed—the right, she'd observed, did well enough for his champagne flute and water glass, and he used it without any self-consciousness, but clearly the fine manipulations of cutlery were painful. "I did warn you I have no manners."

"How is it that you know what orphans look like?" Gemma parried hastily, before he could take another stab at her past.

"Because I see the look in my mirror every day," he replied, no evasion or self-pity. "My father was a wastrel, Miss Garland. He died with a fine New York name and a great many debts. My mother died not long after of shame, and a boy who sees everything in his childhood home go under an auction hammer soon learns that there is nothing in life that cannot be taken away from you, except what you build and safeguard yourself."

Not so very different from how Gemma's own childhood had disintegrated, though there had been no fortune or old name involved—only a small farm, a few small lives at stake. The destruction had been just as complete, however. "I'm so sorry, Mr. Thornton."

"I've come out all right." He sat back, toying with the spoon. "I suppose it hardened me, but is that a bad thing? We live in a hard world, after all. Soft people are crushed by it. So I make sure that will not ever be me."

"Or me," Gemma heard herself say. "The stage is such a capricious world in which to make one's way . . ." From the very beginning she'd known just how precarious it was, the lifeline of her own voice and talent that she had hoped might haul her out of Nebraska and a lifetime of hired-girl drudgery. But it was the only lifeline she had, the *only* thing she could do besides roll out piecrust and milk cows, so she'd thrown it out there and prayed. "I've seen so many singers fall by the wayside. They sink into the same old traps: greedy husbands, spendthrift friends, dishonest business managers, bad investments. Before they know it they have nothing."

"And you determined that would not be you?"

Gemma raised her chin. "Just so."

They drank to that. He stretched his arm along the back of his chair, and Gemma couldn't help but notice how many eyes covertly watched him in this big dining room full of San Francisco's finest. He was far from the handsomest man in this room, and certainly not the best-dressed . . . But everyone here, not just the waitstaff, seemed to know who he was. "This idyllic Nebraska farm family of yours," he said now. "What do they think of their very own Jenny Lind?"

"My mother had a glorious voice, probably better than mine will ever be—she taught me to sing, and then when I was old enough she even allowed me to get proper lessons with a good teacher in the next town. But she never thought I'd want to do anything more than sing in the church choir. By the time I was fourteen, she was beside herself. She couldn't understand why I dreamed of the stage, when I could have Arne Nilsson from two farms over, and eventually fat babies who spoke Swedish as well as English, and win a blue ribbon every year at the county fair for my apple butter."

"Your career is clearly a great loss for the county fair and the church choir," Thornton said piously.

"Arne Nilsson, at least, was not inconsolable." Gemma spooned up some vichyssoise, which slid down her throat like satin. "He married my cousin Etta." Once the influenza had taken Gemma's parents and everything else followed like crashing dominoes, Arne had somehow disappeared as well. He wasn't so keen to come calling on a girl who lived in an orphanage, and no one else had been, either. Strange how an entire town full of friends could disappear so completely, even when you all still lived in the same town.

"Clearly a man of no taste."

"He's stuck with Etta, which is punishment enough. She raises prize goats and her blueberry cobbler is famous across three counties, and she has a tongue that could strop a razor."

Thornton laughed. That lean, almost homely face was very nearly handsome when he laughed. "Did you ever find a replacement for Mr. Nilsson?"

"No husbands so far, if that's what you mean." And she was not going to answer questions about lovers, if *that* was what he meant. She was thirty-two and she worked in the theater; she'd never let herself be taken up by a wealthy man as so many singers did, to pay their bills, but that didn't mean she'd spent all her nights alone, either. She'd come a very long way from the starry-eyed nineteen-year-old from Nebraska, after all. But none of that was any of his business.

"No temptation to marry, then?" he persisted.

"I did get rather close to tying the knot with a tenor from Swampscott," she said. "We sang a lovely Susanna and Figaro together in a Worcester *Nozze di Figaro*, and it's easy to fall in love during a performance run. It's a very intimate thing, making music. All that time spent getting yourself into a perfect rhythm with someone else, all those late postrehearsal suppers." That tenor, he really had wrung Gemma's heart rather badly— her first serious love affair at twenty-four, after holding herself so cautiously in reserve for years. He'd kissed her wrist after the last performance of *Figaro* and taken off to sing a *Messiah* in Boston just as she left to perform a *Fledermaus* in New York, and he'd promised to write so they could discuss marriage plans, but never did.

Darling Sal, they never write, Nellie had said when Gemma cried into her lap, running her fingers consolingly through Gemma's hair. *Men in the arts are horribly unreliable for romance. Get what you can out of them, but don't expect them to stick around.*

I don't see any of your endless parade of girls sticking around, either, Gemma had replied, scrubbing her eyes. Nellie went through gallery owners and art collectors on one side, curvaceous dancers and clay-smeared sculptresses on the other (and hadn't *that* shocked little Sally Gunderson the first time she saw a half-naked artist's model come yawning out of Nellie's bedroom in their Bronx flat!). *You have a new* amour *every week, Nell.*

Maybe it's just artistic types in general who make for unreliable lovers, Nellie admitted. *Men or women, it's all "I love you forever" when you're sharing rehearsals or studio space, but then they're gone to the next show without a backward glance. You forget that tenor, farm girl. He isn't worth your tears.*

Well, he hadn't been. A lesson Gemma had learned well. "It's a bad idea, singers marrying each other," she told Thornton now, brightly. "Scarves and jars of throat lozenges on every surface, and a lot of squabbling about who gets the piano first to warm up. Just dreadful." Short affairs during a production were all right, perhaps. No one got hurt as long as no one fell in love. But in the long run, theater men let you down twice as reliably as the ordinary kind.

"You're married to your career, then." Thornton nodded, spooning up the last of his gumbo.

"Most men disapprove."

"Most men are idiots. They have no idea how hard it is for a woman to smash her way to the top."

"And you do know?" Gemma raised her eyebrows.

"Not in the slightest. I know how hard it was for me, though, as a young man with nothing, to smash my way to the top. I can only imagine it would have been doubly hard for you, a young woman with nothing. At least I have the law on my side, the world made conveniently for me and those like me. Nothing in this world is made convenient for women."

He said it so matter-of-factly, Gemma wasn't sure quite how to respond. "I thought you had a business proposition for me tonight, Mr. Thornton," she asked, laying down her spoon. "Perhaps you'd better make it."

One side of his mouth quirked upward. "In time."

"You've already heard a great deal about my work." The early days rooming with Nellie in the Bronx, the auditions and lessons, the chorus roles leading to larger roles. Now Gemma marshaled some questions for him, but Mr. Thornton was signaling for the soup plates to be taken away.

"How lucky I am that this friend of yours praised San Francisco to the skies and lured you out here," he said as the waiters disappeared again. "I'll have to thank her if I ever meet her."

"Perhaps you already have. A female artist, who tends to make a splash wherever she lands. Dark-haired, wears trousers—"

Gemma listed off half a dozen of Nellie's various artistic *noms de plume*. If her new dinner companion turned out to be the one who could tell her where Nellie had flitted off to, rather than Nellie herself, Gemma really was going to give Nell an earful when they finally met up.

"I haven't seen anyone like that in San Francisco." He refilled her champagne himself this time, clearly not interested in Nellie. "May I ask you something? It's not a nice question, and I'm not really sorry for that, because I already warned you that I'm not very nice. Why aren't you a star, Miss Garland?"

Gemma's smile faded, and she felt her cheeks heat. "If I knew the answer to that, wouldn't I have done something about it by now?"

"I'm quite serious. That instrument you have is extraordinary. Someone else by now should have recognized it for what it is."

"There are a great many sopranos in New York."

"Not like you. You should be headlining opposite Caruso, not swishing your petticoats in the chorus."

Gemma rotated her champagne flute. She was used to flattery, stage-door suitors gushing over *your brilliance, Miss Garland, quite incomparable!*, and she knew how seriously to take such words. She wasn't used to praise stated as fact rather than flattery: *The sun rises in the east. Chinese royalty wear kingfisher feathers for jewelry. You are extraordinary.*

"I work hard," she found herself saying. You weren't supposed to admit that; a voice was supposed to be *a gift from God*, or maybe more like a god itself—a capricious, fickle deity of skin and cord that had been whimsically placed in your throat, which it was your duty to nurture and placate. "People think a singer's life is all champagne parties and lovers, but I sing nearly two hours a day, and I easily spend another four studying roles, languages, diction. Training my lungs."

Delicate Meissen platters arrived: hers golden-skinned squab swimming in mushrooms and madeira, his blood-rare filet mignon béarnaise. Gemma's menu had not listed any prices, but she was willing to wager the entire meal cost more than the month's rent she'd just put down for the room on Taylor Street. Mr. Thornton sliced into his filet, manipulating the knife in his scarred hand without much grace but with long practice. "How exactly does one train lungs?" he wanted to know.

"I go out to the nearest park for a run every morning—"

"A *run*?"

"Yes, running. Only I do it holding my breath between lampposts, and seeing how many I can rack up before I have to take a breath." She picked up her fork, trying a bite of squab. It all but melted on her tongue. "Olive Fremstad trains her lungs that way, and so do I."

"You should be putting Olive Fremstad out of a job, not copying her practice methods." He was making short work of the filet mignon, eating like a man who appreciated his food. He took a moment to savor the béarnaise on his tongue, and the small sound of appreciation deep in his throat mesmerized Gemma just slightly. "You were on your way to leading roles in New York, if the night I saw you sing Zerlina is any indication. So why are you singing in the chorus in San Francisco eight years later?"

"It's the Metropolitan Opera." Gemma sipped the claret that had come with their dinners. It was like drinking a ruby, but suddenly her tongue only tasted sourness. "Hardly a career slide."

"It's still the chorus. Some might say your time is running out."

"Being a singer isn't like being a dancer or an actress, Mr. Thornton." Gemma allowed her voice to cool. "Voices mature later, and so do careers. A soprano of my age has her best vocal years ahead of her, not behind. I have plenty of time left in my career to reach the spotlight."

"But if you haven't made it out of the chorus yet, in a decade of singing . . ." He sat back in his chair, eyes unwavering. "It tells me either that you aren't very good—and I know you are—or it tells me something else."

"What?"

"That you have been unlucky."

Gemma watched a woman in a wine-dark Worth dress glide past, watched a waiter present a platter of crêpes suzette to another table with a flourish. "Yes," she said at last, pushing the final bite of squab around her plate. "I have been unlucky."

"How so?"

She was trying to find a polite answer, something to get around the ugly truth of it, when a *whoosh* of flame sounded at the next table: the sauce for the crêpes suzette had been lit with a flourish. Gemma had never seen the point of food that had to be set on fire and turned back toward Mr. Thornton with a shrug—only to see that his face had gone white under its tan, and his scarred hand balled into a fist on the tabletop.

"Excuse me," he said rapidly before she could utter a word. "I need a moment—just please give me a moment." His eyes squeezed shut, and she could see the pulse of his throat. He sat with his head turned slightly away from the crêpe pan where the flames were already dying down, his hand flexing on the table, scars ugly in the candlelight. Gemma hadn't meant to, but she reached across the plates and covered his hand with her own.

It all happened very fast—she doubted anyone else in the restaurant had seen a thing. At the next table, the guests were tucking into their crêpes. Thornton opened his eyes, seeming to feel her hand for the first time. Quietly, Gemma pulled back. His thumb squeezed hers in a brief, fierce pressure, and then he let her go. "You'll have noticed these," he said with another painful flex of his hand.

"Yes . . ."

"Thank you for not asking. I'm amazed how many people think it perfectly within the bounds of propriety to gape and make rude remarks." He raised the hand in question, signaling for their plates to be taken away. "The injury happened at the Park Avenue Hotel fire in New York, in '02."

Gemma had heard of that particular disaster. A fire at one of the city's finest hotels raging out of control; men and women stumbling through smoky corridors in their nightclothes, choking and looking for a way out. More than twenty people had died. "You don't need to explain anything to me, Mr. Thornton," she said, but he was already speaking.

"It leaves me vulnerable. I wish it didn't. I don't mind the hand; what I mind is quivering like a child whenever the smell of fire surprises me." He tried to smile, but he was clearly still shaken; color was only slowly coming back to his face. "A fire in a bedroom grate or a kitchen stove is one thing, but that *rushing* sound when flame goes up unexpectedly . . ."

He trailed off—something Gemma already sensed he did not do often. She looked down at her lap, pleating her napkin between her fingers. "To be vulnerable is not the same as being weak."

He cocked his head. "I don't follow."

"I am an orphan, Mr. Thornton. You were right about that. Around the time I lost my parents, I began to suffer from migraines. Not headaches," she said, heading off the inevitable question, "migraines. Quite different. They go on for hours and hours, and all I can do is lie in a darkened room until they finally go away again. That's why I'm not a star, Mr. Thornton. I never know when these attacks will hit, but if they do, I can't go onstage. I had to cancel at ten minutes to curtain-up, the day I was due to sing my very first Countess in *Nozze di Figaro*. The next year, my understudy had to go on for me when I was in the middle of a run of *La Bohème*, and the conductor said I was being lazy and fired me. I lost out on a contract in Boston last year because the director had heard I was a drunk, or maybe a hysteric—someone who couldn't be counted on, anyway." She raised her eyes to his. "Being unreliable, that's the great unforgivable sin in the theater, Mr. Thornton. Opera companies will forgive you for throwing tantrums or slapping your pianist or demanding roses in your dressing room—that's what divas do—but they won't forgive you for being unreliable. There's always another soprano, and maybe her voice isn't as good but she won't collapse into a shivering heap because her brainpan is on fire when she's supposed to go on in twenty minutes. So she'll get the job, and you'll still be singing in the chorus at the age of thirty-two."

Gemma couldn't tell what the look on his face was. Concentration? Fierceness? She looked back at the napkin twisted in her lap. "But it isn't my fault," she said with some difficulty. "It's not something I can stop from happening, if I were just a little more disciplined or harder-working. I get migraines, and I can't perform. You were in a fire, and now you need a moment to breathe when the smell of smoke surprises you. That's a vulnerability, Mr. Thornton. Not a weakness."

It wasn't the sort of thing she usually shared with men—with anyone, really. Nellie was the only one who knew how bad the migraines were; Nellie would darken the room and rub Gemma's temples gently with lavender oil when the pains hit their worst.

This isn't your fault, Sal. She'd been the one to say that first, to make Gemma believe it. Everyone else just seemed to think Gemma was faking it, somehow. Or that if she just *applied* herself sufficiently, the pain would go away. *Prayer will ease your discomfort,* the matron at the orphanage had said when fifteen-year-old Gemma had vomited from the agony right in the middle of catechism. From the doctors in New York she'd consulted one after the other, it had been *These female vapors go away in time* or *It's just headaches, m'dear, have you tried willow-bark tea?* or *There's one surefire cure for womanly agues, Miss Garland, and that's marriage and motherhood!*

"How do you make a career with"—Mr. Thornton made a wordless gesture—"that hanging over you?"

"The best I can." A shrug. "I try medicines that don't work. I pray it won't hit at the worst time possible. I live with it. What else is there to do?"

She could see him struggling not to say something—not to insist, probably, that there was a solution. Something she hadn't tried. People so often told her that. But instead he shook his head a little and said, "I won't offer you advice. I imagine you're swimming in it. The well-meaning do love to give advice, don't they? As if they know so much more than you, about something you've been living with for years."

"Yes." Gemma sat up straighter. "Yes, exactly. 'Just *will* the pain away.' As if I've never thought of that before—"

"Right. I've been afraid of fire since '02, and somehow they think it's never occurred to me to *just control the feeling*?" He smiled, and Gemma smiled back. "I hate idiots. Yet the world is so full of them . . . It was about that time I decided that I'd make a fortune, the kind of fortune that means I can say whatever I like to idiots."

"And have you?"

"I have. I work long hours, I believe in being ruthless, and I don't suffer fools. I'm not very kind, but I'm honest."

"I will take honesty, Mr. Thornton."

Dessert arrived at the table: crystal dishes of peach Melba, velvety vanilla ice cream and golden peaches with a lacework of raspberry sauce, accompanied by tiny cups of ink-dark coffee. "I have a proposition for you," Thornton said once the waiter retreated.

Oh dear, here it came: the indecent proposal. Gemma sighed silently. And she'd been enjoying this dinner so much. Well, perhaps *enjoying* wasn't the word. Old wounds and lonely childhoods weren't exactly the happiest topics of conversation, but it was certainly the most interesting dinner she'd had in a long time. "Mr. Thornton—"

"I'm not offering to make you my mistress. You're a lovely woman," he added, eyes resting briefly on her bare shoulders over the gauzy black mousseline, "but I don't mix business and pleasure, and my proposition for you is purely business. I'm hosting a small gathering soon to display some of my latest acquisitions—some rare *chinoiserie*, not to mention my Queen of the Night plant. Mayor Schmitz will be in attendance, also the Floods, the Kohls, the de Youngs—" reeling off more names that even Gemma recognized, little as she knew of San Francisco society. "I want you to perform for the occasion, Miss Garland."

"So I'm to be the entertainment?" Gemma knew what that could be like. Shown to the servants' entrance; made to wait hours in a stifling-hot corridor, then singing through a tired collection of opera standards while tipsy guests chattered to one another and chewed their apple tartlets.

"You'd be my guest of honor." Mr. Thornton rotated his coffee cup. "A voice like yours deserves a setting worthy of a jewel, and an audience who can appreciate it. No one whispers during the concerts at *my* house, let me assure you."

Gemma felt her pulse quicken. Something different, then, from the usual tired dinner-party entertainment. Maybe the kind of concert that changed careers. The right ears at the right time in a soprano's life could make all the difference. "How many guests?"

"Perhaps fifty. I'll invite the director of the Grand Opera House for you, and the directors of the Tivoli and Columbia theaters as well."

"Why would you do that?" Gemma asked, thinking of gift horses. *Am I expected to pay for the opportunity afterward, overnight?* For all his fine words about not mixing business with pleasure.

"I'm just a businessman," he said. "I can't create art, but I can fund it. Rockefeller and Gould and Carnegie in New York put their names on concert halls and museums; I want to do the same in San Francisco. I've worked hard so I can be a patron of the arts in this city, and I'm perfectly willing to include you in that patronage."

Just a businessman. Never in her entire career had Gemma heard a man describe himself that way. Businessmen were far more likely to say she was *just* a singer. A step above a racehorse, perhaps, but not quite a human being. "When is this party of yours?"

"Monday."

She dropped her spoon into the half-melted ice cream. "Three *days*?"

"You're a consummate professional, Miss Garland. Don't tell me you couldn't perform this minute if you had to."

She could. Still, three days. She'd need a program, a pianist, rehearsals . . . "I am a professional," she agreed. "So there is the matter of my fee for singing."

He named a good sum, one that would handily pad out Gemma's meager account.

"Thank you, I'd be happy to—"

"No." He cut her off. "You would *not* be happy to. You know what you're worth, Miss Garland, so double your fee. Rake me over the coals here; I can afford it. Extort me."

She burst out laughing—she couldn't help it. "Are you *asking* me to charge you more?"

"Begging you. You're too nice for your own good, Miss Garland. You'd like to be hard, because you told me yourself that the world of the stage is a capricious one, but I don't think it comes easily to a Sunday school farm girl like you." He steepled his fingertips under his chin, gazing at her. "I am not nice, and you don't have to charm me. Charge me double."

Gemma looked him in the eye. "Triple."

"Done."

Chapter 6

April 7, 1906
Ten days, thirteen hours, thirty-one
minutes before the earthquake

Suling had met Alice Eastwood at the second of Thornton's parties, a month after the first. That time the party was a fundraiser for the California Academy of Sciences, held in the octagon house's spectacular conservatory. The main attraction at the event was a collection of flowering succulents, but it seemed to Suling that the guests were more intent on impressing one another than admiring the rare plants.

Stationed near the conservatory's door beneath an arching stem of scarlet bougainvillea, Suling surveyed the room. A middle-aged woman examining a plant caught her interest, partly because the woman's plain dark dress contrasted with the other guests' sumptuous finery and jewels, but mostly because Thornton was giving her his full attention.

"Succulents are not my specialty," the woman was saying, "but I'm certain I've never seen one with such characteristics, quite unusual. From the Argentine, you said? I'd like to come back and make a sketch for David Prain, the director of Kew Gardens. He has a particular passion for succulents."

"No need to come back, Miss Eastwood," Thornton said. "You'll have your own cutting tomorrow, delivered to the Academy."

The woman beamed, the smile deepening the lines on her sun-weathered face. "That's most kind of you. Well, I've stayed longer than planned, thanks to the many fine specimens in this conservatory, Mr. Thornton. But now I really must go."

"Your kind words about my collection mean more to me than anything else at this event," Thornton said. He sounded very sincere.

Suling straightened up as they approached the conservatory door and held the tray of champagne flutes a little higher. Thornton smiled at her and picked up a glass. He bowed to the woman and rejoined his other guests.

The woman, however, did not leave. She stared at Suling, puzzled. No, not at Suling. At her hair.

"Is that an iris? But it's October, how is this possible?" She leaned down and peered at the blooms in Suling's hair. The woman smelled faintly herbal, of rosemary and bay leaf.

"They're artificial, ma'am," Suling said. "Silk." Sensing an opportunity, she added, "I made them."

"How astonishing," the woman said. "They're entirely lifelike until you get this close. Have you made other plants in silk?"

"Flowers for arrangements in vases," Suling said, "or hair ornaments like this. I also embroider."

The woman pulled out a card from her bag. "I'm Alice Eastwood. Would you come see me sometime? I'd like to commission some silk flowers if you have the time. Now I really must go."

Alice Eastwood. Curator of Botany. California Academy of Sciences.

A woman in charge of something. How very intriguing.

A FEW DAYS later, Suling had gone to the Academy. The guards at the museum entrance eyed her dismissively, her laundryboy's clothes and rough boots, and refused to let her in.

"The Academy is open to the public," Suling pointed out, "and it's free."

"There's the public, and then there's the likes of you," one of them said without rancor. "We've got garden club ladies visiting and they wouldn't want to see you in here. Give it an hour till they're gone, China boy."

Her journey from Chinatown, while fairly short, had not been easy and Suling wasn't in a mood to wait for society ladies. She held out Alice's card. "Miss Eastwood wants to see me."

"Miss Eastwood." He sighed. "Of course. Sam, you stay here. I'll walk this boy to Botany."

She followed him along back passages and stairs to the sixth floor, where a sign on the black-painted door read BOTANY. He pushed it open and Suling breathed in the scent of pine needles, a sharp resinous odor, and something that reminded her of roses. Men in shirtsleeves—and quite a few women—worked quietly at large tables, some writing notes, others carefully laying strips of tape over sheets of thick paper that held what looked like pressed leaves.

"This little Chink is here to see Miss Eastwood," the guard said, to the room in general. "Can I leave him here?"

A young woman got up from the table. "I'll take him."

The door to Alice's office was open. She was seated by a large window, looking into a microscope. "Miss Eastwood," the woman said, "you have a visitor."

"Thank you, Emily," Alice said. She looked up smiling, then looked again at Suling, a frown of confusion creasing her forehead as she crossed the room. "Come in. Where do I know you from?"

Suling stared at Alice Eastwood, at the woman's odd attire, a brown belted jacket with large box-pleated patch pockets. Strangest of all were the denim trousers, so roomy and wide that if Alice stood still you'd think it was a skirt. And was she in stocking feet? Suling surveyed the office and spied a pair of muddy boots drying on a wooden crate. The scent of roses was stronger in this office, but glancing around the room Suling couldn't see any such flowers.

She removed the fedora. "I was at Mr. Thornton's party, Miss Eastwood. My name is Suling. Suling Feng."

Alice's smile returned, grew wider. "The young beauty with out-of-season iris in her hair. Come in. But why are you dressed as a boy today?"

"Better to come as a boy," Suling replied, as nonchalantly as she could.

She wasn't going to tell this woman about the men who had pulled on her pigtail and pushed her to the ground, laughing and singing "ching chong Chinaman." She was lucky they didn't realize she was a girl. Lucky, too, that it was daytime and the men hadn't started drinking yet. Not that they needed to be drunk to get dangerous. A white woman wouldn't understand.

But Alice understood. Suling could tell by the change in the botanist's face, the flush on her cheeks when she realized how thoughtless the casual question had been.

"Well, Miss Feng," Alice said, all business. "What I have in mind are models of plants made from silk. I don't know how detailed and accurate you could make them, but let's see how it goes. By the way, have you ever seen a rose-scented geranium?"

She picked up a small potted plant from the windowsill. "Smell those leaves," she commanded. "Delightful."

A quiet but urgent knock from the open door interrupted her. A young man stood at the doorway with an inquiring look on his face.

"What is it, Seth? Oh, that delivery from Colorado. Wait here, Miss Feng, I won't be long." Alice bustled out and hurried down the hall with the young man.

Alice Eastwood moved with such purpose, every stride giving the impression that she was prepared, *eager*, to tackle any challenge. What sort of woman was this, that she could be a curator at such a prestigious institution? That she commanded the respect of a man like Thornton?

AFTER THAT FIRST meeting, Alice had Suling come to her boardinghouse on Taylor Street. "After all, I only live three blocks away from the edge of Chinatown," Alice said. "A shorter walk for you."

Shorter, and safer.

"These are remarkable," Alice Eastwood said when Suling dropped by the house on Taylor Street with her latest offering. The botanist sat at her dining table and squinted at the stamens on a yellow silk poppy. "Can you get my handbag for me, dear?" She waved vaguely in the general direction of her dressing table and held the flower closer to inspect the leaves.

The curator of botany at the California Academy of Sciences lived in a spacious room on the top floor of the boardinghouse, a bedsit with its own small kitchen, large enough for a settee and dining table. The dining table was always covered with books and stacks of pressed plant specimens. Faded curtains in a paisley print were pulled back from windows that gazed out over the city.

The first commission Alice had given Suling was a white flower, a Catalina mariposa lily. Suling crafted it by studying the photographs and drawings Alice provided. Then a pink bush mallow, from drawings and an actual plant. Suling then offered to repair Alice's one and only evening bag, first replicating its beaded embroidery on a semicircle of heavy black satin, then patching it onto the bag. By Thanksgiving, Alice had persuaded her landlady, Mrs. Browning, to use Fenghuang Laundry for the boardinghouse's linens.

Suling handed Alice a green leather bag. Alice counted out two quarters.

"No, no, Miss Eastwood," Suling protested. "Twenty-five cents is plenty."

Alice shook her head. "Suling, you must value yourself and your work more. Take it."

"Miss Eastwood, I feel truly terrible for what I must ask," Suling said, accepting the coins. "I've had an order from Mr. Thornton for silk flowers, quite an urgent request. Is it all right if I put off making the Douglas irises?"

She did feel terrible. She would work as quickly as she could on Thornton's flowers, but the day after he paid for them, she would get on a train for Boston. Or New York. She would never make those irises for Alice.

"Of course. There's no hurry. May I ask what you're making for Mr. Thornton?"

"It's a white flower with rather strange leaves," Suling said, "and I only have drawings to work from. The name on the drawing is *Epiphyllum oxypetalum*." She stumbled over the Latin.

"Queen of the Night flower!" Alice clapped her hands, delighted. "He must've acquired a specimen. I've never seen one in bloom. Those strange leaves aren't leaves at all, you know, they're flattened stems. I must call on Thornton and get a look. The flowers are very complicated, I hope he's paying you well."

"He pays very well," Suling said, "and he's ordered twenty-five flowers, Miss Eastwood. If I could earn that much every month, I could leave the laundry. But embroidery and silk flowers are just a hobby."

"Your skills are too good to be considered just a hobby." Alice snorted. Her praise gave Suling courage.

"Could I ask you a favor, Miss Eastwood?" Suling said, heart thumping. Alice had been so kind to her, but how much of that kindness could she draw on?

The older woman nodded. "Of course, my dear."

Suling hesitated a moment before speaking. "I would like to support myself, leave the laundry and Chinatown. Perhaps go to the Midwest or the East. Do you know anyone who might need a domestic servant, one who can sew and embroider?" Suling had heard it was more common in the East for white families to hire Chinese women as domestic servants rather than just men. Perhaps Alice had friends in Chicago or New York.

Alice looked thoughtful. "Actually, I do have an idea," she said, getting up from the dresser. "Just a moment."

A faint hope stirred in Suling. Alice was so practical. She wouldn't suggest anything unrealistic.

Alice pulled something out from a steamer trunk, something large and carefully wrapped in tissue paper. A dress. "Here, let me hang it up so it drapes properly," Alice said, holding it up.

The evening gown was simple and modest, a mossy black silk velvet with a V-shaped bodice. Cream lace over white silk gauze filled the bodice and rose to cover the throat. A pleat of the same lace was set into bell sleeves. The skirt was plain except for some smocking that gathered the lower half of the fabric into just the suggestion of a train. The embroidery around the neckline, however, was what caught Suling's attention.

Two bands of black velvet crossed to form the V-shaped bodice; the bands were densely embroidered in silk with tiny jet beads that repeated the pattern on the creamy lace. The effect was subtle and at the same time, elegantly opulent.

"This dress is nearly ten years old," Alice said. "I only wear it to the opera and special parties. It's from France, the Callot Soeurs atelier. Look at the embroidery and beadwork. Your work on my evening bag is just as good, Suling. I hear that the Callot Soeurs workshop in France employs six hundred people. Apparently they plan on opening a store and workshop in New York soon."

Suling examined the dress, then looked up at Alice. "The women who do this, do they earn enough to live on?" In Chinatown, women did piecework, embroidered panels of linen and gauze that garment factories used for dresses. The low wages supplemented family incomes, but they weren't enough to survive independently.

"My dear, the women who do this at fashion houses are considered artists. And you are an artist with the needle." Carefully, Alice folded her gown into the tissue paper and placed it back inside the trunk. "Your skills are worthy of a career, Suling. There are fashion houses in New York and in Chicago that would value your talents."

"Do you know anyone at these fashion houses?" Suling asked timidly. In her world, nothing happened without *guanxi*, connections. Unless Alice could pull strings for her, she couldn't imagine a fashion house hiring her.

"Let me work on it," Alice said. "Some of the garden club ladies I've gotten to know are also society women who order Paris couture every season. In the meantime, take this." She held out a Callot Soeurs catalog, a year old.

Suling tried not to look disappointed. *Let me work on it* didn't sound as though anything would happen soon. All Suling wanted was to leave San Francisco and support herself; not just to avoid marrying Dr. Ouyang but because every street corner mocked her with memories of Reggie.

"SHOW ME YOUR world," Reggie had said, and Suling agreed, on one condition. That they would only see how normal people lived. No opium dens or gambling parlors.

"Evil and decadence. It's what white people think of first when they think of Chinatown," Suling said, "and yes, there are dozens and dozens of those places. But Reggie, ordinary people also live here, people like me. Shopkeepers and factory workers, children who go to school, men who go out with the shrimp boats. Perfectly ordinary families leading ordinary decent lives. That's what I want you to see."

They couldn't stroll together, not without drawing stares and gossip, but before each little expedition Suling would explain about the streets and buildings, which shops and establishments to enter and what to look for inside. She would walk several paces in front, pause at storefronts or doorways of the places she had described, then wait while Reggie went in and came out again.

The Chinese Theater. The temples, which white people called "joss houses." Herbalists and restaurants, broom factories and barbers. The Tung Wah Dispensary, a large herbalist shop with a clinic at the back, the closest thing Chinatown had to a hospital. Neighborhoods where children walked hand in hand along the sidewalk, basement diners where the smell of cooking wafting up made them both so hungry that Suling bought some steamed buns stuffed with chopped pork and pickled mustard greens. Then they hurried down to the waterfront and gobbled down the buns, laughing at each other's greediness.

"So many gambling houses," Reggie said, after one such day. "Are all Chinese natural gamblers?"

Suling stopped in her tracks. "No. Nor are we inclined to opium. There are hundreds, thousands of unmarried men in Chinatown. They have no families, they don't speak English well, and they aren't comfortable going to American theaters or sports stadiums. What can they do for amusement but gamble or go to brothels or the Chinese theater? Most of those who smoke opium do it to forget the misery of their lives." She was almost shaking with indignation.

After a long silence, Reggie said quietly, "What a bigoted idiot I am, Suling. Please forgive me."

Suling looked into those green eyes, the concern and affection in their depths, and burst into tears. Tears that soaked into the shoulders of Reggie's coat as she pressed herself against a warm and comforting embrace. That was when she realized she was falling in love. Something that wasn't supposed to happen, not with a foreign devil.

But Reggie made it so clear the feeling was mutual, teasing her at first, giving her silly nicknames. China doll. Eastern Lotus. Then, seeing how much Suling disliked these nicknames, Reggie learned how to pronounce her name properly in Chinese. Then how to say Chinese greetings such as "good morning" and "good evening." How to say "goodbye." Endearments such as *bao bei, airen*. Precious treasure, lover.

And then one day, how to say "I love you."

Something had clenched in Suling's heart, joy and delight. And dread. She couldn't say it back. She wouldn't. But her hesitation didn't seem to deter Reggie. Who didn't mind if she pulled back when their kisses grew too passionate, their hands too eager to explore. Sometimes their bodies pressed so close, so deliciously curved together that Suling wanted nothing more than to give in completely. But she fought the desire and Reggie simply said "only when you're ready."

And Suling had felt herself ready, felt herself willing to give in. But in February, when they were supposed to meet on Valentine's Day, Reggie didn't come to the rendezvous. Suling waited, went back again and again to their usual meeting place, searched for a note. Whenever she and Old Kow delivered laundry to the Thornton mansion, she inquired as discreetly as she could of the servants, but they just shrugged. Apparently, it was a common thing. Their master's protégés came and went.

There was something strange about it all. Reggie had been so excited to win Thornton's support, an unexpected and thrilling career boost. Reggie could be impulsive, sometimes annoyingly unpredictable, but when it came to career obligations, Suling had never known Reggie to be anything but dead serious. It must've been Thornton's decision. Had Reggie been disheartened, enough to leave San Francisco without contacting her?

And now the familiar streets of Chinatown taunted her with memories. Reggie, leaning back to look at the gold lettering on Wah Hing Restaurant's sign. Reggie, watching the sword dancer perform for tourists. Reggie, kneeling down to speak with the fish seller's daughter, a pretty ten-year-old in pigtails.

"I'D BETTER GET home," Suling told Alice. "The sooner I finish those flowers for Mr. Thornton, the sooner I get paid."

Suling opened the door, and a cascade of music rolled up the stairs. Singing. A beautiful voice, and unmistakably a trained one. A voice that elicited emotion even just singing scales.

"Our new tenant," Alice said, coming to stand beside her. "An opera singer. Glorious." She sighed happily and sat at the top of the stairs. "I'm going to just sit here and listen for a bit."

There was a pause in the music and then the voice started up again, this time a melody that made Suling's heart yearn for some unnamed desire. She found herself wishing she could sit on the steps with Alice, just for a few minutes of beauty. But she had to go. She needed that twenty-five dollars. In less than two weeks, she had to be out of San Francisco.

And one more thing. She was done mooning over Reggie. She'd drown any such thoughts the moment they surfaced. No more regrets or yearnings, only plans for her future and the steps she must take. With the Callot Soeurs catalog tucked firmly under her arm, Suling marched down the stairs.

Chapter 7

"You remembered how to pronounce my name," George Serrano remarked around a half-smoked cigarette when Gemma greeted him for their practice session. "Even a proper flip on the 'r.'"

"It's not so hard to properly roll a Spanish 'r,'" Gemma said. "I've studied Italian, French, German—"

"How well can you speak any of those?" the pianist asked, moving a pile of scores off the music stand. His rehearsal room where she'd first found him practicing backstage at the Grand Opera House looked like the den of a musical pack rat: pages of sheet music scattered like snowflakes, half-finished cups of cold coffee everywhere, discarded opera props (Papageno's birdcage and Susanna's wedding garland, if Gemma wasn't mistaken) lying around like old friends.

"Oh, I'm as multilingual as any opera singer. My conversation is extremely limited if it comes to anything useful like how to order a meal in a bistro or ask where the train station is, but I can sigh, die, or cry at the drop of a hat, Mr. Serrano."

"*Muere mañana, practica hoy,*" he said, exhaling a stream of smoke. "What do you want to rehearse? And call me George," he added.

"Do you prefer *Jorge*?" Giving that the proper Spanish roll as well.

"I came to San Francisco at nineteen, and most Americans couldn't pronounce it. I'm used to *George* by now." His eyes crinkled. "What are you rehearsing, Miss Garland?"

"*Gemma*, please. And I'm performing tomorrow at a house on Hyde Street in Nob Hill . . ." No time to waste: Gemma had been consumed since Friday night with her octagon house afternoon concert. She'd spent all yesterday going over scores, drawing up song lists and tearing them up, running vocalises—she wasn't missing this chance to impress the high-society cream of San Francisco, not to mention the musical directors of at least two grand theaters. "I'm working up some old standards, no time to polish anything new, but of course I'll need a proper accompanist. I'll pay twice your fee for the short notice."

He stubbed out his cigarette in an old rhinestone-spangled goblet that looked like, Gemma thought, the love-potion cup in Act I of *Tristan und Isolde*. "Done."

They were knocking Strauss's "My Dear Marquis" together in no time. "I'll sing it in English for a nice lively start," Gemma said, pushing back her sweat-damp hair. She'd jogged all the way to the opera house, nearly three miles, collecting stares the whole way—even in San Francisco, streets jammed with drunken sailors and Chinese errand boys, it was surely rare to see a woman in a shirtwaist and a home-shortened skating skirt running (well, running with no one after her), face scarlet as she counted *six lampposts . . . seven lampposts . . .* But even if she looked a fright, she'd arrived warm and perspiring with her voice positively tingling to sing.

"Not sure I've ever played for a soprano who took that whole last phrase in one go like that," George commented after they'd finished the first run-through. "You've got lungs like an elephant."

"I'd like to see an elephant tackle a Mozart concert aria. Do you have the music to 'Vorrei spiegarvi'? I thought I'd go to that after the Strauss . . ."

"Bit long for a short concert. Have you got 'Non curo l'affetto' under your belt?" George asked briskly, and Gemma sighed in relief. Rehearsal pianists were a mixed bag: you might land a worn-out cynic who yawned his way through every phrase or a complete incompetent with no idea how to partner a voice. But George played beautifully: sensitive phrasing, knew how to follow, elasticized his beats when she breathed. "I'm no conservatory brat," he said, laughing when she asked where he'd studied. "A few good teachers here and there, but I learned to play on out-of-tune pianos in Buenos Aires bars when I was a kid. How are you finishing your program off? I have a feeling you could burn a barn down with 'Martern aller Arten.'"

"I can, but not for this crowd," Gemma decided. "It's not a seated concert, so I'd better leave them tapping their toes. I thought the drinking song from *Traviata*—I'll sing it solo rather than a duet. Release them into their champagne humming."

George nodded, already launching into the big swinging 3/8 chords. He wasn't a large man—burly rather than tall, shirttail hanging out—but he had the biggest, broadest hands Gemma had ever seen. He could stretch an eleventh on the keyboard without even seeming to try. "Perfect for choking someone on a dark night," he said when she commented as much, throttling an imaginary throat with his left hand as his right covered both parts on the piano, and Gemma was laughing so hard she missed her entrance. Rehearsal really could be fun—how much she'd missed that.

"Can I take you to lunch?" George asked as they finished. "A plate of sand dabs at the Oyster Grotto goes down a treat after a long rehearsal."

"No, thank you." He had a warm admiration in his grin that Gemma thought best to nip in the bud. No romances with theater men for now; ill-timed love affairs were the Achilles' heel of sopranos everywhere, and she had no intention of being derailed when such a good opportunity had dropped into her lap. "I have too much to do before tomorrow's recital."

"*Crudele*," he said, plinking some tragic chords. "You sopranos are cruel."

"Hard as nails." Gemma grinned. If she practiced *that* just as she practiced her vocalises, it might even become true.

They were just wrapping up their session, Gemma rummaging in her sealskin handbag for her coin purse to pay him, when she felt the first pulses of another impending migraine. *Oh no, not now*, she thought, but since when did her body care when it let her down?

"Is something wrong?" George was running through the introduction to one of her arias, handily adapting the long orchestral lead-in to a tidy three-bar entrance more suitable for a recital.

"Not at all," she managed to say, pushing a handful of coins over. "Meet me tomorrow at my boardinghouse on Taylor Street? Mr. Thornton is sending a carriage to collect me; we can ride over together"—and she dashed out, cramming her old straw hat back onto her head. Let this *not* be one of those migraines that came on like an express freight crashing through every barrier in a matter of minutes . . .

"Package arrived here for you, Miss Garland," the front-house manager called out as she rushed past. "You really shouldn't be using the opera house for your personal correspondence."

Gemma thrust the brown paper parcel under her arm and headed back toward Taylor Street without stopping, neck already throbbing. The whole ordeal always began with pulses at the neck and base of her skull, which would gradually move higher. Things would start vibrating with their own light, sounds would take on an extra resonance in her ears, her stomach would begin rolling with nausea. That stage could last for a good hour, her vision narrowing as the pain moved up her neck and settled in like a cat kneading a cushion in front of a cozy fire. Flexing its claws, curling deeper, until it was well and firmly expanded through the left side of her head and ready to squat there for the next three hours at least. *Just let me get home*, Gemma prayed.

"Miss Garland," Gemma's landlady called out as she stumbled into the Taylor Street house—the woman was handing a packet of mail over to Alice Eastwood, but she straightened eagerly as Gemma passed the sitting room. "Could I beg you to join us in the parlor this evening for a little musicale? I do like gathering my ladies round the piano for a bit of song! Do you know 'Bill Bailey, Won't You Please Come Home'? Or 'Break the News to Mother'?"

"No," Gemma said shortly. "I'm preparing this evening for my concert tomorrow."

"Will it get a mention in the *Call*?" Alice asked, interested. "I always take the *Call* with my morning tea. Right now it's all articles on that Pinkerton detective who went missing. I'd much rather read about musical concerts—"

"It will be a private concert. No press write-ups." The pain was moving fast up from Gemma's neck now. "If you'll excuse me, I need to press my performance dress."

She tried to move toward the stairs, but Mrs. Browning patted her arm. "Maybe you can grace us with a song some night after your concert, then? I can't tell you how much pleasure it would bring us all—"

"But what's it going to bring *me*, Mrs. Browning?" Gemma snapped, feeling the throbs of pain all the way to the tips of her ears now. "Maybe a reduction in rent?" and she finally managed to escape upstairs, ducking Alice Eastwood's startled glance.

Vee-vay-vah-vo-vooohhh, Toscanini sang as Gemma staggered into her room, imitating her daily warm-up.

"Oh, shut up," she told him, opening the cage. He took off like a small green bullet, fluttering around the room twice before finally landing on top of the mirror. Gemma held her hand up with a coaxing chirp, but he ignored her, grooming under his wing with a flip of green tail feathers. "I do wish budgies *cuddled* more." Gemma sighed, plucking out her hairpins. She couldn't stand the slightest pressure on her scalp when the migraine really sank in, and it was sinking in fast now. Pulling the window shade down, she curled up on the bed and finally took a look at the square paper-wrapped parcel she'd hoisted all the way up the hill from the opera house. The handwriting on the label wasn't one she recognized . . . Gemma hesitated, massaging the back of her neck, then tore off the brown paper.

A painting maybe a foot square, unframed, heavy drawing paper mounted on stiff cardboard. A Chinese boy and a Chinese girl standing side by side, drawn in vivid watercolors, with a wallpapering of Chinese symbols and shapes behind them. Nellie's work—not only did Gemma recognize the style, it was Nellie's sigil on the bottom, the little mark she used to sign all her paintings. Turning the drawing over, Gemma saw an envelope taped to the back and her heart squeezed at the sight of it. *Finally,* a letter from Nellie—she hadn't really let herself dwell on just how hurt she'd been feeling at the way her oldest friend had left her in the lurch, but she could feel the hurt now as it eased. She was smiling as she broke the seal.

Welcome to San Francisco, Gemma! Who knows where you're living now you've arrived, but I knew you'd head to the opera house first thing. Sorry I can't be there in person to greet you—well, I'm not really sorry, because I got a chance to go sketch mountain scenery in Colorado, and I just had to jump at it. You understand—or you would, if you could see the views here! Anyway, I thought you'd like this sketch, the last one I did before grabbing the train out of town. Must dash!

Gemma looked at the typed letters on creamy, expensive paper, feeling her smile leak slowly away. "I'm doing very well, thanks ever so much for asking, Nell," she muttered, cramming the little painting back into its paper wrappings. That was all she was going to get, after being abandoned in a strange city by her oldest friend? A sketch and an offhand *I'm not really sorry?*

Pain bisected her temples like an iron wire, pushing Nellie's careless callousness away in its spiked wake, and Gemma pressed the heels of her hands against her head as if she could hold it together. She really should start sponging the faille dress she'd planned to wear to the octagon house tomorrow—it had been badly crushed in her trunk; she'd have to press out every single pleat, and who knew how long the migraine would lay her out once it really settled in. But her eyes were suddenly swimming, and her stomach wouldn't stop roiling, and it was all she could do to wring out a cloth in the washbasin and drape it over her face as she huddled on the bed. "It's just headaches," she remembered one doctor telling her in bracing tones. "We all get headaches, Miss Garland, so do try to buck up!"

I'm so tired, Gemma thought, squeezing her eyes closed under the wet cloth, *of bucking up.* Wasn't it hard enough to be a woman alone, trying to make a career in a hard business and a harder world, without this? Without a sleeping beast living inside her own head, who might at any moment wake and sink its fangs into her brain?

Don't be self-pitying, a savage little voice scolded inside. *It's not all about the migraines. That's not the only reason you're still singing in the chorus at thirty-two.*

"Stop," she mumbled, listening to Toscanini twitter on top of her mirror. Her vision was narrowing now; she could feel it even behind her sealed eyelids: if she opened them it would be like staring through a tunnel, blurry and sparkly at the same time, with a flare of pain if she tried to focus on anything directly rather than looking at it sideways. "Stop."

The truth is, if you weren't such a trusting little ninny—

"Stop—"

You wouldn't be in such a pickle, would you?

"I was ill—"

You were stupid.

Ill *and* stupid, Gemma supposed. Her old theater agent, the one who had plucked her out of a cattle-call audition at twenty and gotten her into the chorus of a second-rate production of *La Bohème . . . I don't like him*, Nellie had declared. *He's oilier than a roast duck.* But Gemma had laughed that off. He'd never made indecent advances (and how rare was that, after she'd had her bottom pinched all over New York trying to find representation?); he kept her working; he sent her to doctor after doctor to try to get the migraines under control—of *course* Gemma had stayed with him. It hadn't seemed unreasonable when he suggested she add him to her financial accounts. She was so careful with her money, he pointed out; what if a migraine laid her out for days and she wasn't able to get her rent paid or a doctor summoned? He could do those things for her. And she'd built up a modest nest egg over the years, so determined not to be the diva who bought mink stoles and French champagne but never saved for the future. No, Gemma had been determined to be *smart*. Always thinking of that home she wanted to have someday: the piano, the terrace, the garden.

She wondered dully now what her agent had bought with her nest egg, when he scooped it all. He'd certainly timed it well: a particularly bad attack that had laid her up for nearly four days at the beginning of a New York *Nozze di Figaro*. It should have been her first Countess, a role that suited her to her fingertips, a lavish production, her first real chance at Dressing Room A. Instead her understudy went on, and four days later when Gemma managed to stagger upright, she found she'd not only been fired from the company, but her bank accounts were empty. Empty to the last penny.

It's not your fault, she tried to tell herself, *it's not your fault.* But wasn't it? The migraines, those were not her fault. Trusting the wrong man, though—that was a tale as old as time. Stupid Sally Gunderson, who would never cheat anyone, and had been so very easy to cheat. She had made herself sound more courageous, talking to Mr. Thornton over glasses of claret that tasted like rubies, than she really was—the orphan who had become a diva, despite her brave battle against bad health. That sounded so much better than a story about a dim, trusting farm girl who got conned.

Stop wallowing, she told herself. *You aren't exactly in a gutter. You dusted yourself off and got the chorus job before the month was out, didn't you? You're still working for the Met, for God's sake. You're in a brand-new city, getting a brand-new start. Isn't that the American dream?*

The nausea was moving in, now. Gemma sat up, vomited competently into the chamber pot under the bed, and lay back down again. The pain had settled in now, purring, flexing—it wouldn't shift for hours. She turned carefully onto her back, even that gentle motion throbbing through her skull like a railroad spike. "Why couldn't you be here, Nell?" she whispered into the darkened room. "You promised you'd be here for me. You said we'd fix everything." She hadn't been able to write Nellie about losing all her savings—she'd hoped to confess that over a flask of brandy, in one of their old late-night heart-to-hearts. Nellie would get furious on her behalf, would stride up and down vowing bloody revenge, would make her laugh and then swear to her that none of it mattered, that Gemma would make her fortune twice over here in San Francisco.

But Nellie wasn't here. She was in *Colorado* of all places, and Gemma was left lying in a darkened room with no one but a budgie for company. Alone in a new city, on a new coast, no opera company yet, no comforting routine of rehearsals and performances, no familiar cafés for postpractice coffees and familiar restaurants for late postcurtain suppers. Alone—except, she was supposed to have Nellie.

I really need you. She'd written as much in her last letter, right after she'd been fired and swindled, underlining the words for emphasis . . . and her oldest friend had sauntered off to Colorado without a backward glance.

You don't *need her*, Gemma told herself, forcing her eyes open to stare into the blurring, sparkling, painful dark. Forcing herself to be hard, to be practical, to never be called *nice* again. Because friends let you down, even the oldest of friends; men let you down; colleagues let you down. But her voice hadn't, not yet, and she had a chance to let it shine tomorrow, so as soon as she could stand without vomiting—as soon as she could move without wanting to dig her eyes out with a soup spoon—she had better heat up the irons and press all the wrinkles out of her biscuit-colored faille.

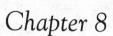

Chapter 8

Suling slipped up the back staircase of Hing Chong Tailors and pulled the chain by the heavy wooden door. This time it was Hyacinth and not Amah Chung who opened it. Hyacinth wore a flowered cotton tunic and comfortable, loose trousers. By now the women who worked at Thornton's parties dressed very casually in clothing that was easy to slip on and off, knowing they would change into sumptuous garments at the octagon house. They took elaborate care with their hair and cosmetics though, and Hyacinth hurried Suling into the large room where the others were getting ready.

"Different this time, isn't it?" she remarked, seating Suling in front of a mirror. "An afternoon party instead of evening." She began brushing Suling's hair.

"Yes, and on a Monday rather than a weekend," Suling said. "Same money, though. Where is Madam Ning?"

"She's left Pearl in charge downstairs," Butterfly said with a giggle. "Mr. Clarkson just came for an unexpected, umm, inspection."

If not a friend, Suling at least counted Michael Clarkson as one of the more sympathetic policemen. It had been Clarkson who brought her home from Mile Rocks the day her parents died. He had wrapped a blanket around her and didn't try to make her speak as she sat, silent and numb, eyes dry and staring. Clarkson waited at the laundry while one of the workers ran to find Third Uncle. Chinatown gossip traveled faster than any telegram service, and on the street outside, people were

converging at the laundry. The small crowd parted to make
way for a woman who wailed as though pursued by demons.
Madam Ning had charged through the door, hair disheveled
and makeup smeared.

"Tell me it's not true. It can't be true!" She dropped to her
knees beside Suling, who simply continued staring into space.
Madam Ning turned to look up at Clarkson. "Mike, what happened? This girl's mother, she is my best friend."

"I'm sorry, Nina," he said, "both her parents are presumed
drowned."

Suling didn't need to pound on the policeman's chest or
scream out her grief. Her auntie was doing enough of that for
them both. Clarkson just held the sobbing woman, hushing her
quietly with a tenderness that spoke of more than mere acquain-
tance.

Later, Dr. Ouyang came to the laundry with a packet of herbs
and brewed a soothing drink, which Madam Ning coaxed Suling into swallowing. When Suling woke up, Madam Ning was
asleep beside her in a chair by the bed. Dr. Ouyang was there,
too, a silhouette at the open door, silently regarding her.

SULING SHOOK THE memory away with a lump in her throat,
checked her makeup one more time, and followed the others
into the carriage. She glanced up at an open window on the
third floor of the brothel. Madam Ning was there, looking out
to make sure her charges were on their way, on time for the
engagement. Then the stern face turned from the window and
smiled, and as the carriage pulled away, Suling saw the madam
lift her face to Clarkson's kiss. *Perhaps some white devils are
faithful in love*, Suling thought.

At the octagon house, they followed Mrs. MacNeil as usual
to the room where they got changed. Thornton had provided

different garments this time. There were simple silk tunics decorated only at the neckline, hems, and sleeves with wide bands of embroidery; others were formal court robes weighed down with gold and silver thread. The one thing they all had in common was their color: blue.

Suling picked out a pleated skirt with a matching tunic blouse, blue damask woven with a pattern of clouds and bats. The skirt's flat panels on the front and back were embroidered with flowers, fruit, and butterflies in the most intricate knot stitching she had ever seen. The side panels were pleated, each tiny pleat the same exact width as the others. How many hours of sewing had gone into this ensemble?

"It's called a 'fish scale one-hundred pleat skirt,'" Butterfly said, tying the skirt tapes at the back for Suling, "because when you walk, the pleats along the sides swing and ripple like fish scales."

Out on the spiral staircase, garlands of fern, ivy, and hothouse flowers hung from wrought-iron railings. Guests arrived, mounting the marble steps to the third-floor mezzanine where a buffet had been laid out on linen-draped tables. There were platters of oysters on ice, slices of meat pie, cold salmon in aspic, lobster salad, cheeses and fruit. Niches in the wall held pedestaled marble basins filled with ice and bottles of wine, jugs of water and fruit juices.

Suling and the others moved through the rooms carrying trays of sparkling fruit drinks and champagne. They moved slowly and deliberately between the guests, walking as quietly as they could on the marble floor.

A hand bell tinkled, cutting through the hubbub of conversation, and the butler cleared his throat. "Ladies and gentlemen, Mr. Thornton requests your presence in the music room upstairs, if you would be so kind."

Suling rounded up the other girls and they took the service

stairs up to the next floor. The tall windows in the music room were hung with deep blue velvet, drawn closed to keep the afternoon sun from angling in. Six chandeliers blazed from the coffered ceiling, lending the large room a theatrical ambiance. There was a grand piano on the dais, and round tables, each draped in blue-and-gold damask, had been set with dessert plates and silverware.

A footman changed out her tray, and now Suling's silver platter held a selection of dainty sweet confections. Tiny fresh fruit tarts, meringues, and little cake squares beautifully glazed and covered in swirls of lacelike icing.

A smattering of applause and Mr. Thornton stepped in front of the grand piano, the jacket of his gray afternoon suit open, his shirt a blinding white. A blond woman stood quietly beside him. He rested one hand on the piano.

"My dear friends, honored guests, Mayor Schmitz," he said. "My original excuse for this party was to show off a new plant, an *Epiphyllum oxypetalum*, a Queen of the Night. And indeed, it is on display in the Chinese Room. However, my excitement over acquiring this specimen has been unseated by another discovery. Please welcome Miss Gemma Garland."

The blond woman bowed at the polite applause, took a long breath, and smiled. The pianist, an olive-skinned man with broad shoulders and dark, unruly hair, began to play.

Suling recognized the woman. *Gemma Garland*. Whose luggage she had helped carry to the boardinghouse. She studied the woman, her peach complexion and hair like summer wheat. The shapely figure, the modest smile.

The modest smile grew dazzling, confident, and the woman began to sing.

Suling recognized the voice. The new tenant at Taylor Street, who Alice had listened to with such bliss.

Even the most obnoxiously talkative guests fell silent as the soprano's clear, thrilling voice reached out to the audience. Rapt and enthralled, every single guest turned to gaze at the performer. Suling didn't understand the words, but the melody and Gemma's clear, elegant soprano stirred a wistfulness in her, an awareness that there was beauty amid the sorrows of this world, and that some of it was right here in the marvelous voice that directed itself straight to her heart.

After a standing ovation, members of the audience surged toward the low stage while others returned downstairs where the buffet tables had been replenished during the performance. There were dainty sandwiches, fruit sorbets, and more champagne. Suling herded the other women downstairs where the butler pointed them at silver trays of little cakes and pastries, and it was back to work.

Suling glimpsed Thornton standing off to one side, watching as Gemma drifted down the staircase flanked by admirers. He gazed at the soprano, a triumphant gleam in his eyes. There was something else in the intensity of his gaze, something Suling couldn't quite put her finger on, not yet.

"Marvelous, Mr. Thornton, simply marvelous!" Thornton was no longer alone. He'd been accosted by a society matron, her status on display in the ropes of pearls wound about her neck. "Where on earth did you find her?" Not waiting for an answer and still talking, the woman tugged him out to the mezzanine.

Suling slipped into the Chinese Room; she visited the Phoenix Crown whenever she was at the octagon house, never tiring of its elaborate beauty. Today, however, the doors to its display case were shut. But the glass case adjacent held a new item that made her breath catch: an exquisitely embroidered robe. A dragon robe in heavy blue silk brocade. She could hardly take her eyes off the intricate details. Had it been looted from the Forbidden City? Which empress or imperial concubine had worn it? Perhaps it had been touched by an emperor's own hands as he presented it to a favorite consort.

Her eyes inspected the embroidery as critically as she had examined the fine gowns worn by Thornton's guests. There was no comparison between what she saw on those women's dresses and the superb work on this dragon robe. Of course it was still daytime and the women at the party were not wearing their finest evening gowns so she should reserve judgment, but still. Her eyes took in the tiny couching stitches that anchored gold and silver threads to the heavy blue silk. At the stem stitching, used to outline shapes, at the tiny Peking knots used to color in small areas.

In naming these stitches, she could hear her mother's voice, her gentle instruction. "The Peking knot is also called the seed stitch, and sometimes the forbidden stitch because it's so fine it is said women have gone blind using it too much."

Suling stepped away from the glass case as a cluster of guests entered the Chinese Room, led by Thornton, Gemma on his arm. They moved from one cabinet to another, Thornton giving a tour of his treasures. To Suling's delight, Alice Eastwood strolled in after the group, a plate of pastries in her hand. She looked at each dainty confection approvingly before taking a generous bite, apparently unconcerned about the crumbs falling on her bodice. She winked at Suling, who held out her platter of petits fours.

"I invited myself," Alice whispered, taking two of the little cakes. "I telephoned and said I wanted to see his Queen of the Night. Thornton suggested I attend this party and view the plant at the same time."

Alice strode over to a niche where a plant with luxuriant

green leaves grew out of a large porcelain pot. "Look at her, Suling," the botanist said, gazing fondly at the stems of dangling buds. "The Queen of the Night. More interesting than most people here. Oh, what I'd give to see this in bloom. They're extremely fragrant, you know."

They both backed up as Thornton's entourage moved in their direction and stopped in front of the blue robe.

"Now, this one is called a dragon robe," Thornton said.

"But why, when there's not a single dragon on it?" said the society matron with the pearls.

"Dragons represent royalty in China," he replied, "and dragon robes are what gowns of a particular design are called. They can only be worn by a member of the emperor's family or a member of the court. Every embroidered symbol, even the colors on a gown, are regulated according to the wearer's rank. This one is turquoise blue, indicating it was for an imperial consort. But there aren't any official symbols in the decoration. Only butterflies and flowers, so this was a gown for private occasions such as family celebrations."

"It's beautiful," Gemma breathed, gazing at it. "I can't imagine anyone actually wearing this. It's a work of art."

"Well, Miss Garland, I must confess I brought this out from my collection for you," Thornton said. "Perhaps one day you can wear it to sing in *Madama Butterfly*. I saw it last year at Covent Garden in London and I'd be willing to fund an opera company for a San Francisco run."

There were excited murmurs, more small talk, and the guests gradually drifted away, leaving only Gemma to stand with Thornton. Gemma spied Alice and beckoned her over with a smile. Suling tried not to look as though she was eavesdropping, held out her tray of petits fours, and smiled vacuously at passing guests.

"I've heard so much about *Madama Butterfly*," Gemma said. "I'm terribly envious Henry saw it in London."

Henry. They were on first name terms already.

"I'm certain that any production with Gemma singing Cio-Cio-San would be an even more sublime performance than the London production," he said.

Then Suling saw it again, the triumphant gleam in his eyes. This time she could put her finger on it. There was ambition in that look, something avid and acquisitive. As though he had bought a precious vase or painting no one else had been discerning enough to find. She wondered if Gemma had noticed that look. She wondered if she would've noticed it herself if Reggie hadn't told her of Thornton's blazing ambition to make a name for himself as a patron of the arts. Dance or music, painting or sculpture, the millionaire was always alert to talent. Clearly, he had made Gemma Garland his next project.

A stout man with owl-like features interrupted the conversation, bowing to the ladies. "Miss Garland, Miss Eastwood," Thornton said, "may I introduce you to Mr. Martin Beck, owner and manager of the Orpheum Theater?"

The bespectacled man bent over Alice's hand, then Gemma's, then drew her away to speak in private.

"*Madama Butterfly* is set in Japan, not China," Alice remarked, finally brushing the crumbs from her bodice. "This dragon robe would not be authentic to the setting."

Thornton shrugged. "The only thing that matters to me is the music. When I saw that opera at Covent Garden, believe me, authentic costume was the last thing on my mind. The music was breathtaking."

He looked at the dragon robe and sighed. "But this gown will not take part in that opera anytime soon. It's been damaged at the back and my housekeeper has yet to find a needlewoman equal to the task of repairing the embroidery. Such skills are apparently unobtainable this side of the Pacific. I may send it to Hong Kong."

"Nonsense," Alice said. "It would be child's play for Suling. Her embroidery work is the finest I've ever seen. I doubt you'd find better even in Paris. If anyone this side of the Pacific can repair this robe, it's Suling." She beckoned Suling to come over.

Thornton stared. "You mean *this* Sue? From that . . . establishment in Chinatown? Who makes silk flowers?"

"She's not a prostitute, let's be clear on that," Alice said. "Her family owns a laundry. What do you think, Suling? Could you repair this robe?"

Suling put her tray down on an inlaid table and moved closer to the glass case. "May I see the damage on the garment, Mr. Thornton?"

Without hesitation, he pulled out a key chain and unlocked the glass case. He turned the dressmaker form around and pointed to the damaged section, a rip along the hem, part of the embroidered edge torn off as though by greedy hands. Suling knelt down and examined both sides of the hem.

It was not a large piece of work. It was the intricacy of it that excited Suling. She looked up at Thornton. "The motif of cloud, wave, and mountains at the bottom is embroidered separately on a band of silk attached to the hem. I would need silver thread and silk floss in the same colors to replicate the design on a band of silk. Then I'd attach it to the hem using the same stitching to blend old with new."

"Good lord," Thornton exclaimed. "Your voice. You're the laundryboy!" He looked amused rather than shocked. "Well then, how soon can you start on this dress?"

"Not for another week," she said. "I'm still making those Queen of the Night flowers for you, Mr. Thornton."

"Well, I'd like you to work on the dress instead." Thornton's voice held barely contained excitement. He looked across the room at Gemma, still talking to the Orpheum's manager. "I have an idea, and it involves this robe and the opening night of *Carmen*. Eight days, Sue. Can you make the repairs in eight days?"

Suling hesitated. "I could. But I'd have to work day and night to do it."

"Name your price," he said.

Her mind added up the hours, the dollars, wondering what Thornton might be willing to pay. He could afford anything, of course, but what did he consider reasonable? How did one deal with the very rich?

"I'll name a price," Alice interrupted, not waiting for Suling to reply, "one hundred and sixty dollars."

One hundred and sixty dollars. Suling held back a gasp. She was still kneeling beside the glass case. If she'd been standing, her legs would not have held her. She forced herself to rise from the floor. Thornton would never agree to such an amount.

"Done," Thornton said. "In eight days, when you've finished. But that robe does not leave the house. It's worth too much. I'll have a room set up as your sewing room. You'll come in every day to work."

Thanks to Alice, Suling now knew that whatever she asked for was nothing to him. "I'd prefer twenty dollars a day," she said, "payment after each day's work." In case she had to make her escape before finishing the robe.

"Done," Thornton repeated. "Twenty dollars a day, eight days." Then he chuckled. "You Chinese, as sharp as Jews."

The clock chimed four and Thornton gave Alice a nod, then

sauntered to the staircase to bid his guests farewell as they left, the perfect host.

"Now, that's something I never expected him to say," Alice murmured, a frown creasing her forehead.

But Suling barely heard Alice's words. She had to bite her lip to stop herself from screaming with delight. Eight days to earn more money than she could steal from the laundry cashbox, more money than her little collars and cuffs could ever sell for. She'd find a way to evade Third Uncle. Oh yes, whatever it took, she would find a way.

Chapter 9

Gemma was still humming a bit of Verdi when she walked Alice Eastwood out at the end of the party. Her train rustled deliciously over the Savonnerie carpets as they descended the winding staircase toward the front doors—every painstaking minute she'd spent this morning pressing each frill of her biscuit faille reception gown with its bands of bronze velvet had been worth it, worth it, worth it. The afternoon, despite the previous day's migraine, had been an utter triumph.

"I know opera singers frequently have admirers," Alice Eastwood was saying as they reached the big entrance hall. "You didn't mention yours was the man who owned the octagon house botanical collection!"

She cast a longing glance at the glassed doors to the conservatory, and Gemma laughed. "I didn't know you'd be here, Alice, but I'm glad you were." She'd made an effort to be more friendly tonight, feeling a flush of embarrassment that Alice had seen her be so abrupt with their landlady yesterday, but Gemma still hadn't been able to hide her surprise to see the botanist among Mr. Thornton's high-society guests. Alice stood out in her old-fashioned black dress like a musty silk flower in a bouquet of hothouse blooms, but Mr. Thornton had greeted her with hands outstretched. *We last met at my fundraiser for the Academy, didn't we, Miss Eastwood? I sent you a cutting afterward of one of my new succulent varietals. How is it faring? . . .* He'd drawn her out respectfully about her latest expedition, asked about the Academy's newest acquisitions, answered her questions about the reblooming yellow rose in his front garden.

"Most men would regard Alice Eastwood as a fusty old maid

with an odd hobby," Gemma had said afterward, as Alice went back for another look at the Queen of the Night plant. "You treated her like a queen, Mr. Thornton."

"I prefer her to half my guests here," he replied. "I like to surround myself with people who have a purpose in their life—a passion. There's nothing more boring than people who are perpetually bored."

"Share my cab back to Taylor Street?" Alice asked Gemma now, shrugging into her old cloak. Carriages were pulling up in front; Thornton's guests were already streaming out to their theater engagements, their dinner invitations, their evening parties.

"You go on, I need to make sure my accompanist receives his fee." Gemma waved Alice off into the late-afternoon sun and went in search of George in the trail of departing guests, still trying not to gape at this incredible house. The onyx marble floors, the polished mahogany paneling glowing with jewel-like tapestries, the crystal chandeliers throwing off a million diamond points of light . . .

"There you are," George said, music folder under his arm, meeting her halfway down the spiral of stairs. "You weren't climbing all this way back up this man-made mountain to find me, were you?"

"I don't mind climbing a staircase like this." Gemma gave a twirl on the landing. "Men ask themselves what women want—well, I have never met a woman who didn't yearn to sweep up a really magnificent staircase in a really elegant gown." She swirled her velvet-banded train so it flared like a toreador's cape.

"Easy there." George caught her arm before she missed the step. "How much of that champagne did you swig?"

"Hardly any, I'll have you know." She'd been too busy getting her hand kissed by half the room, after her final encore. The director of the Tivoli had actually had tears in his eyes as he told her he'd never heard a better Violetta. He'd pressed his card into her hand and asked if she might come to his office to discuss her future plans in San Francisco. It didn't do to leap too eagerly on such openings, so Gemma thanked him with a demure smile and tucked the card in her sleeve, but her heart had been thudding with triumph. She might have awakened this morning with a migraine-tender head, but she had never sung better.

"You aren't leaving, too?" George asked as she passed over the envelope with his fee and made to head back upstairs. "You don't have your cloak."

"Mr. Thornton can call me a hansom cab, after I've collected my fee for performing." The old Gemma would have waited uncomplainingly until her host felt like paying her, even if that wasn't for days or weeks. The new Gemma wasn't going home without extracting the payment she'd earned, and she'd make no apologies for it, either. And she grinned a little, because she thought Mr. Thornton would approve. *You know what you're worth*, he'd probably say with that glint in his eye. *Make me fork over.*

She intended to.

George was still studying her, leaning against the mahogany railing. "You sang beautifully today."

"Yes, the voice behaved herself tolerably well."

"Why do singers do that?" He spread those huge piano-playing hands. "I don't say 'The hands behaved themselves' when I play well."

"Hands are external. With voices, it's like you're housing a tiny ill-tempered god in your throat, one that might just decide to take the day off if you displeased it."

"You clearly made it just the right offering today."

"Flatterer!" Gemma waved goodbye to George, then waltzed back upstairs with a rustle of taffeta petticoats.

The last guests had gone, and servants were sweeping away the detritus of the party: marble-topped buffet tables cleared of silver dishes, discarded champagne flutes whisked off mantelpieces. One of the ever-present clerks was locking up his employer's private office on the second floor, wedging the key in the potted palm by the office door—he looked stricken when he saw Gemma watching. "Don't tell Mr. Thornton? I'm not supposed to leave it out, but the other clerk needs it and I'll be waiting hours—"

"Your secret's safe with me." She put her finger to her lips with a smile as he shoved the key farther back at the edge of the pot, and Gemma went up the next turn in the staircase. On the landing she saw the Chinese girls headed for the servant stairs in a line, their faces still painted but their sumptuous blue silks changed for ordinary cotton robes. As they stood back for Gemma to pass, one lingered behind the others, eyes suddenly panicked as she began searching the floor. She asked something of the other girls in rapid Chinese, then turned to a parlormaid carrying a tray across the landing. "A ring, did you see a ring?" the Chinese girl asked in English.

"No." The parlormaid shrugged, not bothering to look. The Chinese girl dropped to her hands and knees, feeling along the carpet, and Gemma couldn't help but flinch, her soaring mood darkening for a moment. She knew exactly what it felt like to be down on your hands and knees scrabbling for your things as people stepped past in complete indifference and your toes curled in shame. *If you could just give me a week to find the rent, ma'am,* Gemma had asked her landlady back in New York after she'd been cheated of her savings, never anticipating she wouldn't get that week's grace. She'd been a model tenant, after all; she'd never once been late with rent until that day; she kept her room immaculate; she'd spent hours over cups of tea sympathetically listening to the woman complain about ungrateful children and slovenly boarders. *Surely a week is no issue, ma'am?*

Gemma had just lost her job at the opera house; she was still reeling from realizing how her agent had robbed her blind. She barely had more than ten cents to her name, but she had an audition for the Metropolitan Opera chorus in five days. All she needed was a week's grace. A week, that was all.

And the woman had walked upstairs to Gemma's room with a face like stone and begun physically tossing her clothes out onto the grimy stair landing. *Get out, you stupid caterwauling bitch. I don't run a charity.* Getting down on her hands and knees on that oily scrap of landing carpet had been the worst moment of all—worse than realizing she'd lost her job, head still rolling sickly with postmigraine tenderness as the house manager told her to clear out; worse than realizing her savings were gone. Gemma had scraped up her scattered belongings as fast as she could, eyes burning as the other women in the boardinghouse averted their gaze. Not one offering to help—not one. She'd felt ashamed, somehow, like it was her fault she was there. *Stupid caterwauling bitch.*

"Here," Gemma said quickly now, dropping to her knees on the landing next to the frantic Chinese girl who was still running her hands over the rich Savonnerie carpet. "Is this what you're looking for?"

A ring on a cord, just a little thing—Gemma hardly got a look at it before the girl snatched it with palpable relief. "Thank you, ma'am," she said in perfect English, slipping the cord around her neck and tucking the bauble under her collar. She looked somehow familiar, though Gemma couldn't be sure with all that white powder smoothing her face into an ivory mask. A small bow, and the girl dashed away with the rest of her friends. Gemma continued up the stairs, forcibly putting the ugly memory aside. *Stupid caterwauling bitch.* She wasn't that woman anymore, and she never would be again. Not ever.

"THERE YOU ARE." Thornton stood alone in the Chinese Room, hands in his pockets, gazing at his collection. His back was to Gemma; he must have known her by the click of her heels. "I love a party, but I love it even better when all the guests go home."

She found a laugh, feeling the lightness of her afternoon's triumph come fizzing back with the sound of his voice. "I'm afraid you won't get rid of me until I receive my fee, Mr. Thornton."

"How very hardheaded of you." He turned with a grin, passing over a white envelope from his pocket. "Be sure to count it."

"Why? Have you cheated me?"

"No, but you should always assume someone is going to."

Gemma opened the envelope and flipped through the bills. Accurate to the last dollar, of course. "Did anyone break any of your curios?" she asked, moving closer to the lavish display shelves full of jade and porcelain and lacquer. "I was holding my breath every time my skirt brushed past all these priceless relics—you have an astonishing house."

"I can't claim to have built it." He came to join her, burned hand turning his jade watch charm over. "I bought it off a silver magnate who'd gone bankrupt, stripped everything out as I began building Thornton Ltd., and filled it with everything beautiful I could find. I wanted it the moment I saw it was an octagon."

"Why?"

"Eight means good luck in the Chinese tradition, and a businessman needs luck. These Astors and Rockefellers may boast about building their empires by the sweat of their brow alone, but they're idiots. Hard work is required, yes. But no empire is built without luck." He nodded at his display cases. "What's your favorite piece here?"

Gemma pointed to a watercolor on a scroll of silk, hanging down a strip of wall. "That one." A trio of Chinese women in layered court robes and elaborate piled hair, making music—one had some sort of pipe, the other a stringed instrument. "The third woman—I want to know if she's the singer, or if she's the audience. I wonder what she's thinking, because the oddest things sometimes go through my head when I'm performing, and I wonder if it was the same for them all those centuries ago." The woman had painted peony lips and perfectly arched eyebrows, like the girl she had spoken with on the landing. "What's your favorite piece here? The dragon robe?"

"Mmm, no." He led her to the display at the center of it all, opening the cabinet that had been closed during the party. Gemma caught her breath at the sight of it: an ornate jeweled crown in shimmering, iridescent, electric blue. "From the Old Summer Palace in Beijing—a phoenix crown, and a very unusual one. Seven phoenixes, blue-and-white two-tone jade, fifty-seven sapphires, thirty-six rubies, and over four thousand pearls. And these loops of pearls dangling from the crown, with the carved pendants?" He lifted one for her to examine. "They're Queen of the Night flowers, carved out of ivory. That's why I wanted a Queen of the Night for my conservatory."

Gemma touched the crown with the lightest fingertip. "Who was it made for, I wonder?"

"An empress." He turned away from the shimmering thing, looking down at Gemma for a moment. Then he said, "Wear it."

"What?" She tore her eyes out of the grasp of that hypnotizing kingfisher blue. "I'm no empress."

"Do you want to be an empress of the stage? It can happen. This, today"—gesturing at the detritus of the party all around them—"this is just the beginning of what I can do for your career."

"What are you offering?" Gemma kept her voice brisk, businesslike. "Let's be clear with each other, Mr. Thornton."

"By all means." He squared off against her as though they had a phalanx of lawyers each and a contract on a board table between them, looking as though he was going to enjoy every minute of the wrangling before they both signed it. Gemma squared off, too. Hadn't part of her known this was coming? It hadn't only been her performance fee she lingered to collect after the party, had it? She opened a hand in invitation: *Your offer, sir?*

"I heard you sing in that empty opera house when you first arrived in this city," he began, "and I knew that voice was something special. Watching you mesmerize an entire room today, I knew it for certain: you can be a star. And I want my name known in this city as a patron of the arts, so allow me to make you one."

Gemma couldn't help a faint, reflexive bristle. "You think I can't make myself a star?"

"I think you've been trying. By your own admission, though, you've been unlucky. But that's not your fault," Thornton said, forestalling her objections. "Why not let me balance the scales? With someone like me behind you, no opera house would dare fire you for having to cancel when one of your migraines hits. They'd send roses and apologies to your room instead, and they'd kick your understudy off the stage the moment you were well again."

What would it be like to rehearse a role in that kind of security? Gemma wondered. Not always balanced on a knife edge, wondering if her own body was going to betray her and then if her employers were going to punish her for it.

"In eight days, Caruso and your new company arrive in San Francisco and open with *Carmen*," Thornton went on. "You can sing in the chorus and travel on afterward to Kansas City or wherever else is on the schedule, hoping that the director sees the gift you have in your throat and promotes you. Or you can let me sponsor you instead, knowing you'll rise up the ladder a great deal faster with my patronage. You decide: What do you want?"

I wanted to do it on my own, Gemma thought. But where had all that independence gotten her? Knocked down the ladder over and over again, cheated by people she trusted, and still singing in the chorus at thirty-two when singers with half her voice went waltzing on to bigger roles and private terraced apartments and jewel boxes full of pearls. They might only have half her voice, but they knew how to play the game better than good little Sally Gunderson from Nebraska who would never compromise that fine upbringing of hers and let a man pay her way.

Well, maybe she was tired of being good. Maybe she wanted to play the game for once, and play it for all she could get. So that she'd never be on her hands and knees again, scrabbling on a greasy hallway carpet for her scattered underclothes and burning with shame.

"I accept, Mr. Thornton." Gemma stepped forward and wound her arms around his neck, drawing his lips down to hers. She'd been wanting to kiss him since the Palace Grill, had been wondering since that night why he hadn't made the slightest attempt to do so for all his evident admiration—but now her toes left the floor altogether as he collected her against him in a grip like a steel bar.

"I don't mix business with pleasure," he said eventually, once his mouth released hers.

Her lips felt bruised. "I think I want to, Henry."

"Gemma." He said her name lingeringly, but released her waist. "Don't feel you have to buy my patronage with anything but your voice. I may be a tough trader, but I don't attach those kinds of strings to my deals."

Gemma shrugged, feeling giddy. She'd just launched herself off the cliff, and now she was flying instead of falling. "You want me; I want you. You want to make me a star; I want to be one. That's a deal I'm more than happy to make."

"Then drive a hard bargain with me." He bent his head with a low laugh, nibbling along the line of her neck. His burned right hand wound around her wrist and found the mother-of-pearl buttons on her glove. "What do you want, Gemma? Rake me over the coals. Don't be nice."

"I'm not breaking my contract with the Met. And I'm keeping my room at Taylor Street, paid in full in my name." Trusting men and their promises blindly, that was how sopranos ended up singing in bottom-level music halls. She was keeping something in reserve, a fallback no one could take away.

"Good girl." He thumbed open one glove button, then two, still nibbling along her neck below her ear. "There will be a suite here in the octagon house at your disposal: pianos, gowns, maids . . . But a woman should always have something of her own that no one can touch. What else do you want?"

"A voice teacher, the best in San Francisco. Lessons every day. I can't always be singing for you and your friends; I need time to practice and improve on my own." Time and leisure to make herself the best she could be.

"A voice teacher, language coaches, a daily pianist to rehearse you. Done." Thornton tugged off her glove and dropped it to the floor. "What else?"

"A role." She took a deep breath. "Buy me a role, while the Met is in San Francisco. I've been bumped off the stage for so many understudies—I want someone bumped off the stage for me for once. I want to sing opposite Caruso while he's in town."

"Ruthless," Thornton approved. "I like it."

"I think I do, too," Gemma breathed, standing on tiptoe to kiss him again. She bit at him and he bit back, the two of them swaying and clinging.

"I'm not going to be content seeing you go when the Met traveling company leaves town," he growled in her ear. "That's only a few weeks away. Are you sure you won't break your contract?"

She pulled back and looked him in the eye. "You arrange a series of solo concerts for me here in San Francisco, in the best theaters in town. Advertising. Posters and billboards. Whatever it takes to sell out every single one. When you show me the signed contracts with the theaters, and I meet with the theater directors myself to know they're serious about showcasing me, then I'll know I have a reason to leave the Met chorus and stay here. But I won't break one contract without more in hand."

The flare in his eye was pure, naked admiration. "You drive a hard bargain."

"I learned from the best."

"You haven't asked for jewels yet. Don't you want diamonds?"

"Right now what I want is security, as much of it as I can get." Gemma wasn't fool enough to think this was going to last forever, but when you never had any security at all, security for now was good enough. Maybe it would only last a few months— she'd still take it with both hands and eyes open. What did she have to lose?

"I can give you security." His rough, burned fingers sifted through her hair, dislodging hairpins one by one. "And I'll give you something else. When the curtain comes down on *Carmen* in eight days, I'll throw the biggest party San Francisco has ever seen. A grand ball to put this afternoon's gathering to shame. I'll deck you in that imperial dragon robe that matches your eyes and put the Phoenix Crown on your head, and I'll introduce you as my Queen of the Night. Today's performance whetted society's appetite—in eight days, when I bring you out with that crown on your head, they'll be clamoring for you. Every one of those concerts you're asking for will sell out to the last ticket. By fall, the masses will be fighting to hear you the way they're fighting now to hear Caruso."

And everyone will say you bought it for me, Gemma couldn't help but think. Harder to silence that little starchy voice inside than she'd thought.

"Gemma." His thumb traced the frown that lined itself between her brows. "There's no shame in an artist relying on patrons. It's been that way for centuries. Who cares now that Michelangelo had sponsors for his paintings, his sculptures? People only marvel at the art. If you can demonstrate you deserve to be at the pinnacle—and you do deserve that—then no one will question how you arrived there."

Gemma felt her eyes blur. A tumble of images whirled kaleidoscope-like through her head: curtain calls, encores, roses, her name on Dressing Room A . . . but the tears weren't just for the dream castles he was conjuring up. It was for the *belief* in his eyes. Making a career on the stage was all about believing: that you were good enough, that your turn would come, that your time to shine was almost here. That until it came, the music was enough.

But at some point someone else had to believe, too, and had

anyone done that for Gemma? Not since Nellie, and Nellie had traipsed off without caring, without a backward glance. It could wear down even the steadiest heart, trying to believe in yourself day after day, year after year, until you were no longer young and you'd just been beaten down until you no longer believed you were anything but a *stupid caterwauling bitch.*

And here was Henry Thornton, who believed she was a star in the making. And he wanted to do the making.

She twined her fingers through his burned ones and led him from the Chinese Room.

MUCH LATER, HENRY padded naked across the Persian carpet of his bedroom and took a lacquered box off the mantel, opening it to show a jade opium pipe with a small lamp and a porcelain jar. "Did I wake up in a den of iniquity?" Gemma laughed, shaking back her loose hair over the sheets of the big bed. Her body was humming like a perfectly tuned harp. Not that harps were ever in tune—harpists did nothing but fiddle with their harp pegs, while the conductor looked increasingly incensed. *But this harp,* Gemma thought with a languorous stretch of her arms, *is* perfectly *in tune.*

"You haven't been asleep yet, pet. We've been too busy." He leaned down to softly bite the side of her throat, then opened the porcelain jar to show the small gummed balls of opium. "Have you ever tried the dream stick? I like to think an emperor dreamed grand dreams of celestial conquest with the aid of this one."

Gemma looked at it and shivered, part pleasure and part something else. "I don't think . . ."

"It's not dangerous in moderation." His hands were preparing it: the pipe bowl, the spirit lamp, the ball of opium. "And it might help with those migraines of yours." He finished preparing everything, took a leisurely inhalation through the pipe, then lounged back in the sheets and drew her leg up over his shoulder, which tipped her back against the pillows with a shriek of surprised laughter. She inhaled, smelling the strange sweetness of opium smoke. "Try it," he said, kissing the inside of her knee. "And dream of singing your favorite roles on all the greatest stages of the world . . ."

"Mozart's Countess at the Vienna Staatsoper," Gemma said, the pipe's cool jade in her hand. "Gounod's Juliette at the Paris Opera. Verdi's Gilda at Covent Garden."

"Keep going." Kissing his way higher.

"Puccini's Tosca at La Fenice in Venice . . . they call it *the phoenix* because it's burned down so many times." Gemma bent her head and took a long deep inhalation off the pipe, body juddering, Thornton's mouth between her legs and his smoke in her lungs, and why had she ever hesitated? It was all delicious. A dream, a dream, a delicious dream with no end in sight.

Chapter 10

It was Fate, Suling decided. The gods approved. How else to explain that after she decided to forget about Reggie, Henry Thornton had as good as tossed a bundle of money into her lap? For work she loved to do, longed to do. Or that Third Uncle had believed so readily when she told him she'd spend most of the week at Hing Chong Tailors working on her wedding garments? Better equipment and better light, she'd explained.

Third Uncle hardly noticed her these days. The gambling parlor did all it could to keep him playing happily and he was rarely home. Ever since Dr. Ouyang set the wedding date, Third Uncle had been living large. All Chinatown knew Ouyang was paying him a huge sum for Suling, so Third Uncle's favorite gambling parlor was being generous, advancing him large amounts on credit. Once Ouyang paid up, however, Third Uncle would begin losing. He was the only one who couldn't see this.

Suling could finish the repairs on the dragon robe in time, she knew she could. The torn border didn't need a large replacement piece of embroidery. She knew how she would embroider over the edges of the patch to blend it in with the original stitches, picturing the swirling outlines of silver and blue above diagonal lines of silver, gold, and blue. She knew exactly what to do and the prospect made her shiver with delight.

Only two years ago she had helped her mother sew a dragon robe for Madam Ning, who liked offering her clients new fantasies. A dragon robe, and men could pretend they were enjoying an imperial consort's favors. Suling and her mother didn't embroider an entire robe, that would've taken too long and cost too much. A mere costume didn't require rigorous authenticity. Ming Lee sewed a robe in heavy cherry-pink brocade and stitched a pre-embroidered panel of birds and flowers onto the garment. The traditional motif of stylized waves, clouds, and mountains at the hem, however, they embroidered themselves. Ming Lee wanted to teach Suling some special stitches. Suling accompanied her mother to Fung Tai Dry Goods store, the only shop that carried the special gold and silver thread.

"We don't ever actually sew using gold and silver thread," her mother explained, showing her the metallic thread. "It's too thick and brittle to pull through a needle. We use this, a couching stitch in pale yellow or white silk floss, and just attach metallic threads to fabric. Think of them as tiny basting stitches that apply thread to fabric."

Now Suling chatted with Fung Tai's owner and purchased thread for the dragon robe; the shopkeeper assumed Suling needed them for her wedding wardrobe. The entire neighborhood seemed to know about her upcoming nuptials.

At the Thornton mansion, Mrs. MacNeil met her at the tradesmen's entrance. She looked at Suling, dressed in her delivery boy clothes, and shook her head in wonder. "Bless me, I never would've guessed you were a girl," she said. "Well, the master has given you one of the smaller rooms on the third floor. Come with me."

The room wasn't small, not to Suling. And to her relief the light was excellent, sunshine streaming in through two tall windows. The dragon robe was on a dressmaker's form placed away from direct light. A worktable and chair were positioned by the window. Mrs. MacNeil opened a door to reveal a tiled bathroom with a water closet.

"These are the facilities, in case you've never seen one for indoors," she said. "It's not because you're special, every bedroom has one. And I expect you to clean it right after using."

She pointed at a tea trolley. "Pitcher of water, some biscuits. You can go downstairs to the servants' hall for your meals, but mind you use the back stairs and corridors, never the central staircase."

"Thank you, Mrs. MacNeil," Suling said. "I have everything I need."

"Mrs. MacNeil, Mrs. MacNeil!" An auburn-haired maid rushed into the room, cheeks red with excitement, the unruly curls escaping from her cap at odds with the severe black dress and starched white apron.

"Kathleen, what have I said about running? Only in the servants' areas. What is it?"

"I'm sorry, Mrs. MacNeil. But a wagon has come with Miss Garland's things," the maid said. "Did you know she'll be living here now?"

"Yes, I did," Mrs. MacNeil said. "Who do you think sent the wagon? Who do you think got the Blue Suite ready first thing this morning? Tell the footmen to bring everything to the third floor."

"Oh, there isn't much luggage at all," Kathleen said. "But there's a birdcage!"

"Let's hope Miss Garland's not as messy as the other one," Mrs. MacNeil said, shaking her head as she left the room.

The maid hurried behind the older woman. "Who will you assign to be her lady's maid?" she asked, sounding hopeful.

Suling closed the door. So Gemma Garland was Thornton's new mistress. Suling wasn't naive enough to think a woman could move into a beautiful suite of rooms in a home like this, with an owner like Henry Thornton, and not be expected to share his bed. And Gemma Garland, if Suling was not mistaken, most certainly was not that young or that new to this business.

Suling changed back to her usual garb in the tiled bathroom, glad to be out of the tight-fitting vest. She inspected the padded chair beside the table, gave the seat an experimental spin, and adjusted the height. She assembled the slats of wood in her bag into a square frame and attached the blue silk to the frame by lacing heavy thread through the edge of the fabric and the row of holes in the frame, carefully keeping the tension even on all sides until the blue silk was stretched as taut as the surface of a drum.

Then she took a large sheet of onionskin paper from her bag and cut off a piece slightly larger than the section of damaged border. Only then did she approach the dragon robe. She held the thin paper against the border and with a thin stick of charcoal, traced the pattern on the hem.

HOURS LATER, SULING looked up from the embroidery frame, disturbed by loud trilling laughter outside the door. She stretched her arms toward the ceiling and shook her head. She had only stopped once to eat the buns she'd brought and drink some cold tea. The sun had angled around, telling her it was late afternoon and time for her to leave. She had done a satisfyingly good day's work. She had drawn a detailed pattern on the paper then transferred it to the fabric. She had stem stitched most of the outlines for the intricate motif. She couldn't take the robe home, but she could work on the strip of blue silk at night in her bedroom. Tomorrow, Wednesday, she would begin the hard work of tacking silver thread to heavy blue silk. That would take the most time.

THE DAYS FLEW by, the work so engrossing Suling barely noticed interruptions. She often stood up to rub her neck or look out the window to rest her eyes and only then would realize there were fresh plates of food and fruit on the tray, that the teapot had been filled with hot water and fresh tea leaves. Someone had done all this without disturbing her. She suspected Little Fong and Big Fong, one filling the plate in the kitchen, the other bringing it quietly into the room.

There was loud conversation out on the mezzanine. She opened the door and peered out to discover Alice, striding up the staircase behind an anxious Mrs. MacNeil.

"I know Mr. Thornton is out, I only want a few minutes with Suling. I have other errands after this, so rest assured I won't stay long."

With a wide smile, Suling threw open the door and her friend swept inside the room. Mrs. MacNeil returned down the stairs looking resigned, as so many people did when confronted with Alice's resolve.

"It's Saturday. You've been at this for five days now, am I right? Are you happy with your progress?" Alice scrutinized the embroidery frame, circled around the blue dragon robe, and helped herself to some fruit. The curator was looking cool in a crisp white blouse and navy skirt. Her blouse would've been as austere as a man's shirt if not for the tiny pleats on its bodice. Suling longed to embroider a blouse for Alice, tiny pale green fern fronds in silk on white linen, not the usual daisies.

"Yes. It's quite amazing how quickly it goes when there's no one to bother you," Suling said. "And I continue working at night back home, too."

She didn't tell Alice about other things, not exactly interruptions, but momentary distractions. Noises, music. The chords and arpeggios each day from the music room as the dark-haired piano player warmed up. And then the singing; Gemma's practices and voice lessons went on for at least two hours. The long music sessions were followed by a seemingly endless stream of dressmakers and milliners who traipsed up the stairs carrying bolts of fabric and ribbons, laughing and talking excitedly at the prospect of an entire new wardrobe for Henry Thornton's new mistress. And in the mornings when Suling first arrived, she could detect the lingering but unmistakable sickly sweet smell of opium. Opium, the sin that corrupted lives and ruined San Francisco's reputation, according to politicians and newspapers. Except when used by rich white men and their mistresses, apparently.

"And Mr. Thornton is honoring the agreement?" Alice asked. "You're being paid every day?"

"Yes, there's money on the worktable every morning," Suling replied, "you can rest easy on that. Miss Eastwood, I am so grateful you jumped in to negotiate for me. I still can't believe anyone would pay so much."

"We both heard him at the party, my dear. If not for you, he'd be sending the robe to Hong Kong. That would cost far more and take much longer. Men like Thornton like things to happen right away and will pay for it."

Suling rummaged in her bag and held out the Callot Soeurs catalog Alice had lent her.

"Ah yes. We were talking about you finding work at a fashion house," Alice said. "I've given it much thought. I'm delighted you want to spread your wings. You need an employer who truly values your skills."

There was going to be a "but," Suling thought. There was always a "but," a "however," an "unfortunately."

"As you know," Alice continued, "I'm not interested in fashion, but I have a very stylish friend in New York who's on the board of a garden club. Such a knowledgeable group of women, any of them would make a wonderful botanist. But I digress."

Mrs. Julian Vanderhaeghe of New York had dropped in on Alice while touring through California. Over lunch together Alice had spoken of Suling and her desire to work at a fashion house. Mrs. Vanderhaeghe was intrigued by the notion.

"She's headed back to New York now, but Mrs. Vanderhaeghe offered to introduce you around if your embroidery impresses her enough," Alice said. "Have you any samples you could send her, Suling? You don't need to go there yourself just to show her your work."

"I can take samples to New York and show her myself after I've finished the dragon robe," Suling said, giddy at the thought. "Oh, Miss Eastwood, thank you!"

"But my dear, nothing is settled, it's only a possibility." Alice's brow furrowed. "And what about your family? Do they approve of you leaving home?"

Suling wasn't going to tell Alice she was being married off in five days. "I can leave San Francisco anytime. The only family I have is my uncle. He just wants to be rid of me." That much was true.

"But I don't like the idea of you traveling alone, Suling," Alice said. "Why not wait another month? I'll be giving a lecture in New York. We can travel together and I'll introduce you to Mrs. Vanderhaeghe myself."

Suling smiled. "Yes, of course I can wait a month." But of course she couldn't. And she wouldn't. New York had telephone directories. Surely she could find the Vanderhaeghe home address and surely Alice's business card would get her in the door. Just knowing Mrs. Vanderhaeghe's name made Suling's plans more feasible. She would take the next step and buy a train ticket.

SULING FINALLY WENT to the train station on Monday morning and paid for a ticket to New York City, the first eastbound train on the morning of April eighteenth. By then she'd have all the money from Thornton. She closed her eyes for a moment and clutched the little piece of cardboard tightly in her hand, then tucked it into her pocket. Next, the octagon house. She was so close to finishing the repairs, she might even be a day early. Leaving the station, she found herself pushing through a crowd. Two men elbowed past, nearly knocking her down, running toward a train that had just pulled in, the locomotive still puffing small bursts of steam. The crowd was converging onto the same platform.

"Is that his train?" a female voice said, anxious and somewhat out of breath. "We haven't missed seeing him, I hope."

A group of women hurried by, almost running, purses clutched tightly to their chests. They skirted past a Chinese man in a dark blue tunic and trousers, a servant. He was looking at Suling with a puzzled frown. She ducked her head and turned around, made her way to the steps by the station exit. A roar of applause from the crowd made her stop and turn back around to look.

"Mr. Caruso, Mr. Caruso!"

"Welcome to San Francisco, Mr. Caruso!"

A dark-haired, mustachioed man stepped out of the carriage. He waved and bowed. So this was the great tenor who would be singing at the Grand Opera House in two days' time. Well, in two days' time Suling would be on her way to New York.

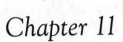

Chapter 11

April 16, 1906
One day, sixteen hours, seven minutes before the earthquake

Gemma didn't want to get all metaphorical about birds in cages, but her eyes welled up every morning when she came downstairs to release Toscanini into the glass-paned, green-scented, blossom-heavy jungle that was the octagon house conservatory. The way her budgie always flew a delirious lap around the glass walls, testing the limits of his new world and finding it so much bigger than the one he was used to—the way he perched himself on the highest branch of a potted orange tree and just sang and sang . . . "I know exactly how you feel," she told him. Ever since coming to the octagon house she had been delirious, singing and singing and *singing*. Free as a bird.

"Mr. Serrano has arrived, Miss Garland," the housekeeper said from the door of the conservatory. "Oh my, that bird . . . Is he allowed in here?"

"He's too small to make a mess. I take him back to his cage in my room at night." Toscanini was one of the few things Gemma had brought from her room on Taylor Street. She'd originally thought she might be going back there at night but . . . She smiled. No, she had not been leaving here at night. "Mr. Serrano is here, you said?"

"Waiting in the music room. As for the rest of the day," the housekeeper rattled off, "you have fittings with the dressmaker at four, and dinner with Mr. Thornton at eight."

"Excellent." Gemma stretched up to scratch Toscanini's fluffy chest with a gentle finger, then waltzed out of the conservatory. "Could you please send some ice water and hot tea up to the music room, Mrs. MacNeil? If it's not too much trouble." The house was humming like a huge well-oiled machine with preparations for the ball tomorrow: delivery carts coming and going from the servants' entrance, enormous vases of flowers being carried upstairs, workmen arriving to prepare the ball-room floor . . . "Oh, and there's another package of my things coming from Taylor Street," Gemma called over her shoulder as she headed for the sweeping stairs. "Can you send it up to my rooms?"

"Of course, Miss Garland." The housekeeper's face gave no hint at all if she found it distasteful to take Gemma's orders. Henry, of course, took that kind of thing for granted. He was used to being obeyed. Gemma still found it a novelty. But it was one she thought she could absolutely grow accustomed to.

Because as much as she loved *la vie bohème* and had even lived it—life in a rented garret, crammed together young and delirious with all your artistic friends—it was not actually possible to *live for your art alone*. You couldn't live for art when you were consumed by the difficulty of everyday *living*, no matter how many garret-living poets like Rodolfo from *La Bohème*, subsisting on cigarettes and philosophy, said you could. How could you practice two hours a day when you had to work ten hours a day to get your bills paid? How could you focus on the purity of your German diction or the cleanness of your trills when worry drilled in the back of your mind about where dinner was coming from?

Here, all that worry had been sliced away from her in one stroke. If her best gown was torn, she could ring to have it mended or replaced. If she was hungry in the middle of practicing, she could call for a meal and then go back to work. If she woke in the middle of the night, it wasn't out of worry that she'd never make it out of the opera chorus, it was because Henry had decided to wake her up by kissing along the line of her breasts under his crisp linen sheets.

"Hello, George," Gemma said, beaming as she swept into the music room that had been made over entirely for her use. Pale buttercream yellow walls, shelves of opera scores, a vast concert grand with its great lid raised like the sail of a ship . . . And her accompanist, already seated and playing. She always knew George's mood by what he was playing when she arrived for their rehearsal: today it was a melting bit of Chopin, which meant he was feeling introspective, but he looked up with a grin and went lilting off into some rollicking music hall tune.

"Lazybones," he accused, looking her over. Her hair was still loose down her back, and she hadn't dressed for the day, just come up in an ivory lace tea gown threaded with pale green ribbons. "Did you only just fall out of bed?"

"Anytime you see a soprano voluntarily awake before tea-time, you should suspect demonic possession." Gemma grinned, taking the tray from the maid at the door. Since she'd more or less moved to the octagon house a week ago, George had been hired to rehearse her daily—something Gemma had thought might be awkward, as he could hardly have any illusions as to her position here, but he hadn't said a word about it. "I thought you were practicing with that string quartet this morning—"

"No, this evening. It's slow going; Jesus, that cellist is a mule—"

"Is he still insisting on the Telemann? You hate Telemann—"

"—I'm trying to persuade them into some Granados, but you'd think I asked them to eat a beehive. Getting Western musicians to play *anything* from south of the equator . . ." George's hands nimbled off into an Argentinian tango. "How are the migraines?"

"Mr. Thornton wants to take me to a doctor in Chinatown. He says they do something with needles that might help. I don't like needles, but I'll try anything." Gemma poured herself a glass of ice water and George a cup of tea, doctoring it up with three sugars just the way he liked it. "Did you hear from your mother after her birthday? Is she still angling for you to go home to Buenos Aires?"

"Always. Someday I'll do it."

"Just not before my concert series," Gemma begged, moving an enameled cigarette box off the windowsill to within his reach. "Here, I managed to get those *cigarillos* you like, even if they do smell like a dead matador—"

"*Gracias, princesa.*" He pushed back his rumpled sleeves and began warming her up, and soon they were diving into her program for the midnight ball.

The midnight ball, that was what Henry was calling it. Thousands would flock to see Caruso in *Carmen*, but only a select three hundred would flock in all their diamonds and velvets, the moment the Grand Opera House's curtain came down, to the octagon house for the ball at midnight. The ball where Gemma would sing the second "Queen of the Night" aria and be launched, officially, as San Francisco's new nightingale. It should not have been possible to pull off such a thing in a week, but money and willpower, Henry said, could pull off almost anything. *Let me take care of the ball*, he said, writing an almost offhand list of instructions for four hundred bottles of champagne, a full orchestra, massed camellias and lilies decorating the ballroom, three hundred engraved invitations dispatched in a single day. *You just focus on the voice.*

And she had—despite the luxury of the past week, Gemma could honestly say she'd never worked harder on her music, preparing for this performance. No easy program of old standards this time: she'd throw down her best.

Tomorrow night.

"Nervous?" George caught the little frisson that went through her voice as she ripped through the Queen's final snarling notes.

"No. Yes?" Gemma sighed. The Metropolitan Opera traveling company had arrived this morning, two long trains pulling into San Francisco according to the servants' gossip—nine sixty-foot baggage cars, followed by sleepers, diners, private cars, everything required to convey the great Caruso, an entire chorus, the orchestra and its instruments, the scenery and sets and costumes necessary to stage more than a dozen opera productions on the road. A traveling city that could perform any one of those operas with no more than a day's rehearsal to adjust to a new stage space. Tonight the singers would be shaking off their travel dust at the Palace Hotel, but in the morning—"I wish I didn't have to rehearse *Carmen* all tomorrow." Normally she would have been looking forward to it; now her Metropolitan debut seemed an unnecessary distraction.

"Real life intruding on your daydream," George remarked with a mocking little scamper of notes over the keyboard. "Inconsiderate of it."

She made a face, but took his point. "I don't mean to be ungrateful. Sharing a stage with Caruso, chorus or not—it's something to dream of. But with the ball right after, I can hardly think about it."

"Twelve nights the Metropolitan company will be staying in San Francisco." George's hands wandered into something melancholy. Debussy, she thought. He was looking at the piano keys, though she knew he didn't need to watch his hands to play. "Then they're off to . . . Well, somewhere. A new city. Are you going with them?"

Gemma fiddled with the pale green ribbon on her sleeve. Henry was setting up the string of concerts she'd asked for; she'd seen the contracts. "We'll see what happens after the ball."

George took a slug of sweetened tea and began to play again, soft arpeggios singing out under his hands. Definitely Debussy. "Mr. Thornton never comes in to hear you practice."

"He doesn't want to distract me. He knows I'm working hard this time of day." Which frankly Gemma found refreshing. So many seemed to assume that *practice* was something a singer did for a lark, rather than something essential to a professional—but Henry took it for granted that just as he kept business hours, so did Gemma. He would have been irked if she'd come sweeping into his study in the middle of the day expecting attention while he was hard at work reviewing land reports and shareholder figures; likewise, he wouldn't have dreamed of interrupting her daily rehearsals. Their time together was at the end of the day, when work was done. "Besides," she added, "he says my voice drifts through the whole house even from two floors away. He quite enjoys making business telephone calls to the sound of Delibes."

"Gemma . . ." George's big hands paused on the piano keys. "I don't mean to meddle in your private affairs."

"Yet somehow I think you're going to do just that," Gemma said, trying for a joke.

He didn't smile. "All of this"—a gesture at the big rehearsal room, the piano, beyond it the suite of rooms given over to her use—"it's dazzling. Generous. But I hope I don't see you . . ."

Her eyebrows climbed.

"Hurt," George finished.

Gemma wavered a moment between being annoyed and being touched. George Serrano hadn't even known her for two weeks, and he felt qualified to comment on her private life? But in a way, yes, he was: few things were more intimate than making music together, and the two of them had been working closely for hours every day, for nearly all those two weeks since she'd arrived in San Francisco. She knew George's mother was from Guatemala but his father from Argentina; she knew how he hummed under his breath when he played and that he had all of Beethoven's piano concertos at his fingertips but preferred playing chamber music. In return, he knew her: how hard she'd fought for those first voice lessons in Red Hook; Toscanini and Nellie; her migraines and what was likely to set them off. Nonstop rehearsal was the fastest way in the world to make friends—and when you made friends, they felt entitled to comment on your private life, even if it annoyed you.

So Gemma sat down on the piano bench beside her accompanist. "Are you worried I'm in over my head?" She began playing a bit of *Carmen*, the death theme, deliberately gothic. Her chords clunked far more than George's. "Not to worry, darling. I'm a realist. I know what to expect here."

"And what's that? Third finger down a note," he couldn't help adding, wincing at a sour chord.

She rearranged her fingers. "Men, in my experience, do not ever marry the opera singer. They enjoy her. And as long as I'm enjoying myself in turn, no illusions, what's the harm?" Gemma knew she was not the first woman to be expensively installed at the octagon house—she'd overheard two of the maids remarking "At least this one doesn't stay up till all hours like the previous one" when they tidied her room—and she doubted she would be the last, either. Not to mention the fact that at some point, an empire builder like Henry Thornton would decide it was time to found a dynasty, marry some little nineteen-year-old from a good family, and begin filling his octagon house with sons.

By that point Gemma might already be gone, hopefully touring the great opera houses of Europe, or perhaps they would still have something between them, which she would bring to a graceful end (and then tour the great opera houses of Europe). Henry would probably kiss her hand in farewell, send roses to her dressing room whenever he saw her perform, invite her periodically to intimate dinners, and shake his head ruefully when she refused (for the sake of that nineteen-year-old bride at home).

That was probably how it would all go, and Gemma didn't mind a bit. "If you aren't silly enough to fall in love," she said now, "then no one can be hurt."

George began adding some little tremolos below her basic chords, embellishing the Death theme. "Do you really think no man ever marries the opera singer?"

"Darling, I'm sure of it. And really, it's quite all right. Because no man likes to share his wife, and anyone who married me would share me with this." Patting her throat. "Not to mention the fact that I cannot cook."

George smiled. "Not a bit?"

"Not a bit. I live on honeyed tea and oysters."

"I live on steam beer and *choripán*."

"What on earth is *choripán*?"

"Chorizo—that's cured sausage, the best in the world—split open and slabbed together with chimichurri on fried bread. *Casi tan delicioso como tu boca.*"

"What did you just say?"

George took over the piano keys, shifting her deftly down the bench with a bump of his burly shoulder. "I said let's get back to work."

"That is not what you said," Gemma accused, but got up with a laugh. "All right, let's run 'Der Hölle Rache' again."

"The long run of triplets, it could be cleaner. You've got the lung power, I know you do, but you sound like you're running out of breath there for some reason."

"Maybe with a better launch off the E . . ."

Another hour, and Gemma bid George goodbye with a kiss on the cheek, promised to see him tomorrow morning at the Grand Opera House (he would be back to his usual job, rehearsing the visiting opera chorus in the blocking rehearsal), and trailed to her octagonal pale pink dressing room where the best dressmaker in San Francisco waited to discuss the new wardrobe of imported Worth gowns being refitted for her immediate use. "Six evening gowns, six dinner gowns, six walking dresses, six traveling suits, six tea gowns to start, Miss Garland, and then we'll see to the *real* wardrobe. What would you say to an empire gown of pale green liberty satin, with puffs of white tulle and silver embroidery?"

"It sounds divine." Gemma didn't think she'd ever be one of these society women who changed their frocks six times a day and wouldn't dream of being seen in the same gown more than once, but it was heaven not to eye the fraying seams on her old biscuit faille and wonder if it would survive one more pressing.

When the dressmaker finally bustled away in a stream of assistants and tapes and pincushions, Gemma wandered into her bedroom—ice blue, with acanthus leaves picked out in white and gold wreathing the high ceiling; a massive bathroom next door with pale green walls like a mermaid's grotto, and a huge tub in white Carrara marble. A dinner gown had already been laid out, silver gray velvet edged with chinchilla—Henry was taking her to the Palace Grill again; he swore they'd run into Caruso there. *I have a little surprise for you and the* maestro *both, concerning* Carmen . . . There would be champagne and foie gras, and Gemma looked forward to it, but for just a moment she wished she could order up some chorizo and chimichurri slabbed together on fried bread and eat it in her dressing gown with a mug of steam beer.

"Miss Garland?" A maid curtsied at the door. "That Chinese girl has brought your robe for the ball tomorrow. The embroidery repairs are completed, she says."

"Send her in. I'd love to see it." Gemma caught sight of a parcel sitting on an octagonal side table—the package of things she'd had sent over from her Taylor Street room. Rummaging through the bundle of clothes and trinkets, she pulled out the wrapped square packet that was Nellie's last sketch. She frowned, tempted to toss it in the trash considering that careless, callous note that had accompanied it, but it really was a lovely thing, the Chinese boy and girl with the backdrop of Chinese symbols behind them. Sighing, Gemma propped the sketch up on her dressing table in front of the triple mirror.

"Your robe, ma'am." The young Chinese girl named Susie slipped into the room, holding the embroidered silk reverentially across her arms. The same girl who had dropped her ring after the afternoon party, looking very different without rice powder and paint—Gemma had grown used to the sight of her in the octagon house this past week, generally whisking around a corner of the servants' stairs, or slipping into a spare bedroom where she was ensconced with her embroidery needles and reels of silk thread over the blue dragon robe. Now she spread it carefully across the bed and then stepped back, eyes lowered.

"I can't even tell where you mended it." Gemma hardly dared touch the bands of raised gold-and-silver embroidery, the scrolled waves and mountains and clouds. She still wasn't sure exactly how she was supposed to sing in something so heavy and grand, but Henry was insistent. "You do beautiful work."

"Thank you, ma'am." The girl's eyes flicked up, her face never moving from its polite mask.

"I just got done being fitted into a dozen gowns made to the latest French fashions, and not one had embroidery as good as this. You could work in Paris— Susie?"

The girl's face was already impassive, but now it had drained of color so she looked like a waxwork. No longer looking at Gemma, or the robe—her eyes were fixed over Gemma's shoulder, on the dressing table.

"The sketch?" Gemma blinked, looking at Nellie's drawing. "Why . . ." and her voice faded as she saw it.

The Chinese boy and girl, standing back to back, faces turned to look at the viewer. Not brother and sister, as Gemma had thought—a mirror image. The *same* face, oval with winged brows and sculpted chin, level eyes and grave mouth, only on the left that face was surrounded by a fedora and a boy's knot-buttoned tunic, and on the right the hair fell loose and soft around an embroidered collar. The same face.

Susie's face. Gemma didn't think she'd have seen it if Susie hadn't been standing there gazing at herself, those winged brows drawn together and her grave mouth a taut line. "It's you," Gemma heard herself say inanely. Susie the sewing girl, but also Susie wearing a fedora, dressed as a boy . . . Gemma remembered that fedora. "Y-You helped carry my trunk up to Taylor Street my first day in town," Gemma stammered. "That was you, too." Answering Gemma's eager questions about San Francisco, taking a tip, smiling.

The Chinese girl jerked a tiny nod. She didn't seem to be able to wrench her gaze from the sketch. She had a red silk cord around her neck, Gemma saw . . . And so did both of the painted depictions of her. "Excuse me, ma'am. Would you mind me asking where that drawing came from?"

"My friend Nellie sketched it. Did she hire you as a model when she was in San Francisco, or—"

Susie's head whipped around, and Gemma nearly took a step back. No more ivory-faced servant or impassive seamstress—her eyes *blazed*.

"What are you talking about, Miss Garland? Reggie painted that."

Chapter 12

Reggie? Who is Reggie?" Gemma said.

Suling pointed at the watercolor. "Regina Reynolds. Reggie. My . . . friend."

Gemma looked at the painting again, then back at Suling. "The artist," she said, not using any names. "What does she look like?"

Rumpled coal-black curls, cut to fall just below her ears, Suling thought. Full lips, the top lip slightly wider than the lower so that her mouth curved sweetly when she smiled, a smile that enveloped you in exuberant joy or tender intimacy. A slight crease between her brows that deepened when she concentrated on the canvas in front of her or bent down for a kiss. Pale skin that sunburned easily, Reggie was careless about wearing a hat. And eyes that could shift from light green to a deep and mesmerizing emerald.

"Perhaps six inches taller than me," Suling said, her eyes still fixed on the painting. "Curly black hair. Pale skin. Green eyes. A strange accent, Bronx, she said." Flat words, a bland description that conveyed nothing of Reggie's vivacity, her dash, her wild and passionate soul.

"That sounds like Nellie. Reggie." Gemma had a very odd look on her face, a mixture of confusion and distress. "Do you know when she's coming back to San Francisco?"

Suling looked up. "I don't know. She left without telling me." She couldn't keep the forlorn note from her voice, and the blond woman seemed to look at her more closely.

"Well, I'm sure she'll be in touch when she comes back from Colorado," Gemma said.

"What is she doing in Colorado?" Suling said, startled.

"Painting mountain scenery, apparently." There was a bitter edge to the singer's voice.

"Why is she painting mountains in Colorado?" Suling said. She touched one corner of the watercolor. "This is what she was working on, a San Francisco series. This is one of her Chinatown scenes. She was preparing for a solo exhibit."

And this, *this*, was the discrepancy that kept bristling at the back of Suling's mind. Reggie might've abandoned Suling, but she wouldn't have walked out on the biggest break of her career. Unless Thornton had decided not to back Reggie anymore—yet there had been no indication of that, not as far as Reggie could see. "Then Mr. Thornton canceled the exhibit. No artist, no show."

"What does Henry have to do with Nellie . . . Reggie?" Now it was Gemma's turn to look astonished.

"Mr. Thornton rented a gallery for her exhibition," Suling said. "He was going to surprise San Francisco society with Regina Reynolds, a fresh new talent in American painting. Her launch was going to be the cultural event of the year."

"He was launching her?" Gemma sat down on the bed. She looked around the room, dazed, a little queasy even. "Was . . . was she living here?"

"Do you think you're the first to occupy these rooms?" Suling couldn't hold back her scorn. "You're not the first of his artistic discoveries and neither was she. The difference was, she knew it." She didn't know whether to laugh or feel pity for Gemma.

"Of course I know he's had others. I'm not a fool." Gemma sounded defensive. "But Henry never said anything about knowing Nellie. That first night at dinner, I told him about looking for a friend. I said she was an artist, a painter, ran down a list of names she had used. I didn't know 'Regina Reynolds,' but I described her. *I described her!*"

"If you don't believe me," Suling said, "go upstairs to the top floor. There's a room with skylights that was her studio. How would I know that unless she told me? Unless she'd been here?"

A long pause. Then, "I do believe you." Gemma sat up straighter. "How did you meet Nellie?"

"Here. At one of those parties," Suling said. "Last fall. September." Pause. "She never referred to you as Gemma Garland. The name I knew was Sally, who would be a famous opera singer one day." Sally, a name between friends, which Reggie had shared with Suling.

"If you were . . . friends," Gemma said, "didn't she tell you her real name was Nellie Doyle?"

Suling shook her head. "I asked. She just made a face and said she'd left that life and that name behind." *I was Reggie when I met you,* she'd said, *so I will always be Reggie. Whoever I used to be doesn't matter.*

"Do you know how she met Henry Thornton?" Gemma looked away when she asked this.

"At an exhibit," Suling said. "Reggie only managed to get one painting accepted to the show. Mr. Thornton bought it and told her it was the best painting of San Francisco he'd ever seen. A dozen stories lived on that canvas, he said. Then he took her out for lunch and proposed to make her famous."

"She never told me she had a patron," Gemma said. "I don't understand. Why didn't she write to me about . . . this?" She looked around helplessly at the room, its soothing soft blue colors and luxurious furnishings, the door that opened to a huge bathroom.

"Reggie was going to wait until after she'd sold some paintings and could call the show a success. She said you didn't approve of certain . . . conditions when it came to patrons." Suling looked rather pointedly at Gemma, who flushed.

"Were you and Nellie, I mean, Reggie, close?" Gemma said, her words and tone careful.

"It doesn't matter anymore," Suling said. "It seems she's done with me." She reached inside her tunic and pulled out the red silk cord, yanked it over her head, and dropped it in the wastebasket by Gemma's dressing table. Something she should've done months ago.

"Wait!" Gemma cried. She ran to the wastebasket, knelt down, and took out the silk cord. She stared at the ring dangling from the red loop.

"I thought it looked familiar the other day when I picked it up," Gemma said. "It never occurred to me it might be Nellie's. Did she give you this?"

"She said it was her most precious possession." Suling shrugged. "Turns out it's a cheap thing, churned out by the factory load. Not even real silver."

"But it *was* Nell's most precious possession," Gemma said slowly. "And it's cheap because they were very poor. This belonged to her mother, who she loved more than anyone in the world. If Nellie gave you this, then you truly meant something to her." She held it out to Suling, who after a moment's pause, took it back with trembling hands.

"She told me she loved me," Suling said, looking down at the ring. "And you're saying this proves she really did. So why did she go to Colorado without a word?" She held the ring to her lips before slipping the red cord over her head. It just didn't make sense.

"I don't know." Gemma shook her head. "Nellie is many things and sometimes she fibs to get out of trouble, but she doesn't hurt the people she cares about." She looked thoughtful. "The only reason I even know she's in Colorado is because of the note she sent with this painting."

"She sent you a note, but she didn't contact me?" Suling closed her fist around the ring a little more tightly. "May I see the note?"

Gemma shuffled through a box of belongings, then gave Suling the letter. The paper was heavy and expensive. Creamy, formal. So different from the colorful stationery Reggie favored, like the sheets of writing paper she'd bought at Fung Tai Dry Goods, pale pink speckled with gold. Suling's mind tore through the possibilities, growing more worried by the moment.

Gemma paced around the room. "Why didn't Henry tell me he knew Nellie? There couldn't be more than one painter in San Francisco of her description. How did he not guess she was Regina Reynolds? And the staff never said anything, not that I knew to ask, and I suppose they wouldn't be indelicate enough to mention a previous . . . protégée."

"The entire note is typewritten," Suling said, looking up. "There's no actual handwriting."

"Wait, let me see that again," Gemma said. Then looked up, her blue eyes agitated. "It's addressed to *Gemma*, but when we write to each other, it's always 'Nellie' and 'Sal.' No one else uses my real name; it's between us."

"If not for the painting that came with it, there'd be nothing to prove that Reggie—Nellie—was the one who sent it, right?" Suling closed her eyes for a moment.

"But then who?" Gemma was almost whispering.

What dangled in Suling's mind was a hatchet about to fall. She gestured with her hands, taking in the room like a magician's assistant presenting a trick. She lifted an eyebrow at Gemma. "Who do you think?"

All color left Gemma's face. Her features shifted from confusion, to anger, then fear.

A gurgling fountain of panic welled up inside Suling. Who else but Henry Thornton could have had access to Reggie's paintings? But why hadn't he admitted to knowing Reggie? Suling felt her spine turn to ice.

Gemma reached for the servant bell hanging beside the tufted headboard and pulled.

"Wait, what are you doing?" Suling said.

"I'm going to get Mrs. MacNeil and ask her about Nellie," Gemma said. "Straight out ask her."

"No, no, no," Suling said. "Don't. Not Mrs. MacNeil. None of the senior staff. Reggie once asked her who used to live in this room and was told the staff wasn't allowed to discuss such things."

No discussion of previous mistresses, on pain of employment. Suling remembered it was the first time Reggie felt uneasy about Thornton. Furthermore, the housekeeper said, if Miss Reynolds asked her again, she would be forced to report the conversation to Mr. Thornton.

"Say you rang for lemonade or something," Suling said. "And ask for the maid Kathleen to bring it up." Footsteps sounded on the marble floor outside and Suling vanished into the bathroom just as a discreet knock rapped on the door.

Gemma smiled at the maid who entered. "I'd like some lemonade, please. And some of those lovely biscuits the cook has been baking. And please have Kathleen bring it up."

Suling came out when the maid left. "Why Kathleen?" Gemma whispered.

"She was friendly with Reggie," Suling said, sitting on the bed. "Reggie refused to have a lady's maid, but she called Kathleen if she needed help dressing."

Not fifteen minutes later, another discreet knock and a smiling, auburn-haired young woman came in carrying a tray with a small crystal jug, a crystal tumbler, and lavender biscuits on a footed dish. Suling peeped through the partially open bathroom door, at Gemma's smiling face, the maid's careful curtsy.

"You asked for me, Miss Garland?" Kathleen asked.

"Yes, Kathleen," Gemma said in a friendly, cheerful tone. "I've a question about the lady who stayed here before, Miss Regina Reynolds."

A shadow came over the freckled face, curiosity struggling with apprehension. "I can't say, Miss Garland. I really couldn't."

"The thing is," Gemma continued, as if she hadn't noticed Kathleen's concern, "I really like this little painting and I'd like another by Miss Reynolds. Do you know where she went?"

Still looking troubled, the maid hesitated. "No, miss. Mrs. MacNeil told us to clear her things out of these rooms two months ago. Miss Reynolds had already left and we packed all her belongings in a steamer trunk to be sent on."

"And did someone take the trunk to her new address?"

"One of the footmen took it away to be sent on, miss, but I don't know where."

"Which footman?" Gemma asked. "Please don't worry, Kathleen, I won't say a word to anyone." She gave the girl a friendly wink. "Just as you won't say a word to anyone that I was asking."

"It was young Jonathan that took the trunk away," the maid said, warming to Gemma's confiding air.

"The thing is, I do like this painting very much and would love another. Miss Reynolds is a fine artist, isn't she?"

"Oh, that she is, miss," Kathleen agreed enthusiastically. "She did my portrait, just a pencil sketch, and it was lovely. But as for more of Miss Reynolds's paintings, there ain't any here now. The master had them packaged up and young Jonathan took those away, too."

"Goodness, Jonathan is a busy young man. Is he here today?"

"Oh, he was let go, Miss Garland," the maid said, "the day after he took away the paintings." Then in a dramatic whisper, "He'd been drinking on the job. He said he never drinks but Mr. Thornton had the butler fire him."

"Well, Kathleen, I suppose that's that. Thank you for your help."

"You're so welcome, miss," then rather anxiously, "Mrs. Mac-Neil will be wanting to know why you asked for me. What should I say?"

"Tell her I wanted to ask you about a missing chemise," Gemma said. "But by the time you came up, I'd found it. My mistake."

The bedroom door shut and Suling slowly emerged from the bathroom.

"You were right," Gemma said. "I was still hoping there was some other explanation, but there isn't. Nellie didn't run away and Henry is deliberately deceiving me. He must know where she is, Susie . . ."

"Miss Garland," Suling interrupted, "my name is Suling, not Susie. My family name is Feng. Please remember that. Suling Feng."

Gemma flushed, and Suling continued, "Whatever Thornton did with Reggie, he doesn't want anyone to know, so it's something underhanded and I only hope she's still alive." Because in San Francisco, with enough money, anyone could be made to disappear.

"No, don't say that. He can't be a murderer on top of everything else!" Gemma said, practically wailing.

Suling sighed. Gemma was as Reggie had described. *Sometimes she can be unbelievably naive*, Reggie once said. *It's as though all that corn-fed goodness insulated her brain from recognizing how awful people can be. Especially the powerful.*

"Maybe he just sent her away somewhere against her will," Suling said. "Let's search these rooms, see whether anything was left behind that might offer a clue." She began opening dresser drawers.

They spent the next half hour peering into the backs of closets and drawers, even looking inside the compartments of the revolving shoe rack. Then Gemma straightened up.

"Money," she said. "My uncle Halvor was a bookkeeper. He always said he could deduce a man's character and activities by looking through his checkbook. Henry must've paid someone to have her . . . disappear. We need to get into his office when it's empty."

But Thornton was always working. Suling and Madam Ning's girls sometimes saw Thornton cross the second-floor mezzanine from his office to his bedroom only minutes before a party. He would emerge dressed to perfection, ready in time to greet his guests.

"Tomorrow night during the performance of *Carmen*?" Suling said. Their only option.

"Yes, yes, tomorrow night," Gemma exclaimed. "Henry's leaving the house at seven. The staff will be busy on the third and fourth floors getting the rooms ready and the second floor will be empty. That's our best chance to sneak in there."

"You'll be singing, so I have to do it." Suling's fear of getting caught struggled with her fear for Reggie's safety. "Does Thornton lock his office?"

Gemma looked downcast, then straightened up. "The potted

palm. His clerks share one key between them, but it's inconvenient so they hide it in the potted palm outside his office door. Henry— *Thornton*," she corrected herself, biting off the name, "he doesn't know."

"Then let's hope the key is there," Suling said. "I'll come just before seven. I'll wait on the street until his automobile leaves."

"I'll tell Mrs. MacNeil to take you upstairs to wait for me," Gemma said, "because I want you making sure all's well with the dragon robe when I put it on."

It was about as good a plan as they'd get. Then Suling looked directly at Gemma.

"Breaking into Thornton's office could be dangerous. I need to know what you're willing to risk. How much does Reggie mean to you?"

"She's the one person in my world I could always rely on," Gemma said, without hesitation. "When I thought she'd traipsed off to Colorado even though she knew I needed her—that was the loneliest feeling in the world." She shook her head. "If I couldn't depend on Nellie, I couldn't rely on anyone. Now she's in trouble and I must be the someone she can depend on."

"That makes two someones," Suling said. They smiled at each other, their smiles tentative, a bit shy.

Suling didn't voice the question she most wanted to ask Gemma. *What* did Reggie truly mean to her? She wanted an answer that would allay the twinge of jealousy she'd always felt when Reggie spoke so fondly of "my Sally," but it could wait until they'd found Reggie. And if they never found Reggie—and at this, a dark abyss of despair cleaved her heart—then it didn't matter. Nothing would ever matter again.

"If I'm not in your room when you get back from the opera,"

Suling said, getting up to leave, "I'll write a note and tell you what I found, if anything at all."

SULING MADE HER way to Chinatown, so much tumult in her thoughts she barely noticed the streets she crossed, the vehicles she avoided. *Reggie didn't abandon her.* This would've made her skip all the way home if she weren't so worried. *You make me want to take care of you, Suling,* Reggie used to say. *You're like a pineapple, spiny leaves and a rough rind. But inside, you're all sweetness.*

Now it was her turn to take care of Reggie, wherever she might be. And whether or not Gemma was competent to help solve the mystery, Suling wasn't leaving San Francisco until she'd found the woman she loved.

Chapter 13

Y ou look pale, mademoiselle," ventured the girl who had been assigned as Gemma's lady's maid at the octagon house. Not the chatterbox Kathleen, who had innocently confirmed so many of Gemma's fears. This maid was French, or said she was—sometimes her accent slipped but her hands never did as she piled Gemma's blond hair into a pompadour while Gemma sipped tea and tried to keep from shaking. "Are you feeling up to the rehearsal today?"

"I'm quite well, thank you." Gemma had begged off dinner at the Palace Grill last night, claiming a migraine when Hen—Mr. Thornton; she refused the intimacy of using his first name, even in her mind—knocked at her bedroom door. He hadn't been terribly pleased. "I have a treat for you," he cajoled through the door, like he was dangling a bone before a dog, and Gemma's stomach roiled. She made some retching noises as if she were vomiting her guts out, just to make him go away . . . But that was just postponing the inevitable. Tonight was the midnight ball—and before that, *Carmen*. She'd promised Suling she'd get Henry Thornton out of the house; the only way that was happening was if he was seated in his box in his carelessly donned evening clothes, watching her flutter a fan to Bizet's brilliant faux-Spanish melodies. She'd promised Suling. She owed it to Nellie.

Nellie, oh God, *Nellie*. Reggie. Whatever she was calling herself now, she was still Gemma's Nell. *I should have known you wouldn't have left town like that. I should have known.* Nellie's dark curls and Bronx clip, the crackle of energy she gave off like sparks of electricity, the dab of red or yellow paint always clinging to her cuticles, the trousers and the poet's shirt she liked to wear to shock men. *Did Henry buy you French gowns, too? Or did you laugh and tweak his nose and tell him you'd never wear such beribboned rubbish?*

Gemma squeezed her eyes tight shut, aware that the maid was putting the final touches on her hair. No time to think of Nellie, not now. She had a performance to put on—three of them, in fact. Tonight in *Carmen*, then at midnight as Thornton's Queen of the Night . . . And over it all, she had to act as if nothing was wrong. She'd never before wanted so badly to just crawl into bed and stay there with her burning eyes, her betrayed heart, her scared bones. But she thought of Suling's voice: *How much does Reggie mean to you?* The way her own face softened at the name.

Hard to believe that was the woman who had somehow won Nellie's elusive heart. Nellie had always liked women— something that had shocked Gemma at first; of course it had. *Don't worry.* Nell had laughed, kissing her latest model and seeing Gemma's face afterward. *You aren't my type, farm girl. Though you really should give it a try. Men might be useful, but women are fun!*

Fun was not exactly the word Gemma would have used to describe the cool, polite Chinese seamstress with her impassive face. *Hard* would have been the word she chose, once she saw those dark eyes drop their studied blankness and suddenly blaze like a phoenix. Well, maybe Nellie would like that. She was hard herself, in so many ways.

Gemma was the weak one.

She flinched, drawing another curious look from the maid. Tried to smile reassuringly, as the words screamed inside her head: *Nellie, where are you? What did he do to you?*

Well, tonight they might have answers. And all of today, with the flurry of the coming rehearsals at the Grand Opera House, Gemma at least had a reason to be good and far away from Henry Thornton. Yesterday she'd been looking on the rehearsal as a chore, having to rehearse the *en masse* routine of castanets and skirt swishing—right now, it sounded like a blessed relief.

Until she got to the opera house and faced a barrage of cold stares.

"Good morning," Gemma said to the stagehands smoking outside the street entrance, getting down from Thornton's very new, very modern Rolls-Royce, which had chauffeured her over from Nob Hill. They all stared, not replying. "Good morning," she tried to a group of laughing women near the dressing rooms, who looked like they might be fellow chorus singers. "I'm Gemma Garland, do you know the rehearsal order for today's—" But her voice faltered under their suddenly cool gaze. She'd come in a pleated street suit of plum cheviot with an Irish lace blouse, smart enough to impress, not so smart she couldn't get it a bit dusty onstage when the blocking rehearsal began. Why did they glare as if she had a scarlet A on her chest? Yes, she was new here; yes, she had a rich patron and gossip had certainly spread about that, but hers was hardly an unusual situation. Three-quarters of the women here undoubtedly had a stage-door admirer or two they relied on for rent money and expensive late suppers—who were they to judge?

"George, good morning," Gemma called across the busy corridor inside, spotting her accompanist hurrying somewhere with a folder of sheet music, but he just gave her a long look before disappearing into one of the rehearsal rooms.

What in the world, Gemma wondered—*George* giving her the cold shoulder, when he'd never once gotten censorious about her move into the octagon house and up the ladder? Trying to ignore the sliver of unease threading her stomach, Gemma took herself out to the main house to see if she could track down the chorus master. As usual on the day of a performance, all was chaos: the spotlight wandering all over the stage like a stray cat as the lighting technicians practiced their cues, stagehands cursing as they attempted to unfurl a stuck backdrop, prop swords for the smugglers and prop wine bottles for the tavern scene being tripped on right, left, and center . . . And onstage, *Carmen*'s two leads: a buxom brunette in a Spanish shawl and a foul temper, snarling at a tubby man with curly dark hair and a round red face. "—supposed to appear onstage with a soprano who screeches like a hoot owl?" the great Enrico Caruso was screaming.

"You'd screech, too, if the stagehands nearly collapsed a backdrop on you, you overpaid Neapolitan windbag," shrieked the singer Gemma assumed was *the* Olive Fremstad, Gemma's heroine in the flesh, those world-famous lungs expanding like a bellows as she jabbed a pointed nail into Caruso's puffed-out chest.

"*Overpaid?*" howled the great tenor, dancing up and down like a scalded alley cat. "Whose name draws the *le folle* to this theater? Answer me that, you fringed Nordic cow—"

"If your fees weren't sucking the budget dry we could afford stagehands who knew their way around a theater," the diva bellowed back. "A thousand three hundred fifty per *performance*, and you have the gall to— *Get that spotlight out of my eyes!*" she shouted up at the lighting booth. The wandering spotlight froze, then inched offstage as if trying to be casual. Carmen and Don José continued spitting epithets at each other, and Gemma tiptoed around the orchestra pit where a cluster of bored violinists were completely ignoring the fight as they yawned over their instrument cases and their morning coffees.

"Do you know where I might find the chorus master?" Gemma began to ask, only to run nearly headfirst into the conductor. It wasn't hard, when you'd been in as many traveling opera companies as Gemma had, to identify the conductor. It was always the man shaped like a barrel who looked like he hadn't slept in a year and was about three missed oboe entrances away from an apoplectic stroke. "*Maestro?*" Gemma made the little reverence always owed to the man with the baton. "I'm Gemma Garland, the newest chorus—"

"So you're the trouble," he barked, face going as plum as her skirts. "Caruso and La Fremstad are already going at each other like dogs in a ring, and then they saddle me with you."

Gemma stared, forgetting for an instant about the troubles back at the octagon house. "I beg your pardon?"

"I don't care how much Mr. Thornton's paying management," the conductor snapped, "this kind of thing is bad for a company's morale. But it's out of my hands, so get yourself onstage in twenty minutes, and we'll run you through 'Je dis que rien.'"

"I'm not singing Micaëla, I'm in the—"

"Don't think for a moment we've had time to get the programs reprinted with your name," the conductor said, and he rushed back toward the stage as if his hair were on fire. "Olive, *cara mia*, put down the prop sword, Enrico didn't mean it, please don't stab him—"

Still mystified, Gemma plunged backstage looking for a rehearsal room to warm up—and stopped. The dressing rooms, all in a row: the largest bearing the name DON JOSÉ/ENRICO CARUSO; the second CARMEN/OLIVE FREMSTAD . . . and the third largest bore a sign saying MICAËLA/BESSIE ABOTT. Only the name "Bessie Abott" had been crossed out, and "Gemma Garland" had been scribbled in. Micaëla. The second female lead; the primary soprano part in *Carmen*. Gemma knew the role; she'd sung it before. A rather boring village girl part—the good girl to Carmen's bad girl; no surprise which one the tenor picks—but Micaëla had a lovely aria and an even lovelier duet, and you could work some fire into the village maiden if you weren't hamstrung by a director who wanted you to simper. And she was singing Micaëla tonight?

Buy me a role, while the Met is in San Francisco, Gemma remembered saying to Thornton. *I've been bumped off the stage for so many understudies—I want someone bumped off the stage for me for once.* She hadn't thought about it since then, that particular request made in the middle of their giddy negotiation on the way toward a bed. She'd assumed the matter of a role would be discussed after the ball—not sprung on the entire production this way, clearly forced down from on high with no tact whatsoever.

I would have hated *anyone who swanned into a new company like this*, Gemma couldn't help but think. Feeling dizzy, she struck the dressing door open and saw the room was filled with red roses. The card on the nearest one was in Henry's bold slash, and it read simply *Surprise!*

"That's one way to get into the spotlight," she heard someone snicker behind her, not very softly. "I wonder what he paid?"

"Her? Or the management?"

More snickering.

"If I can take your measurements for Micaëla's costume, Miss Garland?" A wardrobe assistant, looking harassed. "We'll be hours letting the hems down. You're two inches taller . . . have to let everything *out*, too. Miss Abott is slimmer," the woman said with a hint of spite, whipping her measuring tape around Gemma's waist, her rib cage.

I didn't want it like this, Gemma wanted to protest. But she had asked for it, hadn't she? All part of her plan to be more hard-edged. To look out for herself, no one else.

"Did you know?" George leaned against the doorframe, music folder under his arm.

"No." Cheeks flaming, Gemma shook her head. "I mean, I wanted a role, but—" At the other end of the corridor she thought she could see the displaced Bessie Abott—whom she recognized from opera photographs and posters, who had reigned over the Paris Opera for years; a career Gemma would have given her eyeteeth to have—standing in a cluster of angry friends, crying. *I'm sorry*, Gemma wanted to tell her, but who was going to believe that? She was a soprano promoted from the chorus to second lead, she had a dressing room full of roses with her name on the door—and by now, the company would have heard about the ball in her honor tonight. "I didn't want it," she managed to say, gesturing at her name on the dressing room door, the roses. "Not like *this*."

George sighed. "Come on," he said gently. "You've got a lot of blocking to learn before curtain-up tonight."

No, Gemma almost said. *I can't go out there*. But she'd made her bed and now was the time to lie in it, so she gulped some cold tea and started warming up.

"So you're the one with the patron," Olive Fremstad greeted Gemma in the wings, sweeping off in her fringed shawl as Gemma waited in a peasant skirt and a prop basket to go on and run her aria. The diva's heavy lashes swept her up and down, and Gemma shriveled. *The one with the patron*. Not *the one with the thrilling high F's* or *The one with the electrifying stage presence*, but *the one with the patron*. Had she actually realized how crushing that would feel, when it was applied to *her* and not to someone else?

But Olive Fremstad looked almost approving. "You burned

some bridges today," she said. "A real diva needs to be willing to burn things up, if she has to."

"Is it worth it?" Gemma heard herself ask. Somehow she doubted Olive Fremstad had ever had to tell herself to be more hard-edged.

"It's worth it if the man keeps his promises." La Fremstad shrugged. "My new husband, he owns every gold mine in Tierra del Fuego. That's worth any number of friends in this business." She checked the watch pinned to her bosom. "Don't try to maneuver me out of the center spotlight in Act III, will you? I don't care if the director wants you downstage, you stay out of center."

"Yes, ma'am," Gemma said meekly and shook out her hair to wander onstage as Don José's lost, desolate village fiancée. How she was going to get through an entire day of learning this role and then the performance tonight, she didn't know, but she was going to do it—even if the thought of facing Henry Thornton afterward made her skin crawl.

Suling, she prayed, arrowing the thought at the slight Chinese seamstress, *you had better find what we're looking for.*

Chapter 14

She had finished repairing the dragon robe ahead of schedule, so Suling accompanied Old Kow on his rounds for the last time, gave him his wages for the last time. Walking beside him all day, listening to him talk about his family and his little village, it seemed impossible to Suling that so many revelations had come crashing into her life only yesterday. Impatient to get back to the mansion on Hyde Street and search through Thornton's office, she was short with customers and with Old Kow and his rambling.

When she finally hauled the cart inside the laundry and pushed it under the staircase, Suling knew something was wrong. It was completely quiet. No grinding of machinery or loud conversation from workers shouting over the noise. Then from upstairs, the sound of a door opening, and Third Uncle's head leaned over the railing.

"Get up here," he shouted. Her luck had finally run out.

"Third Uncle," she replied, ascending the steps. How bad would this be? "What can I do for you?"

"You can stop shaming me!" he roared. He grabbed her by the shoulders and slammed her against the wall. "You can stop lying to me!"

He gripped her elbow and dragged her into her bedroom where he threw her on the bed. He was panting, so angry that spittle ran down his chin.

"I had lunch with Dr. Ouyang," he said. "He was concerned because his manservant saw you at the train station, dressed like a boy. I said his man was mistaken because you've been at Hing Chong Tailors all week sewing your wedding garments. We laughed about it."

But after lunch, Third Uncle immediately went to Hing Chong's to assure himself that Suling was indeed there. He found that the only women working there were the tailor's own wife and daughters. Suling had not been there in weeks.

"But unlike you, I saved face for our family," he said. "I didn't act worried or angry, I pretended I was just passing by. Where have you been this past week? Should I have gone to the Palace of Endless Joy? And why are you wearing a boy's jacket and trousers?"

She was not going to get Old Kow in trouble. She wouldn't say anything to defend herself. She needed to finish this argument, get her uncle out of here. She had to get back to the octagon house by seven.

"I'm sorry you were worried," Suling said, as calmly as she could.

"Worried?" he screamed. Saliva flew in her face. "Do you know why I invited Dr. Ouyang to lunch? To thank him, to show gratitude. Your cousins are getting out of Immigration today, and it's because of his generosity they weren't detained for months. But you, you're just shitting on all he's done for us."

"I don't want to marry him, Uncle," she said, temper rising, "and my parents would never have forced me to marry anyone I didn't want, especially a man whose wives hated my mother and who would hate me just as much. But you know that and you don't care."

"It's not your decision. Did you think you could run away?" He held up a small rectangle of cardboard, a triumphant sneer on his face. Her train ticket to New York, which she had tucked in her pillowcase. She hoped in a surge of utter dread that he hadn't found her money. "Break the contract and ruin our family's reputation?"

"You mean, ruin your chances at paying off your gambling debts?" Suling couldn't hold back anymore. Her fists clenched. "If anyone has ruined our family's reputation, it's you, Uncle. You've squandered our family business, lost all our good and loyal employees. Do you know what people say when your name is mentioned? *A piece of rotten wood cannot be carved.* What will you do once you've gambled away the money you get for selling your only niece?"

He slapped her across the face. "You're marrying a man everyone respects, a man who will provide for you and your children. What more could any uncle do for a niece? I'm going to the Pacific Mail Steamship terminal now to bring your cousins home. And you will be here to welcome them."

No, she would not. She would be at Thornton's house.

"Get dressed properly to greet your cousins. When I come back, we're going for dinner with Dr. Ouyang at the Shanghai Loh Restaurant and you will behave. Or I'll beat you silly."

He tore up the train ticket and slammed the bedroom door shut. The key turned in the lock from outside. The squeak of floorboards, heavy footsteps down the staircase, and another door slammed. The front door.

Knees trembling, Suling climbed up on the chair and reached for the top of the wardrobe. She didn't think Third Uncle had found it, but still it was a relief when her fingers touched the brown paper envelope hidden behind the cheap crown molding.

Her money. Her savings. Safe. Her heartbeat slowed and she breathed more easily. The train ticket didn't matter, not anymore. It had been foolish of her to leave the envelope in her pillowcase, it had given away her escape plans. It had been her fault for assuming her uncle would follow his usual routine of stumbling to the gambling parlor after breakfast and not coming home until supper—if at all.

Suling worked quickly. She put her cloth-soled shoes and some extra clothes in a laundry bag, tucked the envelope of money inside her shirt. She wrapped a few pieces of jewelry in a scrap of chamois cloth: a coral brooch, a hairpin set with a pink enameled butterfly, pearl earrings her father bought from a vendor going door to door. She paused for a moment, remembering the leathery brown skin of the pearl seller's hands as he opened paper packets of jewelry, the longing in her mother's eyes, the smile in her father's as he opened the cash drawer.

Suling tied up the canvas bag, looping the thin rope so she could sling the bag over her shoulder, then rattled the doorknob just to be sure it really was locked. Taking a deep breath, Suling opened the window. Just looking down made her dizzy and she shrank back. But she had to get out before Third Uncle and her cousins came home. For Reggie's sake she had to conquer her fear of heights. Madam Ning's words flashed into her mind. *Are you sure this girl is worth it?*

SULING HAD BROUGHT Reggie to meet Madam Ning at the Palace of Endless Joy. Suling and Madam Ning had both enjoyed the astonishment on Reggie's face when she realized the most infamous brothel owner in Chinatown was practically an aunt to Suling. A day later, Suling hurried over to see her auntie. Now she could talk to someone about Reggie. Madam Ning had frowned over the state of Suling's hair and made her sit at the dressing table so she could brush and braid it properly.

"Isn't she wonderful?" Suling asked. "Did you like her, Auntie?"

Madam Ning gently teased a snarl out of Suling's hair. "Very much. She's not like most white women. In more ways than one. Are you sure this girl is worth it?"

"She loves me, Auntie," Suling said. She touched the front of her blouse, felt the ring she had strung on a silk cord. "I have not been happy since my parents died, but when I'm with Reggie, life feels new again."

"You should enjoy it," Madam Ning said. "First love only happens once, after all. But my precious, since your mother isn't here I must say what I know she would say. Remember to hold back your emotions because there's no future with her. You're from two different worlds."

"Well, what about you and Mr. Clarkson? What about your future together?"

"I don't need to marry him or live with him," Madam Ning said, looking through a drawer of hair ornaments before picking one out for Suling. "But think of what else you'd have to contend with out there. For us, at least before the missionaries came, love between men or between women was not a crime and some of us still feel this way."

It wasn't terrible for a man to have male lovers so long as he fathered a son to carry on his family lineage. If women had close friendships, what did it matter since there was no danger of pregnancy? If wives and concubines in a large household occasionally took comfort in each other when their husband was in some other bed, where was the harm?

"Americans are not so tolerant," Madam Ning said. "You'll be crossing so many lines, Suling."

"Reggie doesn't care about any of that," Suling said. "She wants us to live together once her exhibit is over." Once Reggie no longer lived at the octagon house. Once they'd left San Francisco and were free of Thornton.

"Do what you will with Reggie, but don't give your heart away," Madam Ning said. "Promise you'll hold back something for yourself, just in case."

"I promise," Suling said. And meant it.

Madam Ning coiled Suling's long plait into loops at the nape of her neck. "I like Reggie, it's just that the world is bigger than the two of you."

"Don't think I haven't considered that," Suling said, with an almost inaudible sigh.

SULING HAD TRIED explaining to Reggie what a Chinese person lived with every day. The virulent hatred Americans had for the Chinese in their midst, blaming them for crime and disease, branding them as lazy and corrupt. Not all Americans, Suling conceded, thinking of the Mission Home and Alice Eastwood. But enough of them so that most Chinese felt safe only in Chinatown, lived there in crowded conditions out of need for mutual protection. Enough of them so that politicians seeking votes made laws that punished the Chinese. Immigration, taxes, schools, and more.

"There are women who live as couples, you know," Reggie said, kissing her neck. Tempting, so tempting to let those lips rove farther, kiss lower. "Their friends don't care and strangers just think they live together for companionship, or to share living expenses."

"If I were white, perhaps your friends wouldn't care," Suling said, returning the kiss, "but I'm Chinese. Perhaps it would be easier if I posed as your maid."

Reggie's eyes blazed emerald. "If they don't accept you as an equal, they're not my friends."

Are you sure this girl is worth it?

SULING LEANED OUT the window again. It was at least a fifteen-foot drop to the alley below. Taking scissors from her sewing box, she cut the coverlet on her bed into strips. She tied together the long strips into a makeshift rope, which she hoped would reach the ground. After some thought, she tied a knot every few feet. Then she tied one end of the rope to a bed leg and flung the other out the window. It dangled a yard or so above the ground, but it would have to do.

The main thing, she decided, was to not look down. In fact, she would close her eyes.

Laundry bag over her shoulder, she sat on the window ledge facing the room, rope between her trousered legs. Not looking down. Fists gripping the rope, she backed off the windowsill slowly until she was hanging out, knees still resting on the windowsill. Then with eyes squeezed shut, she pulled one foot over the sill and felt for the rope, twisted her ankle through it. Then the other foot. A small yelp and she was hanging, swaying, but she pressed her knees together against the rope and felt its reassuring thickness. Only then did she open her eyes, but she only looked straight ahead. Not down or up, just straight ahead at the wall, at the peeling brown paint and the white splash of dried seagull shit.

Then gripping for dear life with hands, knees, and feet, Suling slid down the rope, the knots along its length slowing her descent as she braced momentarily against each one, but it was a terrifyingly fast journey that somehow also lasted forever. A scream of terror when her shoes kicked at nothing but air, and then the last knot slipped through her hands and she fell onto the ground.

And then she was running, not caring anymore who saw her, running for Hyde Street and the octagon house.

"THE BLUE DRAGON robe is already in Miss Garland's room," Mrs. MacNeil said as Suling followed her up the servants' stairs, "and Mr. Thornton will bring up that blue feather hat himself later."

The Phoenix Crown, Suling wanted to say. It's not a hat.

"You know where to go, your sewing room," Mrs. MacNeil continued, "and you know where not to go. Stay in there till Miss Garland comes back. I've got enough to worry about tonight."

Suling closed the door to the sewing room and changed into cloth-soled shoes. She peeked through the door and slipped out quietly, her shoes sliding across the marble floors. Linen-draped tables were already set out on the third-floor mezzanine but it was momentarily empty. She ran to the circular staircase, leaning on the handrail as a moment of vertigo swept over her. She gripped the handrail tightly and looked down. The second floor was equally empty. She breathed more easily knowing none of the servants would come up or down the winding staircase.

The potted palm to the right of the office door, Gemma had said. Suling hurried to the graceful rosewood stand and reached behind the arching fronds, feeling along the inside of the porcelain rim. She exhaled with relief when her trembling fingers touched cold metal.

And then she was inside Thornton's office, locking the door behind her.

There were cabinets of files, shelves filled with ledgers. Each shelf was labeled with the name of a company. Thornton's wealth was all documented here. Where should she even start? She opened the door to the adjacent study. There was a large desk and the room looked more personal. Perhaps she would start here. Her hand reached to turn on the desk lamp, then stopped. It wouldn't do for someone to notice a light. She pulled the drapes closed and shut the study door before turning on the lamp.

There weren't any checkbooks in any of the drawers. Suling looked around the room, frowning. At random she pulled down a document box from a bookcase marked "Cerro Gordo Silver Mine." The box contained a checkbook, a bank book, a packet of receipts and invoices, and a ledger. She looked at the date column in the ledger, then looked through the checkbook. The only information written on the check stubs was amount and payee. The ledger entries, however, listed more details for each check and deposit. All very efficient.

And just how many bank accounts did Thornton have anyway? One or more for each of his companies, judging by the labels on the document boxes. But with the ledger books, she could scan the entries on a page rather than turn over every check stub. And, she realized, she only had to look for payments since February. That was when Reggie had disappeared.

But was it likely Thornton would pay through a company account? She scanned for boxes with labels that seemed more personal, more likely used for hiding secrets.

She looked carefully through the document box marked "Personal: Bank of California." There were payments to his tailor, boot maker, and hatter. Payments to art galleries and antiques stores, membership dues to a number of athletic clubs, businessmen's clubs. When the clock struck nine, she looked up, rubbing her eyes. The performance would be in full swing now at the opera house. Gemma would be singing and prancing about the stage as if there was nothing more important in her life than the performance.

Suling opened a document box marked "Philanthropy." Thornton maintained a bank account just for donations. Including the Mayor's Fund. He paid for political connections out of this account. She skimmed the pages. There were payments to a dozen cultural and arts associations, society fundraisers, various church groups and hospitals. Now, if only she could find a document box labeled "Nefarious Deeds."

She put the Philanthropy ledger back in its box and was about to shelve it when she pulled the ledger out again. Something nagged at her. She opened the book to April. Her finger tapped on the most recent entry on the page: a donation of twenty-five dollars just a few days ago on the fifteenth of April to St. Christina's Convent and Hospital. Suling knew it well, a long building of brick and stone on Filbert Street opposite the Sts. Peter and Paul Church. It was a Catholic convent unpopular with Chinatown laundries because the hospital ran a competing laundry business.

What made her look twice was that she knew enough from attending the Mission Home school to recognize the churches and foundations listed in the book. Presbyterian, Methodist, Baptist—they were all Protestant. Only St. Christina's was Catholic, an aberration. She turned to the page for March. There had been a donation in mid-March to St. Christina's, also twenty-five dollars. Another one in February, the week Reggie vanished. And nothing before that to St. Christina's or any other Catholic charity. No detailed description beside the ledger entries. Just "Donation."

Suppressing panic as a horrible suspicion crossed her mind, Suling opened the checkbook and flipped through the check stubs to February. Twenty-five dollars to St. Christina's. No more information than what was in the ledger. She turned it over and froze. On the back of the stub was a single line in pencil. *Monthly. RR.* The same on the other check stubs for St. Christina's. No details in the ledger, only on the back of check stubs.

She had been looking for a single large payment but now another explanation stared at her. The hospital part of St. Christina's Convent and Hospital was an insane asylum. What if these were not donations? What if Thornton was paying to keep Reggie in an inmate's cell?

Suling stuffed a fist in her mouth to keep from crying out. She rocked back and forth on the chair. She wanted to throw the box of documents at the wall. Reggie, imprisoned. Reggie, unable to lift her face to the sun, to run up sand dunes and slide down to the beach. Reggie, so lively and in love with life, shut in a small room. Had Thornton pretended to be a guardian of some sort, her husband or a brother? He would've had to lie about her mental state to have her committed. But why? What had Reggie done to upset him so much? Why hadn't Thornton just dismissed her?

Suling stifled the impulse to rush out of the house, run as fast as she could to the convent. But first, she had to let Gemma know what she'd discovered. There was stationery in Thornton's top right-hand drawer. Heavy, expensive cream-colored paper, just like the typewritten note that had accompanied Reggie's painting. She dashed off a few lines.

The clock chimed the half hour. Nine thirty. Suling left the office, locking the door and hiding the key again, then ran silently up the circular staircase and into Gemma's room.

Where could she hide the note so that Gemma was sure to see it? She berated herself for not agreeing on a place to hide messages. She cast her eyes around the beautiful room. The walnut desk with its crystal and gold desk set, pale blue notepaper on the blotter. The little table with the marble top beside the bed. The chest of drawers. The dragon robe was on one side of the tall mirror, a pair of evening shoes arranged in front of it.

Suling slipped the note inside one of the shoes. Then after a moment's reflection, moved the shoe so that it was at an angle, pigeon-toed, no longer perfectly placed.

Not too long after, a Chinese boy carrying a laundry bag walked away quickly from the octagon house on Hyde Street. When the boy reached the corner, he broke into a run.

Chapter 15

April 17, 1906
Five hours and twenty-two minutes before the earthquake

B ravo! Bravo!"

Gemma drew a shuddering breath as the curtain came down for—hopefully—the last time. How many times was the audience going to call Caruso back? How many times was he going to step forward in his velvet breeches and sash, chest heaving with emotion, and make his sweeping bow?

As many times as he wants was clearly the answer. He'd brought the entire theater to its feet in a roaring storm of applause the moment his final hair-raising cry sang out and he slumped over Olive Fremstad's body on the stage. The society matrons in their diamond tiaras and pearl dog collars, the groundlings who had packed into the back seats—all had risen as one throughout the orchid- and narcissus-decked terraces, applauding till the roof resounded. And that applause had washed over to the rest of the cast: even Gemma had received a generous hand when she came forward in Micaëla's blue peasant skirt and took her curtsy, and she knew she hadn't sung particularly well.

"Goddammit," Olive Fremstad snarled as soon as that curtain looked like it was going to finally stay down, stamping offstage, hurling her Spanish fan somewhere off into the wings. But Caruso paused in that sudden onstage crush of chorus members trailing off to their dressing rooms and stagehands rushing to secure the props and gave Gemma a pinch on the chin.

"Very nice, *carissima*," he said kindly. "Next time not so nervous, *sì?*"

"You carried me out there," Gemma told him with complete

honesty. The tantrum-throwing boy-child of the day's rehearsal had completely vanished by the time the curtain went up; during their duet he'd been quick to cover up her blocking mistakes and effortlessly melded that glorious tenor with hers even though they'd only had a single run-through that morning. The company's star had been the only one not ignoring Gemma onstage or actively trying to sabotage her—the chorus baritone who pulled her hair unnecessarily hard during the scene between Micaëla and the teasing guards, the stagehands who hid her prop basket from her until she missed her entrance cue.

"Don't mind the bitches," Caruso told her now, kindly. "Another scandal comes along, they forget you."

"And I won't forget that I've sung with the great Caruso," Gemma answered. Something any soprano would have walked on broken glass to say. She just wished she could be prouder of how it had happened.

"I will see you after at this *ballo* on Snob Hill? I promised I stop by." Caruso gave her another pinch (this one *not* on the chin) and swanned off to his dressing room, which was undoubtedly already packed with adoring admirers. Gemma went off more slowly to her own dressing room, dreading who she'd find there—she hadn't looked for Thornton in the dazzle of the stage lights, but she'd *felt* him up there in his box, devouring her with his eyes. The pride of a creator, Dr. Frankenstein gazing down at the creature on his laboratory table: *I made that.*

You didn't make me, she thought with a spurt of anger, heading backstage, yanking off Micaëla's namby-pamby blue headscarf. *And you don't own me, either.*

"Miss Garland." Thornton's chauffeur waited by her dressing room door. "Mr. Thornton will be heading directly back to Hyde Street to see to last-minute preparations for the ball, but he's left the Rolls for you. I'm to drive you back as soon as you're ready."

"And my pianist." Gemma vibrated between relief at not having to see Thornton quite yet and apprehension that he'd return to his study before Suling was done searching it. "I'll be quick."

It didn't take long to scrape off her stage makeup and climb out of her costume: no line of admirers waited for her as they did for Caruso or Fremstad; she had no friends in this chorus to breeze in and out of her dressing room wanting to borrow a hairpin or ask for help with their laces. As she hurried into her clothes she could hear the others chattering and making plans down the corridor: a group of chorus singers were heading to Zinkand's where they'd heard the macaroni was cheap; some of the dancers were arguing for the Oyster Grotto on O'Farrell Street. No one invited Gemma along. Why should they? She'd stolen someone else's role, and then she hadn't even sung well enough to justify stealing it; of course they all despised her. Some probably envied her, too—*I wouldn't mind heading off to a swanky ball in my honor,* she could imagine the other chorus sopranos thinking resentfully. But right now, Gemma would have traded Thornton's ball in a heartbeat for one of those laughing postcurtain midnight suppers: a cluster of friends and a plate of macaroni, everyone laughing too loudly and looking forward to the rest of the run.

Well, that wasn't going to happen, and she still had a very long night to get through.

"SULING?" GEMMA CALLED as soon as she slipped back into her huge ice-blue bedroom at the octagon house. She'd heard Thornton's voice in the conservatory when she entered the front doors, but the whole place was in enough of an uproar (kitchens sending out a steady stream of dishes to be carried upstairs, guests arriving any minute) that he hadn't noticed her slide past up the main stairs. Toscanini greeted her with a vocal trill; someone had brought him back from the conservatory to his birdcage for the night. "Suling? Did you find anything?" Gemma had checked Thornton's study door as she passed it: locked, and the key was in the pot, so surely—

But Suling wasn't waiting for her, here where the embroidered dragon robe hung on the dressmaker's form, or in the octagonal pink dressing room or pale green bathroom. Gemma took a deep breath and began to search. She was rifling the last of her bureau drawers when she noticed the embroidered evening slippers set below the dragon robe—one had been placed at an angle, not carefully in alignment as the maid had done earlier.

The note was stuffed into the slipper's toe. Suling's handwriting was copperplate, and the brief message had Gemma's skin trying to crawl off her body and slink cringing under the bed:

He's had her committed to the asylum at St. Christina's. I'm going there now. If I manage to get her out, I'll take her to Alice Eastwood on Taylor Street.

An asylum. Vibrant, irrepressible Nellie in a madhouse. "No," Gemma heard herself muttering, "no, *no.*" Nellie was mercurial, impulsive, reckless, but unstable? Never. If he'd committed her there, it wasn't for her well-being. It was to get her out of the way.

What made him turn on you, Nell? What did you see, hear, find out? What—

Oh, for God's sake, why did it matter? Thornton had turned on Nellie, for whatever reason, but he hadn't killed her. Hadn't been able to kill a woman he'd admired, bedded, been fond of . . . Or maybe, with his intense love of beauty, he hadn't been able to destroy an artist like Nellie who had brought such color and life into the world through her canvases.

But locking her in a madhouse—trapping Nellie inside bleak

colorless walls, no vibrant vistas to paint, no palette knives and brushes at her disposal . . . she would rather, Gemma knew, be dead. It really would be a fate worse than death to Nellie.

"Mademoiselle?" A knock at the door; the French maid's voice. "Shall I help you dress?"

"A moment, please." Gemma turned the note over, but there was nothing more. Suling was supposed to be working the ball tonight, but Gemma knew she wouldn't be among the cluster of Chinese girls who'd be arriving shortly to take up their serving-girl robes and champagne trays. The seamstress was long gone, off to St. Christina's, wherever that was.

I should have gone with you, Gemma thought, crumpling the note, but that small, brutal voice at the back of her mind demanded, *Really? What good would you be, exactly?* The old Gemma had been too softhearted and trusting to be useful; the new Gemma she'd tried to create was just the same, only more selfish. She should have known from the beginning that Nellie wouldn't have left her in the lurch. She should have *known*, because Nellie for all her faults had always been the most loyal of friends—just as she'd said to Suling. *You knew that, but all you did was wallow in self-pity instead of trying to find out what really happened.*

The guests were arriving downstairs, judging by the rising buzz of chatter and the swirl of orchestral music starting up from the ballroom. Gemma put her head down and cried three or four hard, gulping sobs—mostly for Nellie in her cage, one tiny sickened thread for herself. For how horrendously, how *shamefully* she had failed her friend.

Well, she could still keep Henry Thornton busy, his mind very far away from his office or his former mistress. Until the small hours of the morning, if necessary. How much time did Suling need? How could she possibly extract Nellie from—

"Mademoiselle?" the maid called again.

Gemma smoothed her face. Another costume to put on, another performance to give. "Come in."

She found herself staring at the dragon robe as the maid brushed out her hair from its Micaëla plaits and did it up in a low, elaborately braided knot. Or maybe it felt like the dragon robe was watching her. She remembered a night this past week, in Thornton's bedroom, languid with poppy smoke, listening as he drew winding circles over her naked skin and told her where so many of his treasures had come from.

"The Forbidden City, at least my more recent acquisitions. So much collected from the imperial palaces after the recent rebellion. It's said the British legation was holding auctions every afternoon. All those civilized lords and diplomats and their wives, bidding in a frenzy, then turning around and accusing the French and the Americans and the Germans of doing *so* much worse."

"Looting?" Gemma remembered wrinkling her nose, heavy-eyed, nearly asleep.

"Spoils of war, pet. Even in civilized nations, it's held that a city that doesn't surrender and is taken by force can be looted." A shrug. "Six years ago it was the Forbidden City; back in 1860, it was the Old Summer Palace in Beijing. My grandfather was there, he had connections in the British military, and he made good use of them. The Old Summer Palace, that's a place I would have liked to have seen before it was all burned. Bronzes and porcelains three thousand years old, pleasure gardens where imperial beauties strolled in dragon robes like that one"—bending down and delivering a bite to Gemma's shoulder—"jewels by the trunk-load. The things my grandfather brought home . . ."

That was when Gemma had fallen asleep, heavy-eyed from opium, his words sliding into the ether. They came back now with a vengeance as she looked at the dragon robe, and her stomach roiled. Had an empress worn that, a fierce-eyed woman like Suling? Or a concubine like Gemma—*That's what you are*, the thought whispered viciously, *a goddamned concubine*—singing for her supper with one of those lutelike instruments she'd seen in scroll paintings? What had happened to the woman who wore that robe, once the British and French soldiers broke inside? Had she managed to flee, or had she met the fate so many women suffered when cities were sacked?

"Let's just get you into this, mademoiselle," the French maid said, moving to take the embroidered robe off the dressmaker's form. "I thought the Chinese girl was going to stay and help you with it? Mrs. MacNeil is kicking up a fuss downstairs about her; the other Chinese girls arrived and not one of them speaks English, so if she's not here . . ."

"I don't know where she is," Gemma said. "And I'm not wearing that. Too heavy." Not just in gold and silver thread, but in history. It wasn't hers, even to borrow, and it wasn't Thornton's to loan, either. Gemma was sorry to waste all Suling's painstaking work with her embroidery needles, but she couldn't put that robe on. It would feel like wearing a shroud.

"What's this?" A disapproving voice sounded behind her as the maid was doing up the last of her hooks, and Gemma barely had time to school her face before turning. Thornton stood in his evening tails, tie carelessly knotted as usual, frowning at her midnight-blue velvet evening gown glittering with diamanté paillettes.

"Much more comfortable to sing in," Gemma said brightly, pulling up one long kid glove. "How is the ball?" The clock had long struck midnight; the dancing should be in full swing. Her entrance, late and devastating, had been carefully planned.

"All the expected luminaries are present," Thornton said, still frowning. "I suppose it's too late for you to change."

"I don't wish to change," Gemma said and saw the line between his brows deepen. She didn't remember seeing that line when he'd been courting her attentions—was he just not bothering to hide it now, how much he disliked being told no? How often had Nellie seen that line groove itself, before he decided she was too much trouble and had her committed? Gemma had been too sick, too shaken, too shocked to feel much anger earlier, but now a curl of rage flickered to life in the pit of her stomach. She clung to it. Rage was much more stiffening than tears. "You don't get absolutely everything your own way, you know," she added coolly, pulling on her other glove.

"Cross at me for springing the Micaëla role on you?" His frown cleared; he sounded amused. "I wanted to see if you'd rise to the challenge. I must say, you didn't sing at your best."

Like she was an employee getting a mild reprimand. Gemma buttoned her glove, giving him a long, level stare. He'd been so good at egging her on when they were first getting to know each other—urging her to look out for herself, letting her be the one to initiate things between them, letting her be the one to take charge. Only after he'd gotten what he wanted did he get out *this* tone, the tone of an employer calling a paid subordinate to heel.

"Don't pout, Gemma. It doesn't suit you." He came closer, kissed her bare shoulder over her midnight-blue bodice. "I brought something for you."

"I don't want—" But he wasn't listening. He lifted his burned hand with a snap, and a footman came in with a velvet tray. Nestled on it . . .

"I can't wear that," Gemma said at once, looking at the Phoenix Crown. She wanted no part of it, any more than she did the dragon robe. Another beautiful thing from halfway around the world, the spoils of crowing men who'd wrenched it out of a woman's jewelry box or off her head, seeing it only for its pearls, its sapphires, its kingfisher feathers in gold wire. "It will be too heavy, and—"

"I'm going to present you in it," Thornton said, and the line was back between his brows. Something prickled in Gemma then, the warning not to deny him any more. Not to say no again. Not until she could get away.

And she *was* getting away. At dawn when the party wound down, when Thornton went to bed and the house was asleep, she'd pack her things and head to Taylor Street. She wasn't taking one more crumb from Henry Thornton. The only thing she was going to take from him was Nellie, however it could be done, whatever she had to do to help Suling accomplish the impossible.

Nellie. It was Nellie's voice now, rather than the poisonous one—Nellie's dear, familiar voice whispering, *Don't make him angry. At least not yet.*

So Gemma bit her tongue when he lifted the Phoenix Crown and lowered it onto her head. She shivered a little, feeling the weight of it, the heavy swinging ropes of pearls that dangled from its elegant points and swung carved ivory Queen of the Night flowers about her shoulders.

"Beautiful." He stood back and admired her: the blue, jeweled gown; the blue, jeweled crown. "You're going to dazzle them."

I'm not going to dazzle this time, Gemma thought, making herself place her hand on his arm. *I'm going to burn this thing between us to the ground.*

Chapter 16

$\mathcal{S}$ he had to stop running. Suling rested against a tall fence, doubled over from the stitch in her side. Her thighs and calves burned. She'd always thought her legs were strong from walking up and down the steep streets of Chinatown every day of her life but running was a different matter. The moon was a thin sliver of waning brightness so feeble a mere haze of passing cloud doused its light. Nob Hill was quiet, the neighborhoods nearly empty of automobiles and carriages. Its wealthy residents were probably all at the opera, eager to appear cultured or at least to say they had seen the great Caruso. Fortunately, it was all downhill now to Washington Square Park, which wasn't very far from the convent at the corner of Filbert and Stockton. Suling took a deep breath and set off again.

She paused when she saw the bell tower of Sts. Peter and Paul, the Roman Catholic church near St. Christina's Convent. She had no plan, she realized, only some vague notion of pounding on the door and demanding to see Regina Reynolds. Or Nellie Doyle. And then—then what? The moon finally peeked out as she approached St. Christina's. Under its cold silver light, the convent hospital loomed large and intimidating, a long stone building with tall arched windows that ran the width of the second and third stories, iron bars across the windows on the ground floor. Up on the second floor, someone was walking along the corridor with a lamp, illuminating each window for a moment, a narrow Gothic arch of light.

The deep portico at the entrance was dimly lit by a small electric bulb. Suling pulled on the chain, heard the loud clanging inside. After a few minutes, the panel behind the small grilled opening in the heavy door opened a crack.

"It's very late, visiting hours are over. Come back in the morning," a young woman's voice said. The small gap didn't let Suling see her face.

"Please, I'm looking for a friend, a patient," Suling said.

"Come back in the morning," the voice repeated. "And a girl shouldn't be out on the streets this time of night. Go home, my dear."

"Please, Sister," Suling said. "Can you at least tell me if Regina Reynolds is in this hospital?" She moved directly under the light. The panel opened wide and through the grille Suling looked at a nun's face.

"Oh. You're a boy," the nun said. "What was that name again?"

"Regina Reynolds," Suling said. "Please, is she here?"

From behind the nun, "Who's ringing the bell at this hour, Sister Anne?"

"It's a Chinese boy, Sister Margaret, asking for a Regina Reynolds."

An older woman's face moved into view behind the grille.

"Or Nellie Doyle," Suling called in desperation. "Have you a Nellie Doyle in the hospital? Curly black hair, green eyes. She would've come here in February, the middle of February."

"Why, that sounds like . . ." Sister Anne began, but the older nun interrupted.

"Go home," she said. "Get out or I call police. Police, you savvy?" The panel shut.

Suling sank to the stone floor of the portico. The younger nun had been about to say something about Reggie, she was sure of it, but the senior nun had cut her off. Suling was willing to bet Reggie was in there. She could try again in the morning, perhaps get in through the servants' door, pretend to be picking up laundry. Then she remembered that the convent ran its own laundry business.

She wanted to curl up on the threshold and weep, but she couldn't stay in case the older nun made good on her threat to call the police. Suling wiped her eyes and nose on a sleeve, slung the laundry bag over one shoulder, and crossed Filbert Street to the church. It was an awkward building, with additions and enlargements that marred the original architecture. Its portico was squat and ugly, but more welcoming than the asylum's, with two wide marble benches facing each other like an offer of rest.

Perched at the end of one bench, Suling gazed across the street. The windows on the upper floors were utterly dark now. She tried not to think of Reggie locked in a cell. Did her room look down into a courtyard or was she in some windowless room? If Suling couldn't get into the asylum tomorrow morning, she would have to get help. Not from Gemma. She needed someone who had authority, a reputation. Donaldina Cameron at the Mission Home. Reggie wasn't Chinese, but she was a woman in need of protection; surely Miss Cameron wouldn't refuse.

It meant going back to Chinatown, possibly running into her uncle or Dr. Ouyang, or any number of people who might inform them. But this was Reggie. Suling would risk anything.

A thousand worries churned through Suling's mind, but exhaustion took over and she sank down on the bench, pulled her jacket tighter around her. She wished her mother were still alive. Ming Lee would reassure her that all would be well. That it was all right to love Reggie. Suling's eyes closed, her mind wandered; she remembered a day when she had been at Madam Ning's with her mother, helping fit Hyacinth for a gown.

SHE RECALLED THE dress clearly, pale blue satin with tiny pink rosettes embroidered on a skirt that ballooned out over Hyacinth's knees. Hyacinth was just stepping out of the dress when Butterfly burst in, screaming. The two women argued, then fell into each other's arms, kissed passionately, and left the room together. Suling gave her mother a querying look, but it was Madam Ning who spoke.

"Have you spoken to your daughter about Butterfly and Hyacinth, Ming Lee?" she asked, and not waiting for Suling's mother to reply, she turned to Suling. "Do you find it strange that two women should be in love? Or two men, perhaps?"

"I'm . . . not sure," Suling said. "I thought that since Butterfly and Hyacinth entertain men . . ."

Chinese and American men. Men of every nationality, since the world passed through San Francisco. Men who paid just to enter the Palace of Endless Joy's glossy doors, then paid even more when they selected one of the eight beauties. Suling was sixteen and understood this. In theory.

"That's what they do professionally," Madam Ning said, "and nothing to do with who they love. Little Coral, our youngest, loves a man from her hometown because they speak the same dialect. As for Butterfly, she's had enough of men. It's as simple as that." She chuckled.

"Love is hard enough to find in this world," Ming Lee said. "If the gods have tied their fates together with a red silk thread, who are we to judge Butterfly and Hyacinth?"

"A silk thread?" Suling said.

"There's an invisible thread of red silk," Ming Lee said, "that the gods tie to the fingers of two people whose destinies are meant to be joined. The thread brings them together eventually, no matter how far apart they are. No matter what hardships they face, no matter how much strain is put on that thread, it will not break."

NO, MY MOTHER *wouldn't mind*, Suling thought, falling asleep. *She would know that Reggie and I are joined by that red silk thread.* Right now, that thread was being tested and strained but it would not break.

Chapter 17

April 18, 1906
Three hours and fifty-one minutes before the earthquake

There were so many great songs for sopranos, Gemma thought—yet so few of them were *angry*. When a woman in an opera sang, she was transported by love, by grief, or by death, but rarely by fury. Sigh, cry, or die, just don't *rage*.

But there was Mozart's Queen of the Night, who got to spit rage for three minutes in d minor, hitting those four stratospheric high F's that (if done right) made the audience shiver as though an exquisite silver knife had just been slipped into their ears. And that rage saved Gemma, because she'd never felt shakier in her life before getting up in front of an audience, but she was *angry*.

And for three minutes, she got to look Henry Thornton in the eye and tell him what she thought of him.

Hell's vengeance boils in my heart. She ripped off the beginning like she was ripping off his head, and maybe she hadn't impressed anyone very much tonight as the dippy village maiden in *Carmen*, but her vengeful queen silenced the entire ballroom within half a phrase. *Death and despair blaze about me.* She tore through the translated German words as if she were shredding flesh, the long pearl loops of the Phoenix Crown swinging around her throat, and launched into those high staccato runs like she was leaping off a mountain. She fired off her high F's like crystal bullets, every one perfect, and when the Queen's last guttural vow snarled across the room—*hear, gods of vengeance, a mother's oath*—she had a moment's disembodied remoteness, coming back into herself on that tidal roar of fury as the room exploded into ecstatic applause.

Hear a woman's oath, not a mother's, Gemma thought, breath still heaving, looking straight at Thornton's smug, oblivious face. *Hear* my *oath. For what you did to my friend.*

She had no idea how she got through the entire program, but finally her last aria was over and for once she refused an encore. When she came off the ballroom stage in a surge of applause, her hand was seized and kissed over and over. Mayor Schmitz and his cadre of City Hall cronies; the chief of police; James Flood, the mining tycoon with his wife beside him glittering in diamond tiara, diamond dog collar, diamond stomacher. A languid, handsome actor smelling lightly of whiskey kissed Gemma's wrist: "John Barrymore, you glorious creature. Those are the most beautiful blue eyes I've ever seen . . ." Caruso descended on her, a more welcome presence, and kissed her on both cheeks: "*Carissima*, you are magnificent! Micaëla, she is not for you, but I think you and I will sing a beautiful *Traviata* together someday."

The mayor pressed a glass into Gemma's hand, some potent blend of Peruvian brandy and pineapple and lime: "Pisco Punch, a drink invented right here in San Francisco—" A tower of crystal coupes was presented to *ooh*s and *aah*s, piled high in a glittering pyramid, more punch poured into the topmost glass and cascading all the way to the bottom as all the glasses filled. The orchestra struck up "The Merry Widow" and dancers swirled out onto the floor again.

"You were magnificent," Thornton said in her ear. "I had a tribute for you, you know. The Queen of the Night plant in the conservatory was supposed to blossom tonight—I intended to pick the flower once it opened and tuck it between those beautiful breasts of yours. A Queen of the Night, for my queen of the night, on the evening of her triumph." *How did I ever think you were charming?* Gemma wondered. "But it's a day late flowering," he concluded, frowning.

"Even a millionaire can't make a flower bloom on any schedule but its own," she quipped, just for the pleasure of seeing that frown deepen. Some sapphire-decked matron rapped at Thornton's arm with her fan—"Do promise my daughter a two-step, Mr. Thornton"—and Gemma took the opportunity to remove her looted crown and pass it to a hovering footman to be locked back up in the Chinese Room.

More gossip swirled along with the music: "Did you see Louisa Ward trip on her hem at the Cotillion Club ball?" "—dropping that story of the Pinkerton detective who went missing, there simply isn't any—" But Gemma let it eddy through one ear and out the other. This carnivorous city . . . if even a Pinkerton detective could vanish without a trace, what chance did she and Suling have of finding Nellie?

"You aren't dancing," Thornton cajoled, but Gemma just blinked at him. During the last party here at the octagon house she had flitted through the crowd of guests like a champagne bubble, infatuated with the radiant sunlight, the luxury all around her, with Thornton himself. Tonight she didn't flit: she stood at the edge of the dance floor in her sparkling night sky of a ball gown, gazing at the spectacle that was more nightmare than daydream to her exhausted eyes. The dancers seemed to tilt and stagger like badly operated puppets; the music lurched through her ears, a feverish calliope—like the party at the beginning of *La Traviata*, she thought dizzily, the soprano's home crowded with guests who care nothing for her, the hollow glittering shell of her life whirling like a top.

"*Buona sera, carissima,*" Caruso shouted over the shrill laughter of the dancers, pinching Gemma's cheek like he had after the Grand Opera House's curtain came down. "Enough oysters and champagne for me, I need a plate of *tagliatelle* or I'll never sleep!" He whirled off in his opera cloak, and Gemma envied him. But she'd stick this out till the bitter end. Two o'clock, three o'clock . . .

"What's wrong?" George spoke quietly, hand at her arm, black brows knitted. "You look like an exhibit at Madame Tussauds."

"I'm quite well," she managed to say, lying through her teeth.

He looked at her for a long moment, fingers grazing her bare arm above her long kid glove. "Maybe all this is exactly what you thought it would be," he said at last, jerking his chin at the crowded ballroom, the stage where she'd sung, Thornton presiding over his guests like a king. "But if it's not—if this isn't what you want after all—you can leave it all behind, Gem. Walk out of here now, with me. I've got a room south of Market Street; you're welcome to stay as long as you like. I'll bunk with my landlord, even though he snores *and* farts. As long as necessary, if you need space to get things straightened out." A smile. "No one owns you. You've got friends. Walk out of here, if you want. I'll be right at your side."

You'd take me away from here if I so much as thought it at you, Gemma thought. She wouldn't even need to nod. A skilled pianist didn't need any signal from his singer to know it was time to begin—he'd know, just from the lift in her body, that she was ready.

So she kept her body still, kept her smile in place. "Thank you, George. You have no idea how much I appreciate that. But I'm quite all right, you know. Go home and get some sleep; it's gone four in the morning."

He went, still looking troubled, and he wasn't the only one making his way toward the staircase and the night outside. The orchestra was starting to saw through the dance tunes, the massed camellias and lilies were wilting; the American Beauty rose in one bejeweled matron's hair was listing over her ear.

"I've started herding them out," Thornton murmured in her ear. "I want you all to myself." And even though he made her skin crawl, some small, treacherous part of Gemma couldn't help but respond in quite a different way—her knees wanting to weaken, her lips wanting to curve in an answering smile. *Why can't we just turn emotions off like a hot-water spigot?* she wondered, biting down savagely on the inside of her cheek. *Cut off the flow the moment we realize what's coming out is burning us?*

Maybe because so much of what he'd given her *was* real. Oh, he'd probably thrown out that first dinner invitation as bait—looking back, she'd realized he no doubt had heard about her imminent arrival in San Francisco from Nellie, had probably been keeping an eye out for her, wondering if she'd raise the hue and cry for her missing friend, and if so what he'd have to do about it. But his admiration after that Palace Grill dinner *was* sincere; Gemma had heard enough praise in her life to tell true from false. He devoured her in bed with palpable desire; he listened to her sing with real tears in his eyes; he truly wanted to throw her into the heavens and see her shine like his own personal star. *That was all real*, she wanted to cry, beating on his shirtfront. *So why did the rest of you turn out to be monstrous?*

Of course, he had warned her the first time they met: *You look like a nice girl, Miss Garland. I'm not very nice. Better steer clear of me.*

You didn't have to be nice, she wanted to say now. *But did you have to be a monster? Was that too much to ask?*

If you aren't silly enough to fall in love, she'd told George blithely, *then no one can be hurt.* How stupid that had been. There were so many ways the powerful could crush those under them to smithereens.

The final waltz finished with a plinking discord of indifferent bows on tired strings, the musicians barely putting in a token effort, the last of the guests not listening as they yawned and chattered, collecting their fans and heading for the stairs. Thornton stood bidding his goodbyes, the perfect host sending them off to their wraps, their carriages, and their waiting silk sheets. Gemma faded back discreetly out of sight down the servants' staircase—not that she gave a damn if these sharp-eyed society matrons knew she slept here; it was more to get out from under Thornton's eye. Checking on Toscanini in his cage, she found him agitated for some reason, squawking and hurling himself around the bars, so she fed him some seeds and then trailed the rest of the way downstairs, coming out into the great octagonal center atrium on the first floor. Thornton's butler was just closing up the doors, the last guest's carriage rattling away outside.

Looking up, Gemma realized dawn light was seeping grayly through the glass cupola far overhead. The great clock was chiming five in the morning. An exhausted stream of maids trudged in the direction of the servants' quarters. The night—and the ball—was over.

"Gemma?" Thornton's voice floated down from the top floor. Looking directly up, she saw him leaning on the staircase railing four floors up, his head a dark silhouette against the glass. "Come to bed."

"In a moment," she hedged. She was going to have to go up there and let him peel this ball gown off her, but she couldn't make herself move toward the staircase yet. Not quite. "The morning newspapers will be here any minute," she improvised hastily. "I want to see what the critics said about *Carmen*."

"Sopranos!" He laughed. "You have five minutes, pet, then I'm coming down and dragging you off to bed by the hair . . ." To her relief he disappeared in the direction of his bedroom. She listened for the click of the door before releasing a long breath. The air in the octagon house seemed too close, suddenly, smelling like tobacco and flat champagne and the sweat of dancers hoping to cover their exertions with perfume. Gemma threw her midnight-blue spangled train over one arm and slipped out of the house.

She might have been up all night, but the rest of San Francisco was waking up. The milkman and his cart were already rattling down Hyde Street as Gemma walked through the manicured gardens and out to the gate, and yawning kitchen maids and cooks were trudging out for their milk bottles. Farther down Nob Hill, horse-pulled wagons were plodding toward the produce markets. A church bell sounded sweetly, somewhere in the distance—Old St. Mary's in Chinatown, maybe. A policeman ambled past on the way back from his night rounds, and he tipped his helmet to Gemma, standing at the gate stretching her neck—the muscles ached from carrying the Phoenix Crown, all that weight of pearls and kingfisher feathers and history. She nodded back. Overhead, the sky had already faded from dawn gray to misty blue.

"The *Call*, ma'am." A paperboy handed Gemma a copy of the morning paper, almost literally warm off the press. She didn't much care what the music critics thought of *Carmen*, but she had a wan hope that if she dawdled long enough out here Thornton would fall asleep in bed waiting for her, so she unfolded the newspaper: "'*Carmen' rechristens itself for San Francisco last night. For the season, at least, it may as well be called 'Don José.' Caruso is the magician . . .*"

"La Fremstad won't like that," Gemma murmured, amused despite herself. She glanced up as a cacophony of dogs began barking, but the street looked peaceful, so she skipped to the end of the review. "*Bessie Abott sang the music of Micaëla as if terrified, yet enlisted some sympathy for her pretty vocal quality and the intelligence behind it.*" Well, if she was going to be damned with faint praise by the *San Francisco Call*, it might as well be under the wrong name.

"Whoa—" Across the street, the milkman stopped to soothe his horse, who was nervously jerking his head and switching his tail. "Easy there."

"What's wrong with him?" the paperboy called, already at the next house.

"Dunno, he's usually quiet—"

Gemma raised her head again, this time at the sound of a strange rumble like far-off ocean waves. "What—" she had time to say, before realizing that the cobblestones of the street were *rippling*. She thought absurdly of oil drops leaping in a hot pan. The milkman's horse let out a shriek, rearing in its traces, and the distant rumble crescendoed to a deafening roar. The ripple was tearing up the paved street like a shark knifing through deep water. All Gemma could do was stare at it.

Then the earth did a great curtsy underneath her, a diva sinking into her onstage death throes, and flung Gemma to her knees—and the ground tore itself apart.

Chapter 18

Suling came to with a jolt. The church bells were tolling, but it was a wild uneven jangle of noise. There was a din of crashing timber and a final metallic reverberation. She stood up and immediately fell down again as the ground heaved. You couldn't be a native of San Francisco without recognizing an earthquake, and this was a big one. There would be aftershocks to come, ones that would do more damage than just rattle china cabinets.

Still on her hands and knees, Suling peered through the dim morning light, straining to make out St. Christina's, but she couldn't see through the dust in the air, not all the way across the road. She could only see as far as the streetlamps on the sidewalk. And the streetlamps were swaying, tilting madly. Filbert Street surged and buckled to the sound of shattering glass. The tremors were getting worse. Suling dived under the marble bench. She shut her eyes and pulled the laundry bag over her head. Deafening roars and crashing sounds of falling masonry. Then came the screams. Screams of terror, screams for help. A sickening fear clutched her insides, not for herself but for Reggie, locked in, unable to escape.

When the ground finally stopped shuddering, Suling rolled out from under the bench and saw that the entrance of the portico was blocked by a chest-high pile of timbers and brick. In a panic, she began tossing aside pieces of rubble. The dust was so thick she had to tie a kerchief over her nose and mouth. With strength she never knew she had, Suling dislodged a wooden beam from the wreckage and used it to push away the debris.

She finally cleared her way out, kicking aside broken bricks as she ran to the street.

She paused to look back. The church's bell tower had fallen and so had its walls. Dust still drifted up from the ruins. But squat and solid, the portico that sheltered her still stood intact. She had no idea how much time it had taken for her to break free, but the sun shone brightly overhead in a clear blue sky, revealing a scene of unimaginable destruction. Sections of the street had warped, rising and falling like a broken roller coaster. A strip of cobblestones curled back as though peeled away by a giant hand. Wooden houses tipped at precarious angles, their brick chimneys collapsed. Some had been lifted several feet above their foundations and residents were jumping off and helping one another get out.

Milkmen and delivery boys had been on the streets when the earthquake struck. Now they joined in excavating the debris, with shovels and axes if they had them, with bare hands if they didn't. Some shouted at passersby for help uncovering people from under the wreckage. Apart from these shouts for help, people were strangely quiet, whether from shock or disbelief. One man soothed a whinnying horse, hitched to a wagon that had fallen down a wide crack in the ground, while two others worked to cut free its harness.

Dreading what she might see, Suling crossed the intersection. The bulky outline of St. Christina's jutted through a haze of dust and in front of it, an avalanche of bricks and stonework poured across the road. The convent's entire streetside wall had fallen down, leaving the interior intact, all the rooms and their furniture visible, as though a huge dollhouse had been opened up.

But the people coming out weren't dolls. Some women were half-dressed, others fully clothed, and they were weirdly calm clambering over the fallen bricks. The ground-floor rooms and connecting hallways were open to the street, yet the women were leaving through the front door. Perhaps they were dazed or perhaps it was out of habit.

"Take it slowly, Sister," one of them said, "watch out for those iron fence posts poking up through the bricks."

"I'm all right," the other nun said. "I can get to the street myself from here. You go help Bridget, I saw her in the cloister. She looked confused."

Nuns, novices, and workers were picking their way through the rubble. But what about the patients? Suling scanned the second story of the convent. Outside walls and arched windows gone, a row of doors was visible, spaced along the corridor that stretched across the width of the building. Doors to patients' rooms. Even from where she stood, she could hear cries, but she couldn't see anyone opening those doors, couldn't see anyone getting the patients out of a building that could fall apart any minute.

Suling scrambled over the wreckage toward the hospital. She had to get Reggie out of there before the next aftershock. It was coming and when it did, it would be bad.

"Stay back!" a man shouted from the street. "Stay away from the building!"

She ignored the warning cries. Climbing over a pile of bricks and stonework, she clambered into a room simply furnished with a narrow bed, a chest of drawers, and a wooden chair. A crucifix hung on the wall above a calendar. She opened the bedroom door and stepped into a long hallway steeped in darkness and looked to the right, where a well of light shone dimly through dust. It was the stairwell, open to the second floor.

A door close to the staircase opened and a nun stepped out, holding a long key chain.

"Hello?" Suling called. The nun swung around. She was a young woman, cheeks plump and face unlined.

"Are you hurt? Do you need help?" she said, hurrying toward Suling. "What are you doing here?"

"I'm looking for my friend," Suling said. "Please, Sister, I don't know what name she was admitted under, perhaps Regina Reynolds or Nellie Doyle, but she's tall with curly dark hair and green eyes. She's an artist."

The nun looked at her more carefully. "You're the boy who was here last night. But you're not a boy, are you?" A pause, then, "Well, what does it matter now. I think your friend is here, she's on the third floor. I'm going to get all the patients out. Come with me."

The nun cautioned Suling, "Stay near the wall when you climb the stairs." They reached the second floor and heard cries for help from behind the doors, sounds of pounding fists.

"It's all right," the young nun called. "There's been an earthquake. I'm unlocking all the doors."

In the first room a woman with cropped gray hair sat in a chair, back to the door. She faced what had been a wall, now open to the courtyard below.

"She's looking at the courtyard garden," the nun said. She spoke very calmly, as though giving a tour of the facilities. "The building is a quadrangle and all the patients' rooms have windows looking onto the garden. We have rooms on the north and south sides, staircases at either end." As conversationally as though it were just an ordinary day.

She shook the woman by the shoulder. "Genevieve, please go down the stairs then out to the street. You'll see Sister Margaret there."

The woman looked up, her face blank. "Yes, Sister Anne," she said, but made no move to get up.

Sister Anne sighed. "We must release as many as we can. Either they'll leave or they won't."

Suling paused when the nun turned to look at San Francisco, their view unobstructed by walls or window frames. She had known this was a bad earthquake, the severest she'd ever experienced. And now she realized it was infinitely worse than she ever imagined. A shattered city stretched as far as Suling could see, plumes of smoke in the distance. Her ears caught the faraway jangling of alarm bells.

Suling followed the nun, who now moved swiftly along the corridor unlocking doors as she went. Some of the patients needed coaxing, others refused, but most burst out and ran as fast as they could down the staircase.

Sister Anne turned to Suling. "At first, I thought it was the Apocalypse, but it's only an earthquake. We can save our patients from an earthquake." It occurred to Suling that the young woman must be in shock, her calmness unnatural and unnerving.

"We can save them faster if both of us do it," Suling said. "Sister, give me your keys to the third floor. I'll run upstairs and start unlocking. Which room is my friend in?"

The nun slipped a ring of keys off the long chain dangling from the crook of her arm and handed it over. She gave Suling a stern look. "*All* the doors, do you promise? Not just hers. The door numbers are on the keys. Just tell them to get out. It's not safe." As if to emphasize her words, a remaining section of window arch crashed down to join the wreckage below.

Suling sprinted up the stairs. It was a good thing Sister Anne hadn't told her Reggie's room number because she would've gone straight there and ignored all the others, the ones pounding and crying to be let out, the ones who were silent. She unlocked doors as fast as the keys could turn, hoping this one, this time, would open to show a familiar, beloved face. She shouted into each room, "Get out, get out! Earthquake! Down to the street!" then ran to the next, working her way along the corridor.

And then, with only two rooms left, she found Reggie.

Suling couldn't believe the woman sitting on the narrow bed was her beloved. The black curls were gone, her hair clipped close to the skull. And she was so thin, so pale, her lips dry and cracked. She opened her eyes and that was the worst of all. Flat, dull green, like stagnant water. There was no sparkle, no spirit. The woman turned away from Suling and closed her eyes.

Suling fought the urge to run to Reggie's side, to stroke the poor, shaven head, to pull her close. Because she knew that if she did, she would never get to the two remaining rooms and two women might die trapped in their cells. She wrenched herself away and unlocked the last two doors, shouted at the women to leave, not bothering to see whether they did or not.

Then she returned and knelt in front of Reggie, kissed her hands, trying not to weep over the broken nails, the scarred wrists. And then Reggie's grip tightened.

"Suling?" she said. "Are you really here? Is this real?" Her voice was hesitant and it made Suling want to cry even more, the absence of all that breezy confidence.

"Yes, Reggie, it's me," Suling said, stifling her sobs. She had to be strong for Reggie, strong enough for them both. "I'm here. Oh, I've been so afraid for you. It's all right now, but we must get out of here. There's been an earthquake. Let's get you dressed."

"Suling," Reggie said, clutching at her hands. "I've seen you so often but it's never been real."

"I'm real, I'm real," Suling said, "only we can't stay here. We must get out of the building." But Reggie just smiled the tiniest of smiles and slumped on the bed as though exhausted.

Suling took a flannel dress from the small chest of drawers by the door and slipped it over Reggie's nightgown. She found socks and shoes, an ill-fitting coat. She prayed Reggie was cognizant enough to understand the urgency of their situation. The timid, slow movements, the uncertain voice. What had they done to her?

Taking Reggie's hand, Suling led her out of the room, murmuring reassurances. At first, Reggie didn't even seem to notice the entire side of the building was missing. Then she whispered, "Suling, what's happened?"

"Earthquake," Suling replied, guiding her toward the stairwell. At the top of the stairs, she saw Sister Anne coming up.

"Oh good, you've found her," the nun said, from the landing below. "I think all the patients are safely on the ground floor now. We're getting them out onto the street." She turned to go back down.

Suling coaxed Reggie to follow, then stumbled back as an aftershock shuddered through the building. She fell forward, hands clutching the edge of the top step. She saw the wooden landing under Sister Anne's feet detach from the wall. The young nun didn't make a sound as she fell backward, just looked up as she dropped, bricks and timbers raining around her, her mouth a round "O" of surprise and disappointment.

Suling screamed and rolled away from the staircase, clutching Reggie's arm.

"Oh my God, oh my God, oh my God," Reggie moaned, crumpled on the floor, hands covering her face. Bits of wood and plaster showered down on them. Suling didn't know what frightened her more, the prospect of dying under a wall of bricks or seeing Reggie like this. She crouched down and hugged Reggie.

Finally, the building gave a sigh and settled. "Dearest love," Suling whispered. "We must somehow climb down and get away from this building."

"I want to sleep," Reggie announced, closing her eyes.

What kind of drugs had they given Reggie? All she could do for now was leave Reggie curled up against a door. Walking quickly to the other end of the corridor, Suling paused at the other staircase. But after what had happened to Sister Anne, could she trust it to stay up? Heart thumping, she turned her gaze down to the street where brick and stone lay in heaps below, none of the piles high enough to reach the third floor. But perhaps there was a way to get down from the second floor. The main thing was to get there.

One floor at a time.

Reggie stumbled but didn't complain. Suling could barely shoulder her weight as they shuffled along the corridor to the remaining staircase. She prayed it would hold until they got down to the second floor. She made Reggie clasp the handrail beside the wall. The journey was agonizingly slow; the wooden risers under their feet creaked ominously. She moved as gently as she could. Hardly daring to breathe she coaxed Reggie onto the safety of the second-floor corridor. There Suling leaned against the wall to rest, panting. Reggie gave her a dreamy smile and closed her eyes, sinking down to the cool tiles.

Did she dare continue down the staircase? The wooden planks had groaned and rasped with every step. Sister Anne's face haunted her, the plump cheeks and look of bewildered disappointment, and Suling couldn't bring herself to take the stairs. She pulled Reggie up again, arms already aching from the strain.

"Come with me, dearest," she said. "I think there's another way, messier but probably safer."

Again, she half dragged Reggie along the corridor, sparing just a quick glance at Filbert Street, which was busier now, police and ambulance carts moving through obstacles in the road. She pulled Reggie around the corner to another passageway. Here, the outside wall facing Stockton Street had also collapsed, covering the sidewalk all the way to the intersection with Filbert. Stockton was steep, sloping up alongside the convent, and because of this—as Suling had hoped—the drop from the second floor to the sidewalk did not measure two full stories in height. It was more like ten feet. And only six or seven, if they could fall on the pile of rubble below. Without breaking any bones.

But how could they fall and not hurt themselves?

Suling ran back to the open door of the first cell and grabbed the mattress off the bed. It was only a few inches thick, cheap striped cotton ticking stuffed with kapok and straw. But there were plenty of them, she thought with grim humor as she dragged it to the corridor. When she came back hauling two more mattresses, Reggie had fallen asleep on the first one. She went to the cells, again and again, until she had nine more.

Ten mattresses. She dropped them down one after another on the mound of rubble, trying to cover an area large enough to cushion their fall. She considered waking up Reggie, but what if she refused to follow, refused to step off?

"Forgive me, dearest," she said, kissing the dark brow. She dragged Reggie, mattress and all, to the edge of the building. And pushed. The mattress, Reggie still lying on it, vanished over the side. There was a clatter of tumbling masonry.

And then with eyes closed, Suling rolled off the edge.

Chapter 19

M a'am? Ma'am, are you hurt?"

Gemma focused her blurring eyes and the round mustachioed face of the passing policeman came into view, the one who had been coming off his night rounds. He raised her up by the elbow, saying, "That was a big 'un! Thought for a moment we were all going into the bay."

"A-a big 'un?" Gemma echoed faintly. The quake had seemed to go on forever: she had clung to the ground on hands and knees, feeling it buck and heave beneath her like a mule. That terrible roaring, backed by the sounds of falling roof tiles and shrieking timber—dogs baying and horses screaming—it had gone on and on, until suddenly everything fell still. For ten agonizing seconds, Gemma could hear again, the *chink* of stray bricks hitting the ground and the cawing of startled birds and her own voice muttering *stop, make it stop, make it stop*, as though she were a small child huddled in a closet against the terror of the night. She'd just begun to struggle to her feet when the ground shrugged, throwing her down with a cold chuckle as the earth began to twist and dance all over again. One of the gate's stone pillars collapsed with a crash, pulling its iron railings down in a snarl of black spikes. A sharp spearlike point chipped the pavement three inches from Gemma's face—she stared at it, hypnotized, as the last wrenching spasm pulsed through the earth, dying off in smaller shuddering gasps.

And then it was finally done, the world gone ghastly still, and this policeman was talking about *a big 'un*.

"Easterner, are you?" the policeman guessed. "Lord love you, ma'am, earthquakes happen around here all the time. That one was a rattler and no mistake, but everything's built solid up here on Nob Hill. It'll all be fine, you'll see."

Gemma jerked a nod. She couldn't take her eyes off the twisted iron spikes of the octagon house's fallen gate. A few inches the other way, they'd have plunged into her face.

"You go inside, ma'am. Likely you'll find you haven't lost much more than the dishes and a window or two." He looked a little more pale than his confident words indicated, but he set Gemma on her feet and began moving down the street. Hyde Street had filled up with strange white figures—for a moment Gemma thought they were ghosts, and then she realized it was her neighbors, men and women alike rushing down into the street in their white nightshirts. "All right, everyone, back inside, now. Careful of broken glass—"

People were beginning to talk in hushed whispers, breaking the silence, and Gemma saw the octagon house's servants streaming out into the gardens. Incredibly, the house didn't seem to have been badly damaged, at least from the outside: the cupola crowning the domed roof now canted at an angle, and most of the chimneys were on the ground rather than the roof. But like most of the buildings she could see along Hyde Street, the house still stood tall.

Staggering inside, she saw that the grandfather clock had crashed over in a snarl of broken dials and brass gears. Two chandeliers had plummeted to the floor and shattered, but two more still hung, chiming faintly with vibrations from the aftershocks. Half the panes from the skylight had broken and showered down all over the central atrium. Three of the maids were weeping, bleeding from glass cuts, and Mrs. MacNeil was clapping her hands to restore order: "—sweep up this mess while the kitchens get a cold breakfast set out." Gemma's ears still buzzed, and she couldn't seem to stop her thoughts from racing like her heart. Absurdly, she found herself wondering about the Chinese Room three floors up. All those porcelain urns and delicate bronzes, the jade and the thousand-year-old figurines—had they all smashed into slivers? So many beautiful things, born in care and artistry and craftsmanship halfway around the world, looted from burning palaces and loaded into crates by thieves, finally meeting their end here swept into a San Francisco rubbish bin . . .

And then she thought of the screaming horses and baying dogs, the roar that was surely the sound of buildings collapsing south of the slot where houses had *not* been raised over solid Nob Hill foundations, and she began to shiver. She didn't care how nonchalant that policeman had sounded; people had died this morning. How many were trapped, how many were—

The sharp sound of running footsteps snapped her mind back into focus: Henry Thornton, coming down the staircase in his evening tails, loading a pistol. He had evidently not changed for bed yet when the earthquake hit. "Gemma," he greeted her distractedly. "Try to keep order here, will you? I'm off to my offices in the Financial District."

"You're going to *work*?" she couldn't help asking, incredulously. "Are you going to dock a day's pay if any of your clerks are late? What is *wrong* with you?"

"Don't be hysterical." His burned fingers were stiff, manipulating the handful of bullets, but he still managed to load the gun with ease. Gemma knew hunting rifles, the sort of weapon common on a Nebraska farm, but she couldn't identify this sleek model he was tucking in his pocket. "I'm going to assess the damage. The greatest danger in earthquakes isn't the quake, it's the resulting panic—that, and people who spot the opportunity for looting. Stay inside, I'll be back when things are calmer."

And he left without a backward glance, shoes crunching over

the broken glass and out through the front doors to the shattered street outside, calling for his Rolls.

When things are calmer. What on earth was happening to Suling in the middle of all this chaos, making her bid to find Nellie? And Nell, a Bronx girl to her bones, no more experienced with earthquakes than Gemma, was she scared out of her wits in her cell in St. Christina's? Were the inmates rioting, maddened by the chaos, or—

"H'lo, you." A shaky voice sounded behind Gemma, and she blinked to see the handsome actor from the ball last night. What was his name, John Barrymore? "Fell asleep on a sofa outside the ballroom, woke up thinking I'd been tipped into a saltshaker. Got rattled and rolled right off that sofa . . . hey, you're the singer." He tried a smile, clearly still shaken. "Sorry I can't give you a kiss, my lovely. I'm still a bit unsteady on m'pins."

Gemma caught him by the elbow as he staggered, steering him to a tapestried settee by the wall. "You just endured an earthquake, Mr. Barrymore, and so have I. That'll be something to tell the folks back East, won't it? These San Franciscans seem to know what to do, so we Easterners should probably just keep calm and let them get on with it."

She eased him down on the settee, talking lightly until he stopped shaking, then she pointed him at Mrs. MacNeil—"She'll see you get a glass of water and a sandwich, some food will set you right"—and ran up the stairs. The chandelier in her ice-blue bedroom had plummeted down onto the bed with a crash, though somehow all her glass bottles of perfumes and powders were unbroken. Toscanini's cage hadn't fallen over, but the budgie was screeching and hurling himself against the bars. Gemma took him out and cuddled him to her breast, stroking his downy head until he ceased flapping and curled into her palm. The bird's tiny heart was thrumming in one fast, continuous pulse. Gemma didn't think her own was going much slower. Another shock of tremors hit, much smaller than the first, but she went to her knees anyway, shielding the bird with her body. The windows rattled in their frames, but nothing broke as the tremors died away.

I am supposed to be running away, Gemma thought. Packing her clothes and the birdcage, leaving the octagon house forever, heading for the boardinghouse to see if Suling had managed to spring Nellie out of the asylum. That had been the plan, admittedly desperate. But now the whole city was a mess, and no plan sounded like the right one. Was the house on Taylor Street even still standing?

Shivering, Gemma tucked Toscanini back into his cage and drew the green baize cover down to calm him, then pried off her evening dress and taffeta petticoats. She buttoned herself into a plain skirt and shirtwaist, hooked up her sturdiest boots, threw her jewelry and a few other things into a bag. She hesitated for a long moment, but left the bag and the birdcage in her bedroom as she ran for the stairs. Who knew if the streets beyond Nob Hill were safe to walk, and a woman stumbling through rubble laden with baggage would be such easy prey—Thornton had mentioned looters. At least the octagon house was standing solid and well guarded by servants; her bird would be safe for now, until she knew for certain where she could take him for shelter.

Gemma tore back down to the atrium, past Mr. Barrymore, who was munching a sandwich between a pair of sympathetic parlormaids, past Mrs. MacNeil, who was supervising the footmen and their brooms, and set off down Hyde Street. Less than half a mile to her old boardinghouse—men and women in their nightshirts were trailing back into their homes now, Gemma saw, looking sheepish at their alarm. Servants were heading out with brooms, sweeping up smashed glass and grumbling: "Better fire up that stove, the missus will screech if she doesn't get her morning ham and eggs, earthquake or no . . ." Another chimney lay toppled in the street like a beached whale, but Gemma saw a man in a homburg and a smart suit clamber right over it, checking his pocket watch, clearly on his way to work. *Am I going mad?* she wondered, making the turn onto Union Street. Was it utterly normal to feel the earth shudder this way and just—go on about one's day?

"Gemma," Alice greeted her as Gemma came round the back of the Taylor Street house—which, thank God, was still standing. "Slow down, what are you babbling about—Suling? No, I haven't seen her. Or your friend Nellie or Reggie or whatever she's calling herself. How would Suling know her? Here, take this bucket."

Disappointed but hardly surprised, Gemma took the bucket as Alice began filling another at the cistern. "It doesn't look like you lost a single window here." Gemma was starting to feel somewhat alarmist for panicking the way she'd done, but the inside of her head was still such a whirl, she could barely think straight. "Everyone seems to be taking things in stride. You San Franciscans really are blasé," she tried to joke.

"Too blasé for their own good." Alice looked ready to head off to the Academy for work, her hair rolled in its neat pompadour, her shirtwaist crisp, but her face was grim as she hoisted another bucket and started off toward the kitchen. "Here, dump your bucket in that tub there. We want all the pots and utensils filled, as much water as we can. I tried to get Mrs. Browning on it, but the stupid woman's having the vapors upstairs. No time to lose—"

Squinting into the distance when they came back out onto the porch, Gemma made out three or four twists of smoke rising into the blue morning sky. The sight of those lazy black swirls over the rooftops twisted her stomach into a knot. She might not know much about earthquakes, but with all the years she'd spent in open Nebraska grasslands and then cramped New York tenements, she knew something about fire. "Oh God . . ."

"Don't fall apart now." Alice filled buckets until the cistern clanked empty; Gemma helped her lug them. Snatching up her bag, Alice then set off down Taylor Street toward Market, beckoning Gemma to follow with a jerk of her head. Her air of command was so matter-of-fact, Gemma followed in a daze without even thinking why. "It might be a good time to pray, if you're devout. San Francisco is going to burn."

Chapter 20

The moment she fell, Suling reached out instinctively to grab something, anything. She landed facedown on a mattress, arms and legs flung in all directions. It hurt to land on bricks and timber, but at least nothing stabbed through the mattress. She felt rubble shift and crumble under her weight, opened her eyes and saw the mattress sliding slowly down the mound of wreckage. When it stopped moving, Suling pushed herself up and picked her way through ankle-deep debris as quickly as she could to Reggie, who was only just sitting up, one hand still clutching the edge of her mattress, silent and terrified.

Drugged or not, who can blame her? Suling thought as she cradled Reggie in her arms. Every face on the street was filled with confusion and fear. Some bore a look of wariness, a look Suling recognized because she knew what to expect: more aftershocks, jolting buildings and foundations already weakened by the first quake that would terrify an already terrified populace.

Reggie was in no shape to weather an aftershock; she could barely stand. And Suling realized she herself wasn't light-headed just from the morning's exertions. She hadn't eaten since lunch the day before. She had to get food and water. Reggie would need plenty of both, too, when the drugs wore off.

The portico of Sts. Peter and Paul Church was surrounded by debris, and behind it, what remained of the church stood barely higher than its windows. The wooden bell tower had toppled over and lay in the street. If more shocks were to come, at least there wasn't much of the church left to fall.

"Please stand up," she begged, tugging at Reggie's arm. "We need to get somewhere safe, where you can sleep off whatever they made you take. Just across the road, my darling, and then you can sleep all you want."

And for what seemed like the hundredth time that morning, Suling shouldered Reggie's weight and tottered across the intersection into the shelter of the church portico. She settled Reggie on one of the marble benches, then crossed the road again, this time to grab two mattresses. No one stopped her, no one questioned her. People stood in front of their homes contemplating the damage, engrossed in their own problems. She dragged the mattresses onto the portico's stone floor and coaxed Reggie to lie down. Then she went to find food.

Suling made her way past the convent and up Stockton Street since there seemed to be less damage in that direction. At the end of the first block a man in front of a grocery store was hauling out a trash barrel filled with broken glass. Pickle jars, soda bottles, some painted dishes.

"Do you have bread?" she said, hoping he wasn't the sort who refused Chinese customers.

"Do you have money?" he replied in a heavy Italian accent. She rummaged in her tunic pocket and held out some coins.

"If you have fruit and bottled drinks," she said, "I'd like some as well. I'm buying for a sick woman."

The shopkeeper took off his tweed cap and ran his fingers through curly gray hair. He took the coins and jerked a thumb toward the store. "Take what you need. It don't matter what it costs." He began sweeping broken window glass from the sidewalk. "There's some bottles of soda sitting in crates by the wall, those didn't break."

Inside, the floor was wet with what smelled like vinegar and brine. Suling found a loaf of sourdough bread beside the cash register and took some canned goods from a shelf by the wall.

Peaches, corned beef, and baked beans. The cans were randomly stacked, as though the shopkeeper had picked them off the ground and put them back without looking. There were two crates of bottled beverages on the floor. She picked two bottles of plain soda water and two ginger ales, mostly because the bottles had wired cork stoppers that would be easy to open. The shop window contained flat crates of oranges and small baskets of strawberries. She took four oranges.

Before leaving, she paused by a display of kitchenware and pocketed a can opener and two forks. Her bag was heavy, but she had to be sure Reggie had enough to eat. On her way out, she handed the shopkeeper another quarter. He nodded his thanks and continued sweeping.

Suling was halfway to the church when another aftershock struck. She staggered to the nearest lamppost and clung to its base with one arm and clutched the bag against her with the other as the ground shook. People on the street flailed about trying to keep their balance, houses crashed against one another, and the convent's remaining walls slid to the ground. Suling only had eyes for the church portico, watched its ungainly outlines shiver with every tremble of the earth. But the squat edifice, its roof held up by six stout and unlovely wooden pillars, remained upright. She prayed that Reggie was sleeping through the commotion. That she wasn't awake and terrified, wondering if Suling had abandoned her.

As soon as the tremors ceased Suling dashed the rest of the way to the church. She huddled beside Reggie's sleeping form and ripped off a chunk of bread, which she devoured quickly. She carefully worked the wire bale and cork stopper off a ginger ale bottle and drank deeply before replacing the cork. Then she lay down, exhausted, and put her arms around Reggie. Nothing else mattered. She was where she needed to be. No, where she *wanted* to be.

FOR THE SECOND time that day, Suling woke up. But it was to the scent of citrus, not the jangling of a bell tower careening down. Reggie sat across from her, peeling the skin off an orange. She wore Suling's fedora and a wide grin. She was herself again. Suling threw herself into Reggie's arms.

"I didn't want to wake you," Reggie said, once they stopped kissing long enough to draw breath. "It was heaven just watching you sleep."

Suling's emotions had been a hard, tight knot for the past two days, a knot pulled tighter than it had ever been during the long weeks since Reggie's disappearance. And now, seeing Reggie back to normal, she could feel the knot loosening and tears welling behind her eyes. A sob rose in her throat.

And then she stopped. Realized that Reggie was *not* back to normal.

Despite the familiar grin and the jaunty angle of the hat, Reggie's emerald eyes still lacked luster. They were no longer flat and vacant, but the sparkle in their green depths was missing. Suling hugged Reggie again, felt how her body was so much thinner than before, felt the tremor of her limbs.

"There's so much to tell you," Suling said, "and we need to get you back to Taylor Street. But let's eat first or we'll never have the strength."

"Oh lovely," Reggie said, her smile still bright as Suling emptied her bag and put the food and bottles on one of the benches. "Let's pretend it's a picnic. When was the last time you went on a picnic?"

The day my parents drowned, Suling refrained from saying. "I don't remember, so it must've been a long time ago."

They sat side by side with their backs against the church door. Suling made a sandwich but Reggie said the thought of corned beef turned her stomach, so Suling opened a can of peaches and Reggie ate slices of fruit, fishing them out with a fork, then drinking syrup from the can. The color was returning to her cheeks and from time to time she turned to kiss Suling, her lips sweet with the lingering taste of peach juice.

"I could be perfectly happy here," Reggie said, "while San Francisco falls around our ears." She laid her head in Suling's lap and smiled up at her.

"You slept through much of the quake," Suling said. "What did they give you?"

"I think those nuns fed me every selection in their menu of tinctures and tonics." Reggie made a face. "I don't know what they gave me. Can we not talk about that place? Tell me how you knew I was . . . in there. I didn't think anyone would ever come." The last sentence was nearly a sob.

Suling stroked Reggie's stubbled head, tried to think of a way to tell her, words that wouldn't crack the brittle facade Reggie was working so hard to maintain. "You went missing," she said, "and I couldn't understand why. I thought you'd left San Francisco without telling me."

"Never," Reggie said.

That one word swelled Suling's heart to bursting, erased all her weeks of doubt, and cracked open the last hard shell of her resolve. She slid down to lie beside Reggie and wrapped her arms around the emaciated frame. "I love you, too," she whispered. After several blissful minutes of silence, Suling continued. "And then your friend Gemma Garland came to San Francisco."

Reggie sat up. "Gemma? Sally's here right now?"

"Between us, we guessed Henry Thornton was behind your disappearance," Suling said. "We found he'd sent you to

St. Christina's. Why, Reggie? Why did Thornton have you committed? What did you do?"

"I didn't do anything, Suling. Except see him kill a man." Reggie closed her eyes.

It was the evening of February 13. Reggie had agreed to have dinner with Thornton at a café in the Financial District, not far from his office building. The next day was Valentine's Day and she looked forward to an evening with Suling. Reggie arrived at the café quite early and decided she'd stroll the few blocks to Thornton's office and meet him there instead.

"I did like him at first, you know," she said now. "He was good company, always interesting and knowledgeable. But after I met you, I think he sensed something, that he didn't have my full attention anymore."

Thornton Ltd. occupied modest premises, a two-story brick building. The doorman on duty that day was a huge Irishman with the squashed nose of a pugilist and shoulders that nearly burst out of his coat.

"Good evening, Desmond," Reggie said, as he opened the door for her. "I take it Mr. Thornton is still working?"

"That he is, Miss Reynolds, always stays late when he's here," the man said. "He's got a meeting in his office. A last-minute visitor."

"Do you need to get home? Mr. Thornton and I can lock up on our way out."

"Nay, nay," he said. "Mr. Thornton asked me specially to stay until his visitor was gone."

Thornton's office was at the end of a long corridor at the very back of the ground floor. The first time Reggie visited his office and saw his window facing the alley, she commented that he should move up to the next floor where he could enjoy a view of

the water. He grinned. "Lift up the edge of that Turkish carpet."
When she did, it revealed a safe set into the floor. "The clerks
can have the million-dollar view," he said, "while I stay close to
my worldly goods."

His door was shut but she could hear two voices, one excited
and increasing in volume, the other even and measured. Thornton. Then she caught words that made her pause. *Park Avenue
Hotel fire.*

She had been in New York four years ago and remembered it
well. The famous hotel had gone up like a torch at three o'clock
on a February morning, the corridors pitch-dark because the
lights had gone out. Twenty-one had died, guests who had no
idea which way to turn and couldn't escape.

"The thing is, Mr. Thornton"—the man's voice was almost
squeaky—"it seems that wiring for the hotel's lights had been
cut deliberately. The hotel safe was emptied of all its money and
the guests' valuables. Whoever did that probably set the fire to
create confusion. They stole a fortune from the safe and are
responsible for the deaths of twenty-one people."

"Perhaps hotel staff was involved." Thornton sounded bored.
"Mr. Langford, forgive me for ending this conversation but I
have another engagement soon."

"We have witnesses who saw a man leave the hotel manager's
office carrying a large suitcase and one of the hotel guests in the
register is unaccounted for . . ."

"You've given me a very comprehensive account of the fire,
Mr. Langford," Thornton said, "and that the insurance company
has hired the Pinkerton Detective Agency to investigate. But I
still don't know why you need to see me."

"Sir, if you'd be so good as to tell me where you were the morning of February twenty-second, 1902 . . ." The Pinkerton detective sounded very nervous. And young. He had a young voice.

There was a choking cry. Reggie pushed open the door just in time to see Henry Thornton pull a knife from the detective's chest. She gasped and turned to flee back up the corridor to the front door. But Thornton called out very calmly, "Don't let her get away, Des. Bring her to my office."

Struggling was no use. Nor were pleas to let her go. "Nay, nay, I can't do that," the Irishman said, almost kindly, hands of steel gripping Reggie so tightly he lifted her off the floor and brought her along the hallway, feet dangling. "Mr. Thornton is the one who gives orders here."

Then Thornton clamped a cloth over her nose and mouth. Reggie tried not to breathe in the sickly sweet, slightly disinfectant smell. It was chloroform, she was certain of it. She screamed through the cloth, kicked at nothing because the burly Irishman was holding her from behind. "Keep her still, Desmond," she heard Thornton say. "Just five more minutes and she'll be quiet as a sleeping baby." She could only hold her breath for so long. The world went black.

She came to lying on the Turkish carpet, feet tied, hands tied behind her. A sharp pain throbbed through her head. She'd never felt so nauseated, so hideously queasy.

"Yes, Sister Margaret," Thornton was saying, "I would be truly grateful if I could bring my sister tonight. The situation is unbearable. She's made advances to me, and I can't stand— yes. Yes, in about an hour." Then the sound of a telephone hanging up.

She opened her eyes just enough to look through her lashes. Desmond entered the room with a Chinese man nearly as tall as he was. The man's hair was cut short, no queue, and he wore Western clothing: flannel trousers and a leather vest. Together they stuffed the Pinkerton's body into a large canvas sack. Thornton was at his desk, writing. He stood as they tied up the bag.

"Tomorrow morning, first light," he said, dropping some coins into the Chinese man's open hand. "No questions."

"Fishing boat go very far out," the man said, "ocean do the rest."

"Come off it, Danny. Speak English." Thornton laughed out loud. Laughing while the man he'd murdered lay at his feet.

Danny chuckled. "Sorry, boss. I forget sometimes. My cousin's boat is heading out in the morning. Just me and him, it's all sorted. One of these gold coins and he'd throw the mayor of San Francisco overboard." Desmond hoisted the canvas sack over his shoulder and the men left.

Reggie couldn't fight the waves of nausea anymore. She began retching. Thornton crouched beside her with a wastebasket and held her head over it, supported her gently until she'd emptied her stomach. He wiped her mouth with his handkerchief.

"And are you going to kill me, too?" she said, her voice hoarse.

"I wish you'd waited at the café, Reggie," he said. "Would you like some water? Let me put you on the settee. You may as well be comfortable while we wait for Desmond."

Thornton rarely talked about his past, and when he did, it had only been small snippets. Now he regaled her with his life story. How much he'd admired his grandfather, who brought back treasures from China to replenish their family fortunes. Less so his father, who had promptly squandered his inheritance and then died, but not before teaching Thornton how to enjoy the finer things in life.

"Thornton isn't his real name," Reggie said now, gazing above Suling's head. She took a swig of ginger ale. "He built this fortune under the name Thornton because some of his schemes were illegal. He doesn't want to taint his family legacy. He used what he stole from the Park Avenue Hotel safe as seed money to buy his first silver mine."

Then he'd boasted to her that one day, he would return to New York under his real name, a wealthy man who owned fine art and antiques. He'd marry an aristocratic wife. Every word out of his mouth terrified Reggie more, because why would he risk telling her unless he was certain she'd never tell anyone else?

When Desmond came back, they put her under again with chloroform. And the next time she woke up, it was to Sister Margaret's face hovering over her, lips pursed in disapproval.

"He took me to St. Christina's claiming he was my brother," Reggie said, "saying I suffered from all sorts of delusions as well as extreme promiscuity." She fell silent and looked away, hands trembling. "I want to kill that man. He's a murderer, a criminal, and a fraud."

Suling shook her head. "We'll kill him later. Let's get to the house on Taylor Street and hope it's still standing. I told Gemma I'd take you there if I found you. She's rented your old room, you know."

"Mrs. Browning must be thrilled with her," Reggie said, sitting up. She put the fedora back on her head, stood up to stretch. "She's so tidy, it's the farm girl in her. Your turn. How did you meet Sally? How did you figure out my connection to Thornton?"

"I didn't know who she was when I first met her," Suling said. "Kow and I helped take her luggage to Taylor Street. Then I saw her again at one of Thornton's parties. We only realized two days ago that we both knew you." Suling took a deep breath. She could only keep the facts from Reggie for so long. "Your friend is Thornton's latest mistress. He was going to make her the toast of San Francisco's opera society."

"She's with him?" Reggie's drawn face went utterly white

and her legs gave way. Her hands shook. "We must get her out of that house!"

"Hush, dearest love," Suling said, as soothingly as she could. "She knows now what sort of man he is, that he's responsible for your disappearance. She's leaving him. That's why we're meeting at Mrs. Browning's."

"But she doesn't know he's also a murderer!" Reggie's voice rose and Suling could tell she was on the verge of hysteria. "Suling, we must get to Thornton's house. I must know she's safe!"

"Reggie, please." Suling held Reggie's hands and kissed them. "If Thornton sees you, neither of you will be safe. He thinks you're still locked up, that he hasn't got any witnesses to the murder."

"I don't care, I don't care." Reggie was starting to weep. "I wasn't there to meet her when she arrived in San Francisco. I'll go get her now all by myself if you won't come with me."

Suling pulled Reggie close. Reggie wasn't going to listen to reason. Who knew where Gemma was now that the earthquake had struck? Suling wasn't strong enough to prevent Reggie from staggering off to Hyde Street. And she had to stay with her; Reggie was liable to collapse on the way. The main thing was that Thornton shouldn't see Reggie.

"All right, *bao bei*," Suling said with a sigh. "We'll go to the damned house together. But when we get close, I'll go in first to see whether Thornton or Gemma are there. Promise me you won't go barging in until I've looked around. But we're not leaving unless you have something more to eat."

Chapter 21

Almost there—" Alice scrambled over a whole front of stone cornicing that had fallen off a building onto the street. Gemma scrambled after her, ears buzzing, feet sore from rubble; they had been making their way down California Street for what seemed like hours. *What am I doing?* Gemma wondered, passing a couple smeared in brick dust and dragging a trunk between them. *Suling and Nellie could be anywhere. I should have waited at Taylor Street. Why am I here?* The shock of the earthquake had dazed her senses so completely, she'd followed Alice's hastily snapped order without even asking where they were going.

The eerie silence over the city still held, but as they made their way off Nob Hill, Gemma's initial shamed feeling that she had overreacted to the earthquake disappeared. Here, even the quake-hardened San Franciscans were wandering in complete stupefaction or scrambling in utter panic: distracted mothers tugged hastily dressed children along at a worried clip, dogs trotting behind on makeshift leashes attached to belts, and men hurried past with bundles tied in sheets under one arm. The street was fissured with cracks, and the tidy houses leaned against each other or over the street below like listing drunks.

And everywhere, everywhere, the smell of smoke. No more blue sky to be seen—smoke from the lower Market Street area had blotted out the sun.

"Alice, I need to go back. I can't just—" But Gemma's protests were drowned out as someone shouted *Miss Eastwood!* Alice began to run, Gemma ran after her, and then there it was, the looming bulk of the California Academy of Sciences. Two of Alice's subordinates ran up, dust grimed and panting.

"—Museum locked—" a frazzled brunette Alice addressed as Emily groaned. "Seth couldn't find anyone with keys—"

"—vestibule door blocked by wreckage—" That was Seth, a wild-eyed young man in waistcoat and shirtsleeves.

"—but I looked through a crack, Miss Eastwood, and I saw sky. The roof is *gone*, it is just *gone*—"

"We'll try the bridge on the sixth floor of the Commercial Building," Alice soothed. "It leads to the scientific quarters—" And she drew them off like panicked ducklings. Gemma ventured around the building to Jessie Street at the rear, hearing a roar and wondering if another quake was coming—but this wasn't the sound of ripping bricks and mortar. It was the rush of fire.

Now she could finally *see* the flames putting out all that smoke. Red-orange tendrils were creeping their way up Mission, crawling like ivy. Men with hoses and smoke-grimed faces stood on the roof of the United States Mint, spraying down flaming lengths of timber as they dropped, but over everything was the greedy roar of fire.

And Gemma felt her scalp shrink as every nerve in her body shrieked *Run*.

A balding man in an incongruously neat morning suit rushed past, and she seized his arm before he could disappear into the chaos around the Academy. "Where are the fire engines?" Gemma demanded, her earlier daze now utterly burned away. "The firemen? This city is supposed to have the best fire department in—"

"Quake broke most of the water mains," the man said brusquely. "They're hooking their hoses up, but there's no water flow to be had anywhere."

"But the men on the Mint over there—"

"Mint's got an artesian well under the building. Rest of the city isn't so lucky."

"This city is surrounded by *water* and you're saying there isn't any way to douse the fires?" Gemma heard her voice scaling up. "Doesn't that seem like just the tiniest design flaw?"

"Take it to the mayor, ma'am." He jerked out of her grip. "If you can dig him out. The entire dome of City Hall came crashing down."

He hurried off around the corner back toward Market as Gemma ran behind calling "Wait—" and there was Alice again, covered in brick dust, still trailing the white-faced Emily and Seth.

"Bridge on the sixth floor collapsed," she said calmly, "but I ran into the Academy director and he stopped having hysterics long enough to give me the keys."

"Miss Eastwood, you *mugged* the keys off him," Emily objected.

Alice waved a hand, heading for the vestibule with a clanking key ring. "We need to get out of here," Gemma said, panic racketing through her veins now, the urge to go, go, go, *anywhere* that wasn't here. "All of us—" But Alice was already kicking rubble out of her way, jamming a key in the lock, and throwing the weight of her body against the museum door. "*Alice*—" Gemma yelled, but the damned woman heaved the door open with one shoulder and vanished into the museum without a backward glance.

The massive staircase inside was shattered, chunks of marble littering the floor like fallen gods. Piles of timber, planks, shingles—the roof overhead was gone, a vast jagged hole showing smoky sky above. The huge stuffed head of a horned mastodon sagged drunkenly on one wall. "The collections," Emily whispered, her gaze traveling in agony up the listing, ruined museum. "Can anything be saved?"

"We're about to see," said Alice, hands on hips, gazing up at the smashed, sagging staircase.

"Alice, that is a *death trap*," Gemma began. The open staircase climbed up and around the atrium for more than six floors, the steps mostly crumbled away down to the framework. There was no way on earth to walk or crawl up those stairs.

"Yes, but the banisters look sturdy," Alice said reasonably. "Solid bronze. And look at the space between the banister posts, that's wide enough for a woman's feet. If I go up that way, on the *outside* of the stairs—"

Gemma really did shriek then. "Are you *completely* insane?"

"I am not letting my life's work and a legacy of priceless botanical samples burn up and be lost to the world of science forever just because this city has unstable geological foundations and an inadequate water dispersal system." Alice hung her lunch bag on the mastodon's listing horn. "Seth, you've got feet like boats, you'll never wedge your boots in those banisters, so head back outside and find my workroom window. Emily, go with him, I'll need two of you below the window there. Gemma—"

"Don't bother arguing with Miss Eastwood," Seth advised, heading out with Emily. "You'll never win, ma'am."

"Gemma, I could use your help." Alice swung herself up onto the outside of the stair railings. Her feet in their walking boots wedged between the metal banister posts, and then she began to step upward along the edge of the stairs, foot by foot. "If you could assist Seth and Emily here on the ground—"

"I'm going back to Taylor Street, you mad-scientist lunatic, and so should you! No one here should be risking their life for *plant samples*," Gemma shouted.

"What we risk our lives for is our friends." Alice paused a

moment, hands white-knuckled around the banister. "Lord knows I've tried to be your friend, and I was hoping you might consider helping me save my life's work—work that contributes in some small way to the world of knowledge, which *is* worth risking life and limb for, even if it isn't as glamorous as a spotlit stage. But I haven't really seen you help anyone but yourself, so perhaps I was expecting too much."

Gemma felt a rush of blood sweep her entire face.

Alice gazed up at the climb ahead of her, clearly already forgetting Gemma. "I really do wish I'd lobbied harder for a workroom that wasn't on the sixth floor," she muttered to no one in particular, and began edging upward.

Friends let you down, Gemma remembered telling herself when she first came to Taylor Street, resolving to keep her new neighbors at a distance. *The only person a woman can rely on is herself.*

But somehow she found herself grabbing the bronze rail and heaving herself up, wedging her foot in the gap between banisters.

"You don't have to follow me," Alice said, edging ever higher. "Go help Emily and Seth if you feel like—"

"I don't want you to fall," Gemma said, dry-mouthed. "Besides, someone's got to make sure you get down from there." And she took the first step up as her skirts swung out over empty space.

SOMEWHERE AROUND THE fourth floor, Gemma found herself singing. She didn't want to look down because if she did she might never move again; she didn't want to look up because then she'd realize how much farther there was to go and then she'd *really* never move again. She didn't want to focus on how her sweating hands were beginning to slip on the bronze railings, or how her feet were cramping inside their boots every time she wedged them between banister spokes—if she did that she might stop breathing, and the best way to keep breathing was to sing, so she sang under her breath.

"Beethoven?" Alice asked from three steps higher, edging steadily along. "'Prisoners' Chorus'?"

"Verdi," Gemma said, hauling herself up another foot, then another. "The 'Requiem.' I've studied the soprano solo role, though never performed it. *Libera me, Domine de morte aeterna*—"

"I've heard the Mozart Requiem in concert, but never the Verdi," Alice remarked.

Some chunk of rubble, dislodged by her boot, toppled off the staircase and fell. Gemma couldn't help counting the seconds until she heard it smash on the floor below. A *long* way below. She swallowed, and kept singing, the midregister mutter of the soprano's last-movement lines: *"In die illa tremenda, quando coeli movendi sunt et terra*—"

"What's that part from, in the 'Requiem'?"

"It's the soprano sort of praying at the very end, after all the fireworks and her big B-flat at the climax. Her voice just hovers above the chorus." Gemma risked holding on by one hand for a moment, so she could wipe the other on her skirt. Sweat was creeping down her arms inside their sleeves, down her spine inside her shirtwaist, down her legs under her petticoats. "She's spent the entire movement screaming not to die, screaming for salvation, and now she's begging. *Deliver me, Lord, from eternal death, on that terrible day when the heavens and earth must be moved*—"

"Goodness, that's quite apt." Alice's foot slipped as she edged upward, and she jerked downward, barely catching herself on the bronze railing. Gemma's hand flew out, grabbing Alice's and steadying it on the rail. If Alice fell, she'd pull Gemma with her; they'd fall together, spiraling around each other until they hit marble below—

But Alice's grip held, cords in her wrists tightening as her foot found the shattered step again. "Keep singing, Gemma," she said, as evenly as if she were plucking poppies on a botanical expedition. "Keep singing."

Gemma couldn't remember anything but the last verse, so she sang it over and over. "*Libera me, Domine de morte aeterna, in die illa tremenda, quando coeli movendi sunt et terra. Libera me. Libera me.*"

Save me. Singing it under her breath, as she climbed and climbed and climbed. *Save me. Save me.*

Until there were no more stairs, and no more breath, and Alice climbed over the railing and collapsed onto the sixth-floor landing. Gemma hauled herself over that last banister and collapsed right on top of Alice's legs. She felt a sob building in her throat, and then Alice's hand came down over her shoulder and she reached up to grip it fiercely tight. They lay there a moment, gasping for breath and clutching each other's palms for dear life, and then Alice gave a final hard squeeze and let her go.

"Come on, then. We've got work to do."

"STEADY . . . STEADY . . . PAY out a bit of slack, I need to swing it wide around this chunk of broken cornice—"

"*Libera me* from crazed botanists," Gemma said, as she gritted her teeth and fed out another loop on the cord coiled around her arm. It wasn't a proper rope, just a mix of binder twine and hoarded string and laundry cord Alice had ordered Gemma to tie together even as she scooped botanical samples out of their shattered cases into a basket. The same basket was being lowered out the window now toward the waiting Seth and Emily.

"Almost there!" Gemma thought she heard distantly from outside, six floors down. It was the first time Gemma had seen Alice's workroom, and it looked about as wrecked as the Dutchman's ship at the beginning of *Der Fliegende Holländer*: glass-doored collectors' cases lay shattered, brass weights and terrariums and pots of glue had tipped off their shelves and rolled every which way. But Alice looked positively cheery, pouncing on the piles of flat botanical samples glued to their stiffened cards.

"You know, I couldn't have told you why I was sorting the rarer specimens off on their own, but here they are, all nicely separated out." She began packing up another box as Seth and Emily frantically emptied the basket once it hit the ground below. "Hand me those alphabetized envelopes from the Harkness fungi case—"

"We should go," Gemma said, heart thrumming, after the improvised lift had sent several more loads to the ground below. The smell of smoke was strong enough to scrape her throat, working its way through the Academy's torn-open roof. And Gemma could swear the roar of fire was audible now, over the sounds of the ruined workroom. "We still need to get *down* from here. That staircase is holding for now, but any minute—"

"One more basket." Alice's hands moved with frenzied haste. A rare orchid sample, glued with exquisite care to its card; a new varietal of the golden broom she'd told Gemma was her favorite . . . "Just one."

"*Alice*—"

"One more." A vine sample from the Meeting of the Waters in Brazil; a rare pitcher plant from Madagascar. "Just one more—"

Gemma grabbed Alice's favorite Zeiss lens, hanging around her neck on a long black ribbon, and used it to yank the botanist up against her till they stood nearly nose to nose. "Alice, *enough.* Or you'll die here."

Alice's gaze went over her shoulder to the desk, heaped with papers and notes and scientific journals. "My work," she said, and the blind stubbornness went out of her voice all at once. She sounded small and shaky. "My *work.*"

"You're going to live to be a hundred years old," said Gemma. "You have decades yet to work and make your mark. But only if you *get out of here.*" And she yanked Alice Eastwood bodily back toward the crumbling stairs, because she was very certain now: that distant roar was fire, and it was coming closer.

The descent was faster—maybe just because Gemma had burned through most of the fear she had in her body to feel. Alice, climbing down the balustrade ahead of her, kept muttering "The Trask collections from the California coastal islands, I didn't grab anything from there, I could just quickly—"

"No one's going back," Gemma kept saying.

"Priceless specimens—and the water bottle woven by the last of the San Nicolas Island tribesmen, I *can't* let that be lost—"

"Too late, Alice, just keep *moving.*" Gemma had no idea how they didn't plunge off the staircase to their deaths, because her arms were shrieking now with the effort to pull herself along and her hands were sweating again, and Alice was fifteen years older and had to be feeling it even worse, but somehow they were on the ground, boots on marble, and as she hustled Alice through the rubble toward the outside, Gemma swore she'd never live in a house with a staircase again. Keep it all on the ground, thank you very much. No more *stairs.*

Of course, the octagon house had stairs, and that was exactly where she'd have to go next.

"Is this all?" Alice was crying out just outside the vestibule, now surrounded by museum personnel and Academy staff. "Is this all we've managed to save?"

Emily was making an inventory with a pencil stub, brick dust smeared across her cheeks. "The Academy records, six boxes of Lower California insects, two jars of snakes—"

"Jars of *snakes*?" Gemma erupted. "Why would anyone save *those*?"

"—one folio of bird illustrations and one of reptile illustrations," Emily went on.

"Two Guadalupe petrels," Seth volunteered, toting a stuffed bird under each arm. "And over a thousand botanical samples, Miss Eastwood." Then, looking at the bins Alice had lowered down from the sixth floor, he said, "Closer to fifteen hundred, maybe."

"It's not enough!" Alice made a blind movement as if to go back into the building, but Gemma caught her by the arm. The Fuller Paint plant behind the Academy was billowing flame; sparks were dropping everywhere like malicious fireflies. Across Market Street a block-long line stretched before the bank, desperate people clawing to get at their accounts before the flames consumed everything; a line of soldiers had cordoned off the street. *George*, Gemma thought in a sudden spasm of panic. George had said he lived south of Market; was he safe? *Where was he?*

"We won't even save this much if we can't move it to safety," Emily was shouting over the din of the shouting soldiers, the roar of tumbling bricks, the hungry crackle of fire. A confused storm of people moved, then someone managed to flag down an express wagon, all the samples and documents hurled into it. Gemma trudged back and forth until her arms screamed, wanting to scream herself, wishing she could just hurry back to Nob

Hill but not daring to leave Alice. The glow of the flying sparks was reflecting in the other woman's eyes; Gemma didn't entirely trust her not to rush back into the mouth of the fire and try to save just one more sample, one more plant, one more piece of her life's work. A soldier tried to tell her she couldn't cross back over the cordoned-off street for the folio of reptile illustrations, and Alice's dagger stare sent him stepping backward as if a python had reared up in his path.

"Just take it all back to Taylor Street," Gemma said once the wagon was loaded, cutting off the argument about where the load of museum samples would be safest. Did academic types ever stop arguing, even in a crisis? Evidently not. "Move it all again if you have to, but let's just get it all away from here onto high ground. Taylor and Washington," Gemma told the driver, climbing up into the wagon and perching herself on a box. These fires were still a long way from Nob Hill.

"Three dollars," said the express wagon driver as Alice climbed up.

"That is highway robbery," the botanist shouted.

He smirked. "Three dollars."

Alice threw some silver dollars at him and they were rumbling off. Seth and Emily had climbed into the wagon; the others were all scattering toward safety. *Where* was *safety?* Gemma thought. The smoke was now black and billowing, blotting out not just the sun but the whole sky.

"I can't stay at Taylor Street to get your damned samples unloaded," she told Alice as the express wagon labored up the cobbled hill. "I need to go back to the octagon house, but—"

"No need for language," Alice said, marble dust in her hair, cradling one of the stuffed petrels. "And they aren't *damned*, they are valuable contributions to the world of—"

"Alice, I've risked my neck for you *and* your plant samples this morning, so don't you give me any guff." Gemma fastened a fallen lock of hair out of her face with a jab of a pin. "I have to go back to the octagon house for my things." She could stay at Taylor Street after that, wait there for word of Suling and Nellie—and make inquiries about George.

"Are you quits with Mr. Thornton, then?"

Gemma didn't think Alice would normally be so blunt, but it had been something of a trying morning. "He sent my best friend to an insane asylum," Gemma heard herself saying, ludicrously calm. "So, yes."

Alice blinked. Seth and Emily were trying not to stare, feigning interest in the stuffed petrels. "Goodness," Alice said at last, as the express wagon lurched around a corner toward Washington Street. "Why on earth are you risking going back to such a man's house? Wouldn't it be wiser to avoid him altogether? If you need to borrow some clothes—"

"I'm going back for my *bird*." Gemma found herself near tears, probably long overdue. She was so jangled and tired, so shaky and spent, and this disaster was still unfolding all around them like a hideous fiery rose. "You went into danger for your life's work, Alice? Well, I'm doing it for my bird. I didn't dare bring him out of the octagon house this morning because I didn't know where was safe to go, but now I'm going to bring him to Taylor Street if I have to climb over Henry Thornton's body to do it."

Because what else did she actually have? A wardrobe full of dresses that were not hers; a patron and lover she could no longer trust; a best friend still twisting in the wind somewhere, lost in limbo. The only things she could actually call her own were the shredded remnants of her Metropolitan Opera contract and a budgie. And the contract could look after itself, if she could ever rejoin the company, but her poor bird relied on her, and maybe she'd let everyone else down in her life, but she wasn't leaving Toscanini in Henry Thornton's house, either to burn if the fires eventually got that far, or to have his neck casually wrung by a footman when Thornton had her things cleared out for a new mistress. "I won't leave my *bird*," she heard herself snarling. "I will *not*. So I'm going back to the octagon house."

"I'll go, too," said Alice as the wagon lurched its way onto Taylor Street. "May as well save the Queen of the Night."

Chapter 22

Every bone in Suling's body warned her not to go back to Thornton's mansion. But here was Reggie, marshaling what little strength she had to climb up the streets of Nob Hill toward Hyde Street. And all because of Gemma Garland. Gemma, who Reggie cared about so much she was willing to face down Henry Thornton. Suling told herself to stop feeling resentful, there was no reason for jealousy. Didn't she love Reggie for her fierce loyalty, her valor?

Suling had long since lost track of time. She had no way of knowing how long they'd been walking. Normally it would've taken no more than thirty minutes. But some streets were impassable, others littered with wreckage. They made detours and picked their way through broken pavements, careful to avoid stepping on glass and splintered timbers. No one looked twice at Reggie's odd attire; the quake had forced people to flee from their homes unprepared, in whatever clothes they had pulled on.

They passed women cooking on the street using stoves that had been carried out of their homes. They held a little girl by the hand while her father and neighbors dug the rest of her family out. And at every intersection, they paused to look in all directions, taking in views of the ruined city. The fires were expanding. They could tell from the plumes of smoke to the east. The sounds of blasting in the distance they now knew was dynamite, being set off to create firebreaks between city blocks.

At one street corner, a woman with a baby begged them for food and water, so Suling gave her the rest of what they had: some bread, a bottle of soda water, and two oranges. "Ah, bless you, even though you're a heathen Chinee," the woman said.

"I don't dare go scavenging in anyone's home, the army's been shooting looters. I heard they shot a man climbing into his own house."

Reggie picked up a scarf that had caught on a shrub. She gave Suling back the fedora and tied the cotton square around her head. "One look at my stylish haircut and everyone will know I came out of an asylum," she said, "and I don't want to be sent back to one."

Suling ached at the determined humor, the brave front Reggie was putting on for her, just as she was putting on a brave front for Reggie. Because neither of them could afford to break down right now.

And right now, she couldn't do anything but pray to all the gods they'd find the octagon house empty, or at least its owner absent. And that Gemma would be there so the three of them could head for the safety of the boardinghouse on Taylor Street. Every now and then Suling paused to look south and east. She couldn't help it; Chinatown was somewhere behind that smoke. Her home, the laundry, the Palace of Endless Joy.

"Suling! Suling!" The voice was familiar and she turned around.

"Stop, Reggie, stop," she cried. "It's my auntie." Then switching to Chinese, "Oh, Auntie, I'm so glad to see you're all right." Madam Ning was a vision of elegance in a Western-style ensemble, a jacket and skirt in moss-green jacquard, a hat decorated with dusty pink roses and a veil. In one hand she carried a bag in matching green leather, and a small leather valise with a long shoulder strap was slung across her body.

"Suling," Madam Ning said, hugging her tightly. "Your uncle told me you'd run off when he came looking for you. But I didn't really worry until the girls came home and said you weren't at the party. I was going to send someone to search for you today."

"Auntie, how is Chinatown?" Suling said. "Our laundry? The Palace of Endless Joy?"

"Still standing, but not for long." Madam Ning shook her head. "The police and army are telling people to evacuate, leave their homes. They plan to blow up some buildings with dynamite to stop the fire from spreading. After all, it's only Chinatown."

Only Chinatown. There was bitterness in Madam Ning's words.

Unexpectedly, Suling's throat tightened to suppress a sob. Since her parents' deaths she had felt Chinatown was too small, filled with inquisitive neighbors and obstacles to her future. But where else could she walk about in safety, bump into people who had known her since before she could walk? Where else did evening breezes pick up the familiar scents of everyday life on the streets, incense drifting out from temples, cooking oil heating up as restaurants began their dinner service, pungent aromas drifting out of herbalist shops? She knew Chinatown's streets as well as she knew her own heartbeat.

"Where are the girls, Auntie? Where are you going?"

"The girls are in Oakland, or at least they're on their way," Madam Ning said. "I sent them to the ferry with two of my men. They'll go to the House of Peerless Beauties, which a friend of mine owns. As for me, I'm heading for the Thornton mansion and then up Russian Hill to find Michael Clarkson."

"Suling, did she just mention Thornton?" Reggie broke in.

"Heavens," Madam Ning exclaimed. She lifted her veil to stare at the bedraggled woman, at Reggie's shapeless indigo blue dress, the incongruous bright blue scarf around her head. "Is that your Reggie Reynolds? What happened?"

A quick explanation from Suling, and Madam Ning's lips pressed together in a grim line. "I've heard rumors about that man. You shouldn't take your Reggie to his house. Who knows what he might do."

"Reggie wants to make sure her friend, that opera singer, is safe. I've said it would be dangerous to run into Thornton but she won't listen. But why are you going to Thornton's house?"

"He owes me money. He didn't pay the girls last night," Madam Ning said. "He refused to hand over cash to anyone but you or me, and I am going to need every penny to rebuild my business. Now, do *you* need money?" She patted the valise.

Suling shook her head. "I brought everything I've saved, I'll be fine."

"We need to go now, Suling," Reggie interrupted.

"We'll go together," Madam Ning said. "If he's there, we face him together."

To SULING'S RELIEF, the Rolls-Royce wasn't out in front of the mansion. One of the stone pillars at the gate had fallen down, pulling the attached fence of wrought-iron spikes with it. From the outside, the mansion didn't seem badly damaged. Madam Ning tried the front door. It was locked, the house silent, the doorbell unanswered.

"It's empty," Suling said, coming back to the street corner where Reggie stood waiting. "No one's here. We can leave."

Reggie shuddered, then shook her head. "Let's try the trades-men's entrance," she said. She led them around to the side of the house. There, the door to the kitchen stood wide open. Inside, the kitchen was empty, then a movement in the corner startled them. A man slowly rolled over and groaned.

"Little Fong," Suling said, "are you all right?"

The cook's assistant sat up, looked around. He pointed to the cast-iron skillet beside him. "It hit me on the head."

Mrs. MacNeil and the butler had tried getting the servants

to clean up. But many of the staff fled, some refusing to stay indoors, some rushing off to find their families in other parts of town. The final aftershock sent the rest out the door, including the housekeeper and butler. Little Fong, on his way to the door with a sack of purloined food, was knocked unconscious when a tremor brought the skillet down on his head.

"Don't go home, Little Fong," Suling said. "All of Chinatown will go up in flames soon. Have you friends or family elsewhere?"

"Oakland. There's a Chinatown in Oakland," he said, without hesitation. "But why are you here, Young Miss?" His eyes widened at the sight of Madam Ning, who had seated herself with great dignity on a kitchen chair. Then widened more upon seeing Reggie, her mismatched clothing, the dusty scarf.

Reggie went into the cold storage room and came out with a cold meat pie, which she ate while Suling and Madam Ning brought Little Fong up to date. Tears streamed from his eyes at the thought of Chinatown burning. He shook his head at Suling's story about Thornton. "We hear rumors he's involved with unsavory types, which is no surprise," he said. "No one gets that rich in San Francisco without dirty dealings. But murder. And putting away perfectly sane people."

"Do you know where Mr. Thornton went?" Suling asked. "And when he might come back?"

"The cook said he went downtown to rescue his money," Little Fong said. "His new mistress, the blond singer, left almost right after he did."

Madam Ning got to her feet. "Suling, do try and get your Reggie to see sense. Get out of here. I'm going to Clarkson's home. Hopefully by the time I return Thornton will be back and you'll be gone. Go across the bay to Oakland."

"But Clarkson may not be home, Auntie," Suling said. "The police and fire departments must be working nonstop right now."

"Well, if he isn't home, I can leave him a note," Madam Ning said. "You write it for me." She took a notepad and pen from her purse and gave it to Suling, dictated a brief message. "No matter what, I'll come back for my money," the brothel owner said, putting the note in her bag. "Come to Oakland, my darling girl." She held Suling in a tight embrace, then adjusted her hat and veil before setting off.

Suling stood at the tradesmen's entrance for a moment to watch Madam Ning stroll up the brick path as though at a garden party.

Reggie touched Suling's arm. "Your auntie will be fine. She could survive any number of natural disasters."

Little Fong was also on his way out the door, a sack slung over one shoulder. He had ransacked the pantry. "Young Miss, you should leave now before the boss returns."

"I'll be fine. Good luck, Little Fong. And if you run into Old Kow, look after him. He's not too bright." She felt a pang of guilt over Kow; she'd been short with the old man during their last delivery round.

"We're from the same hometown," he said, "we're like brothers. Don't you worry."

Reggie wiped her hands on her skirt. "I feel better after that food. Let's go upstairs and see whether Gemma took anything with her. If she did, she probably won't come back, and we can head for Taylor Street."

They went up the servants' staircase and came out through the service corridor to the main floor. A quick sweep of the ground floor proved it was indeed empty. Suling started up the staircase, but Reggie stopped her.

"We don't need to go upstairs," Reggie said. "Gemma's coming back."

"What makes you say that?"

"Because that damn bird is still here." Reggie turned her head and pointed up the spiral of wrought iron. There was an indignant screeching noise, which paused, then started again. "She wouldn't leave it behind. She'll come back for the bird."

"We'll wait a bit, then," Suling said. "But not for too long. Thornton." She kicked away some glass. There had been attempts to sweep up broken glass and china, and the brass frame of a chandelier lay on the marble floor, an abandoned dustpan beside it. She peered into the conservatory, which she'd expected would be a mess of shattered glass, but saw only a few broken panes.

There were voices at the front entrance and a key turned in the lock. Suling and Reggie ran to the servants' corridor and hid behind the door. Suling held her breath. What if it was Thornton? *Please, let it be Gemma and we can get out of here.*

The door swung open. Gemma. And behind her, Alice Eastwood.

"Sally!" Reggie leaped out and the two women rushed into each other's arms.

"Thank God," Gemma said, almost sobbing. "You're safe, you're safe. Oh, look at you, Nellie, so thin."

"Look at *you*; is that a rip in your skirt? Your standards have dropped, Sal."

"Tell me everything! Did Suling find you at the asylum?"

"Found me and hauled me out, brave as a lioness. And what's this about you and Thornton? Don't tell me we've both slept with the same man, farm girl . . ."

Laughing and hugging, they talked at top speed, both of them almost in tears from joy and relief. It was clear to Suling how much the two friends meant to each other. She berated herself for the surge of jealousy that sluiced through her body. Of course Reggie didn't love Gemma the same way she loved Suling. The two women were former roommates, longtime friends who'd had more than a decade to learn each other's foibles, listen to stories about their childhoods. Friends who understood each other well enough to know that Gemma wouldn't abandon a stupid bird or that Reggie would only give her mother's ring to someone she truly loved.

It's all right, she said to herself, as Reggie recounted to Gemma and Alice what had befallen her. *When I've been with Reggie for a decade, we'll know each other's little ways and our histories. And we'll have a history of our own.*

"Dear God," Alice exclaimed, partway through Reggie's narrative. "The newspaper stories about the missing Pinkerton detective! Thornton killed him?"

"We have to go," Suling said, quite loudly. "Before Thornton gets back."

"I'll just run upstairs," Gemma said, "I only came back to get Toscanini and my bag. Poor birdie."

"I'll come with you," Reggie offered. She went up the stairs with Gemma, the two continuing their rapid-fire conversation.

Alice gazed longingly at the conservatory. "Somehow the fact that the man's a murderer makes me feel quite justified in stealing his plants. I'll be back in a few minutes." And she vanished through the conservatory door.

Suling sighed. "Does no one feel any urgency to get out of here?"

Reggie hurried down the stairs with a covered birdcage. "Suling, can you put Toscanini outside? And give me your canvas sack, darling. I need it. And then we'll go, I promise. Stop worrying. With any luck, a wall has fallen on top of Thornton."

Suling sighed again and picked up the birdcage, put it outside on the strip of lawn closest to the veranda. And then she froze. A horribly familiar automobile was weaving its way up Hyde

Street. She ran inside and turned the lock on the front door. She called up the stairs, "Reggie! Gemma! Hurry! He's here!"

There was an echoing reply.

Would Reggie and Gemma come down in time for them to rush through the servants' corridor? And Alice. Where was Alice? She rushed to the conservatory, but it was too late. A key clicked, the front door opened, and Thornton entered. His face and suit were streaked with soot, one torn cuff hung down from his sleeve, and his shirt was open to the chest. His boots left grime on the marble floor. Thornton took off his jacket and dropped it on a chair.

When he saw her, he smiled. He actually smiled. "Little Susie," he said. "Are you here to collect for Madam Ning? I won't pay the full amount since you weren't here last night. Just give me a minute to get some money from my office."

"No, there's no need," Suling said, her mind working desperately. She couldn't let him go upstairs, not yet. "I'm only here to tell you that . . . that Madam Ning will come herself later."

"But I may not be around later," he said, "and this house may not be safe later. I'll pay you now. Wait here." He took the stairs two at a time, humming under his breath. As though the biggest calamity of all time had not struck the city. His footsteps silenced as he crossed from the marble of the mezzanine to the thick carpet of his office.

Suling stared up through the spiral of wrought iron and saw Reggie on the third floor, leaning over the railing. Suling pointed in the direction of the servants' corridor but Reggie shook her head, one hand mimed a key turning against the palm of her other hand.

The door to the third-floor servants' stairs was locked.

Now, come down now, Suling gestured frantically, heart in her throat. And almost immediately, Gemma and Reggie ran silently down the circular staircase, past the second floor and Thornton's office.

"Well, the servants are gone," Thornton's voice rang out, "but have you seen Miss Garland?" His footsteps echoed on the marble steps as Gemma and Reggie rushed down the flight of steps below him. But it was too late.

"Why, Gemma," he said, looking down at them, his voice as pleasant as though greeting her at an afternoon tea. The women froze. "And Reggie. What an unexpected delight."

Chapter 23

For a moment, they all just stood staring at each other. Gemma felt her heart pounding slow and hard. Thornton came slowly down the last few stairs, narrowed eyes flickering between her and Nellie. Nellie was drawn stiff and quivering at her side, clutching the canvas laundry bag. Suling stood like a waxwork in the middle of the atrium.

Then a pane of glass from the listing cupola five stories above them suddenly fell inward, splintering on the black-and-white marble floor behind Gemma, and they all scattered. Suling stepped toward them, moving to Nellie's side. Gemma found herself thrusting Nellie behind her—too late, of course, too late, he had *seen* her. Thornton was looking only at Nellie now, fiddling with the white jade charm on his watch chain. "Well," he said. "What do we do now?"

Gemma wanted to scream. Less than fifteen minutes she'd been in this house; another five and they would all have been *gone* . . . She opened her mouth to speak, but a roaring wave of betrayal and outrage and fear had ripped the voice out of her throat. She'd scaled six stories of stairs this morning and sung the whole way, and now she couldn't push out a single word. The sight of him, still in his evening clothes from the midnight ball, now smeared with brick dust and soot, turned her to stone. *Just yesterday I trusted you—liked you—maybe almost loved you . . .*

Suling spoke first. "Please let us go. You don't have to pay me. Just—let us go."

"I'd agree if it was just you, Susie." His eyes were still fixed on Nellie, distantly, as if he was flipping through options in his head.

"Her name is Suling." The words erupted out of Nellie in a snarl. "*Suling.*"

"What are you even doing here? How did— Never mind." Thornton cut himself off, eyes finally shifting to Gemma. "I came back for you."

"You came for your money," Gemma managed to say. *Alice*, she had a splinter's time to wonder—*where is Alice?* "You know the fires are coming up Nob Hill. You came for your cash and your Chinese Room loot."

"Well—" He gave her that rueful grin that transformed his lean, almost homely face into handsomeness. "That too."

Gemma managed to take a step forward, disentangling her arm from Nellie's. "Please let them go. The others. I-I'll go with you." She could hardly hear her own heart over the pounding in her ears. Nellie hissed something at her, but Gemma ignored her. "Just let them go."

"I think we're past that." He hesitated another moment, running a hand through that hair that was always rumpled, and Gemma had a flash of the man who had charmed her so utterly at the Palace Grill: so hard-edged and cynical, but so fiercely devoted to everything the world of art and music had to offer.

"Henry," she said softly.

He sighed, and then he reached for the small of his back and produced the pistol Gemma had seen him load early this morning. "I feel a little absurd waving this around," he said, "but I need you ladies to step into the conservatory."

Another of those hideous silences. The thing looked like a toy in his hand. *This is not happening*, Gemma thought. "You couldn't kill Nellie," she heard herself say. "You couldn't do it. You can't kill me either. Not women you used to care for."

"No." Were his eyes a little misty?

Gemma took another step toward him, heart hammering now instead of thudding. "Henry, please—"

A loud clatter at the front door, making them all jump. "Mr. Thornton?" a woman's voice called. "Mr. Thornton, I saw your automobile, sir." Thornton's head jerked toward the sound, and for a moment Gemma wondered if they might all rush toward him, swarm him, knock the pistol out of his hand. Suling jerked as if she was thinking the same thing. And then the front door creaked and a woman came bustling in—a Chinese woman, older than Suling, in a Western-style green suit and a fashionable rose-laden hat. "Ah, Mr. Thornton," she said in excellent if accented English.

"I don't have time for this," he said, but she kept going stubbornly.

"The payment for my girls, for your party last night—"

He shot her.

The crack of the bullet echoed through the atrium. The Chinese woman dropped like a stone. Thornton was turning away from her before she even finished sliding to the ground.

Suling let out a strangled sound and rushed toward the woman's prone figure. Thornton yanked her back easily, cuffing her across the ear with the butt of the pistol. "The conservatory," he said, "all of you, or Susie here is next—" And they were stumbling around the stairs, toward the back of the eight-sided atrium through the glassed double doors to the plant-filled room. Gemma wanted to fall on him, claw his face open with her nails, but he had the pistol at full extension now, keeping his distance from Suling, whose eyes were filled with tears and who had clapped a hand to her bleeding ear; from Nellie, who had flung her arms around Suling; from Gemma herself, who lost her footing and fell to her hands and knees on the conservatory's threshold. She felt Thornton's hand in her hair, the sparkle of pain across her scalp as he hauled her upright and sent her stumbling inside after the other two. She had a disjointed memory of him this morning, saying he'd drag her to bed by the hair—and during their first conversation, telling her *Pelléas et Mélisande* was his favorite opera. The opera where the soprano is dragged around the stage by her long blond hair, crying, "*Ne me touche pas.*" *I should have known then not to trust him*, Gemma thought dizzily, hearing the conservatory's double doors lock with a click.

Then he was gone, footsteps running lightly back up the stairs.

Suling was rattling the doors, shouting in Chinese. They couldn't see the woman who had been shot; she'd fallen in the arch of the front doorway, on the other side of the staircase. She wasn't making a sound. Nellie was cringing against the glass-paned wall, rocking back and forth. Gemma found herself stumbling backward, farther into the long conservatory, trying to pull Nellie with her. "Get back," she shouted at Suling, "come to the back, we don't know if he—" If he what, was going to shoot them once he came back down? She couldn't think, her head was one huge roar.

"What's happening?" a voice whispered, and Alice stumbled out from behind a potted palm. Cradled in her arms like a baby was a blue-and-white pot overflowing with spiky green fronds—the Queen of the Night, trailing its unopened blooms. "I was all the way at the rear, I didn't hear anything until there was a shot. Is it looters?"

"Stay back, keep out of sight, it's Thornton. Don't let him see you—"

"Are we *locked* in here?"

"We can break the glass," Gemma began, but her voice trailed off. The iron framework between the conservatory's glass panes was sturdy, the grid too small for any of them to slip through.

"Wait, there's a *door* at the back. By the oleander shrubs." Suling, tearing herself away from the locked doors at the front, came flying back down the brick-paved floor, past Gemma and deeper into the conservatory. "I used to sneak in that way." They heard a cry of triumph, then a scream of frustration. Gemma and Alice came running to find Suling beating on a green baize door. She had unlocked it, the key had been on the inside, but the door wouldn't open. Through the glass panes they saw that a section of garden wall had toppled over in the earthquake, bricks and stones heaped against the back of the conservatory. The door was blocked as tight as though it had been mortared in place.

"We'll call for help when Thornton's gone," Alice said in her bracing voice as Suling rattled and shoved. "Someone will hear, surely. Someone will come let us out."

"You think he hasn't thought of that?" Gemma snapped. "*Why did he herd us in here?*"

Nellie's voice from the front of the conservatory, full of dread: "He's coming back."

Alice began to say something, but Gemma whispered at her to stay back, then forced herself to advance toward the locked conservatory doors. Thornton's dark silhouette, a little wavy through the distortion of the glass. A bulging satchel over his shoulder, a crate in his arms . . . Gemma saw a flash of brilliant kingfisher feather blue from the crate, a trailing strand of pearls swinging an ivory flower. The Phoenix Crown, and whatever other valuables he could save from the Chinese Room. He was juggling something in his other hand—a bottle, a can, something trailing behind him as he came down the stairs.

Then in a moment of time-slowed horror she smelled it: lamp oil.

"No, *no*—" Gemma shrieked, rattling the door handles, drumming her fists against the glass. A pane broke, shards tinkling on the bricks below. A sliver pierced her hand, but she didn't feel it. "Henry, *no*—"

She didn't think he would stop, but he did. Looked at her with those dark eyes that used to make her shiver, the satchel over his shoulder crammed with whatever cash and securities he'd yanked from his safe; the crate in his arms brimming with looted Chinese treasures. The things he actually valued, unlike human life. "I'm sorry about this," he said, and to Gemma's astonishment he looked *apologetic*. His face was pale and sweating as he looked from Gemma to Nellie and Suling where they huddled at Gemma's shoulder. "Insurance, you know . . ." His burned hand trembled as he hefted the bottle of lamp oil.

Fire. He was going to burn down his own house. Gemma could smell it, hear it, much closer than the billows of smoke coming from south of the slot: the octagon house was already burning. *But he's terrified of fire*, she thought inanely, still banging at the iron-framed conservatory doors, more glass panes shattering and slicing her knuckles, even as a razor-sharp recollection of the night at the Palace Grill flashed in her mind, Henry Thornton recoiling from the flare of flame in a crêpe pan. *He* couldn't *set his own house alight*—

But her former lover set down the crate and satchel, methodically splashed the rest of the lamp oil on the carpet runner at the foot of the great stairs, managed flinchingly to strike a match—and threw it down.

"I'm sorry," he said, words almost drowned out by the great *whoooooooosh* of fire that leaped up. He stumbled back from it, burned hand flexing and unflexing, his face greenish and dripping sweat. "I'm sorry, Gemma."

He shouldered his treasures again, picked up the crate, and

hurried away, even as she was rattling the doors and screaming, even as Nellie and Suling threw themselves against the glass to do the same. He turned his back on them and left the octagon house. The last thing Gemma heard was his muttered curse as he stumbled over something, probably the woman he'd shot as she came through his doorway. "Dammit, you stupid cow . . ."

Then he left them all to burn.

They went mad. There wasn't really any other word for it, Gemma thought, some distant part of her brain observing even as she flung herself against the glass-paned walls. Take four women as different as four women could be—an opera singer in her thirties, an emaciated artist from the Bronx, a capable middle-aged scientist, a Chinese seamstress not even twenty— and threaten to burn them alive, and they shed everything that made them individual, everything that made them uniquely themselves, and reverted to animals. Gemma was hurling herself against the iron-framed conservatory wall like her bird when he flung himself against the bars of his cage; Nellie was howling and trying to pry up a brick to smash the door handles; Alice was cradling her potted Queen of the Night and keening; Suling had smashed the rest of the glass around the front door lock and had threaded her hand through to jiggle the handle from the outside, like a fox gnawing off a paw caught in a trap.

And fire was running along the staircase all the way up the octagon house, clear to the cupola, and the huge central atrium was filling with dense black smoke.

"There has to be a key," Alice was saying, her voice thin, looking frantically under plant pots. "You would put a *key* here. If we had a key, we could unlock the doors from the outside—"

"We cannot die here," Nellie was saying over and over in a flat, gulping voice, still heaving at the paving stone with her thin, trembling hands. "We cannot die—"

"We are *not* going to die," Gemma snarled, but she didn't believe it, even as she ran back to the end of the conservatory to hammer again on the blocked back door. It refused to budge an inch. Its key fell out with a plink onto the floor, and Gemma kept attacking the door, panting without words now. If they could get the attention of someone passing by—

But the conservatory was set too far back in the octagon house's gardens for anyone on Hyde Street to see, and no one was going to hear their shouts in a city whose air was already thick with pealing bells, roaring fire, and the cries of the injured.

"The back door key." Alice couldn't have heard the sound of the key hitting the bricks at Gemma's feet, but suddenly she was speaking in her mild *I-wonder-if-this-is-a-new-varietal-of-mesquite* tone. "Is there any chance it opens both the back door *and* the front?"

A split second's frozen silence, and then Gemma was scooping up the key in shaking hands and rushing through the oleander and ginger lilies toward the front, stumbling over cracked bricks. Suling tore it out of her fingers and threaded her small, glass-scratched hand back through the broken pane beside the door handle, maneuvering the key toward the lock on the other side with exquisite care. It slipped through her fingers to the carpet on the other side, and they all moaned, a unison sound from four throats. Alice ripped a slender bamboo rod out of a pot where it was holding up a staked vine, and Suling wiggled it under the door, sweeping back and forth until she could inch the key back underneath and into her fingers. "Hurry," Nellie muttered, and Gemma swept her into a violent hug, all their eyes glued on Suling's blood-laced hand as she worked her way even more carefully through the broken pane and inserted the key again. They were all starting to cough now from the smoke oiling its way through the broken glass panes.

"It won't work," Gemma heard herself mutter, "it won't work—"

But then the key clicked, and the door handle turned.

Suling gave half a sob as she wrenched the door open and flung it wide. "Cover your mouth first—" Gemma started to say, but a wall of roiling smoke met them and they all began to choke. Nellie fell forward into Suling, scooping up the canvas laundry bag she'd dropped by the door, and the two of them began to stagger ahead toward the atrium. Gemma pulled the collar of her blouse up over her mouth and headed blindly after them, throwing an arm around Alice's waist when she saw the older woman stagger in the doorway. "*Alice*," Gemma coughed through her blouse, "*drop the goddamned plant*—" But Alice clutched the pot stubbornly against her hip like a baby, and they staggered through the huge atrium, flames leaping overhead.

Forty steps. Forty steps to cross the atrium, hand at the wall to avoid losing her way, Alice lurching against her, blind in the smoke. Forty steps, around the staircase, to the wall—fumbling toward the front door of the octagon house, falling over something at the threshold—and then reeling outside, choking and coughing, into the daylight.

The first thing Gemma saw was the Chinese woman Thornton had shot. She lay where she'd fallen on the threshold, dead eyes staring blindly upward—*I tripped over her, that's what I tripped on.* Gemma steeled herself to seize the woman's limp arms. The muscles of her back shrieked. "Alice, help—" But Alice was on hands and knees beside her plant pot, coughing so hard her whole frame shook. Gemma gritted her teeth, heaving with all her strength, and managed to pull the Chinese woman clear of the doorway, out onto the veranda and then down to the grass. It didn't seem right to leave her to burn in the house, dropped in her tracks where a murderer had shot her simply for being in the wrong place at the wrong time. Straightening painfully, Gemma let go of the woman's limp wrists and finally looked around her. "Nellie?" she called, voice scaling up. "Su-ling? *Nellie*—"

They were still inside.

THERE WAS A moment when Gemma's whole being quailed, looking at the burning octagon house: its double doors retching black smoke, every window leaping with flame, the tilting cupola at its crown burning like a torch. *I cannot*, she thought, her scalp shrinking, the whole surface of her skin crawling. *I cannot go in there.*

But Alice lay half-stupefied by smoke, unable even to stand. And Suling and Nellie were inside.

I cannot do it. She was no good in a crisis, she wasn't brave. She wasn't Suling who had stormed a shattered madhouse to rescue the one she loved; she wasn't Alice who had fearlessly scaled six stories to save her life's work; she wasn't Nellie who had endured two months in an asylum and come out sane and snarling. Gemma Garland wasn't brave, she was selfish—the woman who tried to live by the motto *Rely on yourself, no one else.*

That woman wanted to cut and run in terror. Forty steps across that atrium? It might as well have been a mile. She couldn't do it.

I cannot do it.

Strangely, it was George's voice Gemma heard, compliment-ing the way she could sing a long phrase in one breath: *You've got lungs like an elephant.*

"Lungs like an elephant," she said aloud, faintly. That door-way bellowing smoke. *Just hold your breath.*

She held her breath every day on her jogs down Hyde Street, didn't she? Counting how many lampposts she could pass before she had to breathe. Her record was twelve. Forty steps across that atrium. What was that, two lampposts?

She took a series of long gulping breaths, each one deeper and longer than the last. She breathed in the last one like a sword-swallower, inflating her lungs all the way to the bottom of her rib cage, feeling her whole torso lift with air—and she strode in.

Dark as a tomb inside, smoke roiling. Her eyes began to water and sting, so she shut them. Right hand against the wall. Keep it there, keep going forward, and she couldn't get lost. Follow the wall, half the octagon, around toward the back of the atrium where the conservatory entrance was. Gemma could feel the smoke prying slyly at her eyes, her mouth, her nose, but she sealed herself. Her lungs were full; hot air balloons floating serenely across a blue sky, floating her forward through the choking terror. Above she heard the rush of flames, the dangerous creaking of the staircase. She couldn't look. Forward. Forty steps.

Something at her feet, the softness of a body. She dropped to her knees, finally daring to open her eyes. She couldn't see anything, only hear the sound of someone coughing hopelessly. She couldn't see if it was Nellie or Suling. "Up," she managed to shout without exhaling. "*UP*—"

Arms around her neck, someone coughing. Nellie, it was Nellie's asylum-cropped hair against Gemma's cheek as her head lolled. She couldn't look for Suling; she was supporting almost all of Nellie's weight, turning her by force. Left hand against the wall this time, right arm a band of iron around Nellie, whose feet floundered and wandered and barely supported her weight. Lungs aching now. One more lamppost. The wall was hot, the paper nearly blistering her fingertips. Forward. Thirty-six, thirty-seven, thirty-eight. Forward.

Gemma's breath burst out of her as they cleared the threshold.

The air tasted like wine. Nellie slipped from her arm's grip and tumbled to the veranda, still clutching her laundry bag. She was coughing so hard her throat seemed to be turning itself inside out, but even so she was trying to crawl back toward the door. "Sul—" She coughed. "Sul—"

"I'm getting her," Gemma said steadily, even though she had no idea if she could do that, if it was possible, if she could walk back into that inferno. Better not to think about it; better just to *do it*. She rested her shaking hands on her knees, breathing again in deep, rapid gulps, then slower, longer gulps. Then the last breath, in and in and in.

Lungs like an elephant.

She was lumbering like an elephant now as she staggered back in, scorching her hand on the wall, keeping it there anyway. The air, so much hotter now from one trip to the next. Timbers crackling overhead, glass panes bursting in their frames and showering heated shards of glass. She could feel her eyelashes singeing. Something white-hot hit her shoulder, slicing through her blouse. She kept going. Around the staircase, feeling frantically with her feet, but this time she felt no muffling human shape on the floor. She risked letting go of her contact with the wall, feeling along the carpet. One step, two—was that the sound of coughing?

And there was Suling, crawling blindly around the back of the staircase, coughing and blundering. Gemma managed to haul her up, no breath this time to shout anything. Her lungs were burning. Suling just barely managed to stumble against her, feet tangling. The wall, where was the wall? Gemma had lost the wall. She risked opening her eyes. The atrium was all fire and smoke, the staircase blazing, the drapes at the long windows now sheets of flame, the wallpaper crisping and kindling. She held her breath. She held her breath and moved into the center, dragging the reeling Suling along by the waist. Something fell from four stories up, spinning in the fiery air, a section of flaming newel post—it glanced off Gemma's shoulder, and she heard a crackling sound. *My hair is on fire*, she thought, but all she could do was move forward. Thirty-four, thirty-five. Step, step.

Her breath gushed out. She couldn't hold it anymore. She quickened her leaden legs, and Suling managed to heave a little more of her own weight forward. Another step, lungs burning. A roar, something falling—the staircase, collapsing behind her?—and they were out, bursting into the daylight, and Gemma felt her fallen, flaming hair blazing around her like a corona. She collapsed, coughing, the skin of her neck blistering, Suling's weight sloughing away as she stumbled to where Nellie lay stupefied. Gemma felt Alice's strong hands beating at her shoulders and head, beating out the fire in her hair, and Gemma hit the steps of the veranda and tumbled off them, falling in a heap on the grass below.

She coughed until her lungs felt like they were going to crawl up her throat and out of her mouth, her eyes watering and burning, rubbing at them with a soot-stained hand. When her eyes cleared, she didn't know what she was looking at—bars across her vision, arching upward strangely. Then she heard a chirp and a trill, saw a green blur, and realized it was Toscanini's birdcage. Her bag hadn't made it out of the house, but here was her budgie regarding her beadily from his perch, and behind him she saw the octagon house rearing against the sky, burning like the world's end in the last act of Wagner's *Götterdämmerung*. Gemma lay gasping, fingers looped through the closest bar of the birdcage, wondering if the world really was coming to an end.

Chapter 24

Reggie, Suling, and Alice were on the ground coughing. Gemma sat on the grass, wheezing. But they were all out of the burning house. Everyone was safe.

All except for Madam Ning, lying beside Gemma.

A long smear of blood trailed from the front door and down the veranda steps, testament to Gemma's painful journey to pull Madam Ning from the burning house. Still gasping for breath, Suling ran to kneel beside her auntie's still form. "Auntie, Auntie," she sobbed. The sky hung above, a pitiless red twilight that mirrored the flames leaping up behind them.

Alice came hurrying over. Reggie knelt beside Suling. Madam Ning's dark eyes stared out from her pale face. Her hair, loosened from its chignon, fanned around her head. Her elegant green jacket was soaked in blood and one hand still gripped the strap of the leather valise.

Suling closed her hand over Madam Ning's. "We'll get you to a hospital, Auntie!" She rubbed Madam Ning's wrists. "Miss Eastwood! I can't feel a pulse!"

"She's dead, my dear," Alice said gently. "He shot her through the chest. Her heart." She closed the dead woman's eyes.

Suling held Madam Ning's hand up to her cheek. "There's no one else," she cried, rocking back and forth. "No one else who remembers." Madam Ning was the last remaining link to her parents. There was no one else who carried intimate memories of her mother from her first days in San Francisco to her last. There was no one else who would give blunt and unvarnished advice that sprang from a caring heart. It seemed impossible that anyone so vigorous and forceful could be gone, drained of life.

"What's going on here?" a man's voice called out. "Is someone hurt?" Tall and burly, Sergeant Clarkson strode across the lawn toward the small circle of women. When he saw Madam Ning's body, a low cry escaped his lips.

"Nina? What's happened?" He dropped to his knees and felt for Madam Ning's pulse, lifted an eyelid. Finally he put an ear to her chest. Clarkson rose to his knees, still looking down at the lifeless face, and made the sign of the cross. His features were wooden, only the heaving of his shoulders betraying any emotion. After a few minutes he turned to the women.

"What happened? Who shot her? Looters?"

Suling was still crying, more quietly now, her face buried against Reggie's neck. It was Gemma who spoke up. "Henry Thornton shot her."

Clarkson's astonishment broke through the wooden mask. "Thornton? *The* Henry Thornton?"

"We saw him do it," Reggie said. "He shot her and locked all four of us in the conservatory, then he set the house on fire. He meant to kill us."

From inside the octagon house, timbers crashed and flames shot out from another part of the roof. Alice's crisp voice broke through the roar of the fire. "Sergeant, we can tell you more but right now we need to get away from this house. Are there any fire trucks nearby?"

Recalled to duty, Clarkson shook his head. "It's no use even if there were, ma'am. The water mains broke during the earthquake. Best we can hope is that the wind doesn't push the flames any farther and the fire burns itself out." He took off his coat and covered up Madam Ning, and for a moment his shoulders heaved again.

Then he stood up. "Ladies, have you somewhere safe to go?"

"No, no!" Suling cried. "We can't just leave her here!"

"I know Madam Ning was like an aunt to you, I'm very sorry for your loss." Clarkson knelt beside Suling. "Miss Feng, I wish I could promise that your auntie will get a proper burial. But I can't, even though I want it as much as you do. The city is in crisis and fires are spreading. Our first duty is to the living. Come with me, come with your friends."

"I'm sorry for your loss, too," Suling said after a moment's pause. She wasn't the only one who needed comfort. "She cared about you, Mr. Clarkson. I don't think she wanted to admit it, but she did."

"No, she wasn't one to get sentimental," he said. A small smile crossed his face. "And right now she'd be scolding us to stop wasting time and start walking to safety."

THEY MADE SLOW progress, Alice with her blue-and-white pot leading the way, Clarkson keeping pace, Gemma between them holding tightly to Toscanini's cage. Suling walked as though in a dream, clutching Madam Ning's handbag, the small leather valise slung across her chest, Reggie's hand holding her arm. Clarkson listened while Reggie and Gemma poured out the tale of Henry Thornton's misdeeds. By the time they reached the Taylor Street boardinghouse, the sergeant was shaking his head in fury and frustration.

"So Thornton was behind Detective Langford's disappearance," he said. "Murdered. And you witnessed it, Miss Reynolds. That's news for the chief of police. The Pinkertons have been badgering him since Langford vanished. A Chinaman named Danny, eh?"

"And the doorman, Desmond," Reggie reminded him. "Big, Irish, squashed nose. But it was Thornton who stabbed Langford and had me committed. I would've rotted away in a cell if Suling and Gemma hadn't figured out what he'd done."

"Thank you, ladies," Clarkson said. "I'm sorry you suffered so much at the hands of that devil, but you've done more than the police or the Pinkertons to solve the mystery of Langford's disappearance, not to mention exposing Thornton's criminal past." He pulled a pencil and small notebook from his coat pocket. "Now, I've never actually met this devil Thornton," Clarkson said. "Can I get a description? And how can I get in touch with you all after we've arrested him? We'll need you all to testify . . ."

After Clarkson left, they trooped inside the boardinghouse. Mrs. Browning's tenants milled about in varying stages of panic. Mrs. Browning herself was on a settee in the drawing room, sobbing into a dinner napkin. One tenant had stationed himself in the foyer and was shouting out instructions, that they had to leave and leave now, that they should try Golden Gate Park, where the army was setting up a camp for refugees, or find open spaces such as Portsmouth Square, away from the reach of falling buildings. In the dining room, two women were exchanging information, stories of narrow escapes and which landmark buildings had burned down. A young couple had already packed and were ready to leave, only coming to the dining room to grab some food.

The four women pushed their way up the stairs past a man hurrying down with a wicker trunk and a duffel bag. Gemma went into her room to "get Toscanini settled" and the rest of them followed Alice upstairs to her room, where she set down the Queen of the Night plant on a small table by a window.

Suling sank onto the settee. Whatever reserve of strength and will she had drawn from all day, Madam Ning's death had drained it dry.

"I think you need a wash and some proper clothes, Reggie," Alice said as Suling sat frozen. "We've time for that."

She gave Reggie a damp tea towel to wipe the worst of the grime and soot from her hands and face. After a brief discussion, Reggie put on a pair of Alice's denim trouser skirts and a linen shirt, slipped on a field jacket with roomy pockets. Then Reggie knelt beside Suling with a washbasin and tenderly rubbed a sponge over her face, neck, and hands.

"We'll take a proper bath as soon as we can," she whispered to Suling. "Feeling better now?"

Suling managed a weak smile in reply. Yes, she was better. Despite all that had happened, despite losing Madam Ning, she was with Reggie. Suling reached inside her shirt and pulled out the red silk cord. Wordlessly, she held up the ring to show Reggie.

"I have something for you," Reggie said and reached down beside her. She held up the laundry bag. "Look inside."

Suling untied the rope and opened the bag. The blue dragon robe. She gasped. "This was why you went back upstairs?"

"It was in Gemma's room," Reggie said, "and she told me how much work you'd put into repairing it. It was too beautiful to leave behind and I figured you'd earned it."

"It won't be easy getting to Golden Gate Park," Gemma said, coming in, hair damp, face clean, "but if we have to, we can walk."

Alice glanced at the dining table, stacked with specimens. "Not good enough. I'll rent a horse cart or wheelbarrow. Something, anything. We did not save these just to leave them behind."

Suling sat up. "I'm going to Oakland. I must find Auntie's girls and tell them she's gone. I need to make sure they're all

right." She indicated the valise. "Her money is now theirs."
Then to Reggie, "Will you come with me?"

Reggie gave her a look. Did she even need to ask?

Then they heard Gemma gasp, a sharp, shocked sound. She
was at the east-facing window. They joined her there to look.
"Oh dear lord," said Alice.

Outside, the darkening skies made the inferno consuming
San Francisco seem brighter and closer, more terrifying, each
new fire adding its orange light to the horizon. On the street,
horse carts and automobiles rattled down the hill loaded with
boxes of belongings, bits of furniture, children and pets. In the
distance sirens blared, and then a blast of gunpowder shook the
air and another fire flowered red and gold on the skyline.

Silently, the four women watched San Francisco burn. Suling
sobbed quietly. This was her city, her home. Alice dabbed her
eyes with a sleeve.

It was Gemma who first caught the scent. Delicate, soft, exotic. She turned around and a moment later so did Alice. The
scientist gasped.

The Queen of the Night flower was opening.

Alice rushed to the side table, lit an oil lamp, and placed it
beside the blue-and-white pot. "Like jasmine," she murmured,
"but warmer and sweeter. More potent and yet more delicate."
She sighed happily, flipped open a notebook, and began scribbling. "White central petals open first, releasing more fragrance with each passing second . . ."

The Queen of the Night flower dangled from its stem, white
rounded petals unfurling slowly, a white so pure it glowed like
a small moon in the lamplit room, the blossom surrounded by
a ruff of long, narrow petals. Its sweet scent permeated the at-
tic and attracted a moth flying through the open window. Alice

finally stopped scribbling, and the four women simply gathered around the table and gazed in wonder. For a brief time they forgot about the burning city, forgot the horrors they had endured. Stopped thinking about the hardships yet to come.

Such beauty and grace amid so much destruction. Such balm for their tired souls.

Chapter 25

"This is probably what a beautiful cloudless day in hell looks like," Nellie observed, looking at the sickly orange dawn. *Reggie*, Gemma reminded herself. She'd have to get used to calling her friend *Reggie* now. Though there wasn't much time left to do it.

This morning they were all parting ways.

"You could come with us," Reggie urged. She and Suling stood with Gemma on the sidewalk, the boardinghouse behind them boiling like a frantic beehive. The tenants who had stayed the night were now all fleeing, and so were the neighbors; cats yowled and children cried and their landlady sobbed in her kitchen as she tried to pack a lifetime's worth of possessions into a trunk. The inferno would reach Taylor Street today. San Francisco's fires were eating their way up Nob Hill like a mammoth, implacable dragon, not quickly but steadily. "We'll be in Oakland," Reggie went on. She stood clutching a tiny pot with a cutting of the Queen of the Night—Gemma had one, too; Alice had been up half the night preparing them. *For our new homes, wherever they are*, she'd said. It looked like Reggie and Suling's home would be in Oakland, at least for a little while. "We'll be with Madam Ning's girls," Reggie said. "We'll find room for you—"

Gemma shook her head. "I need to find George. And the rest of the Met cast. I still have a job there . . ." Her tattered Met contract, something she'd achieved herself without Thornton's poisoned assistance. So much had been lost, but she still had that. It seemed wrong to let it go, when she now had so little else. And George, how could she go off without knowing if he was alive or dead? She looked at the waves of acrid smoke and hungry crackling flames rising to the south and shivered.

Reggie sighed, not trying to persuade her. Suling didn't say anything at all. Her eyes were sunken, and she kept staring in the direction of Chinatown. Chinatown, which was now utterly gone. Gemma had heard her muffled weeping in the bedroom an hour ago—steely Suling, weeping like a child when word came just how far the fires had advanced in the night. "Old Kow and Third Uncle, the Mission Home. My poor *cousins* . . ."

"We'll find them," Gemma had heard Reggie murmur back helplessly, but Suling still looked like a ghost, clutching Madam Ning's valise and peering through the smoke for a desperate glimpse of her lost world. Gemma reached out and hugged her awkwardly—felt those slim arms grip her back with fierce strength, and Reggie's arms loop around them both. "Are you sure you won't come with us, Sal?"

"Please come," Suling added, but Gemma shook her head again. Another flurry of hugs and farewells, then Suling and Reggie were making their way up the street. Reggie's big troubled eyes looked back once over her bony shoulder. "Write," she called, "promise you'll write!" And Gemma forced a smile and a little wave.

The smoke-filled air swallowed them all too soon.

It shouldn't end like this, Gemma thought, smile fading away as she clutched her birdcage and her Queen of the Night cutting, thinking of last night's moment of fragile beauty as the plant bloomed. But fire devoured beauty, it devoured peace, it devoured everything. At least it hadn't devoured her friends, even if they were all scattering to the four winds.

"Success!" Alice Eastwood's voice was as brisk as ever as she came round the corner dusting her hands off on her ashy skirt. She'd already bid the others farewell earlier, before plunging out into the chaos to find a wagon out of the city. "The driver's agreed to take me as far as Fort Mason, along with the Academy's botanical samples. We can squeeze you in, too, Gemma."

But Gemma shook her head. "Where will you go after Fort Mason?"

Alice shrugged. "I don't know. What I've built was mostly here. The Academy. My work."

We're all orphans now, in a way, Gemma thought. Herself and Alice, Reggie and Suling—none of them had homes anymore. "You still have your work," Gemma said, helplessly.

"It was a joy to me while I did it. I can still have the same joy in starting it again!" Alice tried to smile but her chin wobbled. For just a moment the older woman sagged utterly in despair, and Gemma stepped forward and held her tight.

And then police were shouting for everyone to move it along, move it along, the fires would be eating their way through here in another hour, and Alice was on the wagon, the Queen of the Night clasped to her breast, wilted flowers spilling over her arms, and Gemma was trudging in the other direction with a birdcage dangling from one hand and a tiny pot in the other.

She had, she realized, absolutely nothing else. She'd borrowed some clean clothes from Alice, but everything else Gemma owned had burned in the octagon house. Two nights ago she'd been draped in pearls and velvet, singing for San Francisco's diamond-decked elite. Today she trudged through a ruined city with barely more than the clothes on her back.

You are not the only one, she reminded herself. Everywhere she looked, people were toiling along with the blank, shocked faces of those who had lost everything. A mother with a little girl on her hip, the girl clutching her doll, the mother pushing a baby buggy piled high with clothes . . . A man with one leg, doing his best to navigate the rubble of the streets on crutches . . .

A drunk sitting on a crumbled wall outside a bar, swigging from a salvaged bottle of whiskey . . . An ancient Chinese matriarch supported by her grandsons, tottering on bound feet no bigger than Gemma's palm . . .

"Vee-vay-vah-vo-voooooohhh," sang Toscanini, imitating Gemma's morning vocalises.

"Oh, shut up," Gemma said, realizing she was weeping.

She'd decided to make for Golden Gate Park—the policemen were directing refugees there; they said the park had a camp set up with tents and cookstoves and soldiers keeping order—but somewhere around burned and desolate Union Square, Gemma wound down. Found herself sitting on a discarded trunk, dragged from who knew where and finally abandoned in flight, sitting and blankly staring at the burned shop opposite. A piano shop . . . She thought of George with a spasm of grief, looking at the burned shells of the instruments in the window, scorched piano keys grinning like blackened teeth.

"*Buongiorno*," a familiar voice said. "Micaëla, I forget your real name. What are you doing here?"

"I could ask the same, *signore*." Gemma blinked up at the great Caruso, hatless in the smoky morning light, his nightshirt stuffed into a pair of trousers, overcoat hanging off his shoulders. She was too weary to muster much surprise at the sight of him. "Where's the rest of the company?"

"Some here with me, we sleep here last night. Some at Jefferson Square, some at Golden Gate . . ." The tenor rubbed a hand over his dark hair. "When the hotel she evacuates, we scatter. The fires come through here in the early hours. My valet, he goes to find me a wagon now. I came back here, there was a trunk I thought I left behind . . ." He looked around at the wasteland of ashes, shrugging. "You, you were safe on Nob Hill I should think?"

Gemma ran a hand over her own hair, mirroring his gesture. So much of it had burned, coming away in great ashy handfuls last night when she tried to ease a comb through the crisped strands. She was lucky the fire hadn't scorched her scalp, but it was hard to feel lucky when she smelled the stink of burned hair and felt the singed ends of that waterfall of corn-blond hair now wisping dully around her ears. "No, I wasn't safe on Nob Hill."

"San Francisco . . ." Caruso sat on the other end of the trunk, beside Gemma. "'Ell of a place. I'll take Vesuvius."

"Vesuvius?"

"I am supposed to sing in Naples this spring, but I say no. Vesuvius, she is right next door and she is grumbling lately. I think I rather sing somewhere the earth doesn't erupt and throw fire into the sky, so I come to San Francisco instead."

Gemma managed a watery chuckle. Caruso laughed a belly laugh, looking at the ruin of Union Square. "I'll be glad to see home again. Italy, my wife, my boys . . ." He began humming the duet he and Gemma had sung two nights ago in *Carmen*, where the tenor yearns for home: "'*Ma mère, je la vois! Oui, je revois mon village*' . . . Come on," he scolded when Gemma failed to come in on Micaëla's entrance. "Why aren't you singing?"

"I can't." Her throat was too raw, and her heart was so heavy.

"You're a singer, aren't you? Or are you a performer?"

Gemma gazed at him, utterly exhausted. "What do you mean?"

"A performer does it for the spotlight." Caruso whipped a little notebook and a pencil out of his pocket and began sketching, apparently idly. "That *civetta* Fremstad, she is a performer—it is all *her*. *Her* voice, *her* spotlight, *her* stage. A great performer," he said, sounding pleased with himself for being fair. "But she does it for herself. A singer, now, they do it for the music.

Because they love it. You know I cry every time Don José stabs Carmen? Every time I think, *Bastardo*, let the poor woman live, she's not for you. Because the music, every time it fools me. I love being fooled. I love singing it, and always it is fresh to me." He kept sketching, and soon he was singing again. "'*Ma mère, je la vois! Je revois mon village*'—"

Gemma joined in. She couldn't *not* join in. "'*Ô souvenirs d'autrefois! Souvenirs du pays*' . . ." Oh, memories of bygone days, memories of home . . .

They finished the duet, and Caruso presented her with his sketch. A caricature, deftly done, of a dejected soprano slumped on a trunk. But with a spotlight on her still, highlighting her in her surroundings. Gemma smiled. "Not only have I sung with the great Caruso, I've been sketched by him."

"We sing together again someday, *carissima*. I think you make a 'ell of a Violetta. Ah—" Caruso bounced upright, stuffing the notebook back in his overcoat pocket. "My valet, I see him waving. Maybe he finds a wagon now. My trunks of things, I'm not leaving them behind. I leave this city, I never come back, that you can be sure. You come with me." Giving her a pat on the rump as she rose—some men never changed, even in a crisis. "However small the wagon, we find room for you and your birdcage!"

Gemma pushed the folded sketch into her pocket and followed him tiredly, cage in hand, pot in the other trailing its dejected, withered flowers. They fetched up not at Golden Gate Park or the Presidio, but some smaller square where a cluster of refugees gathered around some makeshift morning cookfires. She wasn't sure where exactly; the fires now raging north of here had erased every landmark, and there was nothing left but shattered streets and burned black shells of buildings. But a cluster of chorus singers from the Metropolitan were there, and

Gemma found herself greeted with hugs and exclamations. No more hostility toward the new soprano whose lover had bought her way into a starring role—that had been forgotten, given the disaster that had befallen them all. She asked after George, but no one had seen him.

Panic ensued as it became clear that the wagon procured by Caruso's valet would not hold them all and would have to make two trips to the ferry where, apparently, they could rejoin the rest of the company. "Send the wagon back and I'll take the second trip with the baggage," Gemma volunteered and ended up waving Caruso and the others on their way.

Someone passed Gemma a pried-open tin of sardines with a few fish left in the bottom. She slurped the can down to the last drop of oil, wiping off her chin afterward and looking around. A woman in an elaborate ruffled walking suit and high-heeled boots sat on the front step of a burned-out store, drinking water out of a makeshift paper cone and passing it on to a soot-covered street urchin. An upright piano on casters sat incongruously in the middle of the square, canted to one side over a crack in the street—who would try to drag a *piano* away from a raging fire? A woman in an ash-covered toque stumbled past, and Gemma thought for a moment it was the Flying Roller—that stupid woman in the train car who had bleated about how hellfire and earthquakes would swallow the Cesspit of the West if the sinners of San Francisco did not change their ungodly ways. *Not so stupid after all*, Gemma thought, but the ash-covered woman wandered down the street before she could tell if it was really the Flying Roller or not.

A man with a bloodied bandage around his head like a pirate offered Gemma a heel end of stale bread, and she swallowed it down, feeding the crumbs to Toscanini. The budgie was hopping cheerfully around his cage, chirping away. *You dim bird,* she thought. *Singing and singing, as if the world weren't burning down around your ears.*

Caruso's voice: *You're a singer, aren't you? Or are you a performer?*

The grimy street urchin was crying now. The woman in the frilly walking suit tried to embrace him, but he shoved her away. Gemma shifted the Queen of the Night's pot off her lap and went to the upright piano in the middle of the street, striking an exploratory chord. Horribly out of tune, of course. She upended a half-burned crate, sat down, and began the hymn that closed every church service in Red Hook, Nebraska. Even the wretched little services at the orphanage. "'Abide with me; fast falls the eventide; the darkness deepens; Lord with me abide . . .'" Singing steadily through all eight verses. She looked up at the last chord. The street urchin had his arms around his knees, watching her. So was the woman in the ruffles.

"Do you know any more?" the child asked.

So Gemma sang "All Things Bright and Beautiful" and then Handel's "I Know That My Redeemer Liveth," and the shepherd boy's song from *Tosca*. She sang the Countess's aria from Act II of *Figaro*, and "Amazing Grace," and "Home Never Was Nothin' Like This." Her throat was sore and her voice scratchy, but she didn't stop. Someone passed her a little water in a cone of paper, and as she drank it down she realized the square was filling up with more people, gathering silently around the piano. Her fingers, covered in glass cuts and soot, moved painfully over the soured piano keys, but she struck up Mozart's "Laudate Dominum," seeing a tear slip down the cheek of the man with the bandaged head. Maybe she was as dim as her bird, singing when the world was burning down around her ears, but she couldn't do anything else. She was a singer. So she sang.

"Gemma!" She was between verses of "I Am Thine, O Lord"

(the woman in the frilly dress had asked if she knew it; she was a good Nebraska church girl; of course she knew it) when she heard a deep voice shout her name. She barely had time to look around, mangling the hymn chords, when a man's hands lifted her almost bodily off the crate and swept her into a hug. She was crying and smiling before she even saw his face, because she knew those huge cast-iron hands anywhere, those hands that could span an eleventh on a keyboard without even trying, those hands that were now spanned across her back.

"*George*—" She hadn't seen him since the midnight ball before the earthquake, perfectly turned out in his dark suit with a gardenia in his buttonhole, and here he was big and disheveled in an ash-smeared shirt, scorch marks all over his forearms as if he'd walked through flying cinders. Gemma hugged him tight, throat gone thick. He was muttering in Spanish against her hair, and it was a while before he put her down and switched languages.

"I've been all over San Francisco trying to find you," he said, pushing a singed lock of hair out of her eyes. "Up and down Taylor Street, Hyde Street, Nob Hill—"

You came looking for me. Gemma's eyes filled, hearing it. *You came looking for me.* Just as she'd gone looking for him.

"—I went to the octagon house and it's a heap of ashes. I thought you might have gone off to safety with Thornton."

Thornton. Gemma's very bones juddered, as if lead had sluiced into her marrow. "He's gone," she said briefly. Gone into the smoke, and who knew where. "Good riddance to him." It was all she felt capable of saying right now.

George had gone to Golden Gate Park after his own street burned and took his rented room with it; he'd been helping to set up tents and carry stretchers and aided in beating out a few cook-fires before they could rage into more city-devouring maelstroms. "I was doing a sweep near the Palace Hotel in case you ended up there," he said. "And I heard you singing from nearly a block away."

Thornton was wrong, Gemma thought. *I was wrong.* All those hard-edged principles she'd been clutching as she rode into San Francisco, all those cynicisms of Thornton's she'd soaked up . . . It wasn't true, that the only person to ever rely on was yourself. It wasn't true, that friends would inevitably let you down. Hers certainly had not. Not today.

And maybe I didn't let them down, either, she thought, remembering her plunge into the burning octagon house after Reggie and Suling.

"I came looking for you, too," she told George now, softly.

His hands tightened. "Gem—"

"Hey, mister," the street urchin at Gemma's side complained. "Let her keep singing, why don't you?"

George grinned, teeth white in his soot-darkened face. He cocked his head at the piano, and Gemma made a *be my guest* wave of her hand. He flicked imaginary tails over the crate as he sat, flexing his fingers. "Any requests?" he asked the crowd, which was now six-deep around the out-of-tune piano.

Gemma was singing "There'll Be a Hot Time in the Old Town Tonight," the audience singing along on the chorus between fits of shaky laughter, when Caruso's cart finally came back to take her and the rest of the baggage to the ferry. Gemma collected her birdcage, smiling at the thank-yous coming from all sides. She had sung herself absolutely hoarse—a lifetime of safeguarding her voice and she had spent it all in one go. She couldn't think of a better thing to do with it. Much better than throwing it out for those oblivious millionaires in Thornton's ballroom two days ago. Not one of those pampered, well-fed guests had

had tears in his eyes like the man with the bandage round his head, who was now wringing her hand between his.

George handed her up into the cart, then climbed in himself after settling the birdcage and Alice's cutting. Gemma wondered how on earth she was going to keep the thing alive, but clutched the pot anyway. "You think you'll go back to New York?" George asked as the cart began jolting up the street. "After everyone assembles, wherever they are?"

"If that's what the company decides." She didn't really want to go back to New York, but it wasn't like she had much choice. "What about you?" Looking at him, thinking, *You came looking for me.*

"I don't have much more to my name than the clothes on my back." George picked her hand up and kissed it. "So New York sounds fine."

He tucked her against his burly shoulder, and Gemma leaned back against his solid warmth, relief and fear and exhaustion making a stone ball in her chest, Toscanini twittering and hopping in his cage. "You dim, sweet bird," she choked as the cart rolled on, as the fires roared and sent more billows of smoke skyward, as they left San Francisco behind.

Entr'acte

Chapter 26

September 1906
Tahoe region, California

Alice Eastwood had lost her taste for towns. Paved streets could crumple like paper; massive buildings could sway like reeds; all could come tumbling down as soon as the earth shrugged its shoulders. *You silly woman*, she scolded herself, *earthquakes happen in mountains and forests, too!* But she couldn't shake the unease that now filled her when she was surrounded by buildings, lampposts, walls. Arriving here in the Tahoe region, she'd drawn what felt like the first deep breath she'd pulled into her lungs since breathing out the last of San Francisco's smoke.

I've been invited as a guest to the summer camp recently opened by some old friends at Fallen Leaf Lake, she wrote to Reggie and Suling and Gemma, *and I am enjoying the mountain air.* She was hiking herself into near collapse every day, but she didn't mention that part. Her San Francisco friends had their own worries—Gemma in New York, singing in the Met chorus, supplementing with church singing where she could; Reggie and Suling in Oakland, struggling to settle the terrified, displaced cluster of Madam Ning's girls. Alice sent them pressed clips of gentian and pond lilies gathered on her treks, but she didn't write about the rest of it: setting off alone for Desolation Valley and not returning until shadows crawled tar-black over the snowbanks lingering on the higher slopes, gathering spiky red tendrils of snow plants with fingers gone numb and blue-dappled with cold, sitting on a boulder by Glen Alpine and trying to find a reason (any reason) to get up again. Up at five every morning, dawn just blushing the mountain air, to slip a robe over her bloomers and walk down to the lake where she'd plunge into the icy water and float there under the surface until her lungs nearly burst. The only place where, when she closed her eyes, she didn't see her office at the Academy and her life's work going up in flames.

I am quite carefree here was how Alice put it when she wrote to the others, *with no desire to return to San Francisco.* The second part at least was true.

It was a good fortnight since she'd last bothered going into town to collect her mail, so after her morning swim on the first day of September Alice coiled up her wet hair over the collar of her coat and made the trek in. Heading up the steps of the post office, she was nearly bowled over by a pair of boys chasing each other—"Stop that," yelled their sister from the nearest bench, glancing up from her book with an exasperated look.

"What are you reading?" Alice asked the girl, who looked about twelve.

"Not reading. Studying." The girl sighed. "They're supposed to be studying, too, while we wait for Mama"—she glared at the roughhousing boys—"but they won't."

"Don't let them copy your work later," Alice advised. "If they don't study, they don't deserve an easy way out. What's that, algebra? I used to like algebra when I was your age."

"Were you good at it, ma'am?"

"No. But I worked harder than anyone else at it. Several of the boys in my class claimed they'd beat me, and they were all better at it than I was, but I still pitched myself against them." Alice smiled at the memory. Smiling felt rusty. "It was a proud moment, succeeding where they'd failed."

"Mama says pride is a sin."

"Why? If you put in the work, don't you deserve to feel proud?"

The girl frowned, tugging at the ribbon on the end of her plait. "Mama says I shouldn't try to be too good at algebra. Nobody likes a bluestocking."

Alice wanted to smack her mama. Why did it have to be so hard for talented girls, trying to succeed at anything? Why? Young Alice Eastwood teaching school to make ends meet, trying to be accepted on botanical gathering expeditions, forcing that laugh when she was nearly swept over a waterfall in Colorado because if she'd shed a single tear they would have all said *That's what you get for taking a woman along.* Young Suling, now working for a seamstress in Oakland to pay rent for her and Reggie, those talented fingers wasted on cheap calico as she was paid half what a white seamstress would get. Golden-voiced Gemma, glassy-eyed from migraines, singing in a church choir to make ends meet. It wasn't enough for a woman to be talented, clever, or good. That wouldn't save her.

Alice nodded gruffly to the girl with the algebra book and went inside for her post. A whole bundle of letters; she sat down right there on the post office bench to read. Letters from Academy friends like Seth and Emily . . . An invitation to lead a botanical expedition to Yosemite for a group of eastern college girls looking for an adventure . . . A note from Suling; she had burned funeral offerings for Madam Ning at a temple in the Oakland Chinatown, burned more offerings for her uncle and cousins. She and Reggie were talking about heading east to look for better work. Reggie had enclosed a sketch of one of Madam Ning's girls, newly married to an Oakland shopkeeper . . .

That wasn't the only wedding, either—the letter with the New York postmark made Alice smile. *Darling Alice, you will now have to address your letters to Gemma Serrano! It was a very small wedding, but you will be pleased to know I pinned a dried Queen of the Night flower in my hair—my cutting has yet to bloom, but I pressed one of the flowers that opened in San Francisco between the pages of the "Flower Duet" in my Lakmé score . . .*

But the glow of Gemma's cheery letter disappeared when Alice opened the next envelope.

Many apologies for not writing sooner, Sergeant Clarkson scrawled in his downhill slant. Even his handwriting looked exhausted, Alice thought—San Francisco had burned for a full three days after the first earthquake tremors, and any policeman worth his badge had been worn to a nub these past few months dealing with the displaced, the wounded, the dead, the destruction. *But I have news now,* Clarkson went on. *As of this week, Mr. Henry Thornton is presumed dead. No body has been found, but many disappeared in the fires, and since he has not reappeared or otherwise contacted the authorities, his name has finally been added to the list of the deceased. The man's affairs are being settled by his lawyers with the intention of dispersing his assets to whatever family he may possess back East . . .*

Alice jammed the letter back into its envelope, lips suddenly dry. Thornton. She straightened her hat, bundling the packet of mail into her bag and making her way out of the post office. The girl with the workbook was still there on the bench outside, her brothers still ignoring her—Alice found herself pausing, looking down at the small figure poring over her algebra equations. "Don't just be good," she found herself saying slowly. "At your schoolwork or anything else. Be the best."

The girl looked up, blinking. "Why, ma'am?"

"Because life, despite what the Psalms tell us, is not about who is good." Alice pulled her coat closer around her neck, feeling cold. "It is about survival. The ones who survive are not necessarily good."

And Alice Eastwood didn't believe for one moment that Henry Thornton had not survived the San Francisco inferno.

Chapter 27

September 1908
Paris

It was not quite a year since they'd left New York with nothing more than their small hoard of savings and an offer from a madcap American heiress.

"Suling, you're wasted at Saks," the fabled and flamboyant Natalie Barney had declared as Suling knelt with a mouthful of pins, tacking the hem on the heiress's latest tea gown. "It's all very well sewing for an American department store, but you should come to Paris and look me up. I'm going back next week. I'll introduce you to any designer you like. Wouldn't you rather work for a Parisian fashion house where you can embroider your own creations?"

Paris was her dream. Paris and Callot Soeurs. And Paris was not just for herself, it was for Reggie. Suling wanted to put some distance—and a totally different life—between them and San Francisco. Oakland hadn't been far enough and as it turned out, neither had New York. Nightmares still plagued Reggie, who didn't cry out or flail around, but in the morning the sheets would be damp from cooling sweat and Suling would wake up to see Reggie staring out the window, dark circles under her eyes.

By the time Suling finished stitching up the hem of Natalie's new tea gown, she'd made up her mind that she and Reggie would get on a ship to France. And with the address of Natalie Barney's Parisian home in her hand, she'd make sure the American heiress followed through on that offer.

A few months later, Natalie Barney leading the way, Suling walked through the front door of Callot Soeurs, where Natalie

sashayed into Marie Callot's office. One look at Suling's portfolio of embroidery, and after gasping over the dragon robe, the
eldest Callot sister had hired Suling on the spot.

NATALIE'S FRIENDS, MOSTLY writers and artists, helped make
Paris feel—if not yet home—a place where they were welcome.
The French in general regarded Suling with some curiosity and a
near-total lack of hostility. Here she was just another foreigner,
noteworthy mostly for her Asian features and her American accent as she worked to learn French.

Even after a year in Paris, every time Suling opened the door
to their apartment, the sight of the room still sent a small shiver
of delight through her. Because it was their home. Hers and Reggie's. The tall windows, skylight, and secondhand furniture. A
large single room on the top floor of the house that was kitchen,
living quarters, and studio; the bedroom simply a bed and armoire hidden behind a tall folding screen. Reggie had painted
scenes of San Francisco's Chinatown on the screen's panels. And
on a table, away from bright sunlight, their Queen of the Night
cutting grew in a stoneware pot.

Their Montmartre neighborhood and its residents were now
comfortable and familiar, the lodgings were cheap, the cafés
affordable, and the residents accustomed to living with eccen-
tric artists in their midst. Some of their acquaintances thought
she and Reggie lived together for reasons of economy. Those
who knew better didn't even raise an eyebrow. There were many
such relationships within their bohemian community. Some
days Suling felt as though her life were a dream, one where she
worked surrounded by beautiful fabrics and designs, the finest
threads and sequins, every idea she proposed, from silk flowers
to beaded scarves, given serious consideration.

Reggie was another matter. She seemed to have lost interest

in serious work; she dashed off little watercolor sketches of Parisian street scenes and monuments, which a friend sold at a stall beside the Seine. Reggie considered these mere trifles for the tourist trade and never bothered signing them.

"Nothing to show, nothing to sell," Reggie often said, gesturing at half-finished canvases stacked in the corners of their apartment. She always claimed she was too busy or had not yet settled on a new direction for her art. Her most lucrative commission had been one for the Moulin Rouge, a series of posters for a new show called *Rêve Amoureuse*. But it was teaching that brought in the steadiest income.

"In my wildest dreams," Reggie said, "I never imagined teaching Americans in Paris how to paint. Most of them aren't that serious about art. They're more interested in the bohemian life. They sign up for my classes because afterward I take them to cafés where they drink wine and look soulful."

It was a rainy day in autumn when Suling came home to Reggie waving an envelope. She held it aloft tantalizingly while they kissed. "Is it from Alice?" Suling asked, recognizing the stationery.

"Yes, I've been waiting for you to come home before opening it," Reggie said. "Do you want to read it now? Or maybe a little later?" She murmured these last words in Suling's ear before her lips moved down Suling's neck, making it clear what "a little later" might mean.

Later, much later, lying in a haze of happiness and a tangle of sheets, Suling curled beside Reggie. She never tired of tracing a finger over Reggie's body, her thighs, her hips and ribs. On that first night in Oakland when they'd finally found a room of their own, after the fire, after they'd found Madam Ning's girls, Suling had held back her tears over Reggie's emaciated body, her breasts flat, rib cage jutting out, skin so pale Suling could see the trace of blue veins. And now, two years later, Reggie was gloriously voluptuous, her body lightly tanned from an afternoon in August, a picnic at a country estate. Some of their friends had run into the lake, laughing and naked. Reggie had dived right in, of course, legs lean and muscled from walking up and down the hilly streets of Montmartre.

Now one tanned hand held up Alice's letter so they could both read it while lying against the pillows. "Alice seems a bit downcast about the Academy being so slow to build a new facility," Reggie said, "but it sounds like she's enjoying her time in the field."

"Alice loves climbing rocks and wading into lakes," Suling said. "She prefers it to sitting at a desk, so I'm not sure she's that sorry the Academy doesn't have a plan yet for the new location. And she wants to know how our Queen of the Night plant is doing. I swear it matters more to her than we do." But her voice was fond, amused.

"Good news," Reggie exclaimed, reading ahead. "Gemma was offered a role in Buenos Aires, at the new opera house there. The Teatro Colón. I'm sure we'll hear more when we get her next letter." They knew Gemma was hoping for better roles than the small parts she'd been singing in New York. "And Clarkson, goodness!" Reggie said, reading ahead. "Clarkson has quit the San Francisco police and joined the Pinkertons."

"He's doing it because he's never been convinced that Thornton is dead," Suling said. "The police have closed the book on Thornton, but the Pinkertons might let Clarkson keep looking." She immediately regretted her words. Any mention of Thornton and Reggie tensed. Suling knew there was a good chance that Reggie would suffer bad dreams that night.

"Reggie, I think I'd like to have dinner at the café tonight,"

Suling said. With any luck, they'd run into friends and there would be conversation and laughter, something to make Reggie forget the asylum and the man who'd put her there.

Her lover forced a smile, lips tight. "Maybe tomorrow night? I've already started preparing dinner."

But was she also avoiding the past? Suling thought, watching Reggie move around in their tiny kitchen. Was the only difference between them the fact that Reggie still struggled to find direction while she, Suling, had a wonderful, interesting job? No, not a job. A career. A career that helped keep her own nightmares at bay. If not for Callot Soeurs, would she be as haunted as Reggie? Once, just once, Reggie had confided that images from that horrible time invaded her mind at unexpected and uncontrollable moments. Of a drug-soaked cloth being held against her nose and mouth until she blacked out. Of pounding against a heavy door, screaming that she wasn't supposed to be locked in here and realizing no one was coming for her.

Suling had firmly pushed away her own nightmares. Initially, while they were in Oakland, while she was helping Madam Ning's girls move into new lodgings, Suling had experienced dreams so vivid she thought she was back again at St. Christina's, desperate to find Reggie. Dreams of a gunshot and Auntie sinking to the marble floor, Auntie lying on the grass, blood soaking through her beautiful jacket.

And Gemma. Did she have dreams where she ran down an endless circular staircase, all the while knowing she would meet Thornton at the bottom? Did she wake at night gasping for air as when she'd dragged them out of the burning building?

It was hard to imagine Alice, sensible and fearless Alice, allowing the past to overwhelm her. Suling would never be rude enough to ask, but she did wonder. Did Alice wake up suddenly, her arms around an imaginary porcelain pot, carrying her precious Queen of the Night through corridors filled with smoke?

What about the victims of the New York Hotel fire and their families? The dead Pinkerton, they learned, had married only the year before Thornton killed him. What had become of Langford's young widow, their baby girl?

How many broken lives had Thornton left behind?

Chapter 28

July 1910
Buenos Aires

Gemma set down Toscanini's birdcage and turned a slow circle on the sun-drenched terrace, shading her eyes against the riot of blue sky and brilliant blooming bougainvillea climbing the walls. "George, please tell me again that we can afford this."

"We can afford it," he called from inside. Their bags were littered everywhere, their furniture was still on a cart rumbling its way from their old two-room apartment on the other side of town, but the piano was here and he'd already sat down and thrown back the lid. "You're signed to sing *Tosca* this fall, and the Countess after that. The conductor at the Teatro Colón worships the ground you walk on. Quit worrying, *corazón*."

And what if I get a migraine on opening night of Tosca *and ruin everything?* Gemma couldn't help thinking, but pushed the worry away. It was a beautiful day, George was rippling out a Granados fandango, and Toscanini was already fluffing his feathers and cheeping inside his cage. There was no point borrowing trouble, so Gemma moved to the dusty terrace table, already imagining the dinners she and George would eat out here on warm nights. Glass tumblers of malbec and plates of *matambre arrollados*, blood-rare flank steak rolled around sweet peppers and hard-boiled eggs, the sound of Spanish drifting up from the street below . . .

"There you go," she told the potted Queen of the Night plant, setting it down and fluffing its leaves. It had barely survived its first year, Alice's fragile cutting drooping on the windowsill of their rented New York apartment, and Gemma had fussed over it with a care she refused to call superstitious. But it had finally produced its first bloom on an absolutely fetid late summer night, that extraordinary fragrance drowning out the smell of garbage and horse manure from the streets below. And not long afterward, she'd gotten the offer that brought them to South America: the offer to fill in for a Queen of the Night who'd unexpectedly flounced out of a Buenos Aires *Zauberflöte*.

Gemma still thought Caruso might have had a hand in that. Had he dropped a word in someone's ear, somewhere on tour after the earthquake? If he had, she'd owe him forever for opening that door: the conductor at the Teatro Colón adored both her golden voice and her golden hair (she had to swat him off a few times, but he took it with good humor), and the company appreciated the easy Argentinian-accented Spanish Gemma had picked up from George by then. "Most of the sopranos we get from America can't even be bothered to say thank you, much less learn how to say it in Spanish," Gemma's dresser had snorted, pinning the Queen of the Night's starry crown into her hair. "Those rude bitches!"

And now Gemma had a contract here, a good one. Whether it was a whisper from Caruso or Alice's cutting finally blooming that brought the stroke of luck, Gemma would seize her good fortune with both hands. She had starring roles at last, she had a sun-drenched apartment with a terrace to share with the best man in the world, and she didn't have to supplement the month's income by singing hymns in a church choir in Queens.

"Are you rehearsing tonight with those wind players you met during the *Zauberflöte* rehearsals?" she asked George, giving the Queen of the Night's pot a final pat and coming in off the terrace. Half the apartment's main room was taken up by the grand piano, but neither of them would have it any other way. "What was it they wanted you to fill in for?"

"K. 452. The Mozart quintet in E-flat Major, for piano and winds." George's hands wandered briefly from Granados's fandango into Mozart's Larghetto as he grinned up at her. He never seemed to worry about work, but somehow he always found it. He'd wander in behind Gemma when she arrived at a new production, and ten minutes later be filling in for the rehearsal pianist or running recitatives at the harpsichord in the pit, after which he'd inevitably be new best friends with the second violinist, who would invite him to join a local chamber group. He'd play Mozart and Brahms for three months in a small ensemble, wearing concert dress, then spend the next month playing ragtime in bars in his shirtsleeves. "And I already have an offer from the café across the street," he added. "I got to talking with the owner, and he asked if I'd play on tango night—"

"You are too good to be playing in cafés," Gemma scolded, winding her arms around his neck from behind.

"But I like playing in cafés. I don't have to wear a damned tie . . ." He spun around on the piano stool, his big hands sliding around her waist. She lowered her head and kissed him, long and leisurely. The first time they'd kissed had been as they got off the train from San Francisco at the station in New York: filthy, exhausted, still smoke-grimed, Gemma knowing she stank of burned hair. She'd kissed him anyway, surprising herself, and his fingertips had rippled up and down her spine like a piano's keys, melting her against him as she thought, *Home*.

My job in San Francisco burned up along with the Grand Opera House, he'd said back then, shrugging, making light of his decision to stay in New York—but it had been no small thing to Gemma. Singing in the Met chorus, early for every rehearsal, keeping her head down because she knew this was her last chance, her absolute *last*—George had been there for all of it, making her laugh with his stories. His first job playing piano at fifteen, in what he'd assumed was a seedy Buenos Aires lounge and which turned out to be a whorehouse; of playing his way to San Francisco on a luxury liner where the richest of the passengers tipped him in dinner rolls. Falling in love with George had been so simple; deciding to marry him had been the easiest decision in the world.

"I thought we'd invite your mother to lunch here tomorrow," Gemma said, breaking the kiss. "We won't be anywhere near unpacked, but she'll enjoy scolding us. And I'll make *medialunas* from her recipe." George had fretted the way only an Argentinian son with a widowed mother could fret, introducing Gemma to his mother shortly after arriving in Buenos Aires, but Gemma had never worried. *Mothers love me*, she told George, and when she unpacked the wholesome farm girl from deep inside and begged in Spanish for an apron to help in the kitchen, the woman had melted. "In the meantime, have you seen my *Tosca* score? I want to work more *snarl* into the back-and-forth with Scarpia in Act II—"

"You can take a day to unpack, *corazón*. Even two."

"No, I'm going to be sublimely prepared for that first *Tosca* rehearsal. They will never have another soprano as prepared as me." Because the migraines would hit during the performance run, Gemma knew, and there would be times she'd have to cancel at the last moment, and you needed to build up a lot of goodwill in advance for something like that.

The migraines aren't better since you left San Francisco, the thought whispered, insidious. *They're worse.* But she pushed that aside, too, because what could you do? All you could do, living with pain, was *live* with it, as best you could. "We'll have to write our friends," she said, moving a box of George's sheet music off the piano. "Tell them we've changed addresses—"

"I picked up a batch of mail at the old apartment before handing in the key," George said, turning back to the piano and lilting out some more Granados. "In my jacket—"

Gemma dug through his coat pockets and turned up a clutch of battered envelopes. Paris postmarks *and* American postmarks, she was delighted to see.

"Suling is now a senior embroideress at Callot Soeurs," Gemma read aloud, wandering back out toward the terrace as she read. "Reggie has all kinds of rude things to say about tourists in Paris. I wonder if she's showing her work anywhere; she never answers when I ask." Suling had enclosed an embroidered bookmark for Gemma to mark her scores, a beautiful strip of silk embroidered with scarlet blooms from the ceibo trees Gemma saw in the city parks here, but Reggie hadn't included one of her funny little sketches. In fact, she hadn't done that in quite a while. Gemma frowned, moving on to Alice Eastwood's letter. "Alice's eyes are bothering her . . . She's traveling on the East Coast now, working at various herbariums, thinking about traveling to Europe. She wants to see if the English *Wellingtonia* is the same as the *Sequoia gigantea*—"

"What's a *Sequoia gigantea*?" George asked, fingers tripping into a tango.

"Don't ask unless you want Alice to send you an annotated copy of *Hand Book of the Trees of California*. I can tell Alice misses California, I wonder why she doesn't go back." Gemma turned Alice's letter over to the next page. "She said Clarkson is finally with the Pinkertons in New York now." Making inquiries about Thornton, though Gemma didn't say it aloud. She didn't want that name in this brand-new sunny space, this brand-new sunny home.

Just be dead, she begged silently, folding up the letters. *Just let Thornton be dead.* She knew Suling wanted justice for Madam Ning, she knew Reggie wouldn't believe in Thornton's death unless she saw a body, she knew Alice didn't believe in it, either, because a scientist needed empirical evidence, but Gemma was willing to deal in hope. Hope that he was dead, that he would never trouble them again, that they could all just . . .

Move on.

THEY GOT ONE more year.

One year before Alice Eastwood went to London and, after a tour of Kew Gardens, saw an abandoned newspaper folded open to the society column, where two words caught her eye.

Phoenix Crown.

Two words to spark a flurry of telegrams across oceans and continents. Two words to spark frenzied plans, hasty boat tickets, memory-fueled nightmares.

Two words to spur everyone in a single, streaking drive toward Paris.

Act II

Chapter 29

"*Vin rouge*," Gemma told the hovering waiter. She had been sipping ink-black French coffee while she waited for the others, but something stronger seemed called for now that they had all arrived, considering the discussion ahead of them.

No one, however, seemed eager to begin. They sat there, a silent quartet of women on a busy Paris street—late-afternoon sun slanting in dusty summer rays, striped awning flapping overhead, the hoot of French traffic and the rapid babble of French voices flowing past like a busy river. Alice's telegram from London sat in the middle of the café table, and for a moment they all just stared at it.

Gemma finally took the plunge, pearls swinging in her ears as she turned toward Alice. "You look marvelous, Alice. Like no time has passed at all." A few more threads of gray in the botanist's hair, perhaps, but otherwise she was exactly the same from her neat pompadour to her crisp shirtwaist to the lens around her neck. "And all your botanical globe-trotting lately! Are you looking forward to taking up your old position at the California Academy?"

Alice's smile disappeared. "I haven't formally been offered the position yet," she said briefly. "And going back to settle in San Francisco . . . I'm not sure I can make myself do it."

Suling blinked. Reggie cleared her throat. *So much for small talk*, Gemma thought. Alice looked away, clearly uncomfortable, so Gemma turned to Suling this time. "You're looking so elegant, Suling. Paris clearly agrees with you."

Suling nodded her sleek black head. There was nothing of the silent San Francisco seamstress with her girlish plait and buttoned tunic here: the self-assured young woman across the table had glided up to the café in the tiny fluid steps demanded by the most fashionable of hobble skirts, her glossy hair was shingled to outrageous shortness, and her lightweight summer coat was turquoise silk exquisitely embroidered with almond blossoms. But the minutely examining gaze she turned on Gemma was so very Suling, scrutinizing every stitch of Gemma's black-and-white-striped walking suit, the cameo at her throat, her enormous black straw hat with its striped taffeta bow.

"Very fashionable," Suling approved. "Buenos Aires is clearly no more than six months behind Paris. Hobble skirts will be hitting your shores any day now."

"Look out, Buenos Aires." The bright social smile Gemma had pasted into place turned more real when Suling's assessing black eyes shifted to Alice. *I know just what you're going to say . . .*

"Alice, that *hat*," Suling said with dismay. *Knew it*, thought Gemma. "It's the same one you had in San Francisco, and even then you said it was ten years old."

"What's wrong with it?" Alice plucked off her flat pancake of a hat. "You sent me a hat last Christmas for fancy occasions. This is my everyday hat."

"It's dreadful, Alice," Gemma agreed. "Let Suling do whatever she wants to it."

"I was bringing these in for Madam Lydig's latest opera gown . . ." Rummaging in her handbag, Suling produced a tiny sewing kit and a handful of beaded silk flowers. "But this is just too dire to let stand." Alice's hat was whisked into Suling's lap, and soon a silver needle was flashing. Gemma felt herself exhaling. That uneasy, fragile silence that hovered over the table was ebbing away.

"She's never happy unless she's stitching something." Reggie flung a careless, bony arm across the back of Suling's chair, grinning with pride. No hobble skirt for Reggie—Gemma's oldest friend wore a man's trousers and waistcoat like a bohemian, her dark head bare to the summer sun, a red scarf about her neck, her collar bordered with embroidered red poppies that were unmistakably Suling's work. "She may not be the head embroideress at the atelier, not yet, but half the traffic at the rue Taitbout is there for her needle. Not to mention that Paul Poiret himself is trying to poach her for his own atelier."

"Quit bragging," Suling scolded, sounding very wifely.

"Yes, *bao bei.*" Reggie dropped a kiss on her knuckles, quite openly, and no one at the café seemed even to notice. The French, Gemma knew, were far more blasé about this sort of thing than Americans. Or perhaps people were simply blind. Men who made lives together had to be much more careful how they conducted themselves, but if two women made a home together, why, everyone knew it was only for reasons of safety and economy. Women could break a great many rules as long as they did so *quietly. And thank goodness*, Gemma reflected.

"You look like Marcello in *La Bohème*," she told Reggie now, reaching across the table and giving her tanned fingers a squeeze. "In Paris at last, the way you always dreamed! Your letters haven't mentioned any showings; what have you been painting?"

Reggie's smile disappeared. "This and that," she said briefly. Gemma would have pressed further, but the waiter arrived with a carafe of red wine. There was a bit of fussing until they could get rid of him; then Reggie downed half her wine at a gulp,

Suling continued to whip stitches into the band of Alice's hat, and Alice rotated her wine stem between ink-stained fingers. How very far they'd come, Gemma thought, from the fire-singed and exhausted quartet sitting in a dark San Francisco bedroom, watching one of the rarest flowers in the world open its white petals.

"Oh dear," she heard herself sighing. "This isn't how I envisioned the four of us meeting again."

"We meant to catch up with you in New York." Suling's eyes flickered. "But somehow the timing was never right . . ."

"I somehow missed seeing any of you when I first came to Europe, too . . ." Alice's voice trailed off in a very un-Alice-like way, and they were all staring into their wine again.

I didn't mean to lose you all after San Francisco, Gemma almost said. But life had a way of happening, and before you knew it five years had passed and in place of the most important friendships in your life, all you had was a handful of letters where the four of you talked too brightly of your new lives and never, ever mentioned the thing that had sent you scattering in all directions in the first place. *I wrote to tell you three about the good things,* Gemma thought. *My wedding; the fourteen curtain calls I got on opening night* of Tosca *at the Teatro Colón—but did I write about any of the bad?* Like the fact that her migraines were more frequent than ever, and she now missed about one performance in fifteen? No, she had not. She'd simply pretended the bad things weren't there.

Maybe they were all doing that. Alice's reluctance to return to San Francisco when her letters were always so cheerful; Reggie's reticence about her painting when all her scribbled correspondence was full of art world gossip . . .

"Oh, for heaven's sake," Alice said at last. "Maybe this isn't how I hoped to meet the three of you again, either. This certainly isn't how I planned to see Paris—I always swore the first thing I'd do in this city was visit the Jardin des Plantes and investigate the varieties of evening primrose, to see if the edges of the petals are rounded or emarginate. Instead, I'm scrambling to bring a murderer to justice." Alice rummaged in her handbag and slapped a worn-out news clipping down on top of her own telegram in the middle of the table. "Ladies, let's quit dawdling and address the elephant in the room. The elephant named *Thornton*."

A brief silence as they passed the society column around. The one Alice had spotted in London.

"It doesn't say the name *Thornton*." Gemma pushed the clipping away with a black-gloved fingertip. "The name here is William van Doren."

That name meant nothing to her, but the rest of the breathless write-up did: New York millionaire traveling in Paris, having recently gifted his fiancée with a phoenix crown of blue-and-white jade, fifty-seven sapphires, four thousand pearls, butterflies fashioned out of kingfisher feathers, and carved Queen of the Night flowers. *That* meant something to all of them. What man would own that crown except . . .

"Clarkson looks for Thornton for five years and doesn't find a whisper, and Alice stumbles over him in a gossip column." Reggie shook her head. "I'd laugh if it were funny."

"Michael wants to know how we can be sure van Doren and Thornton are one and the same," Alice said. "We exchanged a positive flurry of telegrams. Without proof, he said he can't involve the gendarmes—"

"It's the same man." Suling raised her dark eyes at last from the hat. "Two days ago, I took a stack of dress boxes to the Ritz for a delivery, and I managed to loiter in the hotel court drinking tea for half a morning. He passed right by me, nearly close enough to touch. Thornton is in Paris."

Reggie looked at her, outraged. "You didn't tell me!"

"Because you'd have insisted on coming along, and I wasn't going to risk that. He knows your face, Reggie, but I was just a Chinee sewing girl to him; he never really paid attention to me, and he certainly never saw me in that crowded court at the Ritz. Afterward, when I asked the desk clerk who it was, he confirmed it: Mr. William van Doren."

"How did you know he was staying at the Ritz?" Alice asked.

"Some American ladies were having costumes made at Callot Soeurs for Paul Poiret's Oriental Ball in Versailles tomorrow night." Suling held up Alice's hat, examining it. "They gossiped during their fitting about the van Doren party that's staying at their hotel, the Ritz. All I had to do was volunteer to make the delivery of their costumes and sit discreetly behind a potted palm."

"It really was him?" Gemma said, low-voiced.

Suling's eyes met hers. "Yes."

Another silence fell. Gemma knew they were all imagining the same thing: the almost-homely, always-charming face of the man who had tried to burn them all alive.

"I wonder if *van Doren* is his real name, or another nom de plume," Alice mused.

"I think it must be his real name." Gemma rummaged for some clippings of her own. "Before I sailed from Buenos Aires, I went looking in the New York society pages—"

"You can get those in Buenos Aires?"

"Of course; you know how many wealthy expatriates there are in Argentina? I found a gushy write-up of his engagement: 'William van Doren of the New York van Dorens, replenishing the straitened family finances after spending a decade in Europe.'" Laying the clipping down. "Refurbishing the family home around the corner from Astor House on Fifth Avenue, planning a summer cottage in Newport as a gift to his bride— there were so many details. Whoever wrote it knew a great deal about the pedigrees and lives of the elite New York families." Gemma took hold of her wineglass, feeling her fingers tighten around the stem. "But they didn't know that William van Doren left New York for San Francisco, not Europe. That he took a different name to make his fortune as far from home as possible, then came home to take it all up again."

"But if anyone saw a photograph of him from his San Francisco days—"

"He was very careful about that." Reggie's voice was flat. "He never had his photograph taken. I used to wonder why."

"He certainly looks well now." Suling's needle paused for a moment in its rhythmic flash. "Healthy. Laughing. A whole party of gentlemen and ladies scurrying after him, pretty fiancée on his arm, an expensive automobile waiting . . ."

Very nearly in unison, the four women raised their glasses of rough red table wine and took long swallows.

"We cannot confront him," Alice said at last. "I don't know what any of you have been thinking, but we *cannot*."

Suling shivered, visibly. Reggie crossed her arms across her waistcoat as though she were cold. Gemma made a face. "For heaven's sake, I don't *want* to confront him." The thought made her skin crawl. "I don't ever want to see him again, unless it's in a courtroom on trial for the murder of Madam Ning and that Pinkerton detective."

"Not that anyone will care he murdered a Chinese brothel owner," Suling muttered. "They'll all focus on the Pinkerton." She looked brittle suddenly behind her fashionable facade, and

Gemma wanted to reach across the table and touch her hand. But Suling didn't look like she'd welcome it, her dark eyes suspiciously shiny. *Perhaps you have a few cracks, too, under all that gloss of elegance,* Gemma thought with a twinge.

"Michael Clarkson thinks there is a chance the man can be brought to trial," Alice said. "If things are done properly. We've confirmed van Doren is Thornton; all well and good. We keep our distance until Clarkson arrives in Paris—he's a Pinkerton detective himself now; he can involve the authorities and the police here for a proper arrest."

Reggie looked dubious. "Men like Thornton buy police. And trials."

"And how long will it take for Clarkson to get here?" Gemma asked, as Reggie signaled for another carafe of wine. "If Thornton and his party move on from Paris—"

"They intend to stay through the end of July," Suling said. "If Clarkson is already on his way—"

"He is; he cabled nearly a week ago that he was sailing from New York," Alice said. "He arrives tomorrow morning."

"—then there should be plenty of time since the van Doren party is in Paris through July."

Gemma blinked. "How do you know that?"

"Gossipy American ladies again." Suling sipped her wine. "Poiret is making the trousseau for Thornton's fiancée, but it's taking so long, they've all decided to stay in Paris another few months."

"I wonder . . ." Gemma realized her fingers were drumming nervously and stilled them. "Do you think he believes we're all dead? We haven't exactly tried to lead quiet lives these past five years. We haven't heard hide nor hair of him until now; all Clarkson's inquiries were about a man named Thornton, and we never heard a whisper of him. But has he had any whisper of our survival?"

"He never knew my real name," Suling said, plucking a loose thread off her turquoise silk sleeve. "So he'd only know me if he saw me—*maybe*—and he hasn't seen me."

"He never knew I was in the conservatory that day at all," Alice said. "So if he's been collecting rare botanicals again in the last five years and came across my name, well, he wouldn't blink at it. And you perform under your married name now, don't you, Gemma?"

Thank God, Gemma thought. "For nearly five years, and mostly in Buenos Aires. But what if he's seen one of Reggie's paintings? He has such a good eye; he'd know her style."

A long look between Reggie and Suling. Reggie seemed to shrink, as Suling said briefly, "She hasn't painted seriously since San Francisco."

They all let that lie, painfully, where it had fallen. "I think we can at least be sure Thornton doesn't know we're seeking him," Alice said, clearly realizing Reggie wouldn't welcome questions. "So—"

"So we wait for Clarkson," Gemma finished as the new carafe arrived, "and Clarkson has until the end of July to initiate a proper arrest."

They sat sipping their wine, deflation hovering in the air along with the white dust of a Paris summer. *That's all?* Gemma knew the others were thinking. A slim hope of an arrest, against the man who had left them all to die in the heart of San Francisco's fires, and who could buy judges the way children bought lemon drops?

Reggie spoke, for the first time. "What about his fiancée?"

"Let's see—" Gemma rifled through her collection of news

clippings. "Viennese nobility. She's come to Paris for her trousseau, of course. Her father is Baron August Friedrich Arenburg von Loxen—who knows if I've got the title right, but he used to be a field marshal for Emperor Franz Josef. One of those ramrod-straight old soldiers with a dueling scar. Supposedly he dabbles in chinoiserie and antiques—"

"That must be how he met Thornton," Suling mused.

"That's the father," Reggie said sharply. "What about the daughter? Thornton's future wife?"

"Miss Cecilia Arenburg von Loxen," Gemma read. "Or maybe it's 'Lady,' I don't know. Eighteen, educated in Switzerland, speaks perfect English, so she'll do well in New York."

Suling tied off one last thread and held up Alice's flat black hat, which now sported a scattering of exquisitely beaded silk flowers across the band. "There you go, Alice. Much improved."

"So now I suppose we're in a waiting game," Gemma said, as Alice took the hat back and turned it over with a pleased smile. "When Clarkson arrives, do we—"

That was when Reggie shoved back her chair with a clatter and stormed away from the café without another word.

Chapter 30

Suling jumped up and followed Reggie, who was heading for the metro station. Suling knew the signs of Reggie's distress as well as she knew her own heartbeat: the slight tremble in Reggie's hands, the slump of her shoulders, as though trying to make herself less conspicuous, and worst of all, the way those green eyes lost their light. Everyone else may have just seen Reggie striding away in a bad temper, but only Suling could tell there was more to it.

"I know, I know," Reggie said, when Suling caught up to her. "I'm behaving abominably." Her cheeks were flushed almost as red as her scarf, a sure sign of her embarrassment.

"They understand," Suling said, "and so do I."

"I hate hearing his name," Reggie said, taking Suling's hand and tucking it in the crook of her arm. "I'd rather stay ignorant of his existence."

"We both know better, dearest love," Suling said. "It may be more comfortable not hearing anything of him, but if he's alive, we won't feel safe until he's gone to trial for murder."

For the murder of Madam Ning. For the murder of the young Pinkerton detective. Suling unconsciously touched the jade ring that hung on a gold chain around her neck. Both had belonged to her auntie. They replaced the ring Reggie had given her, the ring she now wore on her finger instead of on a red silk cord.

The flower vendor at the entrance to the Simplon metro station smilingly held up a small bouquet but Suling shook her head. They often bought from this young woman, but not today. In the underground passage to the subway, the busker with an accordion was playing a passable rendition of the "Radetzky

March." When his music was lively, Reggie and Suling often danced in front of him before dropping a few *centimes* in his hat, but today Reggie just handed him a coin and they hurried along to the platform. Neither spoke a word on the ride home to the Barbès–Rochechouart metro station. From there it was a short walk to their apartment on the rue Cazotte.

Their home.

SULING WONDERED WHEN it would *truly* feel like home. *But of course it's our home*, she scolded herself. The studio apartment was becoming known in their little circle of artists and writers, every gathering filled with good conversation and laughter, and more often than not, Chinese food. Sometimes the dinners made Suling miss her mother's cooking and the wonderful variety of food that Chinatown offered. But she'd been so busy learning French, so busy getting to know Paris, so busy with her new career that she never thought of the *missing* as homesickness. Not until the day Marie Callot told her about an antiques store called La Pagode.

"So many exquisite porcelains and beautiful furniture," Marie had told Suling, "and the owner is from Shanghai, a Monsieur Louis Deng, such a pleasant man. His antiques were quite inspiring, they've given me some new design ideas. I'd like you to take a look, Suling, and tell me what you think."

The moment she stepped inside La Pagode, a tidal wave of memory washed over Suling. It wasn't the fine inlaid furniture or carved jades that made her think of San Francisco; it was the scent in the air. She breathed in rose and sandalwood-infused incense, the same kind Madam Ning had used at the Palace of Endless Joy.

And suddenly she missed the gregarious, messy community of San Francisco's Chinatown. She had often wished her neighbors there weren't so inquisitive, that they'd mind their own business and let her keep to herself. She now understood the kindness behind such apparent nosiness, the mutual care and protectiveness that allowed the Chinese community to live in relative safety. In Paris, in spite of Reggie, in spite of their lively dinner parties and the many friends in their circle, Suling realized she was lonely in ways she hadn't believed possible.

She missed the quicksilver laughter of children watching acrobats at New Year's, the talkative neighbors who handed out nuggets of gossip about people and families she'd known all her life. She missed the marine smell of San Francisco Bay on a muggy afternoon. The mouthwatering fragrance of roast pork and garlic in hot oil, incense smoke wafting out from temples. She missed the loud, insistent calls of street vendors. How could Paris give her all that? Barely three hundred Chinese lived in France. There was only one store out by the Gare de Lyon where she could buy Chinese herbs and cooking ingredients.

This wasn't simply a matter of missing the food of her childhood; it was a yearning so strong it nearly buckled her knees. She wanted to weep.

"Is that rose-scented incense?" she had asked La Pagode's proprietor. After nearly an hour of conversation reminiscing about the foods they loved, Louis Deng introduced her to his son and niece, Theo and Pauline. Then he gave her an earthenware jar of pickled mustard greens and a bundle of incense sticks. She went home and burned incense for her auntie. Then for Third Uncle, the cousins she'd never met, and for Old Kow. Perhaps they'd survived the earthquake, but it didn't hurt to make offerings to the gods for their well-being, either in this world or the next.

At least she knew Madam Ning's girls were thriving. Two had returned to China with their share of Madam Ning's savings.

Four had married, their age and beauty—and money—making them highly desirable. Butterfly and Hyacinth were running a boardinghouse at the edge of Oakland's Chinatown.

In return for the antique store owner's kindness, Suling had made him a bouquet of silk magnolias. She braised a side of pork belly with the pickled mustard greens he'd given her and laughed at the expression on Reggie's face upon taking her first delicious, unctuous mouthful.

Reggie then asked Suling to teach her how to cook Chinese food; now she could prepare a few simple dishes. "You're not Amah Chung," Suling said, teasing Reggie, "but it's nice coming home to shrimp sauteed with green peas. Even if you don't use enough ginger."

"I know you miss San Francisco," Reggie said, "and if I can't paint, I may as well cook for you. With enough practice, perhaps I could open a Chinese diner in Paris." It broke Suling's heart to hear those words, even if spoken in jest. Without her art, Reggie was drifting. Suling often worried that Reggie might feel dispirited by the contrast between their career trajectories.

Suling was a senior embroideress at Callot Soeurs, and now, Paul Poiret was trying to hire her away. His fashions often featured simple draped fabrics decorated with lavish embroidery. Inspired, he claimed, by the Orient. He had even invited her to his costume party, so confident had he been that the position he was offering—head of the Poiret embroidery studio—would prove irresistible. That, and his use of Oriental design elements.

"What he calls 'Oriental' is Arabic and Persian," Suling said to Reggie after her first visit to Poiret's atelier. "Harem pants. And there were some coats cut in the style of Japanese kimonos."

"He's offering more money than Callot Soeurs," Reggie pointed out. "Aren't you just a little bit tempted?"

"We have enough to live on, don't we?" Suling said, and Reggie nodded. As senior embroideress, Suling's salary at Callot Soeurs was more than sufficient for their modest needs. "The Callot sisters have been very good to me. If they hadn't given me a chance, Poiret wouldn't even know of my existence."

"I am so terribly proud of you, *bao bei*," Reggie said, pulling her into a big hug. "You took the risk to make your dream real, and here you are."

"Only because you came with me," Suling said, returning the embrace. But she didn't voice the worry that swam constantly at the back of her mind. She had hoped that with time, they could both be proud of each other. But Reggie still struggled to leave behind the horrors she'd suffered at Thornton's hands. Even with the companionship of other artists and the inspiration of Paris's incredible cultural riches, Reggie hadn't finished any serious projects. What Suling truly lived for was the day when Reggie picked up her brushes and began to paint, really paint. And that day had seemed just around the corner.

Until they received Alice's telegram.

Reggie had been drinking more since then. Normally Reggie drank very little. But in the weeks after Alice's first telegram, Reggie had been buying more wine. "What?" she'd said at the look on Suling's face. She poured herself a second glass. "A girl can't have a drink in her own home?"

"It's the third time this week, Reggie," Suling said. "It's not like you."

"Oh, it's very like me," Reggie snapped, "or it would be if I weren't pandering to your irrational worries. Honestly, Suling. Not everyone who drinks is an alcoholic." Suling shrank back, surprised and hurt by Reggie's belligerence.

Would everything change for Reggie once Thornton was behind bars? Let it be so, Suling prayed.

"I'D LIKE TO murder that son of a bitch Thornton. Van Doren. Whatever he's calling himself," Reggie said now, unlocking the door to their apartment. She hung up her coat and red scarf, ran her fingers through her curls. "Someone needs to tell that Viennese fiancée of his. How can she even guess what kind of man she's marrying?"

"Once Clarkson arrests him, his fiancée won't have anything more to do with him," Suling said. "We do nothing. It's Clarkson's job to take Thornton back to San Francisco to stand trial."

"Men like Thornton never have to face justice," Reggie said. "Even if he goes to trial, his money will make sure he's never convicted. He'll buy off judges and bribe witnesses."

"Bribe witnesses? That's simply not possible," Suling said, putting away her coat. "*We* are the witnesses. You and me, Gemma and Alice. He can't bribe us. He'll get the trial he deserves."

Bedsprings creaked behind the folding screen and Suling knew Reggie had flung herself onto the mattress. Reggie's demons began and ended with Thornton. They had all suffered at his hands, but Reggie most of all. She'd seen him murder the Pinkerton detective, watched him shoot Madam Ning in cold blood. Had almost burned to death. Worst of all, had woken up to find herself incarcerated without hope of escape, shut in a cell for the rest of her life, no one listening to her screams of protest because the nuns thought she was delusional.

Suling paused by the corner table that held their Queen of the Night plant; a single stalk of buds dangled over the stoneware pot. She'd show it to Alice tomorrow. Alice would be able to predict when it might bloom. She needed to get out of their apartment for a while because Reggie needed some time alone. "I'm going down to the shops, dearest love," Suling said, putting her coat back on. "We're out of eggs." There was no reply and she stifled a sigh on her way out.

SULING BOUGHT SIX eggs and a pound of green beans from the épicerie on the corner. She wasn't allowed to leave the store until the grocer's wife and daughters had admired and exclaimed over her turquoise blue coat, examined its cut and construction. In Paris, fashion was always center stage and Suling's role at Callot Soeurs gave her cachet in the neighborhood.

Returning to the apartment, she saw that Reggie was sitting under the skylight, a pad of drawing paper on her lap and a stick of charcoal in her hand, a tumbler of wine on the table within easy reach. If Thornton were out of the way, would Reggie be able to complete a painting? She knew Reggie longed to create beauty pulled from the depths of her soul; if she could only paint again, Reggie would heal. Suling didn't have any illusions about getting back the same Reggie she had known in San Francisco but all she wanted was some joy for them both.

For now, all Suling could do was carry on as though all was well. It wasn't the best option, but she didn't know how else to handle it.

"Alice hasn't changed at all, has she?" Suling said in her most cheerful voice as she put the eggs in the food locker. "She'll spend any amount of money to collect some obscure plant specimen but never anything on her own wardrobe. I wish she would come to Callot Soeurs and order a few items. Just a few basic essential pieces."

There was no reply, so she continued. "And Gemma looks well. She's obviously happy in both her marriage and career."

"Didn't you get an invitation to that costume party out in Versailles?" Reggie said, finally looking up.

"Yes," Suling replied, "and I'm glad I decided not to attend." She glanced at the invitation, pinned to the corkboard alongside sketches of dresses with intricate embroideries. A day dress designed for Hortense Acton, a tea gown for Rita Lydig, an evening scarf for Nancy Cunard. She had pinned the invitation from Paul Poiret to the corkboard as a trophy, an emblem of how far she'd come in her career.

"I hear that Poiret wants every guest in costume," Suling said, still attempting cheerfulness, "so he's had extra outfits made up for lending to those who show up in ordinary evening wear. Caftans and such."

Reggie got out of bed and stood behind her. She rested her chin on Suling's shoulder and put her long arms around Suling's waist. "I'm sorry for my rudeness earlier, *bao bei*," Reggie said. "Let's invite everyone to our apartment. Then we can meet Gemma's husband. And I'll apologize for leaving the café so abruptly."

"We can invite the entire Moulin Rouge if you wish." Suling turned and lifted her face up for a kiss, glad Reggie had calmed down.

"It was the thought of Thornton finding himself another victim. That he thinks he can get away with it." Reggie's arms tightened around her. "His bride has no idea who he really is, none at all."

"Try not to think about him, dearest love," Suling said. "Let's think about that little party for our friends."

Reggie remained in a good mood for the rest of the evening and didn't mention Thornton again. She didn't drink any wine and made their dinner, a simple cheese omelette and green salad. When she thought about it afterward, Suling berated herself for not realizing that Reggie had been lulling her into a false sense of security.

Because when she woke up the next morning, Reggie was gone. And so was the invitation to Poiret's ball.

Chapter 31

"Well," Gemma greeted her husband, unpinning her big black hat and tossing it onto the bed, "they're all on the verge of cracking up."

"What's that, *corazón*?" George called absently from the desk. He was practicing—their hotel room didn't have a piano, so he was playing the rolltop desk instead, working from memory. Judging from the way he was sweating through his linen shirt, and from that right hand rattling triplets against the desk edge at blurring speed, Gemma guessed it was Schubert's "Erlkönig." She had a lieder concert this autumn in Manaus, and she liked picking repertoire that showcased George's playing, not just her voice. A pianist as good as her husband deserved better material than just plinking arpeggios as the soprano soared. He banged out the last climactic chords and swung around, raking his sweat-damp black hair out of his eyes. "Franz Schubert can rot in hell for those *moto perpetuo* triplets," George said, pulling her into his lap. "And what gave you that idea about your friends?"

"Alice can't bring herself to go back to San Francisco and her old botany department. Reggie isn't painting. Suling looks tremendously elegant and successful, but there's something just a bit *lost* there." Gemma sighed. "Or maybe I'm imagining things."

"You all survived an inferno. Give them time."

"We've had five years. Why is everyone still so . . ." Gemma nestled her head into his shoulder, wrestling to find the right word. "Stuck?" Henry Thornton had reared his head and it was like they all froze in response, each suspended in their own nightmare like insects in amber. *We shouldn't have left one another back in San Francisco. We should have stuck together.*

George threaded a hand through Gemma's hair. "Next time you meet up with them all, let me come with you?"

I needed to prove I could do it alone, Gemma thought, but didn't say. George adored her, stem to flawed stern; he was only too happy to be leaned on, and for so long she'd had to lean on him—recovering from the octagon house fire, rebuilding her career, fighting always to balance her work with her migraines. But it would be a very bad decision to go on leaning forever, letting him carry her the way his piano carried her voice in so many rehearsals and recitals and practice sessions.

"Not quite the way we envisioned seeing Paris, is it?" Gemma said now, her tone deliberately light. Their room was small, a second-floor bedroom in a cheap Left Bank pension. Alice had found it—she was in a corner room two doors down—and Gemma had been happy to stay somewhere that Thornton (or van Doren or whatever he was now calling himself) would never dream of setting his expensively shod foot.

"Next year when you're back here singing Marguerite in *Faust,* we'll stay at the Ritz and have champagne every day," George said.

"You know I can't take that role, George." Gemma slid off his lap and came round behind him, digging her thumbs knowledgeably into the broad muscles of his shoulders—he always got knotted up after he'd been practicing too long. Especially Schubert and those *moto perpetuo* triplets.

"You could sing Marguerite in your sleep."

"That's not what I meant, and you know it. The Paris Opera—everyone says their management's brutal on new singers. If I get a migraine during a run of *Faust* and can't go on, they'll *end* my career."

"The migraines are getting better. The new medicine—"

"It's half laudanum. I don't like relying on it." And the migraines were worse than they'd been before San Francisco, not that she'd told her friends that. No, she'd put her best face forward at the café today, the elegant diva in her prime. She hadn't said *I'm only getting good roles now because I found a sympathetic conductor who doesn't mind calling my understudy whenever I'm laid out flat in a darkened room with a cold cloth over my head.* And her friends didn't think to ask why she wasn't working elsewhere, because she'd always written so glowingly of the Teatro Colón, one of the best opera houses in the world, so why would she want to take on roles with other companies?

Fear. That was why. She didn't dare risk the Paris Opera or the Staatsoper, even now that she was starting to get inquiries. She'd carved out a place for herself since San Francisco, and she was just barely able to hang on to it. She didn't dare move outside it. If she felt ashamed of herself, well, nearly being burned alive left its mark on a person's soul. She had her life, she had her friends, she had her voice, she had *George*—if she'd lost a little of her courage, maybe that was the price.

George groaned as her thumb found a particularly stubborn knot over his shoulder blade. "How long will we be in Paris, do you think?"

"A few weeks? We'll know more when Clarkson arrives. His ship lands in Le Havre tomorrow, late morning. Do you think you could . . ."

"Yes, I'll meet him when he disembarks. I doubt the man speaks a word of French. Then I'll drop him off to plot and scheme with you four ladies . . ." George tilted his head back and tugged her head down for a kiss, then another.

"I can feel a migraine coming," she murmured against his mouth. Just the earliest signs—the slight initial stiffness in her neck muscles before the pulsing began, the urge to yawn though she wasn't remotely tired.

"Coming quick?" He knew the different varieties as well as she did: the ones that roared in like a freight train, the slower ones that sank deep and lasted so much agonizingly longer.

"It feels like it's taking its time. So—" She peeled him out of his rumpled shirt, let his deft fingers work the buttons on her black-and-white suit, the laces on her corset, her garters. He could play her every bit as well as his piano, fast or slow, surging and crashing or sustaining soft to the last gasp. This afternoon was fast and delicate, a Chopin nocturne, rippling and soothing, as if he could stop the tense rise of pain in her skull by his hands alone.

By the time the migraine hit full force at twilight, the Serranos had the curtains drawn and the cold packs ready, the strictly measured dose of laudanum that could take the edge off. *I hate this*, Gemma thought, curled in a ball on the bed, *I hate this, I hate this*—because why had Henry Thornton and his attempt to kill her made these attacks *worse*? What did the random pain in her head have to do with him? She'd put him behind her; she'd survived and even managed to thrive, so why couldn't she conquer this?

George was talking softly, rubbing a hand along her scalp under her hair, trying to distract her. "Hopefully we'll be back in Buenos Aires by the end of July, in time to see the new Puccini opera premiere. Even if it won't be Caruso starring like he did at the New York premiere."

"Caruso," Gemma mumbled hazily as the pain sank its claws in. "I wonder if we'll ever sing together again. I still think he might be the one who got me that first Queen of the Night at the Teatro Colón."

"Maybe he did," George said. "But anything afterward you earned on your own, *corazón*."

"Maybe." But she had still been lucky, so lucky. She knew it. And, lying in bed in the darkened bedroom, wincing every time the pipes rattled, thinking of Henry Thornton hanging over everything, Gemma wondered if now was the time she was about to pay for all that good luck.

So SHE WASN'T really surprised when Suling came hammering on their door the following morning, wild-eyed and gasping, having run all the way from her apartment in Montmartre, to say that Reggie was gone.

"Oh God." Gemma was still blinking sleep out of her eyes, fragile-headed as she always was the morning after a migraine. George had already left for Le Havre early that morning, to meet Clarkson's boat.

"She's stolen my invitation to the Poiret ball in Versailles," Suling said desperately, Alice already at her shoulder. "Thornton will be there. He can't see her, he *can't*—"

Gemma's hand stole up to her loose hair, nearly grown out to the length it had been before it burned off in the octagon house fire. She took a deep breath, trying to banish the fear, reaching for Suling's shoulder and then Alice's. "How on earth do we get to Versailles?"

Chapter 32

V ersailles-Château, three tickets," Alice said. Her French was fluent, her accent unmistakably American.

The Gare de Montparnasse was most likely the station where Reggie would've caught the train to Versailles. Alice, Gemma, and Suling had searched the platforms and public rooms hoping Reggie was still at the station, but Gemma spoke to a porter who confirmed seeing a tall young woman with dark curls and a red scarf on the platform not an hour ago. The tall woman had asked him whether she was boarding the right train and her accent was obviously American. And yes, the woman had taken the train to Versailles.

Their carriage was full to bursting. The three women sat squeezed together on the same bench, sharing the car with families carrying picnic baskets and couples dressed for an afternoon of walking in the country. An old man and his wife stared silently out the window, their relief at leaving the city visibly etched in every line of their faces. Suling had made this trip before with Reggie, an outing to the palace and its gardens. It had been a day of pure happiness, but now she dreaded what they might find when they reached Versailles. The train hurtled through the outskirts of Paris, houses and back gardens opening up to fields and farmland, lines of poplar trees bordering country roads. Suling tried hard not to spend the entire journey imagining the worst. She would not chew her nails or start crying. Alice gazed intently out the window. Gemma appeared absolutely composed and calm, her only sign of nervousness the handkerchief twisted in her hands.

Suling fought to keep her own hands folded on the bag that contained the dragon robe. She'd had an idea just before running out the door of the apartment. The blue robe had given her entry to Callot Soeurs, it was her good luck charm. And it might be what she needed to get her into the party without an invitation. That, and boldness.

"It's only a ten-minute walk from the station to the Palace of Versailles," Alice said, reading from her guidebook. Of course Alice would remember to bring a guidebook. "Unfortunately, it's a much longer walk to the Pavillon du Butard, which is actually outside the palace grounds. It used to be a royal hunting lodge."

A lodge that became famous when Paul Poiret leased and then renovated it for his fabulous parties, each soiree so spectacular all of Paris society fought to attend.

"I will crawl the entire way if we have to," Gemma said, and Suling knew they were all remembering the same thing: Reggie's voice, grim and hate-filled. *I want to kill him.* Gemma's face was all determination, mirroring Suling's own resolve. They had to prevent Reggie from courting disaster.

When they got off at the Versailles station platform, they saw why their carriage had been so full. Six other carriages displayed placards marked RESERVED FOR PRIVATE PARTY, and passengers from the private cars descended to the gaping stares of other travelers. Musicians with brilliantined hair carrying instrument cases and garment bags stepped out. A troop of dark-skinned, dark-eyed women, each holding a portmanteau, followed. More musicians descended from another carriage, dressed in neat white tunics with red sashes and matching red turbans, instruments in leather cases carefully tucked under their arms. A group of women with identical hairstyles sashayed across the platform, all the while berating the porters who followed behind toting their trunks. The women's words made no impression on the porters since they were chattering in English.

"Goodness, they're from Queens," Gemma said. "Those people are the entertainment for the ball. Let's see how they're getting to the Pavillon."

Outside the station, a long line of horse-drawn charabancs waited, all also displaying placards, RESERVED FOR PRIVATE PARTY. The loud women clambered into one of the charabancs.

"We need to move fast," Alice said, walking rapidly toward the nearest charabanc. Its driver stopped them.

"This is for a private party," he said, eyeing the three women. "Do you have invitations?"

Suling opened her canvas bag to show him a glimpse of the dragon robe, its rich embroidery. "No, but I must get to the Pavillon. My mistress la Duchesse de Clermont-Tonnerre forgot this part of her costume." The duchess had ordered a dress for the costume ball from Callot Soeurs and Suling was betting the staff at Poiret's party had been briefed on the guest list—at least the most eminent ones.

He nodded and waved her on. Suling climbed in beside the dark-skinned women, who shifted silently to make room for her.

Gemma turned her most radiant smile on the driver. "I was hired to sing at the party." He looked dubious. Not even bothering to clear her throat, Gemma sang the opening vocalise from the "Bell Song" in *Lakmé*, her voice rich and thrilling, the notes pouring out effortlessly. The driver waved her on, and she climbed in beside Suling.

Alice simply pushed past and seated herself across from Gemma and Suling. She pointed at the charabanc ahead of them, the women still jostling one another amid shrieks of laughter. "I'm their chaperone."

"But then, do you not want to sit with them?"

"Would you want to sit with them?" Alice said, frostily. He hastened to the front of the charabanc and clucked at the horses.

The horses clopped along the public road, which gave way to a private drive that led them through wooded glades until they reached wrought-iron gates decorated with gilded acanthus leaves. The sun was sinking behind the tall trees that surrounded the Pavillon but within the gates, open-sided tents on the long oval of lawn blazed with candlelight. Torches lined the main driveway and pebbled paths that wound between flower beds. The Pavillon itself stood glowing at the end of the driveway, light pouring out from windows and doors.

The musicians and dancers got out of the hired charabancs and were directed to a large tent. Gleaming private automobiles pulled up to the stone steps of the Pavillon, where a man and a woman, gorgeously bedecked in costumes straight out of *Scheherazade,* stood greeting guests: Paul and Denise Poiret. Liveried servants checked the guests for invitations before ushering them to the Poirets. As the three women watched, two burly servants took hold of a young couple in evening clothes and marched them firmly down the steps of the Pavillon.

"Oh dear," Alice murmured at the sight. "I suppose we could try the tradesmen's entrance."

"If we're to look for Reggie we need the authority to go anywhere we please," Suling said. "We must enter as guests." Carefully, she unfolded the dragon robe and slipped into the garment.

The dragon robe usually hung at the back of their armoire. Suling brought it out occasionally, usually to model the robe for colleagues at Callot Soeurs. She pointed out the different stitches and knots, explained about the special occasions when an imperial consort would wear such a robe. She never put it on without wondering about the original owner, her hopes and sorrows, whether she had also loved this beautiful garment. How many times had this long-dead woman worn the dragon robe before it had been looted from the palace?

Gemma helped arrange the dragon robe so that it draped properly. "It suits you," Gemma said. "I can hold the garment bag, if you like. A woman in a robe like that doesn't heft her own bags."

Suling nodded her thanks and took a deep breath. "Let's go."

In her dragon robe, Suling managed to stroll past the watchful servants, but she paused when the two burly manservants began moving toward her. Suling called up the steps. "Monsieur Poiret!"

Paul Poiret exclaimed in delight. He rushed down the stone steps of the terrace, hands held out in greeting. "Mademoiselle Feng! *Ma chère* Suling! What a spectacular robe! It outshines anything here! This, this, dear lady, is why I want so badly for you to head up my embroidery workshop!"

"Monsieur Poiret," Suling said, pointing behind her, "these are my friends. The soprano Gemma Serrano, toast of the Teatro Colón in Buenos Aires. And this is Alice Eastwood of San Francisco, America's most eminent botanist and curator at the California Academy of Sciences."

"Welcome, welcome," Poiret exclaimed. "Any friends of Suling Feng are welcome."

The two burly servants melted into the background.

"Alas, another automobile," Poiret said, after kissing all their hands. "Ladies, I must greet those other guests, but please, the ladies' boudoir is to the right of the vestibule. Select whichever costumes and dresses please you. That is my only requirement, that you put on a costume. And Mademoiselle Feng," and here he pressed her hand once more, "I hope to see you at my office in the next day or two, so we can discuss employment terms."

As he hurried to the next set of guests, Suling murmured something that sounded like agreement. She had no intention of discussing employment terms with Poiret.

The three women made their way into the Pavillon. Racks of costumes and Poiret's fashions filled one side of the boudoir. Racks on the other side held women's clothing, evening gowns guests had exchanged for Poiret's costumes. Several female guests were looking through the racks, maids patiently standing behind to hang up any clothing they shed.

"I really don't think these are appropriate," Alice said, looking doubtfully at a pair of harem pants in heavy gold satin.

In the end, Alice pulled a black-and-silver caftan over her sensible skirt and blouse; Gemma exchanged her travel suit for turquoise-blue harem pants and a sequined jacket, then tucked her blond hair under a matching sequined scarf. The maid handed Gemma a lacy half mask decorated with jewels and blue feathers, a plain black one edged in gold beads to Alice, and a blue satin domino to Suling.

"Ready?" Alice said. "Let's start looking."

The Pavillon and gardens were chaotic and festive. Footmen circulated bearing trays from the kitchen. In addition to large vases cascading with flowers that filled every niche of the Pavillon, cages of colorful tropical birds hung from wall brackets, their screeches sounding over the music. The svelte, dark-skinned young women had disrobed and now danced in costumes that weren't much more than gold-painted leopard spots. Each of the tents outside featured a different sort of music or entertainment. Dancers from the Moulin Rouge were kicking up their legs in a cancan to a mostly male audience, and the noisy American women from Queens turned out to be a troupe of tumblers and acrobats. Bartenders wearing red fez hats and vaguely Turkish tunics mixed drinks that sparked green and blue flames, then handed the glasses to applauding guests.

But after an hour and four rounds of searches, none of them had spied Reggie. By then several copper tubs of ice and champagne had been emptied and refilled, and it seemed to Suling that all three hundred guests were there, yet more automobiles kept rumbling through the gate.

"It's getting harder to search," she said in despair when she met up with Alice and Gemma. "It's totally dark outside now and more guests are arriving all the time. And so many are masked."

"Should we be keeping an eye out for Thornton as well?" Gemma said. "Has anyone seen him yet? If Reggie finds him first—"

"Let's hope it doesn't come to that," Alice said, "but yes, we must also watch out for that man."

"What if Reggie is watching out for Thornton?" Gemma worried. "She'd be lurking in a spot where it's easy to see new arrivals. I mean, they all stop at the steps to greet the Poirets."

"I'll hang around the guests by the Pavillon entrance," Suling said. "Perhaps you two watch from spots where the entrance is visible, but from a bit farther away."

Three gleaming automobiles were filing up the driveway as Suling took her place. The vehicles stopped beside the stone steps and their chauffeurs fairly leaped out to open the doors. It wasn't an arrival, it was an entrance. Under the shadow of a clipped cypress hedge, Suling dug her fingers into the palm of her hand when a tall figure emerged from the first car. Thornton, no, van Doren leaned down and held out his arm. A small hand gloved in silver lace reached for it and a young woman stepped out. Cecilia Arenburg von Loxen wore one of Poiret's lampshade dresses in a deep, iridescent blue. Gold sandals sparkled on her feet. Her silvery blond hair hung in braided loops at the nape of her neck. An older man followed, lean and commanding, a leonine mane of gray hair, and an evening suit. Not the sort who would deign to wear a costume, not even a mask to hide that dueling scar. Her father, the baron. Two younger men in Arabian costumes climbed out of the next car and trailed behind the baron as he made his way up the steps.

Guests spilled out of the other vehicles while Thornton directed a servant to take a box out of the automobile's trunk. From its size and shape, it had to be holding the Phoenix Crown. Thornton finally made his way up the steps, walking slowly so that by the time he and his fiancée greeted Poiret, their companions had dispersed and only he and Cecilia were there, the focus of their hosts' complete attention.

Poiret gestured, evidently impatient to peek into the box, which the liveried servant carried as though holding a newborn baby. Poiret and Thornton entered the Pavillon together while Denise Poiret took Cecilia by the arm and guided her inside. Then Suling saw a lean man sauntering up the steps, following them into the Pavillon.

Not a man. Reggie.

She wore a long red caftan and a silvery brocade vest over trousers but Suling recognized the loose, casual gait, the dark curls peeking out from the patterned scarf wrapped like a burnoose around her head. Suling didn't call out to Reggie; she didn't want to alert Thornton to their presence. She hurried across the grass and up the steps. Inside, the vestibule and ballroom were noisy and chaotic, the music louder, the party guests more inebriated than an hour ago, the air even more blue and stifling with cigarette smoke. Suling caught sight of a red caftan mingling with a cluster of guests who were shouting encouragement as a man in Turkish costume joined the line of cancan dancers. Suling slipped behind another group of guests.

Then there was applause, members of Thornton's entourage clapping. But not for the dancers. Denise Poiret had emerged from the boudoir with Cecilia, whose delicate neck seemed too slight to hold the weight of the Phoenix Crown. Strings of pearls brushed her shoulders, and the electric blue of her dress almost, not quite but almost, matched the blue kingfisher feathers. Thornton's smile was one of triumph, and Paul Poiret could not hold back his cries of admiration and envy.

Cecilia touched a slim hand to the crown, asked something of Thornton, who smiled indulgently. She looked toward her father, who nodded encouragement. As the young woman straightened her shoulders Suling could almost hear her sigh. Then Cecilia asked Denise Poiret something, and Madame Poiret pointed up the staircase. The ladies' salon. Suling had been there during her first search.

The two young men in Arabian costumes moved to the edge of the dance floor with Cecilia's father. Their costumes couldn't hide their military bearing, and their deportment toward the baron was unmistakably deferential. Perhaps he was their commanding officer? Thornton and his entourage moved toward the open French doors, following the dancers who were now cancanning their way out to the gardens. Suling ducked around a caged pair of scarlet macaws, keeping out of sight.

Then panicked. She'd lost sight of the red caftan.

She spun around just in time to see Reggie disappearing into the ladies' salon upstairs. Why would she be heading away from Thornton? Suling pushed her way through the guests toward the staircase to follow Reggie.

When she arrived, the door to the salon was slightly ajar and she heard Reggie's voice. Not raised in anger, but gentle and patient. Another voice, more shrill and disturbed. Suling was about to push the door when it burst open.

"*Nein, nein, das kann nicht wahr sein!*" Cecilia Arenburg von Loxen shrieked. Then before Suling could move, the petite blonde ran down the stairs with a clatter of swinging pearls.

Inside the salon, Reggie sat slumped on a daybed, looking resigned.

Chapter 33

By the time Gemma and Alice managed to follow the whisk of the blue dragon robe upstairs, fighting their way up the thronged staircase into the salon, Suling was shouting.

"What got into you?" Her short black hair trembled as she looked down at Reggie, who had sunk inside her red caftan on the nearest daybed. "What did you tell that Viennese girl? Why did you—"

"I-I just wanted to warn her." Reggie looked so small and frozen, Gemma thought. Trapped in amber, still fighting to get free of the octagon house. "That the man she wanted to marry was a murderer. I didn't—"

A giggling woman in a kimono coat and ropes of jade beads stumbled into the salon with one of the limber cancan dancers from downstairs. Alice whipped around with a glare; the woman squeaked and backed out. Gemma banged the salon door shut and locked it. Reggie looked up, seeming to register Gemma and Alice's arrival for the first time.

"That girl will warn Thornton," Gemma burst out. "He tried to *murder* us and now he knows we're still alive—"

"I didn't give her our names—"

"He'll still figure it out once she tells him about you! What were you thinking?"

"I wanted to save her." Reggie shrank even further. "I tried to save *you*, Sal—in San Francisco, I tried, and you didn't need it. You saved all of us instead. And Suling had to save me from the asylum, and I didn't help . . . anyone. So I wanted to . . ." Reggie trailed off a moment, then her chin lifted. Tears glittered in her eyes. "You all want Thornton to pay so badly, you're ready to write that girl off. His fiancée. Well, I can't. She *matters*."

"And you have put her in danger," Suling snapped. "Thornton was willing to do anything in San Francisco to cover up what he'd done. What will he do to her if she knows—"

"But she's not like us." Reggie's voice rose. "Her father is a powerful man, he'll protect her. I was just hoping I could make her wary of him so she'd break the engagement—"

"Ladies." Alice stood there in her black-and-gold caftan, glaring. The sounds of the party below filtered through the door: the shrill laughter of guests, sitars and pipes playing what the musicians had probably assured Monsieur Poiret (with much eye-rolling) was *authentic oriental harem music*. "What's done is done. Mr. Thornton at least hasn't *seen* any of us yet, and I suggest we keep it that way. Put your masks back on and let's leave this place."

They hurried out of the salon, past a gilt stand where a pink ibis irritably rattled its leg chains. At least in these harem pants she could move freely, Gemma thought as they moved into the crowd that surrounded an aerialist languidly spinning midair through a ribboned hoop. She followed Alice's black-and-gold shape down the thronged stairs—until she crashed into Alice's back.

Across the floor of whirling dancers below, the hypnotic kingfisher blue of the Phoenix Crown flashed, and a man leaned down toward the girl wearing it: Thornton—van Doren—in dark evening dress, cigar between his fingers as he turned away from a cluster of men idly watching an Indian contortionist twine herself into knots. A black eye mask was Thornton's only concession to fancy dress, but he was perfectly recognizable. Gemma hadn't seen him arrive with his fiancée—this was the first time she'd laid eyes on him, in fact, since the octagon house.

As clearly as if he'd whispered in her ear, Gemma heard his voice: *I'm sorry*, as the whoosh of fire roared up to lick around the conservatory doors, as she pounded and shrieked against the glass. *I'm sorry, Gemma.*

His blond fiancée was pulling at his sleeve, the pearl strands of her crown swinging violently. Thornton covered her hand with his own, smiling, but she wrenched away, saying something Gemma couldn't hear. A flicker of annoyance across his face, eyes darting to his friends, who were starting to glance over . . . The Viennese girl was demanding something now, gesturing toward the stairs.

And Thornton looked up.

Gemma and Alice were concealed behind the spinning aerialist. Reggie's hair was hidden under her scarf and her face behind her mask; his eyes went over her without a flicker of recognition. Yet Suling was on the bottom step, masked, but the lustrous splendor of her dragon robe was like no other, and Gemma saw Thornton's eyes freeze on it in a sudden ripple of shock.

A heartbeat later Suling disappeared behind a throng of shrieking women toasting one another with crystal coupes of some lemon-yellow liqueur. Thornton's eyes hunted for her, his face suddenly pale, and Gemma reached out to grasp Reggie's wrist, yanking her down.

Thornton swept his eyes across the room again, almost frantic. His fiancée in her looted crown plucked at his sleeve. He made a decision, taking her by the elbow and marching her through the crowd, toward the Pavillon's vestibule and the fragrant gardens outside. Gemma saw his fingers sinking into her flesh above the lace glove, thought she could hear the girl cry out, before the sound disappeared into the night.

"He saw me," Suling was whispering as they tumbled down

the last few stairs to join her. The party roared around them like a carousel careening off its wheels. "He saw me."

"He only saw the robe," said Alice. "We can still get out of here."

They could, Gemma knew. Slip out through the kitchens and then to the road. Head back to Paris and meet George and Clarkson, who had to have arrived from Le Havre by now, with his badge and his warrants and his legal shields.

Reggie was staring toward the gardens where Thornton had yanked his fiancée. That doe-eyed little eighteen-year-old. "I don't like the way he was dragging her."

And I don't like being afraid, Gemma thought. Afraid for five years. Afraid of this man hanging over them. And here he was.

"I'm tired of it," said Suling, suddenly. "I'm tired of being frightened."

"So am I," said Gemma, and ran down the steps into the garden.

They followed her, all of them.

The perfumed gardens were overrun by now with tipsy men in caftans and women in bejeweled costumes, flirting and drinking and gawking at the moon. Gemma crossed the dark lawn, Suling and Reggie in her wake, past a row of Persian silk tents carpeted with oriental rugs, under a brace of torches in dragon-mouthed brackets that a designer had probably deemed more exotic than mere candles.

"I don't *understand*." Cecilia Arenburg von Loxen's fretful voice sounded from somewhere behind a potted myrtle tree and a fire swallower's iron brazier still glowing with hot coals. "The things this woman was saying, I don't understand at all. You said you'd never been to San Francisco!"

"I never have." Thornton was trying to sound amused, but

there was a thread of tension in his voice that raised the hair on Gemma's neck. "Darling girl, let's join the crowd on the other side of the fountain. Monsieur Poiret has promised Régina Badet is going to dance on the lawn. The prima ballerina of the Grand Theatre of Bordeaux—"

"I don't want to see a *ballerina*, I want you to answer me! An octagon house in San Francisco, your last *mistress*—you know how my father feels about men who carry on with loose women. You promised him you never—"

"Who exactly have you been listening to, little goose? Don't be so gullible." He chuckled, taking off his half mask with a casual rake of his fingers, but then his smile froze utterly as he saw the women melting silently out of the blackness around the brazier and into the light of the torches. An extraordinary pang of savage rage and equally savage satisfaction wrung Gemma's stomach as she watched all the remaining color drain from his face.

"Good evening, Henry," she said in a steady voice, discarding her own mask.

A burst of applause exploded across the big circular lawn before the Pavillon: the crowds of costumed guests gathering, oblivious, for the Bordeaux ballerina. But here, they were all gripped in the silence of Thornton's stunned gaze traveling from Suling in her dragon robe, to Reggie with her embroidered caftan and haunted eyes, to Gemma in her Poiret harem pants.

Alice, Gemma had an instant to think. *Where is Alice?* Because somehow the botanist had faded away and it was just Gemma and Suling and Reggie staring Thornton down, but there was no time now to wonder any further.

"I have no idea who these women are," Thornton said to Cecilia. He managed to give his words just the right touch of polite bemusement, but his gaze kept stuttering between them in jerky disbelief. Three women, whole, unburned, when he'd left them all for dead.

At the octagon house they'd all run from him rather than confront him, and they'd all nearly burned alive. Now they all took a step toward him instead.

And he took a tiny, involuntary step back.

The Viennese girl's voice was small. "William, why did she call you *Henry*?"

"I don't know any of them," he repeated, his voice firmer. "Why don't we go back inside, my dear? Your father will be wanting to take you home, now that things are getting a bit wild—"

"You like wild parties," Reggie interrupted. "Remember the artistic soirees you used to take me to, back when I was sharing your bed?"

"Or the midnight ball, when *I* was sharing that bed?" Gemma said. "It was me wearing that phoenix crown, then. I imagine you haven't told your fiancée that."

Suling finished, her voice low, "Or that you locked us all in a burning house to die, after we saw you shoot an innocent woman in cold blood."

"This is absurd." Thornton hitched a convincing look of exasperation onto his face, but he didn't seem to be able to step toward them. And Gemma and Reggie and Suling wouldn't move out of his path. Gemma could feel something stoking between the three of them, rising higher and hotter like the torches flaming in their dragon-mouthed brackets.

"We should inform Monsieur Poiret that he has some uninvited guests," Thornton said, taking a sidestep—and his sleeve brushed against the hot iron of the coal-filled brazier. He couldn't possibly have burned himself through his jacket, but he still recoiled.

He's still terrified of fire, Gemma thought. Remembering how he'd flinched at the Palace Grill from a crêpe pan *en flambe*. Remembering how he flexed his burned hand: *It happened at the Park Avenue Hotel fire in New York, in '02*. Not mentioning, of course, that he'd been the one to set that fire that killed so many, all to line his own pockets.

Remembering his greenish, terrified face as he steeled himself to set the octagon house ablaze.

When Gemma's eyes met Suling's she knew they were thinking the same thing.

Suling moved cat-quick toward the bracket of torches, wrenching one loose. Reggie seized the startled Viennese girl by the arm and yanked her away from her fiancé. Thornton wrenched the girl's other arm, trying to pull her back toward the Pavillon, but Gemma moved between them, the hot and violent thing stoking in her breast finally boiling over. She planted both hands at his shirtfront and shoved him backward so hard he released Cecilia. She shoved him again and he tripped, crashing down to one knee. When Gemma looked up, she saw Suling holding out the second torch. Smiling.

Gemma smiled back, taking it.

On one side of the big oval lawn and its banks of flowers, a gauze-draped ballerina glided and arabesqued for a crowd of rapt guests. On the other side, another circle of guests was listening agog as a French actor declaimed from *A Thousand and One Nights*. Here, past a string of Persian silk tents on the side lawn, Henry Thornton hauled himself upright between two women holding torches at full extension like swords, advancing on him with pitiless eyes, backing him against the heat of the brazier.

"Tell your fiancée," Gemma rasped. "Tell her what you've done."

"Tell her now," Suling snarled.

Reggie finished it, still holding the stunned Viennese girl. "Or we burn you like you tried to burn us."

"Dear God," someone exclaimed. "What is happening?" A male voice, speaking English with an accent Gemma couldn't place. Gemma couldn't spare the second it would take to look for the owner of that horrified voice. Thornton didn't seem to have heard the words; he was transfixed by the three women and finally talking, trying to placate, first her and then Suling. A flick of his gaze toward Cecilia standing frozen with Reggie, and he tried to bull past Suling and swat the torch out of her hands. Gemma whirled on him from the other side, jabbing the flames at his sleeve until the cuff caught fire, and he fell back again yelping and swatting until the lick of fire died. "You *bitches*." He was half shouting, half pleading.

"Keep talking." Suling poked the torch at him, jerking her chin toward Thornton's horrified bride-to-be. "She doesn't believe you yet, keep talking—" In her embroidered dragon robe, with her dark blazing eyes and her bared teeth, Suling could have been an empress from that looted Beijing palace, facing down the invaders and their torches. Only this empress had the torch in *her* hands, and she was the one advancing.

Thornton moistened his lips, looking at that flickering flame. "I didn't mean it," he said quickly, holding up placating hands. "It was an accident. I just didn't want you women coming after me. I sent someone to let you out of the conservatory later—I didn't mean for you to burn alive, I'm not a monster—"

"And the woman you shot on your doorstep, was that an accident?" Gemma thrust her own torch at him as he tried to edge away from the brazier. If Suling was a raging, blazing-hot empress, Gemma thought she could bring her Queen of the Night to bear, hurling thunderbolts and ice. "Tell how you *shot her in cold blood*."

"She was just a Chinese pimp. A thief and a whore—"

"W-what?" cried the Viennese heiress. Reggie was holding the girl in fierce arms, protective as a lioness. A deep voice began calling something again, not in English, but Gemma still couldn't turn. One slip of attention and Thornton could be on her like a rabid dog.

But he was mesmerized by the torches darting and jabbing so close to his flinching face and outstretched once-burned hand, spilling words quickly now. He probably still believed he could fix this, Gemma thought in some cooler corner of her mind. He'd assume he could smooth things over with his doe-eyed heiress, if he could only get away from the fires, from these women who probably seemed like they'd stormed straight out of his nightmares. So he explained and explained and explained, wheeling first to Gemma and then to Suling and then to Reggie and his fiancée. *I didn't mean* and *It wasn't true* and *I had a reason*. Explaining, explaining—until a cry burst out of Cecilia Arenburg von Loxen.

"Stop it," she cried, "stop it, all of you, just *stop*—" The glittering Chinese crown slipped forward over her eyes. Stumbling blindly forward, she tore it off and hurled it away, straight into the brazier.

It went up so fast—the gold wires, the strands connecting all those pearls, the brilliant kingfisher feathers flaring up in hungry blue flames like the phoenix it was named for. They could only stare at it—and Gemma thought of beautiful, burning San Francisco, the city that had gone up in flames almost as quickly.

But Thornton looked at the crumbling crown, the treasure he'd rescued from that burning octagonal mansion whose eight sides hadn't brought him as much luck as he'd hoped, and Gemma saw him snap. *What a thing to break you*, she thought.

Murder hadn't done it, even fire hadn't done it, but a demolished crown did.

"You goddamned bitch," he said and slapped Cecilia to the ground.

"*That's enough*," the deep voice behind Gemma roared, and a tall man with a leonine mane of graying hair and a dueling scar slashing one side of his aristocratic face stormed forward. At his side was Alice Eastwood, eyes gleaming like an eagle's, an avenging angel in her damask and her rage.

"You see?" she cried in a voice like a trumpet. "You see how this man treats your daughter?" But Cecilia's august father, Baron August Friedrich Arenburg von Loxen, had already seized Henry Thornton by the throat and began shaking him like a rat, at the exact moment the first of Monsieur Poiret's magnificent fireworks blossomed overhead in a dazzling bloom of ruby sparks.

Gemma sat down rather suddenly on the damp grass as Reggie released the sobbing Cecilia to her father's side, as Suling slid her torch back into its bracket and tripped over the hem of her robe, and Alice quickly steadied her with an outstretched hand. "*Rosa alba*," Alice remarked, watching more fireworks explode into shapes like white roses. Then a series of golden bursts, like blazing California poppies. "*Eschscholzia californica* . . . I think the men are going to storm in and take charge now. Shall we let them?"

WE NEEDED A *respectable witness*, Alice told them a little later when they had a chance to catch their breath. *Confessions are all very well and good, but the right people need to* hear *them.* So when Suling and Gemma cornered Thornton, darling sensible Alice had gone arrowing back inside the Pavillon in search of the baron, a man who had fought duels for imperial honor, a former field marshal in the armies of the Austro-Hungarian Empire. A man whose word wouldn't be disregarded the way the word of a Chinese seamstress, an out-of-work artist, an old botanist, and a loose-moraled opera singer would be disregarded.

"Alice, you genius," Reggie said in admiration. "I want to paint you just the way you looked: the light flooding behind you, upraised hand like the angel of vengeance."

"Arrests first," Alice said composedly. "Paintings later."

"You're going to want to speak to a Mr. Clarkson of the Pinkerton Detective Agency, who should be in Paris by now," Gemma told the gendarmes once they arrived. "He has a great deal of information you'll be wanting to hear . . ."

The men were indeed taking charge of things, everything being done very quietly at the insistence of Cecilia's father. He'd produced several underlings who despite their Arabian costumes had the kind of straight-backed heel-clicking deference that indicated a great deal of time spent in uniform, and many things suddenly began happening at speed: an automobile came to whisk his crying daughter back to the Ritz in Paris; gendarmes were summoned to hold the protesting Thornton, all while the party still continued up at the Pavillon utterly unabated. Monsieur Poiret, once he had been summoned, seemed most anxious to avoid scandal, shooing curious guests away from the lower end of the garden with airy excuses about disorderly revelers being found by the gendarmes, nothing to worry about! More champagne and the promise of an impromptu cancan show had sent all the guests weaving back inside so Thornton could be whisked away toward a vehicle waiting at the end of the road.

And the four women sat on the grass watching the entire spectacle.

"*Gnädige frau.*" The baron waved the gendarme at his side away, making a very correct European bow toward Alice. "I do not even know who you are. Or what is going on, or anything," he burst out, looking agitated the way only a military man finding himself on an unfamiliar battleground can look agitated. Gemma felt sorry for him, but she also felt far too tired to fill him in.

Alice took mercy, escorting him on a short walk around the lawn and clearly bringing him up to date on everything he'd missed. The baron looked stunned by the time they circled back around, muttering in German. "No use talking about it any further until Mr. Clarkson can arrive to verify everything," Gemma heard Alice say, patting the baron's arm. "Now, I understand you have a summer house in the mountains near Kitzbühel, sir. I don't suppose you have an alpine garden?"

Chapter 34

After dinner, Michael Clarkson grew increasingly maudlin with every glass of wine. He prowled around Reggie and Suling's apartment, peering at all the art on their walls. Finally, he broke down in front of the folding screen that Reggie had painted with street scenes of Chinatown, one of which depicted the Palace of Endless Joy.

"Justice. Finally, justice for the only woman I've ever loved," he sobbed. "Justice for my Nina, who I would've married, should've married. My poor Nina."

"Oh no, don't be like that," Suling said. "Auntie would've hated those words, 'my poor Nina.' She never felt sorry for herself. And you couldn't have married her anyway since mixed-race marriages are illegal in California."

"Then I should've taken her to Washington State," he said, "married her there. Made an honest woman of her." He slumped down on the table littered with the remains of their meal, burying his face in his folded arms.

Suling sighed and patted his hand. Madam Ning had had exactly zero interest in being a wife. As for being an honest woman, she had run her brothel as ethically as the profession and profits allowed, and that was honest enough by her reckoning.

George grinned at Suling. "It's time for him to get some sleep," he said and gently pulled Clarkson out of the chair. "Let's go, my friend."

Michael Clarkson struggled upright, then turned to wave from the door, leaning heavily against George. "Good night, ladies," he slurred. "George here, a good man, is taking me out to celebrate some more."

"George here," the pianist corrected, "is taking Michael back to the hotel. A walk in the cool evening air and then a nice, comfortable bed. Good night, ladies. Gemma, stay as long as you like."

The door to Suling and Reggie's apartment shut and the women finally allowed themselves to break into laughter.

There were countless cafés and bistros where they could've dined but none of them wanted to sit amid the clink of glassware and lively chatter. They had reached the end of a strange and disturbing journey together and right now they only wanted the company of others who understood. People who knew what had been damaged and lost. Reggie and Suling's apartment was the one place that felt comfortable right now.

"Did anyone else feel the police station was rather an anticlimax?" Gemma said. She poured herself another glass of wine. They'd finished all the champagne an hour ago.

"Anything would be an anticlimax after you cornered Thornton with flaming torches," Alice said. She pointed her chopsticks at a blue-and-white porcelain plate. "Does anyone else want those last two shrimp?" Alice had taken to chopsticks as though she had used them all her life. Easier than using tweezers to pick up delicate botanical samples, she said.

"Nothing wrong with anticlimactic," Gemma said. "Now that it's over, I'm going to sleep for a week."

When it came to avenging their own, the Pinkerton Detective Agency had made sure their evidence was unassailable. Once Clarkson knew there was a link between Henry Thornton and William van Doren, the Agency's research team had quickly connected the dots to prove van Doren's wealth came from Thornton's estate.

Clarkson had boarded the ship to Le Havre with the evidence, and that morning, in front of Louis Lépine, Paris's prefect of police, and a magistrate, Clarkson had been crisp and concise when laying out that evidence. With George translating, Clarkson showed how Thornton's will had left his entire fortune to a distant relative and business partner, a William van Doren allegedly living in Italy. Upon Henry Thornton's apparent death in San Francisco, lawyers had transferred everything to William van Doren's bank in New York.

"This was a plan van Doren put in place a long time ago," Clarkson said, "that at some point Thornton would supposedly die and William van Doren would return to New York after a decade abroad, a man with investments in railways and mines, shipping lines and real estate. All clean and aboveboard."

Then the four women had sworn in writing that Thornton and van Doren were the same man. One woman had seen him murder the Pinkerton detective, Daniel Langford. Three had seen him shoot a woman in cold blood. All four had nearly perished in flames when he locked them indoors and set fire to the house.

Van Doren was behind bars. And in a few days Clarkson and another Pinkerton detective would escort him back to San Francisco to stand trial.

"I kept wondering if he'd still manage to squirm out of it," Reggie said now, standing up to clear the table. "Wondered whether our sworn statements of witnessing his murders would be enough."

"I worried too, *bao bei*," Suling said, taking more plates to the kitchen sink. "If Clarkson and the baron hadn't been there, Thornton probably would've tried persuading the police we were just angry, jilted women."

There was laughter from the dining table. "Alice, you're incorrigible." Gemma was giggling. There had been more wine, more conversation. "The baron's daughter is in hysterics, his future son-in-law turns out to be a murderer, and you were angling for an invitation to his garden?"

"But the baron has a rare alpine orchid," Alice said, "a *Gymnadenia rhellicani* that blooms a deep red brown. I might persuade him to give me a specimen."

Suling threw all the windows open to let in the mild evening air, and the lights of Paris beckoned. Gemma drifted over to admire the view. Suling suddenly experienced such an overwhelming sense of déjà vu she had to lean against the wall to stand upright. Where had she seen this before? Gemma at the open window gazing out at the city. Alice at another window, Reggie by the sink. But there was something different, too, in the comfortable familiarity between the four of them.

Suling put a thin slice of lemon tart on a plate and brought it back to the opera singer, who smiled and shook her head.

"I've had more than enough tonight, Suling," she said, "everything was delicious. The braised pork belly, the sauteed pea shoots, and that shrimp. This tart. I can't believe you and Reggie managed it all in one afternoon."

"We didn't," Suling said, digging a fork into the tart, "this *tarte au citron* is from the patisserie next door. Are you sure you won't have some?"

"If I eat any more, I'll burst out of these trousers." Gemma had donned her Poiret harem pants for dinner, gleaming and opulent. "And I want to keep them, in case I ever sing Mozart's Konstanze in *Abduction from the Seraglio*."

They stood silhouetted against the window. Below them, streetlamps glimmered, lighting up storefronts and pedestrians. In the distance, church bells rang. A warm breeze wafted through the apartment.

"Gemma, you're so important to Reggie," Suling said. "Let's work harder to stay in touch."

"Yes, we will. And you're good for Reggie," Gemma said. "It's so obvious. She's lost that restlessness, the look of wanting to find something or someone new."

"George told me about your migraines," Suling said. "Would you be open to a different type of treatment? A Chinese treatment thousands of years old called acupuncture. There's a Chinese doctor in Paris who is very skilled. He treats me for headaches from eyestrain, neck pains from leaning over an embroidery frame all the time."

"I'll try anything," Gemma said with feeling. "You think it might work?"

"Even if it doesn't, would those migraines ever stop you performing?"

"Never. You learn to live with the pain. Manage it as best you can."

Suling smiled. "I'll wager the acupuncture could take away at least *some* of that pain. It helps Reggie sleep."

They turned around to look at Alice and Reggie, both laughing softly.

"Reggie told me about her nightmares," Gemma said. "Perhaps now that it's all over, now that Thornton has been arrested, they'll go away."

"I hope so," Suling said softly. "I hope so. Sometimes I think she needs to see him convicted and hanged before she can sleep peacefully and paint again. Will you attend the trial?"

"Not unless we have to." Gemma shook her head. "I've already dragged George through too much of this saga. Will you go back to San Francisco?"

San Francisco. The thought of her hometown tugged at Suling. They'd built a new Chinatown. But if she went back, would Paris beckon to her, the way San Francisco beckoned now?

"Alice," Gemma said, moving to stand beside the botanist as

Suling pondered her answer, "will you go back to the California Academy of Sciences? I know it's just an informal discussion right now, but you know they'll offer you the curator job again."

"You know," Alice said, after a brief pause, "I think I will."

"Maybe we should all go back," Gemma said, suddenly. "Not for Thornton's trial—for us. For each other."

Suling blinked. "Go back?"

"Why not? Since the earthquake we've all been orphaned in a way, cut adrift—you, me, Reggie, even Alice. It's not an easy thing to carry, but it *does* mean we can make our home wherever we want. Choose the people we want to be our family." Gemma smiled at Suling. "You could start an atelier of your own in the heart of Chinatown—you have Parisian credentials now. San Francisco's elite will flock to you for the latest fashions."

Suling's mind raced. An atelier in Chinatown where she could hire women she knew, teach them what she'd learned at Callot Soeurs. An artist's studio for Reggie above the workshop. She would embroider a Japanese kimono for Gemma if she ever sang *Madama Butterfly* and it would be a work of art more stunning than diamonds wrapped around a San Francisco society matron's neck.

"But what does San Francisco hold for you? Have any of the opera houses been rebuilt yet?" Suling said. "You'll need somewhere to sing. And George . . ."

"I can sing anywhere," Gemma said. "Opera companies go on tour all the time. I think I need to be a little bolder about accepting roles away from Buenos Aires. Between tours, San Francisco could be home. And I can give voice lessons when I'm too old to perform. As for George, he loved San Francisco, gets all wistful when he talks about his time there."

"Reggie?" Alice said, "what do you think?"

"I can paint anywhere" was the prompt reply. "I love our life in Paris, and it's easier for Suling here in so many ways, but if she's willing to go back, so am I. Home is where she is."

Suling felt a smile break over her face, bright enough to light the entire city. She held out her hand and Reggie joined her by the window.

The contented silence in the room was broken by a small, excited cry from Alice, who ran to the side table. "Look, your Queen of the Night is going to bloom!"

They gathered around the table, and for just an instant, memory flooded Suling's senses. She saw them all again in a San Francisco boardinghouse, four women who had come through earthquake and fire, pausing for a moment of peace as a white flower opened and softened the smoky air with its honeyed scent, a fragrance richer, deeper, more intoxicating than any rose or jasmine.

Epilogue

From *Women Artists of the Gilded Age: A Retrospective*
(William Morrow, 2000)

12: Regina Reynolds, née Nellie Doyle (1877–1971)

Alice Eastwood

Oil on canvas, 30×40 inches

Location: California Academy of Sciences, San Francisco

Description/Notes:
This work was painted in 1912, when botanist Alice Eastwood resumed her role as curator of the Botany Department at the California Academy of Sciences after the museum was rebuilt following the earthquake of 1906. The subject (a longtime friend of the artist) wears an old-fashioned black dress and sits at her desk before a glued-down specimen of an orange-petaled *Amsinckia eastwoodiae*, a vibrant species of California fiddleneck that was eventually named in her honor. She looks straight at the viewer with a wry, humorous expression, her only adornments a lens hanging about her neck on a long chain, and a flowered hat adding a touch of whimsy. The journal open at her elbow is inscribed with a quote by Shakespeare: "In nature's infinite book of secrecy, a little I can read."

Gemma Serrano as Violetta

Oil on canvas, 30×40 inches

Location: de Young Museum, San Francisco

Description/Notes:
An unusually intimate portrait of opera star Gemma Serrano, another longtime friend of Reynolds, depicting the soprano not

onstage but in her dressing room. Though she is associated with the San Francisco Opera where she would finish her career in the late twenties, she is depicted here preparing for the famous Teatro Colón production of *La Traviata* opposite Enrico Caruso in 1917. Costumed lavishly in the courtesan's white ball gown, the soprano is almost visibly humming through her vocalises as she fixes in her hair a silk Queen of the Night flower (a nod to her most famous role). The scatter of makeup tins, perfume bottles, and opera scores adds a cozy touch, and the overall impression is not one of glamour, but of contentment: the great artist not preening in the spotlight, but focused and happy at her work.

Suling

Oil on canvas, 10×20 inches

Location: de Young Museum, San Francisco

Description/Notes:

A delightfully domestic scene depicting fashion designer Feng Suling (the artist's lifelong partner) at work in her home. She sits at her embroidery frame, head bent over her needle as she works gold and silver thread in the shape of a phoenix—one of the complex embroidered designs that would eventually inspire modern designers like Guo Pei, originally popularized at Callot Soeurs in Paris before Feng opened her own atelier in San Francisco just before World War I. The designer's bobbed hair is mussed above her embroidered dressing gown, a jade ring dangles on a chain around her neck, and the sunlight glowing on her skin shows the intimate warmth typical of Reynolds's work. The artist paints herself slyly into this homey tableau: the mirror on the wall beside the embroidery frame reflects the back of an easel, around which a head of dark curls and a paint-smudged arm are just visible.

William van Doren on Trial

Charcoal on paper, 8×11 inches

Location: private collection

Description/Notes:

A sketch made in preparation for a future painting, depicting railway tycoon William van Doren in the courtroom where he was tried for murder. The artist's characteristic attention to detail is seen in the precise depiction of the judge, the spectators, and the jurors—van Doren himself, by contrast, is a crumpled shell of a man outlined in a few savage strokes. Reynolds was called as a witness in the trial, but never testified, as van Doren hanged himself just days into the proceedings. The planned oil portrait of this sketch was either never painted or destroyed by the artist.

Phoenix

Oil on canvas, 40×60 inches

Location: de Young Museum, San Francisco

Description/Notes:

Reynolds is best known for her portraits, ranging from intimate compositions of friends and family to society commissions like the sumptuous 1913 wedding portrait of Mrs. Gilbert Gould *née* Miss Cecilia Arenburg von Loxen (page 216), but the artist's portfolio includes several notable landscapes. Chief among them is undoubtedly this colorful depiction of San Francisco's Chinatown, painted when the artist returned to the city and opened the studio where she would work the rest of her life. The pagoda roofs and dragon streetlamps are rendered in loving detail, reflecting the artist's lifelong fascination with all things Chinese, and every face along the busy street from the little laundryboy to the sumptuously garbed madam in the doorway is lively, vivid, and individual. Chinatown may have burned in the fires following the 1906 earthquake, but it appears here defiantly rebuilt. Like San Francisco itself, and the men and women who survived that terrible day, it rose again: a phoenix reborn from the ashes.

Authors' Note

San Francisco

On the morning of April 18, 1906, San Francisco was the jewel of the West Coast: a lively, bustling city bursting with self-made millionaires, theaters providing every kind of entertainment, and all kinds of raucous good fun. Three days later it was a smoking ruin, leveled by one of the biggest natural disasters in US history—much to the delight of the Flying Rollers of Benton Harbor, Michigan, who really did send missionaries to call down destruction on the cesspit of the West if San Franciscans did not mend their sinning ways. The quake alone measured an estimated 7.9 on the Richter scale, toppling countless buildings and causing untold damage, but it was the fires that followed that sealed the city's fate. San Francisco boasted what was supposed to be an excellent firefighting system, but the earthquake shattered the water mains: when fires began all over the city in the immediate aftermath of the quake, lit by scattered candles, broken kitchen stoves, and blocked chimneys, the fire department found very few functional water mains to connect their hoses to. Despite a heroic battle from civilians and firefighters alike, San Francisco burned for three days and nights. Nearly thirty thousand buildings were lost, including the massive mansions of Nob Hill, the Grand Opera House, which had hosted Caruso the night before, the entirety of Chinatown, and countless homes and businesses. Refugees fled ahead of the flames to impromptu camps in Golden Gate Park or to Oakland by ferry, and lawlessness gripped the city—the army was ordered to shoot looters on sight, and many sound buildings were dynamited in a fruitless effort to create firebreaks. Despite these precautions, at least six hundred lives were lost, and the true tally is likely in the thousands. Yet San Francisco picked itself up from the ashes and rebuilt in record time, sufficiently recovered to host the world's fair in 1915.

[Kate Quinn: I have been endlessly fascinated with the idea of writing a San Francisco earthquake book, with a heroine who sang at the famous opera house before it was destroyed. But I knew the book would also need a Chinatown heroine . . .]

[Janie Chang: My first response to Kate was "We both just got through writing books set during world wars. How traumatic could it be to write about an earthquake?" After just a bit of preliminary research on the lives of Chinatown women of that era, I could tell that my character would be challenging and complex to write. And I wanted to write her!]

Chinatown

Newspapers and politicians of the time portrayed Chinatown as dirty and sinister, and as such, evidence that the Chinese were a decadent and evil race. They ignored the fact that San Francisco's Chinatown was not a typical Chinese community; it was warped by unfair laws and racism. Fifteen thousand residents lived and worked inside an area of twenty square blocks out of a need for mutual protection, a situation that created crowded and squalid living conditions. An 1885 map of Chinatown's buildings and their usage accompanied a report commissioned by San Francisco's board of supervisors intended to show the supposed moral turpitude of the Chinese. Thus the map highlighted brothels (both white and Chinese), gambling parlors, and opium "resorts," all contributing to Chinatown's notoriety. Yet the vast majority of buildings on the map housed families and shops; there were factories, an opera theater, joss houses (temples), Christian missions and churches, a large herb-alist store that was the closest thing Chinatown had to a hospital, and of course, laundries.

A citizen of Chinatown such as Suling would understand absolutely how gambling, opium, and prostitution ruined lives. She would also possess a nuanced grasp of the reasons why so many fell victim to these vices. One reason was the Chinese Exclusion Act of 1882, which blocked immigration for Chinese, exempting only a few categories of professions. After 1882, most men couldn't bring their wives or children over. They'd come during the gold rush and to build the railways, and now the best they could do for their families was to work and send money home. Living as bachelors, many turned to the comfort of drugs, gambling, or prostitutes to forget their loneliness. Those who could afford it found wives—or married second wives.

In 1890, Chinatown's population was 90 percent male, a gender imbalance that promoted human trafficking. Chinese and white human traders smuggled women from China and sold them to brothels or as indentured servants. It was a chain of tragedy that began with the girls' families (and some *were* just girls). Traditionally, Chinese parents valued sons over daughters, and when faced with starvation some sold their daughters. They may have been naive enough to believe their girls were destined for domestic service in America. Others knew better and sold their children anyway. In Chinatown's cheapest brothels, women were treated brutally and most could expect to die within three to five years from illness, ill treatment, or suicide.

Missionary Donaldina Cameron made it her life's work to rescue these young women by bringing them to the safety of her Mission Home. Sometimes women managed to escape and ran to her Mission for safety. Cameron helped some of the rescued women find husbands, usually Chinese Christians. So scarce were Chinese women that their unfortunate histories barely mattered to men desperate for wives and children. This is the past we gave Suling's mother.

Yet as Suling points out to Reggie, Chinatown was not all vice and exotic bordellos. There were perfectly ordinary families leading ordinary lives. Photos of Chinatown from before the earthquake show children walking along the street holding hands; women strolling together to attend New Year's festivities; a vendor selling pots of narcissus; a grocer standing in front of his store surrounded by crates of vegetables. All this burned down after the earthquake. The Chinatown you see today was designed deliberately to reflect Western notions of oriental architecture. Chinatown's merchants and leaders made a conscious decision to rebuild Chinatown in a way that would attract non-Chinese to exotic-looking streets and shops, a tourist destination that could promote not just business but perhaps cultural exchange. Chinatowns around the world have since followed this template.

[Kate: San Francisco's Chinatown today is wonderful, but it looks nothing like it would have looked in 1906. We both mourned that we couldn't see it.]

[Janie: Something I learned during research was that the spectacular, noisy, cheerful Chinatown New Year's Day parades were not always a Chinatown custom. The first such parade took place in 1953. The Cold War was raging and China, a Communist country, was the enemy. Fearing more discrimination, Chinatown's community leaders felt they needed a platform to emphasize the positive contributions of Chinese Americans. They organized a parade that brought more tourism to Chinatown and San Francisco and that has become a highlight of the year for the whole city.]

Feng Suling

Suling is a fictional character, born in California, the child of immigrants, living in a community that works hard to find success despite racism and exclusion. By 1906, there were Chinese who had lived in the USA long enough to become Westernized and have children who considered themselves Chinese American rather than Chinese. Some of these immigrants owned businesses that served both white and Chinese customers, lived outside Chinatown, and sent their children to public schools. Suling belongs to a demographic in transition: she doesn't reject traditional values wholesale, but wonders how she can live at the periphery of those values while carving out a life completely unlike what her community might expect. At the turn of the twentieth century, there were limited career options for Chinese men and even fewer for women. Sewing and embroidery, which could be done at home as piecework, was a common cottage industry. It seemed only logical that Suling would have such skills, but after researching the art of Chinese embroidery, we just had to use it in the story. Thus, Suling's expertise at creating intricate embroidery became the ticket to her career at a Paris fashion house.

[*Janie: I've always marveled at the courage of pioneers and first immigrants and decided that Suling's courage comes from growing up surrounded by people who had taken a deep breath and made big risks to change their lives completely.*]

[*Kate: From the very beginning we chose Suling's family name Feng ("phoenix") as a direct tribute not just to the title, but to her own bravery in rising from the ashes of an old life to create a new one.*]

Gemma Garland

Our opera singer, Gemma Garland/Sally Gunderson, is fictional, but it is very true that the Metropolitan Opera Company was in town the day San Francisco was destroyed: the great Enrico Caruso (who had rejected the chance to sing in Naples because he was uneasy about nearby Vesuvius erupting!) starred in a performance of *Carmen* mere hours before the earthquake hit. The city's finest (including famous actor John Barrymore, who happened to be in town) turned out in diamond-decked splendor to hear the famous tenor sing, and he earned gushing reviews in the papers, which had barely rolled off the presses by the time the first tremors hit. Bessie Abott as Micaëla was not reviewed well, nor was Olive Fremstad in the starring role of Carmen. Olive, who really did get into a shouting match with her costar during the day's rehearsal, had an otherwise splendid career—and she did indeed train her lungs by holding her breath and counting how many lampposts she could pass at a jog.

[*Kate: I trained as an opera singer in college—a high lyric soprano like Gemma—and my student loans are very grateful I could finally put my degrees to good use! Gemma's character and career are partially based on my wonderful college voice professor, Sally Arneson, a determined blue-eyed blonde who did indeed grow up on a Nebraska farm, make it big in Europe's opera houses with her thrilling high F's as Mozart's Queen of the Night, and marry a wonderfully skilled pianist named George, who partnered her in countless concerts and recitals. I count them as friends to this day.*]

[*Janie: The "Queen of the Night" aria was the piece that turned me into an opera fan—I will never forget falling dumbstruck at those high F's ringing like a bell. Now Kate and I are arguing over which soprano's performance to feature on our Bonus Materials web page.*]

[*Kate: Edita Gruberova.*]

[*Janie: Nope. Diana Damrau.*]

Alice Eastwood

Botanist Alice Eastwood had such a sensational life, she threatened to take over the entire book. She was an extraordinary self-taught scientist whose career roamed the globe, an intrepid explorer who set off on strenuous and dangerous hikes in pursuit of new plant samples, and a meticulous scholar who published hundreds of scientific articles. At thirty-five she was named head of the Department of Botany at the California Academy of Sciences, a position she held until age ninety. When the 1906 earthquake hit and fires threatened to consume the Academy, Alice matter-of-factly hung her lunch bag on a mastodon horn and climbed six stories up the outside of the shattered staircase to her office where she managed to save fifteen hundred botanical samples from the herbarium that was her life's work. Afterward, escaping San Francisco with little more than the clothes on her back and her favorite Zeiss lens, she remarked of her lost work, "It was a joy to me while I did it; I can still have the same joy in starting it again." She did exactly that, returning to the California Academy once it was rebuilt in Golden Gate Park. Over a dozen species would be named in her honor, and her portrait hangs in the Academy's botany department to this day.

[Kate: We invented Alice's adventures in the octagon house with Gemma, but Alice was a lifelong lover of opera and had a huge eclectic circle of friends—why not an opera singer?]

[Janie: When we found a photograph of her wearing an extravagantly flowered hat, we both practically screamed "Suling made the flowers on that hat!"]

Reggie Reynolds/Nellie Doyle

Reggie/Nellie is fictionalized, and so is the epilogue's art book detailing her artistic legacy, but female artists were making a name for themselves both in San Francisco and in Paris in the early nineteenth century. The Left Bank in particular thrived with expatriate women artists (including American writer Natalie Barney) who lived for their art, flaunted romantic relationships with other women, and were socially accepted without a French eyelash ever being batted. The mental institution to which Reggie was unfairly confined is fictionalized, but based on the very real State Insane Asylum at Agnews near San Jose, which collapsed in the 1906 earthquake and released hundreds of inmates to roam free from their cells.

Henry Thornton/William van Doren

Our villain is fictionalized: we found the name H. Thornton on old maps, listed as owner of thousands of acres of land in California, and based his character and background on any number of ruthless nineteenth-century tycoons who accrued massive fortunes (frequently through shady means) and then tried to build themselves up as philanthropists and patrons of the arts. His octagon house is also fictional, though there was a fad for eight-sided houses in the nineteenth century since they were supposed to be luckier and more healthful than the ordinary kind, and more than eighty notable octagon houses exist in the United States today, two of them in San Francisco. Chinoiserie collections were very popular among wealthy Westerners as the fad grew for Chinese antiques—many of them looted first from the Old Summer Palace in Beijing in 1860, and then from the Forbidden City in 1900. The Park Avenue Hotel fire in which Thornton obtains the seed money for his fortune was a notorious disaster taking place in 1902; the fire claimed twenty-one lives, though it is unlikely to have been caused by arson.

[Janie: We researched endless New York catastrophes before finding one that would work as Thornton's backstory.]

[Kate: And we have the Google spreadsheet to prove it.]

The French Fashion Houses

Callot Soeurs where we placed Suling as embroideress was a real fashion house in Paris at the turn of the century, run by four sisters. Callot Soeurs designs were known for their exquisite embroidery. At the same time, Paul Poiret was starting to take the fashion world by storm, becoming known for his hobble skirts, his corsetless gowns, his "oriental" designs, and his over-the-top entertaining. He rented the Pavillon du Butard near Versailles in June 1911 and decked it with exotic birds, gilded furniture, and hundreds of bottles of champagne for one of the century's most sensational parties: guests were provided with Persian costumes, French ballerinas and naked African dancers performed to the music of Egyptian and Indian musicians, and jewel-colored cocktails were spun up at his bar/laboratory for the dazzled crowd.

The Writing of *The Phoenix Crown*

Our primary goal in teaming up to write this book was to turn out a story we could be proud of, *without* ruining a long and wonderful friendship. We're thrilled to have succeeded in that, and we attribute our successful collaboration to three things: Google Docs, a compatible work ethic, and the unshakable belief that a spreadsheet will solve everything! Not to mention a passion for the history we write about—in our history-nerd hearts we mourn all the wonderful historical tidbits that could only be mentioned in passing in this story.

[Kate: *I still regret we couldn't do more with the character of Donaldina Cameron at the Chinatown Mission Home—a legitimate badass who was feared by pimps all over San Francisco.*]

[Janie: *And I only got to mention Tye Leung in passing. As a teenager, she ran away from an arranged marriage and grew up to be a civil rights activist. She was the first Chinese woman employed by the US federal government, working at the Angel Island Immigration Station, and the first Chinese woman to vote in a federal election. But marriage to her coworker Charles Schulze cost them both their jobs because marriage between Asians and whites was banned in California.]*

WE HAVE TAKEN some minor liberties with the historic record to serve the story. Our fictional heroines have been inserted into real historical events: Alice Eastwood rescued her botanical samples with the assistance of several colleagues but not the fictional Gemma; Bessie Abott was not bumped out of her Micaëla role for the pre-earthquake performance of *Carmen*, and Enrico Caruso fled San Francisco somewhat earlier than we have implied here. The roles Gemma sings in Buenos Aires were chosen to suit her voice, not the exact historical performance calendar of the Teatro Colón.

In Paris, Suling pays a visit to La Pagode, a Chinese antiques store. There was a store of that name owned by C. T. Loo, a colorful and controversial antiques dealer. The building still stands and is used as a venue for cultural events. However, the real La Pagode didn't open for business until 1926, and so the store Suling visits is La Pagode from Janie's novel *The Porcelain Moon* and the children she meets will grow up to be two of the characters in that novel.

Alice Eastwood made a number of trips to Europe and we know these dates because she wrote them in little notebooks where she kept meticulous records of her expenses: food, lodgings, transportation. We moved her from London to Paris a little early in her European botanical travels so she could attend Poiret's famous oriental ball.

Our research led us to far too many books to list here. For

more reading about the fascinating history behind this novel, from the San Francisco earthquake to the looting of the Forbidden City and the Old Summer Palace to embroidery stitches and opera houses, please visit the Book Clubs page on either of our websites (katequinnauthor.com or janiechang.com) and look for bonus materials associated with *The Phoenix Crown*. There you will also find discussion questions for book clubs, exclusive Spotify playlists, and recipes for Suling's shrimp with peas, Gemma's lemon tart, and authentic San Francisco Pisco Punch!

~∾~

Acknowledgments

We owe special thanks to so many people who aided in the research and writing of this book. Roy Levin and Jan Thomson, who kindly put us up at their condo during our research trip to San Francisco. Emily Magnaghi and Seth Cotterell, who led us on a tour of the California Academy of Sciences, pulled out library cartloads of books and papers from the archives, and answered countless questions about botany and Alice Eastwood (and they appear in tribute as Alice's colleagues during the earthquake scenes!). Paul Price and Julie De-Vere, wonderfully knowledgeable curators who gave us private tours, respectively, of Carolands Chateau and Filoli Mansion and Gardens and answered many questions about how Gilded Age California mansions operated upstairs and down. Christina Moretta, photo curator of the San Francisco History Center at San Francisco Public Library. The Chinese Historical Society of America, and the Legion of Honor Museum whose fabulous exhibit of embroidered fashions by Guo Pei sent Suling's character arc careening in an entirely new direction. Our friends and fellow historical fiction authors Stephanie Dray and Stephanie Thornton, for taking their red pens to the messy first draft of this book. Our patient spouses: Stephen, who fueled us through two days of feverish spreadsheeting with homemade ramen; and Geoff, who took over the logistics of moving to a new house in a new town so that Janie could hit her writing deadlines. Last, our wonderful agent Kevan Lyon, our patient editor Tessa Woodward, and the endlessly enthusiastic PR and marketing team at William Morrow. Without you all, *The Phoenix Crown* would never have been written!

About the Authors

KATE QUINN is a *New York Times* bestselling author of historical fiction, including *The Alice Network* and *The Diamond Eye*. She attended Boston University, where she earned bachelor's and master's degrees in classical voice. Kate and her husband now live in San Diego with three rescue dogs.

JANIE CHANG is a bestselling Canadian author of critically acclaimed historical fiction. Often drawing from family history and ancestral stories for inspiration, her works include *Three Souls, Dragon Springs Road, The Library of Legends*, and *The Porcelain Moon*.

Keep reading for excerpts from
The Briar Club
by Kate Quinn
and
The Porcelain Moon
by Janie Chang

The Briar Club
Nora

Dear Lisa,

Apparently there's a lair of gangsters just down the street from Briarwood House! Irish mob—I sit in my window hoping to see machine guns and getaway cars. My window overlooks the whole square; the best place on earth to watch people. Though my housemates offer plenty of diversion! Will sulky little Lina ever make a decent batch of cookies? Will old Mrs. Muller ever crack a smile? Who on earth is sending Nora Walsh all these sumptuous flowers?
I wish you were here.

—Grace

Thanksgiving had come and gone, all anyone could talk about was the upcoming Rosenberg trial, and Nora Walsh was moving up in the world.

"You look very smart." Grace March, wrapped in a threadbare robe embroidered with Chinese dragons and waiting on the fourth-floor landing with her toothbrush, looked admiringly as Nora hurried out of their shared bathroom. "That suit's new, isn't it?"

"Hecht Company, sale rack." Nora gave the peplum on her smoke-blue gabardine jacket a pleased tug. It took a lot of sale haunting and bargain-bin shopping to look expensive on a budget as limited as hers, but it was worth it. There were those at

the National Archives who thought Miss Walsh was entirely too
gauche, too green, too Foggy Bottom to have been promoted
out of the file room to personal secretary of *the* Mr. Harris,
executive officer of the Archives. Miss Walsh had decided that
even if she hadn't been raised to be elegant, college-educated, or
top-drawer, no one was ever going to know it by looking at her.
She might live in a boardinghouse shoebox and take weekend
shifts at the local greasy spoon, but the moment she headed to
the National Archives her lipstick was flawless, her clothes up to
the minute, and her voice ironed of every Irish vowel.

"Very nice, Tipperary." Grace had nicknamed Nora that
since hearing her family had originally made its way over from
Tipperary county in the old country and it made Nora grin every time. "Quality gabardine always shows," Grace continued,
rubbing Nora's cuff between her fingers. For a woman who
went about most of the time in peasant skirts and ballet flats,
she had a very sharp eye for clothes. "Coming to the Briar Club
dinner tonight?"

"Wouldn't miss it." Nora's usual dinner was a cup of soup
heated on her hot plate, part of the aforementioned scrimp-
ing and saving. Thursday dinners were usually the best meal
Nora had all week, all the saints bless Grace March and her
Briar Club. (So dubbed by Pete, with an adorable solemnity that
had all the women biting their cheeks in an effort not to laugh.
Well, except Arlene Hupp, who put her head back and giggled,
eyes sparkling as Pete's face fell. "*So* sorry, Pete, you're just *too*
funny!" Claire Hallett had promptly spilled a cup of sun tea
down the front of Arlene's cashmere twinset: "*So* sorry, Arlene,
you're just *too* in the way!" A bit excessive, Nora thought, but
Claire was inclined to overflex her claws at times.)

"I saw you writing a postcard yesterday, Grace," Nora went
on, snatching up her handbag. "Want me to drop it in the mail-

box on my way out, so Doilies Nilsson won't snoop?" *Doilies* was what Grace had dubbed their landlady (when Pete wasn't in earshot) for all those horridly starched little antimacassars she was always crocheting and draping over every blessed surface.

"I'm not done writing it out yet, thank you." Grace smiled her sleepy half smile and disappeared into the bathroom, tousling her golden-brown hair. Nora hadn't seen Grace get a single letter in the five months she'd lived at Briarwood House, or post one either, or mention a single family member back home. For a woman who had such an easy listening air as she welcomed other people's life stories, she was remarkably unforthcoming with her own.

Nora appreciated that. She didn't talk about her family, either.

The square was just waking up as she came through the front door of Briarwood House, pulling on her pristine darned-at-the-fingertips gloves. The drugstore across the street was already open, clerk sweeping off the steps; Dave's Barbershop on the opposite corner already had a fellow rushing in, barking, "Neaten up the sides and leave the top!" Next door, Mr. Rosenberg was out on the front steps of the corner deli, affixing a small sign in the window: *No relation to Julius & Ethel Rosenberg.* "Think that'll do the trick?" he asked Nora as she swung past. "The way people are looking for Reds these days, I don't need any baloney about being the Rosenbergs' Commie cousin . . ."

"I don't know who could think that, Mr. Rosenberg. No one who makes bagels like yours could ever be a spy." Nora waved and kept walking, around the corner and past the Crispy Biscuit, where, unbeknownst to her more refined Monday-to-Friday employers, she picked up weekend shifts—then past the Amber Club where Joe Reiss played six nights a week until three in the morning. The sunlight was golden, the air crisp and cold, and block by block the slightly shabby streets of Foggy Bottom picked up their hems and put out their lace curtains, until she hit Washington Circle and veered onto Pennsylvania, where suddenly the nation's capital began taking itself very seriously indeed. Maybe her hometown didn't have the bustle of New York or the glitter of Hollywood (not that Nora had seen either), but where else could you find a city with the drawling charm of a small Southern town and the electric sense that everything really important in this country was happening right *here*? Nearly three miles to walk to work every day, but Nora wouldn't give it up for anything: the sense every morning that her city was unfurling around her, bright with promise.

Just like her own life finally was, after that horrendous series of bumps that had hit like grenades when she graduated high school.

Down Pennsylvania Avenue past the White House, where Nora sent silent well-wishes to Mr. Truman, then a nip down Ninth to Constitution—and there it was: the National Archives, granite-grand, pillared and pedimented, history breathing quietly from it. Nora had been coming here since she was a freshly minted eighteen, the newest of the file girls. It still made her catch her breath, stand a little taller in her glossy black patent pumps. Mother of God, but she loved this place.

If she had time, she liked to come through the front entrance and into the Rotunda, past the case where the Bill of Rights was reverently displayed—but her feet slowed today as she reached the top of the steps, and all her happy morning goodwill curdled. Because leaning against one of the massive columns was a man in crisp policeman's blues, hair gleaming the same soft brown as Nora's.

"Hello, *deirfiúr bheag*."

"Nearly twenty-one is really too old to be *little* anything,

Timmy," Nora said coolly, feeling her heart start to thump. "And I don't think of myself as your sister anymore."

Sergeant Timothy Walsh clapped a hand to his heart as if she'd shot him. "Come on, darlin', how long are you going to hold a grudge?" He hadn't ironed the Irish out of his voice the way she had—he didn't have to, when half his precinct resonated with accents from Cork, Mayo, and Meath, and when the name *Walsh* had already paved your way because your father had made it from the beat to the rank of detective. No one had paved Nora's way.

"Did I ever tell you how proud I am of you, working at a place like this?" He tilted his head to look up the vast stretch of columns. "Little Nora from Foggy Bottom, hobnobbing with all the bigwigs at the Archives . . ."

As if you've set foot in a library since high school, or even know what an archive is. Nora took a harder grip on her pocketbook, exhaling. He knew exactly how to get under her skin, he always had, and there wasn't any use getting steamed up because it would just entertain him. "Timmy, please get out of my way. I'm going to be late for work."

"If you could see your way to loaning me a bit . . . Catriona's birthday is this week, and Timmy Junior's got to see a doctor about his ears. I've got expenses."

"No," Nora said flatly. He made a good salary, and there was no reason for empty pockets except that he liked the cards and the ponies and the extra dram at Pete Dailey's over on New Hampshire and Virginia. "I am not giving you a dime—"

But he'd already nipped her pocketbook off her shoulder, fast as a pickpocket. Nora yanked back, hissing, "*Tim—*" but he was rummaging through it, and she didn't dare make a commotion. Which was why he'd braced her *here*, right on the front steps of the National Archives, and people were giving them curious looks. The doorman, who was the biggest gossip in the whole building, and Mrs. Halliwell, who headed up the file room and had been the loudest voice opposing Nora's promotion to Mr. Harris's office. What did she see, a jumped-up file girl talking to a beat cop, or a couple of Micks who didn't belong? What would she think if Nora made a scene, shouting at Tim and trying to yank her wallet back?

Nora had made a scene before, the first time her brother braced her on the way to work and yanked her handbag off her arm. She just ended up with a broken handbag strap as well as an empty wallet. Tim was bigger; he was always going to win if it came to a struggle. He knew it, and Nora did too.

"I'll pay you back. Next week, I promise." He never did, and every dollar from her billfold had already disappeared into his pocket. He leaned in and kissed Nora's cheek, or tried to—Nora took a step back. "You're a gem. I won't forget this."

"I won't either," said Nora, feeling her blood pound in impotent rage. "Hard to forget it when your brother *steals* from you."

"Don't be like that, *deirfiúr bheag*. We miss you back home, you know. Mam wishes you'd visit. So does Siobhan."

Siobhan misses me because now there's no one to watch the kids for her, Nora thought uncharitably and accurately of her brother's wife. That was what an unmarried sister-in-law was for: watch the babies, tend the mother-in-law, iron the police uniforms, smile, be grateful. Not move out to a swank job in the capital and start wearing pencil-slim suits and talking above herself.

"I'm working a new thing, you know," he went on, flicking a bit of invisible dust off his badge. "The Feds are looking to wrap up the Warring brothers, the Foggy Bottom gang, the numbers racket—"

"Good luck prying the district away from the Warrings, Tim. They've been here longer than Prohibition. And don't you play poker with Rags Warring every Saturday at Dailey's?" While he collected his weekly payoff, Nora could have added, but didn't bother. Half the local cops were on the take.

Tim shrugged, grinning. "Doesn't mean I won't help the Feds roll 'em up if it gets me a nice promotion come New Year."

Cops and robbers, Nora thought. Every kid in Foggy Bottom played cops and robbers. If you were from a family like Nora's, Mass every Sunday and First Communion photographs in the parlor and a good amount of police blue running through the family tree, you were on the cop side in those games. If you came from a family like the notorious Warrings, where the numbers racket was passed down from brother to brother (and so was the backyard still and the jugged moonshine back in Prohibition days) you played on the robber side. What most people hadn't figured was this: that both sides were utter rackets. That *both* sides, in Nora's experience, understood the game.

"Get lost, Timmy," Nora managed to say evenly, and moved past her older brother into the National Archives, heels stabbing the ground like knives. By the time she was seated at her desk, sorting the mail with efficient speed, preparing her boss's cup of coffee ("Good morning, Mr. Harris—don't forget your ten o'clock and here's that report you asked for on the new preservation case for the Bill of Rights—"), Nora's inner calm almost matched her outward poise again.

So you still get the occasional family hand shoving its way into your pocketbook, she thought, taking possession of her big glass-smooth desk. *You're still on the right track.*

And she didn't ever—after what had happened at eighteen—intend to get knocked off it.

The Porcelain Moon
Camille

Camille peeped through the bedroom curtain, the clenching tightness in her shoulders not easing even after her husband walked out the door. The clank of rusty hinges carried through the still morning air as Jean-Paul yanked open the garden gate. His gait was slightly bowlegged, a legacy of rickets and malnourishment, a poverty-stricken childhood. He turned south, where the road forked toward the village of Noyelles-sur-Mer. A cloud obscured the horizon, dimming the early sunlight, and for a moment all Camille could make out was Jean-Paul's silhouette, the canvas knapsack turning him into a hunchbacked monster.

A slight injury early in the war and his stated occupation of railway worker, essential to the war effort, had allowed him to avoid further military duty. Jean-Paul used to come home between shifts, but as the tolls of war mounted and more men enlisted, the railway put their remaining crew on longer and longer shifts, sometimes for seventy-two hours at a time. But even those absences weren't long enough for Camille.

Moments later a small donkey cart came over the rise, their neighbor the farmer Fournier with a load of winter cabbages. Old Fournier was easy to recognize, his broad figure draped in an indigo-blue smock and driving a red cart, bright slabs of color against the dull yellows and browns of harvested fields. The scene could've been painted by Cézanne.

The cart stopped and Jean-Paul climbed on beside the farmer.

It was market day in St. Valery-sur-Somme, across the canal beyond Noyelles, undoubtedly Fournier's destination. Jean-Paul
would jump off at the Noyelles train station for another long
shift on the Nord, the northern railway line. Camille didn't
know what else her husband might be doing and she didn't want
to know. What mattered was that he would be away.

She lay on the bed and gave in to a moment of weariness,
waited until her churning insides calmed, nausea subsiding as
her body understood it was safe for her muscles to loosen and
breathing to slow. She turned over so that she faced the window,
not wanting to smell Jean-Paul's hair oil on the pillow, the sour
sweat of his body on the sheets. She'd change the bed when
she came home from work. If he was away overnight, then she
could sleep alone in luxury, her limbs sliding under clean linens
scented with lavender, her body longing for . . . no. She wouldn't
think about him. Or about what she had to do on her own.

At the mirror, she pressed more powder above her left
cheekbone. The bruise beside her hairline had faded since the
previous evening and as long as she stayed indoors, away from
bright sunlight, it wouldn't be obvious. She tied a kerchief
around her head and tugged a stray lock to fall across the yel-
lowing mark.

In the kitchen, she boiled some water and dropped a few
dried mint leaves in a mug. Their coffee, carefully meted out
each morning, was reserved for Jean-Paul. She didn't mind going without coffee, but of all the rationed foods, she missed
sugar the most. After a slice of last night's baguette with some
cheese, it was time to go. She rolled up a clean calico smock and
stuffed it in her satchel for the ride into town.

As CAMILLE CYCLED to the post office, the sun finally broke
free of the cloud bank, casting an amber glow across the hori-

zon beyond Crécy Forest. For a moment she thought she heard cannon fire, then reminded herself that fighting in their region had ceased. The rumbling noises more likely came from the reverberation of trucks carrying soldiers to the front. After years of war, her ears were attuned to real or imagined sounds of artillery. Thankfully, since the fighting near Cambrai ended in October, the front lines had been moving steadily east, away from the Somme Valley.

The tide had turned against Germany and its allies, or so the newspapers declared. There were rumors of peace negotiations and news of civilian unrest in Germany, where the kaiser was being pressured by his own government to abdicate. There was talk of an armistice but until then, the fighting continued. But the end was in sight, everyone said. And then their armies would demobilize, their men return from the front.

And she would give up her job at the post office.

Brightening skies promised a clear day, a rare thing this time of year. The walk to Noyelles didn't take long, less than an hour, but after work she wanted to drop by the château in case there was some sewing work to pick up, so she had taken her bicycle and attached the small, homemade trailer to the back. She pedaled slowly through familiar farmland, the shrubbery along the road brown and soggy, bereft of summer's lush foliage. She passed the château and barely gave it a glance. It held too many memories, not all of them pleasant.

Another ten minutes and she reached the fence surrounding the Chinese Labour Corps camp. The yard was already busy, smoke and steam rising from the kitchens, men queueing up outside the mess hall. The camp had been built more than a year ago but Camille still couldn't get used to the sight of its ugly barbed wire fencing. It resembled a stockade more than a camp.

At the post office, she tied on the calico smock and began her half day of work. She started by sorting through mail that had come in the previous afternoon. Her heart clenched briefly at the sight of French Army stationery. In the days and weeks after Rossignol, after Verdun, after the Somme, it seemed as though tragedy cascaded through her hands with every piece of mail. Families destroyed, lives maimed and forever changed. There were only two such envelopes today, thank goodness, but it was still too many.

She paused to look at a postcard addressed to Marie-France Fournier, Old Fournier's youngest girl, from her cousin Thérèse. Thérèse, bolder than most, had left Noyelles to take a factory job in Paris. Camille knew Marie-France had wanted to follow her cousin, work at a factory and earn money of her own, but both her brothers had enlisted and now only she and her mother were there to help work the fields.

Camille read the untidy handwriting.

Ma chère cousine, I spend all day filling artillery shells and the evenings strolling past store windows filled with elegant things. What fun we could have, if only you could come to Paris. Your loving Thérèse who misses you.

If only you could come to Paris. Those scribbled words seemed meant for Camille. She longed to see Paris again. If she had taken a factory job there, she could've spent her days off visiting museums and galleries—the ones still open—to stand in front of paintings that changed how she saw the world. But, of course, it was impossible since she was a married woman. And Jean-Paul was scornful of women who worked in factories.

"No respectable female would leave their husbands and

homes," he said, "only low-class women. Unmarried and willing to work alongside dirty foreigners. Whores."

But when the postal service began hiring women to replace men who had gone to war, it was all right with Jean-Paul for his wife to work at the post office. It was a respectable job in town with modest but welcome wages. Camille suspected the real reason Jean-Paul agreed was that it gave him a chance to get friendlier with the Dumonts, the postmaster and his wife, who were prominent citizens of Noyelles.

Before the Nord railway line got so busy and Jean-Paul was away all the time, he liked to visit the post office around closing time, when Camille was tidying the back rooms, ostensibly to walk her home, but really because he wanted to socialize with the Dumonts. Jean-Paul and M. Dumont talked about the war, the price of food, and often as not, the disruptions caused by foreigners in their little town. British, Canadian, and Australian soldiers were stationed there. And there were also Chinese workers. On principle, Jean-Paul didn't like foreigners, not even refugees from neighboring Belgium, and the Chinese were decidedly foreign. He grumbled at newspaper photographs of brigades arriving in Marseilles from Indochina, at accounts of British troops and Indian Sikhs marching through France on their way to the front. But at least they were soldiers.

"It's one thing to bring soldiers from our colonies to help us fight, even if they're only short little Orientals," he said, "but these Chinois aren't going into battle for us. Digging and carrying. That's all they're doing."

"Digging trenches, loading fuel for tanks and vehicles, repairing roads and railway tracks after aerial attacks. The machinery of war has many parts, Jean-Paul," M. Dumont said. "Napoleon was a brilliant tactician because he understood the logistics of supplying his armies. He could've run a modern postal system." M. Dumont liked pointing to the postal service as a model of efficiency.

He droned on a little longer, reminding his audience that using Chinese labor for the manual work of the war freed up more French and British to fight. That the Allies wouldn't have brought in workers from so far away, at such expense, unless they desperately needed the manpower. Manpower to unload and load cargo at the docks and supply depots, plow and plant fields so that farms still grew wheat for bread, work in armaments factories so that tanks and guns didn't run out of ammunition

But while Jean-Paul didn't like the Chinese, he didn't mind making money off them. When he heard that the workers liked buying Western clothing, Jean-Paul ransacked the armoire in Camille's father's bedroom, then went to the camp on a payday with a sack full of her dead father's clothes.

"They paid me what I asked for, the stupid *chintoks*," he boasted. "So many of them all wanting these old clothes so much they barely haggled."

A few days later, Camille saw a tall Chinese strolling along the main street in Noyelles, one hand straightening the lapels of a familiar waistcoat. Her annoyance faded when she saw how gently the man touched the garment's brocade front and brass buttons, pride and pleasure evident in his face. Jean-Paul shrugged when she pointed at the man, wearing the waistcoat he had sold behind her back.

"They're like children," he said contemptuously. "Dressing up in our clothes, putting everything on the wrong way. He's got it buttoned over that ridiculous tunic."

"But you're the one who sold it to him," she said, her voice just above a whisper. She winced as his fingers tightened on her

33

arm. Then he loosened his grip to make a slight bow as an elderly couple walked past. The mayor, M. Etienne Gourlin, and Mme Gourlin.

CAMILLE SHOOK HER head at the memory.

She finished sorting the mail into four bags and set them down by the back door for Emil to pick up. She put a dried-out carrot from her cellar on top of the bags, a small treat for the donkey that pulled Emil's mail delivery cart.

No, she thought, Jean-Paul didn't have a problem taking money from the Chinese.

And he'd kill her if he ever found out she was in love with one.

EXPLORE MORE NOVELS BY
KATE QUINN

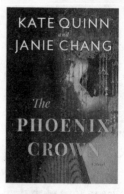

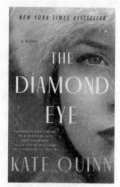